Franklin Horton

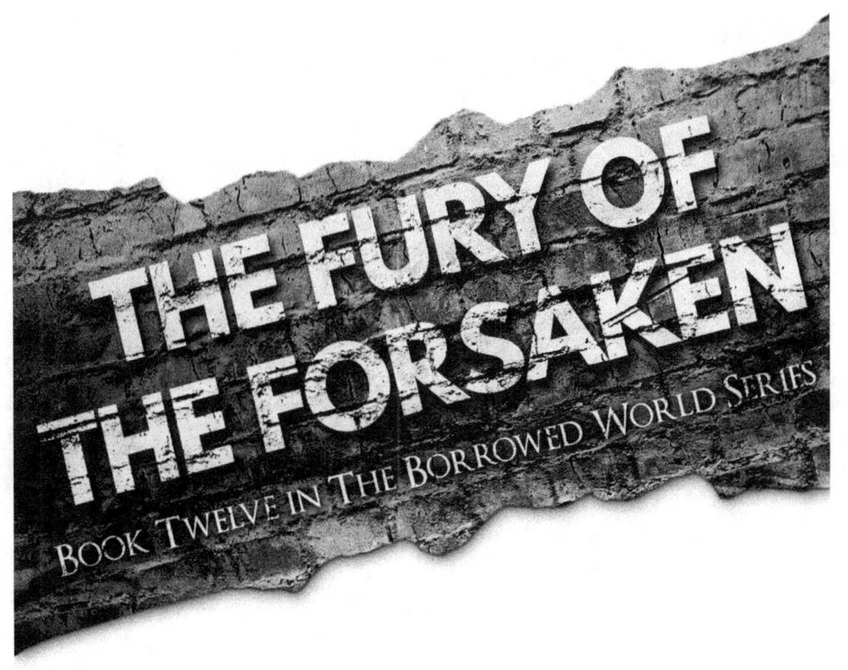

ABOUT THE AUTHOR

Franklin Horton lives and writes in the mountains of Southwestern Virginia. He received an English degree from Virginia Commonwealth University and has written over forty novels. He lives a hermit's life on a remote mountaintop along the Clinch Mountain chain, splitting his day between writing and tinkering in his shop like one of his characters.

You can follow him on his website at franklinhorton.com.

While you're there please sign up for his mailing list for updates, event schedule, book recommendations, and discounts. He's also active on social media so follow him on Facebook or Instagram to keep up with the latest releases.

ALSO BY FRANKLIN HORTON

The Borrowed World Series

The Borrowed World

Ashes of the Unspeakable

Legion of Despair

No Time For Mourning

Valley of Vengeance

Switched On

The Ungovernable

Blood And Banjos

Resurgent

The Reset Roadhouse

The Endarkened

The Locker Nine Series

Locker Nine

Grace Under Fire

Compound Fracture

Blood Bought

The Mad Mick Series

The Mad Mick

Masters of Mayhem

Brutal Business

Northern Sun

Punching Tickets

Ultraviolent

The Death Dealer's Manual

American Oligarch

Shift Point

Dislocated

Hostile Takeover

The Ty Stone Series

Hard Trauma

Child With No Name

Hate Box

The Way of Dan Series

Burning Down Boise

The Path of Water

Boondock Pilgrims

The Oracle

The Rotten Belly Society

The Defeated Creek Series

Willie

Stand-Alone Novels

Random Acts

THE FURY OF THE FORSAKEN

1

Lightspeed Aid Distribution Center
   National Guard Armory
   Bluefield, Virginia

JOSIE FLINCHED at the sound of the rifle shot. She thought she'd be accustomed to them by now. Surely, she should have been, but she wasn't. Maybe it was because of the way the concussive crack echoed around the walls and open spaces of the massive armory, making Josie almost feel as if she was the one being fired at. For as much as she didn't want to know what that particular gunshot meant, she *needed* to know. She was the team leader for this facility, even though it felt like she was less in charge with each passing day.

Josie keyed the mic on her radio. "Alpha Twenty for Alpha One, what's the situation? Are we under attack again?"

"*When are we* not *under attack, Twenty?*"

Alpha One's tone belied his frustration, but Josie let it pass. Alpha One was always frustrated these days and he wasn't the only one.

Josie kept her voice neutral. "I heard a shot."

"Same shit, new day. They're testing the perimeter again. We're bracing for a surge."

"Copy that, Alpha One. I'm headed your way. Alpha Twenty out."

"Whatever," Alpha One replied, his sarcastic tone exposing the disdain he held for her.

Josie stood and clipped the radio to the waistband of her pants. Yes, she knew there wasn't much point in her joining the security team. Yes, she knew she wasn't any good in a fight. Still, she was the team leader and even just a little professional respect would be nice somedays. Apparently, that would not be forthcoming. Not any longer.

"I'm beginning to think help isn't coming." It was Yana, the woman who shared Josie's room at the aid distribution center. Yana was inside her sleeping bag, a book propped on her chest.

Josie let out a long breath. "The people who'd be willing to come for us likely don't have the resources to mount a rescue. The others, the people with the helicopters and trucks, are either not inclined to do so or someone ordered them to stand down. I don't know what that means for the future of this endeavor."

"To hell with the endeavor," Yana said. "I'm concerned for what it means for the future of us and all the other Lightspeed employees left trapped in the field."

"I'm trying, Yana."

"I know you are, but you know the truth here. No one is coming to save us. The sooner you accept that, the sooner we can develop a plan for getting out of here."

"And going where?"

Yana tried to mask her frustration, but it still slipped through. *"Anywhere,* Josie. Anywhere that we're not coming under attack each day. Anywhere that people don't want to kill us just because we're sitting on supplies they want."

"Maybe we just give them all the supplies that are left? It's not much, but maybe it would be enough."

"Those people outside the wire would never believe it. They'd never accept there were no more supplies until they came in here and inspected for themselves. What do you think would happen with us then? Who would receive the brunt of their anger? Who would they take their frustrations out on?"

"I have to go." Josie shot to her feet. "Let's just give it a little longer, okay?"

Josie's mind spun and banged like a dryer full of wet sneakers. What could she say? It was true. With each passing day it became clearer that Lightspeed's organization was not going to be resurrected from the ashes. Their boss was dead. The man with the money and technology to electrify the nation was dead. Lightspeed had been the driving force behind the national recovery and without him, they had nothing. They were literally dead in the water. Those who clung to power had felt it was more important to shut Lightspeed down than to accept the gift he provided. Now they had what they wanted. America was in the dark again, but at least they'd kept an "outsider" from bypassing their presumed authority.

Alpha One's real name was Vince, but he insisted on the use of callsigns on the radio. Even though this wasn't a military operation, it had unfortunately come to resemble one more and more since Lightspeed's grid imploded.

Josie walked down the long hall of bunkrooms, the cinderblock walls painted stark white, and made her way to the giant space that the security team referred to as the drill hall. The room was well lit with natural light coming through high clerestory windows installed around the perimeter of the wall. A catwalk allowed the security team to move along those windows and maintain a 360-degree view of the armory grounds.

The security team heard Josie's footsteps coming across the floor. All four men turned in her direction, then most of them turned back to whatever they'd been watching before she entered.

"Can you come down so we can talk?" Josie called up to Vince.

"That's a negative unless you want us all to die. Shit is going to pop off any second now. I can feel it. If you have something to say, you come up here."

Josie knew Vince wasn't trying to be a jerk in this instance, although he could certainly be a jerk sometimes. He was just intense —all business, all the time. That made him good at his job, but his job had admittedly changed since Lightspeed died. To be fair, though, all their jobs had changed.

Vince's team of four security contractors were originally brought in to secure the site and maintain order at the distribution center while Josie and her people handed out aid. Once Lightspeed's wireless grid collapsed, the locals smelled blood in the water and tried to rob the distribution center, rushing in and overwhelming Josie's people. The locals would have stolen everything and perhaps even harmed them if the security team hadn't opened fire and taken control of the situation. Since that day, nearly every day was the same. Locals tried to attack the armory and the security team drove them back. All day, every day.

Not a fan of heights, Josie took hold of the welded steel ladder and climbed the three stories to the catwalk. Once she'd transitioned off the ladder, she stood there for a moment, clasping the catwalk's railing with white knuckles. She tried to calm her nerves while she waited for her heartbeat to return to normal. The security team was scattered along the rectangular platform, each of them responsible for one avenue of approach.

"I argued for heavier weapons," Vince spat, his face tense. "But Lightspeed said this wasn't a military operation, it was a humanitarian mission. So, we got smoke grenades instead of tear gas. We got flash-bangs instead of high explosive grenades."

Josie pointed at Vince's weapon. "You got machine guns."

"We got select-fire M4s when what we need are SAWs and sniper rifles. I held out hope we'd find some better weapons stashed here in the armory, but whoever cleaned this place out before we got here did a thorough job. You better hope it's not a local wielding those weapons, either. If they show up outside the wire and get turned on us, that's going to be a bad day."

"The mission of this distribution center was to aid the locals, not kill them," Josie reminded him.

Vince smirked. "How do we deliver aid, boys?"

"Center mass! One round at a time!" one of the men recited.

Vince laughed, which made Josie frown.

Her disapproving expression irked Vince. "Hey, you're always pointing out that you're the 'team leader'. Show some leadership. Figure something out before we run out of options."

"I'm working on it constantly. I have a conference call twice daily with other Lightspeed teams around the country. We're all in the same boat and no one appears to have the resources to help anyone else."

"Typical bureaucratic bullshit. Taking conference calls and clutching your pearls isn't going to save us."

Josie gritted her teeth. "I'm doing...the best...I can."

"We can't just sit here on our thumbs." Vince shook his head in disgust. "We're going to run out of ammo eventually. Once that happens and the locals figure it out, they'll find a way into the building and there won't be any stopping them. I suspect they're a little pissed off about all their friends and family we've killed. They'll probably hang us from this scaffolding. Or worse."

"And whose fault are those deaths?" Josie demanded.

"A corpse a day keeps the locals away," one of the security team chimed in.

Josie rolled her eyes.

"Do you think we want to be shooting Americans?" Vince snapped. "We don't! This is just the situation we find ourselves in."

"I'm just saying that you guys shooting locals like they're ducks in a shooting gallery isn't helping matters."

"*Nothing* will help matters!" Vince yelled. "You find us a way out of here or we're all going to die in ways you probably don't want to imagine!"

Their argument was interrupted by a member of the security team abruptly shoving open the window in front of him. He shouldered his rifle, sighted through his optic, and fired off several quick rounds.

"What is it?" Vince demanded.

"They're rushing my sector!" the shooter bellowed.

Vince snapped his head back toward his own window only to find that a group of locals was charging his side of the building too. They were crouched low and zigzagging, making themselves hard targets. "Oh shit!" Vince threw his window open, sighted on the group of runners, and sent several quick shots. Two dropped while the remainder scattered like cockroaches.

All the men in the security detail were firing out their windows, the locals having coordinated a rushing attack from all sides. The explosion of violence was too much for Josie. She latched onto the ladder and began climbing back down to the ground level, wishing she could cup her hands over her ears to drown out the shots.

"Find us a way out of here!" Vince screamed after her.

Josie hadn't even made it back to her room before Lamar intercepted her. He was another member of her team and the one having the most difficulty handling the fact they'd been stranded.

"What's going on out there?" he asked.

Josie didn't even stop walking. "Do you really have to ask? It's the same thing that goes on every day, Lamar. The locals aren't giving up. Some people are slow to learn."

Lamar followed Josie down the hall toward her room. "Which people is that? Them or us? We don't seem to be getting the message either. We need to get out of here."

Josie huffed. "Now you sound just like Vince, so I'll tell you the same thing I just told him. I'm doing everything I can."

"Yeah, well you're the team leader. You're the one who is supposed to interface with Lightspeed Command and the other teams. Not us. You've been very clear since we got here that we all have roles here. *Do yours!*"

Josie stepped into her bedroom, Lamar hot on her heels. She wanted to slam the door in his face but had no chance to do so.

Yana, having overheard the shouting in the hallway, laid her book down and addressed Lamar. "What do you think Josie has been doing for the last few weeks? She makes calls and sends messages all day every day. She's reached out to every satellite phone number and every email address any of us have been able to lay our hands on. No one has any answers, any news, or any way to help us. All Lightspeed's people are in the same boat. What would you have Josie do?"

Lamar groaned and threw his hands up. "I don't know. Something."

"Well unless you can pull a teleportation device out of your ass we're stuck for now," Yana snapped.

Josie took a deep breath, released it, and spoke as if she were relaying information to a child. "There's no news. Everyone seems to agree that Lightspeed is dead, though no one I spoke to has seen a body. We all hoped he'd turn up alive, but he hasn't and that likely means the power grid is down for good. We'll never know why, but Lightspeed was determined that if he died, his technology died with him."

"You've already told us that!" Lamar groaned. "It's old news. The power has been out for six weeks now and no one has come to get us. No one can even tell us if we will be rescued at all. What happened to all the damn helicopters and military trucks that were hauling us around months ago?"

Having heard the shouting, the last member of Josie's team, Brendan, slipped quietly into the room. He put a hand on Lamar's shoulder. "Dude, everyone in the entire Lightspeed organization is the same boat. There are grid installation teams stranded in the field. There are community outreach teams stranded in remote locations. There are hundreds of aid distribution sites just like this one where all the staff have been stranded, just like we are. We should consider ourselves lucky. At least we have food. Some of the teams working in remote areas only had enough for a few days."

"And we have a roof over our heads," Yana said. "We're not somewhere in the woods camping in a tent like the installation teams."

"But how much longer are we going to have that roof over our head?" Lamar demanded. He jabbed a finger toward the hallway. "Locals are out there every day trying to find a way into this building. No matter how many the security team kills, more come back the next day. They *know* there are supplies here and they are determined to get them. They were willing to be polite and stay in line when they knew there would be more helicopters coming, but they're not coming anymore. Now those people are back to being the same band of savages they were when we got here."

"They're not savages," Yana said patiently. "They are desperate, suffering people. If circumstances were different, we could just as easily be out there wanting to get in."

"And we might be soon," Lamar fired back. "Those desperate, suffering people are going to bust down these doors any day now and steal all the supplies. What do you think they're going to do to us? At a minimum, they'll throw us out of here. What are we going to do then?"

"That's what security is for," Josie replied. "They just deterred another attack moments ago. They won't allow anyone through those doors."

Lamar shook his head with disgust. "I hope you're right."

2

The Reset Roadhouse

IT WAS NEARLY dark when Riley Blackwood strolled into the roadhouse with a determined look on his face and a green metal ammo can in his hand. Spotting Jim Powell behind the bar, Riley approached and delicately placed the ammo can down on the bar top. While Jim regarded the can, Riley took a seat on one of the tall barstools and rested his elbows on the counter.

"That your new purse, Riley?" Jim asked.

Riley laughed. "In a manner of speaking. I'm hoping there's enough barter in there to put toward my tab."

Jim did a quick mental calculation. "Well, I don't have the numbers in front of me, but I don't think your tab is too high. You usually pay as you go."

Riley waved his hands. "Oh no, this isn't for what I drank already. I'm wanting to make a downpayment on staying drunk all winter."

Hugh wandered up to join the conversation. "Every man needs a plan and it sounds like you got one, Riley."

Jim lifted the ammo can a couple of inches off the bar, testing the weight. "What's in here? Doesn't seem heavy enough to be ammo."

"It's not." Riley flipped open the latch then swung the heavy lid open. He carefully tipped the can over and dumped the contents onto the bar top. It wasn't ammo but pocketknives that came spilling out.

"Where the hell did you get all those?" Jim asked. "That a personal collection?"

Riley looked uncomfortable with the question. "Not exactly. You know I spent most of my career as a junior high school principal. Those are *confiscations*."

Hugh's eyes went wide. "You didn't just give them back to the kids at the end of the school day? That's what they did when I was in school and they took something away from you. No one was a big enough asshole to keep them." He held up a hand. "No offense."

"None taken." Riley pointed a finger at himself, Hugh, and Jim. "They might've given knives back in *our* day, but they haven't done that in a long time. No one wants to be responsible if they give a knife back to a kid and he does something crazy."

Hugh raked his fingers through the pile. "How many are there?"

"One hundred and thirty-three," Riley announced with the certainty of a man who'd only recently counted them.

Jim looked doubtful. "I don't know. I prefer not to trade in stolen goods—especially those stolen from kids by an unscrupulous principal."

Riley blanched. "Those are not stolen, Jim Powell! They were *weapons* confiscated in adherence with school policy."

Hugh picked up one of the knives and examined it. "The school policy is that the principal gets to take the confiscated knives home and keep them?"

"So, he can trade them for booze?" Jim added.

Riley sighed. "No, taking them home was my policy. I always liked a good pocketknife, and I couldn't stand to see them go in the garbage or be destroyed, so I took them home. You going to take them or not? I figured you could resell them in that store you're running in the back there."

Riley dipped his head toward the section of the roadhouse that had been set up as a retail store, selling everything from guns, ammo, and weapons to clothing and outdoor gear. The goods sold there were spare items belonging to Jim and his people, the spoils of battle, or items traded in by customers of the roadhouse, just like the knives Riley had spread out in front of them.

Hugh stared at the knives on the counter. "Some poor dude might come in here and buy back the knife you stole from him in junior high. How's that for irony?"

Riley groaned. "I didn't steal them!"

Jim leaned across the counter and punched Riley in the shoulder. "We're just giving you a hard time. What do you want out of them?"

Jim actually liked Riley, despite shaming him over the confiscated pocketknives. Riley had never been married and lived in the same home he'd grown up in. He'd worked for the school system his entire life and probably knew every single person in town. His mother had passed away just before the collapse, which they'd all agreed had been merciful since she was in bad health and required a lot of medications. Riley drank at the roadhouse every night, never got out of hand, and was the kind of jovial, conversational drunk that most people liked having around.

Riley stared at the knives as if they might be able to provide the answer. "Those knives have been sitting on a shelf in the basement since I retired. They're worthless to me. I mean, how many knives can one man carry anyway?"

Jim and Hugh looked at each other and shrugged.

"Uh, six most days," said Hugh, "but I could probably carry more if I was expecting a really bad day. That's counting fixed blade, folders, and non-metallic."

"Four for me." Jim exchanged a look with Hugh. "I've always been an underachiever."

Riley's eyes went wide at this information and he regarded his companions with a new wariness. "I guess I was referring to *normal* people. Either way, this many knives is useless to me. I carry the same old one every day, so I'd like to convert these into a winter-long drunk. I'm not sure what the knife-to-liquor exchange rate is so you tell me what you'll give me for them. I'm sure you'll be fair."

Jim craned his head around until he spotted Randi haggling with another customer at the far end of the bar. He cupped his hands around his mouth. "Hey Randi! Can you come here when you get a chance?"

Randi completed her transaction with the customer, poured him a mug of the roadhouse's own beer, then headed in Jim's direction.

Jim pointed to the pile of pocketknives on the bar top. "Can you and Hugh work out a value on these knives? Riley is determined to make a down payment on staying drunk all winter."

"I call my strategy *hibernebriation*," Riley announced proudly. "At the end of winter, if my shadow is blurry, I'll stay drunk for six more weeks."

Randi was all business. She took her job at the bar very seriously. She pointed at the ammo can. "That can come with the knives?"

"I got no use for it," said Riley.

Randy moved the ammo can to her side of the bar. "I got a couple of customers to deal with. Hugh, can you split those knives out into a few different grades? Maybe the good stuff in one pile, the average stuff in another, and the beaters in a third? That might speed things up and you know more about knives than I do."

"Copy that." Hugh began sorting the knives into piles like a man organizing his poker chips. They were all brands he was familiar with —rock-solid companies like Buck, Barlow, Case, Schrade, and Kershaw. School kids typically didn't pack Zero Tolerance, Microtech, Benchmade, Medford, or Chris Reeve knives, which was a damn shame in Hugh's opinion.

"While you're waiting, you want to drink?" Jim asked Riley.

Riley grinned. "I thought you'd never ask. You still have any of that blackberry liquor you guys ran a few months back?"

Jim grew serious. "I don't know if I can part with any of that. It's my personal favorite."

Riley looked downcast, which almost made Jim feel bad for a half second. "I'm just messing with you. We have a decent supply on hand. With corn, potatoes, and fruit coming in all summer, we spent the fall running liquor twenty-four hours a day. We've also been buying from a few local moonshiners out there making their own product. Some of them are pretty damn good."

Riley was intrigued. "You test it all? Somebody has to make sure the quality is up to snuff."

"I let Lloyd handle that. He's the most qualified. Some might say *too* qualified. Sometimes I'll send him out to test a batch and he'll run into another musician, or a particularly good run of liquor, and he'll be gone for days. I've had to send Nooner or Shade out looking for him more than once."

"Sounds like a good rating system," Riley said. "Lloyd's One-Day Drunk would be the bottom tier of acceptable liquor. Lloyd's Five-Day Drunk would be top shelf."

Jim laughed, reached below the bar, and came out with the bottle. The label said Jameson but the liquor inside was purple, and someone had used a permanent marker to relabel the bottle as Blackberry. Jim poured Riley a glass. "Well, if we go by that system, this here is Lloyd's Week-Long Liquor."

Riley took the glass and held it up in a toast to himself. "To a winter that's all *blur* and no *brrrr*."

Jim excused himself. It was the time of day that had once been known as "happy hour" in establishments like this, but the label no longer seemed appropriate considering the circumstances. The mood at the Reset Roadhouse had been subdued ever since Walter Lightspeed's wireless grid system had exploded in front of their very eyes. A dark mood had settled over the entire community. People had died and disappeared at an alarming rate. Suicides were a daily occurrence, and Jim was convinced that a number of others had died from sheer despair. Losing power again after all they had endured was simply too much for some.

Across the building, the back door opened, and Pete and Charlie came in. Jim stepped out from behind the bar and walked toward the boys. Although he always thought of them as boys, they were more like young men these days. Aside from growing taller and filling out, the things they had seen and done had aged them. While this world took a toll on everyone, the young had been changed forever. They'd never know the world of their parents and grandparents.

About half the tables were full already and some of the patrons acknowledged Jim with a wave or greeting. By the time he got across the room and caught up with Pete and Charlie, they were warming themselves by one of the large wood stoves.

"How were Nana and Pops?" Jim asked.

His parents had insisted on moving out of Jim's house and back into their own home during the brief period when electricity had been restored by Lightspeed's grid. Once the lights went out again, when the grid collapsed, they'd moved into Buddy's old house in the valley. It wasn't their home, but it was a home they could make their own until such time as they couldn't live independently any longer. It was close enough to friends and family that people could stop by throughout the day and check on them.

At Jim's question, Pete and Charlie looked at each other and by some unspoken agreement, Pete took the lead.

"They had a fire going and most of the house was shut off. It was warm enough, but they didn't have any water when we got there. Pops thought it was frozen."

Jim looked confused. The night had been cold, but it shouldn't have been cold enough to freeze pipes already. "Did you take a look?"

"The pipes weren't frozen," Charlie said. "They were empty. We checked the spring box and it was silted in with mud."

"Ah, from all those rains we've had," said Jim. "I guess we've been too busy with firewood to keep up with cleaning spring boxes. Did you get the lines open?"

Pete nodded. "We used one of those little tire inflator pumps to blow the line out. Once we had water flowing to the house again, we uncapped the drain on the spring box and did our best to clean it out."

Jim patted the boys on the shoulders. He was genuinely pleased that they'd known what to do and had done it without needing to ask for help. "I appreciate that. I know Nana and Pops did too."

"They gave us each five dollars." Charlie grinned. "I wouldn't have taken it, but they insisted."

"It's not like it's worth anything anyway," Pete added. "Charlie and I have thousands of dollars laying around the house that we've accumulated here and there. It's not good for much more than starting fires and stacking beside the toilet."

Jim frowned. "It might be one day. I'd suggest you hold onto it just in case."

Pete and Charlie exchanged amused glances. Jim could tell they thought they were listening to some old timer rant about something from the old days that they knew they'd never see again in their lifetime. As much as their attitude unsettled Jim, he understood it. There was a strong possibility they'd never see the old normal again.

Although Pops' water lines hadn't been frozen this time, it wouldn't be long before winter was truly making their lives harder. There had been hard freezes that killed most of the remaining garden plants, with the exception of the hearty cool weather crops. Those same frosts caused most of the hardwoods to lose their brightly colored leaves. It was almost as if the physical world itself was experiencing the same bleak emotional and psychological turmoil that the people of the community felt.

Jim and his tribe were among the most pragmatic people in the area and even they were rocked by losing power after having their hopes buoyed by Lightspeed's wireless technology. They had installed his converters on their homes, even as Jim encouraged them to remain skeptical. He didn't want them to place all their faith in this new technology, but it was hard not to. They had all been mesmerized by the return of electric lighting. They had been enthralled by the ability to use electric appliances again. Everyone had appreciated being able to charge old devices, take hot baths, and brightly illuminate every room of their house with wild abandon.

Even after Lightspeed's grid collapsed and took their newfound hope with it, business at the roadhouse remained steady. The apocalyptic establishment was like a neighborhood bar that remained busy despite whatever events impacted the community. Whether it was the economy, layoffs, or marital strife, there were always those who found relief at the local watering hole. Those people continued to come to the roadhouse, even if it was to eat and drink in a much more subdued manner than they had when the lights were on. They drank with the stoicism of people who needed a few beers after work or those who enjoyed a cocktail to unwind from the stress of the day. Booze was a balm for their raw souls rather than a casual way to pass the evening.

Though he enjoyed drinking, booze wasn't part of Jim's coping strategy. He came from a long line of people who treated any mental health condition with an unhealthy devotion to hard work. Depression? Work harder. Anxiety? Work harder. Post-traumatic stress? Work harder. In the same way that some families passed down brown eyes or big feet to the next generation, Jim's passed down an obsession with working until they were too weary to think about the state of their life.

Fortunately, there was plenty of work to go around so the "medicine" for what ailed Jim and the people who thought like him was abundant. They were probably a month away from the coldest part of winter and everything in their world ran on wood. They heated their individual homes with wood and depended on it for hot water. The roadhouse itself was heated by means of several woodstoves, which they also relied on for cooking. At this time of year, with gardening behind them, every spare set of hands was devoted to cutting, splitting, and stacking wood for the coming season.

"What else do you need us to do?" Charlie asked.

Jim didn't even have to look around. He kept a list constantly scrolling through his mind. "Grab a wheelbarrow and restock the racks by these woodstoves. Shade is on his way with the last load of firewood for the day. When he gets here, you can help him unload."

"Good enough," Pete said. "What are you serving today? It smells delicious."

"That's venison chili. There was a woman who came in earlier today that I'd never met before. She lived over in Cleveland and used to have a restaurant. She brought an entire backpack full of spices.

She said she had more, but that was all she could carry. I'll have to send someone over with a packhorse to get the rest of it.

"What did she want to trade for?" Charlie asked.

"Ammunition for hunting. She wanted a caliber that not many people use these days, so it worked out well for both of us."

A loud whistling split the air and Jim whipped his head around to find Hugh waving in his direction. He acknowledged Hugh with a nod, then turned his attention back to Pete and Charlie. "I need to see what he wants. You guys warm up before you head back outside, okay?"

"Can I get a shot of hooch to warm my bones?" Charlie asked mischievously.

Jim cocked an eyebrow at the young man. "No, but I'm pretty sure you could each have a bowl of chili. Would that do?"

Pete answered for both of them. "It sure would."

3

Lightspeed Aid Distribution Center
National Guard Armory
Bluefield, Virginia

CLANG!

Clang!

"Josie!" Yana hissed. When Josie didn't stir, Yana repeated herself louder. "Josie!"

"What?" Josie groaned, cracking an eye open. The interior of their room in the barracks was barely visible in the gray morning light.

Yana was sitting up in her bed. "That noise. How did it not wake you?"

Clang!

"Security," Josie mumbled. "They're fixing something, I guess."

"I don't think so." Yana looked toward the door with fear in her eyes.

Josie pulled her pillow over her head. "Go back to sleep. If it was important, security would wake us up."

The next sound was shattering glass, audible even through the closed door of the barracks. Both women sat bolt upright in bed.

"I think it's an emergency now." Yana tossed her covers off and slid her feet into a pair of Crocs.

Josie reached for her radio on the nightstand. Clutching it in both hands she spoke into it. "Alpha Twenty for Alpha One! Alpha Twenty for Alpha One!"

There was no answer.

Josie heard Brendan and Lamar in the hallway speaking in loud voices. She climbed from beneath her sleeping bag and hurried into the hallway in her socks. "Alpha Twenty for Alpha One! Alpha Twenty for Alpha One! What's going on? What's the situation?"

Yana appeared at the far end of the hallway, her face pale.

"What's going on?" Lamar demanded.

"There are people outside the main door," she said, voice quavering.

Brendan spun on Josie. "Where's security?"

"Not answering," she said cooly.

"What do we need to do?" Yana asked. "They've broken a window and they're trying to get inside."

"The catwalk?" Brendan suggested. "Maybe we should grab our guns and get to the catwalk!"

"That's too far for our handguns," said Lamar.

"The range doesn't matter," Josie said. "The catwalk is too high anyway. We won't be able to see the attackers if they've already reached the building." She raised her radio again, imploring security to answer her. Still there was no response.

Yana was done waiting. She ran past Josie into her room, grabbed the belt with her handgun and spare magazines, and said, "I suggest you all help me drive them away while we still can."

"*If* we still can," Lamar corrected, ducking back into his room for his own weapon.

Brendan was right on his heels. "I knew we should have been issued rifles."

"This was supposed to be an aid mission," Josie said, though no one remained in the hallway to hear her.

Brendan and Lamar sprinted out of their room and followed Yana toward the drill hall. Josie clipped her radio to her pajamas, ran into her room, then pulled on her coat and boots. She took up her pistol belt and strapped it on as she jogged out of the room.

"There's no one up there!" Lamar said when Josie burst into the drill hall. He pointed at the catwalk high above them, where someone from security was always stationed. Today it was empty.

Boom!

Yana fired her handgun through the laminated safety glass on the front door. Outside, a man had been using a crowbar to poke holes through the glass, trying to create an opening that would allow him to hook the panic bar and unlatch the door. Security had talked about chaining those doors but hadn't done so. Now it might be too late.

Yana's round caught the man in the face. He spun and fell backward without a sound. There was a scream from the man's companion. Yana rushed the door and found another man standing off to the side, covering his mouth and staring at the dead man in horror. When he saw Yana with her upraised handgun, he bolted and took off running across the parking lot.

Yana fired at his back, striking him to the left of his lower spine. The man fell and writhed, crying out. Yana was aiming carefully, ready to take her follow-up shot when Lamar pressed her weapon down.

"He was running away! You shot him in the back! There's no need to shoot him again."

Yana's voice was venomous. "Yes, he's running back to tell the rest of those people outside the wire that he and his partner nearly got through the door. What do you think will happen after that?"

When Lamar had no answer for her, Yana shoved him to the side, then raised her handgun with both hands to sight through the hole in the glass. She took careful aim and fired a single shot. The wailing man fell silent.

Lamar turned away with disgust. "I can't do this shit."

"Then you might as well walk out there right now and turn yourself over to them," Yana said. "Are you ready to do that? Are you ready to give up and die?"

"Where the hell is security?" Brendan shouted in frustration.

Yana headed for the ladder that led up to the catwalk. "We need to get eyes on the fence. Even if we can't shoot accurately at those distances, they won't know that. A few warning shots might turn back any attacks." She paused a few steps up the ladder and turned her head toward the rest of the group. "I'll need help."

Josie put a hand on Brendan's shoulder and urged him in that direction. "You and Lamar get up there with Yana. I'm going to see if I can find security and figure out what the hell is going on."

Lamar shot Josie a disapproving look, but he didn't argue. She knew he didn't like heights, nor did he like guns, but this was a predicament no one cared to be in. Yana had presented him with the option of walking out the door and he hadn't taken it. If he was going to stay with them, he had to pitch in and help them defend their position.

Josie waited until Lamar had started up the ladder to retreat from the drill hall. The barracks that the security team used was on the opposite side of the building. They'd insisted on having their own space. Josie ran down the hallway, her unlaced boots flapping on her feet and threatening to trip her. When she reached security's hallway, she found the door standing wide open, which was unusual. They insisted on controlling access to their part of the building.

"Hello?" Josie called down the dark hallway.

There was no answer, but she jerked when a gunshot echoed down the hallway from the drill hall. Someone, likely Yana, was sending a message to those determined to avenge their fallen companions.

"Hello?" Josie repeated.

She removed a flashlight from a pouch on her belt, clicked it on, and directed the beam down the hallway. The doors to every room stood open. Josie headed for the first room, the one she remembered as belonging to Alpha One. The room was an absolute wreck, looking like someone had packed in a hurry.

The pace of Josie's breathing increased as she rushed down the hall, checking room after room. All of them were in a similar state. Her heart sank as she finally understood what had happened. Vince and his people had grown tired of waiting for her to find a solution to their problem. They'd taken matters into their own hands and abandoned the distribution center, leaving Josie and her people to their own devices.

The last of the rooms was what the security staff referred to as their "team room" and the door there stood ajar as well. The metal gun locker was open and all the slots that previously held weapons were empty. Security had cleaned it out. There were hard plastic Pelican cases scattered around the room, sitting open and empty. Josie had no idea what they'd held. Torn ammunition boxes spilled their contents onto the ground. Loose rounds had rolled in all directions, like stray marbles. Jodie nudged the boxes around with her toe, noting that several contained 9mm ammunition. Josie dropped to her knees, found an empty Pelican case, and began loading it with all the 9mm she could find.

"Vince, wherever you are, you're an asshole," she muttered. "You better hope we're not going in the same direction."

4

Lightspeed Aid Distribution Center
  National Guard Armory
  Bluefield, Virginia

HIGH ON THE catwalk above the drill hall, Josie's team was taking as much fire as they were handing out. Apparently the locals sensed blood in the water and were firing upon the armory with an intensity they had not demonstrated when the security team had been in place. Maybe they could tell they were only taking handgun fire now. They might also have noticed that the rounds being fired from the armory were not nearly so accurate as they'd been a day earlier.

Climbing the steel ladder with the backpack of ammunition was more of a workout than Josie had expected. Her legs trembled as she transitioned off the ladder and onto the catwalk. She clasped the handrail tightly and fought to steady herself, afraid her legs would give way at any moment.

"Did you find those security assholes?" Lamar demanded, only briefly cutting his eyes away from the fence he was watching. "You find those fools hid out somewhere, sleeping or something?"

Josie blew out a breath, grasping the railing with both hands. "Those 'fools' appear to have left without us. Their rooms are empty and they appear to have taken their gear with them. All of it."

Lamar curled his lips in disgust. "I knew it! I knew they were going to get fed up with waiting around on you and strike out on their own. What the hell are we going to do now?"

Josie tightened her jaw. "You can't blame this on me. I'm doing the best I can. We're *all* doing the best we can."

Lamar's voice practically oozed with disgust. "Are we, Josie? Are we *really*?"

Brendan raised a hand in Lamar's direction, trying to soothe him. "Come on now. That's not fair. You can't go blaming Josie for those guys abandoning us. We're all responsible for our own actions here."

"Well, my actions can't get me home!" Lamar snapped. "I'm not the one in charge."

"You have internet access just like the rest of us," Josie replied. "And you're welcome to use the satellite phone if you know of someone you can call in to rescue us. For that matter, you're free to walk out the door anytime you want to. No one will stop you."

Lamar either wasn't listening or chose to ignore Josie's statement. He was wracked with anxiety and his eyes were damp with tears. "What the hell are we gonna do now, huh? I ain't built for this shit. People are shooting at us! I didn't sign on for this."

Josie rolled her eyes. She had no patience for people being dramatic. "Surviving this unexpected turn of events might require that you step outside your job description, Lamar. This is what's known as an *emergency*."

Lamar bristled at her tone. "I am not a child!"

"Then quit acting like one," Josie snapped.

Her calm only infuriated Lamar further. He opened his mouth to say something else, but Yana cut him off.

Typically, the calmest of the group, Yana jabbed a finger at Lamar and hissed, "That's enough! Falling apart and turning on each other will accomplish nothing. We have to rely on each other now. Remember that."

Lamar was still glaring at Josie. She met his angry gaze with an infuriating calm, but they both kept their mouths shut.

Yana lowered her voice. "Now, I suggest we come up with a backup plan. Something beyond staying here at the armory. Holding this position until we're rescued is less feasible now that we've lost our security detail."

"A backup plan?" Lamar asked sarcastically. "That implies there's some original plan to back up. If there is one, I haven't heard about it."

Yana ignored him and continued. "Staying here until rescue comes might be fine *if* rescue comes and *if* no one breaks into the building. I suggest we develop a contingency plan, just to be prepared for the worst. A plan for what we'll do when staying inside this building is no longer an option."

BOOM! BOOM! BOOM!

Their conversation was interrupted by an eruption of gunfire from Brendan's handgun. A man had emerged from behind an abandoned vehicle and tried to cross the empty parking lot. The burst of gunfire turned him around...for now.

That moment seemed to provide a punctuation mark to everything Yana said. Everyone was silent for a moment, hearts pounding with anxiety, with the realization of just how bad their predicament had become. When Lightspeed first sent them out here, working at this remote distribution center so far from everything they knew had been daunting enough. Looking from person to person, Josie could see the thoughts spinning through their heads. It was simple to do because they had to be the same thoughts running in a loop through her own mind.

Josie sucked in a deep breath and wiped the sweat from her forehead. She was the team leader, and these people were her responsibility. She'd already wasted so much time in a state of indecision that they'd lost their security team and she couldn't delay things any longer. Rescue wasn't coming. The perfect plan wasn't coming. They needed to do something—*anything*—while they still had options.

"If everyone will listen to me for a moment, I have an idea I'd like to share with you." Josie looked around, met their eyes, and saw she had everyone's attention. "Nearly all the locals who used to come in here had an attitude. They wanted to take as much as they could get, then they complained that they didn't get more. They took their hostility out on us because they saw us as an extension of government, as part of the bureaucracy that had abandoned them in their time of need."

"We all know that," Lamar growled.

"Will you let her talk?" Yana snapped.

"I can count on one hand the number of people who ever took the time to speak to us like humans and ask questions," Josie went on. "I don't know if you remember this or not, but one of them even said that we were welcome to come visit his community if we ever got any time off."

Yana's eyes brightened with recollection and she began to nod. "The big guy. Real country."

Josie smiled. "That's him. His name was Shade. I'd never heard that name before so it stuck out to me."

"I've never heard it before either," said Yana. "Do you even know where his community is?"

"I do. We spoke several times and he showed me on a map. I looked it up on my GPS the other day and it's around sixty miles from here."

Lamar just about blew a gasket at the thought of it. "*Sixty miles*? How long will it take us to walk sixty miles? *Can* we even walk that far?"

Josie held a hand up. "Just hear me out, Lamar. Sixty miles is not impossible. As for how long it would take, it depends on how much we carry and how our bodies hold up to the trip. We might be able to do eight miles a day or we might be able to do eighteen. It could take a couple of days or it could take a week. I believe four or five days would be a reasonable estimate."

"This isn't a race, and we'd obviously let the slowest team member set the pace," Yana added. "Working here kept us all in decent shape. We've been eating well and staying hydrated. Sixty miles is a completely manageable distance."

Josie nodded in agreement. "Obviously, we're all free to make our own choices but we should stick together. It's just like I told the security team. We have a better chance of surviving if we work together."

"How'd that little pep talk work for you?" Lamar cracked. "Where's that security team now? Those bastards left us here to die at the hands of irate hillbillies. I feel like I'm trapped in some horror movie."

"I won't defend the security team's actions," said Josie. "But it was their decision to make. Obviously, I wish they'd said something first so we could have planned accordingly. I'd like to think that the four of us have a bond. I feel an obligation to stick with you three and I'd hope you feel that same obligation toward me."

"I hope we find those guys one day," Lamar said. "I'd love to get a crack at them."

"And what?" Yana said. "You're going to freeze them in their tracks by throwing out some spreadsheet formulas, then beat them to death with your iPad? My suggestion would be that if we do encounter them, you don't engage."

"Are we sure they're gone?" Brendan asked. "What if they just stepped outside to get away for a while. Maybe they're on patrol or something."

"They're definitely gone," Josie said. "Their rooms are trashed from hurriedly packing their gear. They took everything but the ammo they couldn't carry."

"No weapons left behind?" asked Yana.

"No, but we have our sidearms," Josie said. "We should have sufficient ammo for those. They left a lot behind. There's also plenty of food for the trip."

Yana appeared frustrated. "They leave any nightvision? A thermal monocular?"

"Not that I could find," Josie replied.

"You're talking like this is a done deal!" Lamar said. "Nobody has voted on anything. Nobody agreed to go marching across the countryside."

BOOM! BOOM!

Someone tried to skitter through Brendan's zone of fire, but he repelled the charge.

"As you've frequently pointed out, I'm the team leader, Lamar," Josie insisted. "I get to make the official decision here. You can choose to go with me or not, but I'm abandoning this outpost."

"Are we convinced the locals can break in?" Brendan asked. "This might still be safer than being on the road."

"They practically did earlier!" Yana exclaimed. "If I hadn't killed those two men, they might have gotten inside and we'd have immediately been overwhelmed. How do you think that would have ended for us?"

Brendan hung his head like a scolded dog.

"Do you have an alternative suggestion?" Josie asked Lamar. "I'm all ears. Do we wait to be robbed, possibly tortured and killed, or do we save ourselves while we still can?"

Lamar clutched his head in his hands as if trying to prevent it from exploding. He cursed and stomped. "I can't believe this is happening to us. This isn't what I signed up for."

"You're stating the obvious," Yana said. "No one signs up for bad shit to happen. It just does. Grow a pair, dude."

Josie shot Yana a look, a silent warning that she might be pushing a little too hard. She approached Lamar and rested a hand on his shoulder. "As we've discussed over and over again, *everyone* who was working in the field for Lightspeed is in the same predicament. You're not being singled out by the universe. You're letting the stress of the situation get to you, but you need to remember why you're here in the first place. You need to remember why Lightspeed chose you to be on one of his teams."

"What's that supposed to mean?" Lamar asked, on the verge of tears.

Josie couldn't tell if his tears were the result of anger or fear, or perhaps some combination of the two. "We were all picked because we were some of the smartest people in the room. We were chosen because we were exceptional. Don't forget who you are. Don't forget what you're capable of."

Lamar raised his eyes to meet Josie's. "What's that? What *am* I capable of? Because right now, I'm not feeling very capable."

Josie offered Lamar a smile. She wasn't acting from her personal feelings right now, but from her role as team leader. It wasn't her job to soothe Lamar's emotions. It was her job to inspire him to rise to what challenges were presented to them. "Our entire experience as part of the Lightspeed organization was one of being presented with challenges and working together to overcome them. You need to look at our situation as just another of those challenges so we can get on with the business of solving it. You're letting panic and fear disrupt your problem-solving abilities. You need to get control of that."

Lamar wiped his eyes. "I'll do my best."

Josie patted him on the shoulder. "Okay, then let's figure this out. Does anyone want to stay here or are we all going to leave together?"

"I know you said this isn't going to be decided by a majority vote, but my vote is for leaving," said Yana. "The people in this community are resentful at having lost electricity when the wireless grid collapsed. They seem to feel like somebody needs to pay for their suffering and I don't want to be a punching bag."

"I agree," Brendan said. "I'm terrified of leaving, but there's no point in waiting for a rescue that's not going to come. We need to take control of our own destiny."

It took Lamar a moment to find his words. "I'm not at my best right now and I apologize for that, but I don't want to be left here alone. If you think it's best to leave, Josie, then I'm with you. Just tell me what I need to do."

Josie rubbed her hands together. Now that they were in agreement it was simply a matter of organizing the task. This was what she excelled at. "I wish it was as simple as throwing on backpacks and taking off, but I'm not so naïve as to think any of us are in marathon condition. I suggest each of us prepare a two-stage loadout. Take a backpack with supplies critical to your survival and keep it light enough that you can carry it. You'll need food, water filtration, clothing, spare ammunition for handguns, a sleeping bag, and some type of shelter against the weather. For the second stage, I would encourage each of you to grab one of the rolling Pelican cases and pack it with important but less essential gear."

"You're seriously suggesting that we drag a rolling case behind us like it's a suitcase at the airport?" Lamar asked. "For *sixty* miles?"

"We have expertise that could make us very helpful to any group that we join. Those skills and technologies could be the key to us being welcomed into an established group. We bring things to the table that few people in the country have access to right now. We have a satellite phone and laptops with satellite modems. We have GPS and solar chargers for all our equipment. I intend to take all those things because they could be helpful to me, but you can make your own decisions. If you think you'll be welcomed in on the basis of your charm, Lamar, you can go for it." Her tone suggested that was a longshot.

Lamar got the point. "Okay, okay, I'm hearing you. When are we going to leave?"

"Tonight. We already know the situation here isn't going to improve. The longer we stay, the more likely it is that someone breaches the building. How about we go down and pack one at a time?" she suggested. "The rest of us stay up here and keep watch. Things usually slow down around dark since the locals go home by then. I'd suggest we take advantage of their absence and get moving about 2 AM. Questions or comments?"

Josie looked around the room, pleased to see there were none.

"Excellent. Then who wants to pack first?"

5

Jim was behind the bar double-checking that the liquor was adequately stocked for the evening. Randi was twenty feet away, arms crossed and staring holes through Jim. She felt like she had things under control already and didn't require anyone following behind her, even if it was the guy who owned the place. Jim couldn't help it. He wasn't a micromanager, but he'd learned to pay attention to detail. He'd also had a friend once, a local businessman, who had told him that the key to running a good business was not to *expect*, but to *in*spect. Jim had never forgotten that, much to Randi's frustration.

Shade strolled up to the bar, helped himself to a bottle of beer, and leaned on the counter. "You got a minute?"

"Sure, what do you need?"

Shade looked around the room, then shook his head. "Let's take it outside?"

Jim glanced around the room, trying to see what Shade had seen. Although there were few people at the bar, it was far from crowded.

Whatever Shade wanted to talk about must be serious. "Yeah, no problem. Randi wants me out of her hair anyway."

"Damn straight," she muttered, aggressively mopping the bar with a towel.

"Do I need to be worried?" Jim asked. "You gonna kick my ass?"

Shade chuckled. "To hell with that. You've been known to take a gun to a knife fight. I ain't sure what you might take to a fistfight."

"Depends on who I'm fighting."

Jim followed Shade through the tables and they stepped out the side door by the loading dock. The rusty hinges protested and the bottom of the door scrubbed against the concrete. Hugh sat on a stack of pallets smoking a hand-rolled cigarette. Cookie was also there, leaned back against the wall with his arms crossed. Gary was propped against the wall beside him. Shade climbed down the concrete steps to the gravel loading dock, turned to face Jim, and took a sip of his beer.

Jim remained on the steps, studying the situation. "Shade, I know you said we weren't fighting, but in my experience, a scene like this either means an intervention or an ass whipping, and I'm not a drunk."

Hugh snickered, smoke puffing out his nose like he was an old tractor trying to start on a cold day. "Relax. We're not here to kick your ass or ask you to face this forsaken world sober, the latter of which seems particularly cruel."

"I would agree," Jim said. "Then what's this all about?"

Shade cut a look at Hugh. "There *has* been a little conspiracy going on, if that's how you would refer to your friends discussing you behind your back."

"Depends on the nature of the conversation," Jim shot back.

"By mutual agreement, I shall be the spokesman," said Hugh. "Which means I drew the short straw."

Gary raised a hand. "My role here is to pitch in with the occasional amen because I fully support what Hugh is about to tell you."

"We've been talking," Hugh began.

"Obviously," Jim growled.

Hugh continued. "I think it's time for you to do something that you've needed to do for a while."

Jim folded his arms across his chest, then decided that it looked like a defensive posture and uncrossed them. "Well, this can't be about killing somebody. I'm pretty sure I killed everybody I didn't get along with already."

Seeing his opportunity, Gary raised his hand in the air again. "Amen!"

Shade did the same. "I second that."

"I haven't known you as long as Lloyd, but we've been friends for long time," Hugh said. "You never wanted the responsibility of assuming leadership of your people in the valley, but they thrived once you did. You didn't want anything to do with town, but our people were safer once you came into town and opened the roadhouse. You have to agree that it's been a success."

"Very much so," Jim allowed. "It's exceeded my expectations."

Hugh took a drag off his cigarette and squinted at Jim through the smoke. "Then it's time for you to do another of those things you never wanted to do. Somebody needs to take leadership of this community and you're the only man for the job."

"What exactly do you mean by 'community'?" Jim asked.

"The town and the areas immediately surrounding it that consider themselves to be part of this community," Gary explained.

Jim hesitated, considering what his friends were saying.

Sensing he needed to say something before Jim rejected them, Cookie cleared his throat. "Jim, the best man for a job like this is the one who doesn't want it."

"That would damn sure make me perfect for it," Jim said. "I sure as hell don't want it."

Hugh got to his feet. "Shade and I've been talking about this a lot, Jim. We all have, and we have a long list of reasons you'd be perfect for—"

"I'll do it," Jim interjected.

Hugh raised his hand, cigarette pinched between his fingers. "No, hear me out. Organizing this place is more important than ever after all the suicides. Morale is at an all-time low. People need hope."

"By God, he said he would do it!" Shade burst out, eyes wide with surprise. "Quit talking before he changes his mind."

Hugh did a double take and stared at Jim. "You did? You mean you will?"

Jim nodded. "I've been thinking about it too. After Lightspeed's grid went down, I couldn't help but notice how much better our people have done than the people who steer clear of the roadhouse. I'm not saying we're experts, but something that happens here seems to make our folks more resilient and more hopeful. The town needs some of that."

"I've tried to do what I can with the people in town," Cookie said. "You've given us some excellent advice that saved a lot of lives, but people listen to you in a way they won't listen to me. They remember me as the guy who waited on them behind the counter at the hardware store. They see you as the guy who stood on the roof of an RV at the farmers market and cussed them out like dogs. They needed that slap in the face and they respect you for telling them the hard truth."

Jim smiled at the memory of the day he threatened the entire town. "I assumed they all hated me."

"Some of them still might." Hugh grinned. "But if there are haters out there, they are in the minority. They have bigger worries these days than Jim Powell. I see people come into the roadhouse every day wanting you to help them figure out some problem. You give them your time and that's bought goodwill among the community in a way that you are probably not even aware of."

Jim looked around at the group. "If I'm going to do this, I have a condition."

"Let's hear it," Shade boomed. "I'm about done with this beer and no meeting should last more than a single beer."

"I agree," said Jim. "I'll need a council or something, like a board of advisors. People I can bounce ideas off of and get some feedback. God knows I can't roll with every single idea that passes through my head. Sometimes I can be a little harsh."

"Nawwwww," the group chorused, as if shocked by the information.

Hugh pinched his cigarette between two fingers and shrugged. "That's news to me."

Jim rolled his eyes. "Okay, smart asses, but that's my condition. I want a council and I want to hold a town meeting here at the roadhouse to discuss the whole idea."

"How do we make that happen?" Cookie asked. "You tell me what to do and I'll do it."

Jim tipped his head toward the roadhouse. "My wife is in there. Put her in charge of spreading the word. She can get Ariel and the other children to make signs for us. When they're done, we send out teams to post them around town. We set the meeting here at happy hour. That's the busiest time of day, so at least we know someone will come."

Cookie scooted by Jim and headed inside the building. "I'm on it."

Shade chuckled. "That boy wants to move on this before you change your mind."

"I don't think there's any changing my mind at this point. This has been a long time coming and I fought it every step of the way. It's been waiting for me and it's about time I stepped up to the plate."

6

Lightspeed Aid Distribution Center
National Guard Armory
Bluefield, Virginia

IT WAS a nerve-wracking evening at the armory as Josie and her people prepared themselves for escape while it was still an option. There wasn't much discussion, with each of them stuck in their own heads as they contemplated the night ahead of them. For a year they'd lived beneath the safe umbrella of the Lightspeed organization and had hoped they'd remain there until this rough spot in the American timeline had passed. Now they were abandoned, stranded far from their homes, and terrified that they lacked the skills or resources to survive in the world.

They'd all experienced hardship in the months after the initial terror attacks, but they'd quickly put that behind them as they became accustomed to Lightspeed taking care of their every need. Not only had Lightspeed elevated their lifestyle to something better than most people in the country were experiencing, he'd given his new employees better lives than they'd had before the collapse. The prospect of returning to a powerless world filled with desperation and deprivation was difficult for them. It was demoralizing and soul-crushing.

After Lightspeed's wireless grid imploded, Josie and her team had shut their distribution center down. Josie had called around on the satellite phone and spoken to her counterparts at other aid centers. They were all doing the same out of fear. Fear that they'd need the remaining supplies to keep themselves alive until help came, which it hadn't, and fear that locals would overrun the site and take everything.

Those remaining supplies meant Josie and her people would have food, water, first aid supplies, cold weather gear, and more to take with them when they abandoned the center. There would be way more left behind than they could possibly carry. At Yana's suggestion, they decided to leave an emergency stash inside the heating duct-work of the building in case they had to return, reasoning that none of the locals would think to look there once they inevitably managed to break into the building. Among other things, this stash included MREs, freeze-dried food, ammunition, medical supplies, and batteries.

The team fervently hoped they wouldn't have to return to the armory. To do so would most likely mean that their mission to find a community that would take them in had failed. If that happened, if Shade turned them away, Josie had no idea what they'd do next. She couldn't allow her mind to go there. She couldn't assume failure.

Once they finished packing, they took shifts running watch from the catwalk. The hope was that each of them might be able to get some rest before they hit the road, but none of them had much luck falling asleep. They were all planners, which, while that made them good at their jobs, it left them less comfortable with the unknown. There were so many variables in a trip across unfamiliar, unsafe terri-tory that it was impossible to plan for every situation that might arise.

As evening came, the locals surrounding the armory trickled off and went home. Breaking into a building at night when you couldn't see what was going on wasn't worth the risk to them. Even the most determined marauders clocked out and went home for the night. They'd return tomorrow, put in another shift, and hope for better results.

Josie's people had set alarms on whatever electronic devices they were using, having agreed to meet at 2 AM at the rear of the building. Most of them were huddled in sleeping bags until then, trying to stay warm in the cavernous freezer of a building. When their alarms sounded, they forced themselves out of their warm sleeping bags and packed up the last of their gear. They pulled on cold boots and heavy coats, then shouldered their packs. They confirmed they were carrying full magazines in their handguns, just as they'd been trained, and placed them in their holsters. Finally, each of them took up the rolling cases that carried those things they wanted to take but couldn't fit inside their packs. Everything they valued and imagined they'd use was with them when they gathered at the back door.

Josie wished they had access to some of the military weapons that had once been stored at the armory, but they'd been stolen before Lightspeed ever assumed use of the building. Even so, her security team had nightvision devices, thermal scopes, their standard duty rifles, and a couple of sniper rifles. Unfortunately, they took it all with them when they fled without warning, leaving the so-called "nerd herd" behind with nothing but their tech gear and their personal possessions.

"I'm scared to open the door," Brendan said once they when they were ready to venture forth. His hand was on the knob and the others were lined up behind him, ready to go. He just couldn't make himself do it.

"Can we use our headlamps?" Lamar asked. "I have a strong flashlight too. We can make a quick pass of the grounds to make sure no one is out there before we fully commit."

"Remember what the security team told us about that?" Josie said. "Not only will lights draw attention to us in the dark, they'll ruin our ability to see without them."

When Brendan remained reluctant to open the door, Josie moved to the head of the line, dragging her rolling case behind her. "I'll do it.

When I open the door, I'm going to proceed quickly across the rear parking lot and into the weeds. You all should do the same. Don't linger. Walk with purpose. Once we're all there, we'll head for the woods. We'll stay concealed in the trees until we're away from the armory. Once we're on the road, I don't want anyone associating us with the aid center and thinking we have things worth stealing."

"We do," Lamar said. "That's the problem. Anyone who sees these rolling cases is going to wonder what's in them."

Josie shot him a look that he probably couldn't see in the darkness. He was going to have to toughen for the journey. It was time for tough love. "Buckle up, Buttercup," she chided. "Expect we're going to have *nothing* but danger and difficulty for the foreseeable future. If you're not up for that, you're welcome to stay here and take your chances. Your choice."

"No, I'm going," Lamar insisted. "You're not leaving me here by myself."

"Then let's do this." Josie took a deep breath, unlocked the door, and gently pushed it open. When she saw no movement among the dark shapes that surrounded her, she stepped outside and held the door for the others. "Come on."

There was a half-moon, which provided enough light that they could pick out general features of the terrain and see each other in silhouette. Josie had considered waiting to make their escape under a full moon but listening to the locals battering at the door day after day would be unbearable. The rest of the group streamed out of the door, bristling with nervous energy. When they were all out, Josie shut the door gently and made sure that it locked back. Inevitably, they all knew that the locals were going to get inside the armory, but she had no interest in making it easy for them. If they wanted to loot the building, they were going to have to work for it.

The back parking lot was a cluttered mess. When the building was operating as a full-fledged aid distribution center, the back parking lot was where military helicopters and trucks arrived with supply deliveries. There were discarded pallets, packing crates, and packaging of all sorts. Some of it had been heaped into piles and set on fire, leaving behind charred mounds of wood, nails, and melted plastic. The group wove their way through the obstacles, all of them focusing on the edge of the parking lot, which seemed to be miles away.

Though the rolling plastic cases were the only way they could carry all the things they wanted to take, they were horribly loud. The plastic wheels rolling over asphalt made a noise that sounded like it would carry forever. It reminded Josie of riding a Big Wheel in her neighborhood when she was a kid. She couldn't help but feel that the sound could be heard from miles away and would draw the locals in zombielike hordes. That fear of discovery fueled their retreat and put haste in their steps.

Despite their attempt to remain calm, Josie and her people were nearly running by the time they reached the edge of the parking lot. Lamar, the most hesitant to leave, was the first to reach the weeds, where he dropped to his knees, breathing hard. The rest of the group followed his lead, all of them crouching on the cold ground, waiting to see if they'd been followed. Behind them, the parking lot was deep in shadow from the pale moon, yet it was still and silent. Only the sound of their labored breathing reached their ears.

"I think we're safe," said Brendan.

"Let's go with *unnoticed*," Yana said. "We might have gotten away from the building without being detected, but we're far from safe."

Josie held up a hand, though the gesture went unnoticed in the low visibility. She couldn't break the habit of talking with her hands even when they couldn't be seen. "We can't let fear consume us. We need to think more like the security contractors who abandoned us and not the 'nerd herd' they accused us of being. Let's get moving."

As part of their standard gear, each team Lightspeed sent into the field was issued a handheld GPS unit. Whether the team was wireless power grid system installers, aid workers, advance teams, outreach workers, or security contractors, they were each given a BAE systems Defense Advanced GPS Receiver or DAGR. The device was much like the handheld GPS units used by backpackers or hunters except that it was more robust and offered some advanced features that benefitted soldiers and operators working in a combat environment. Those special features weren't of much use to Josie and her people, but she was still happy to have the device.

Josie had preloaded Shade's town as a waypoint based on information she recalled from the conversations they had when he came to pick up supplies. Part of her knew that those random conversations were a small, inconsequential thing, but they were the only thread connecting her and her people to anyone in this region. Most people visiting the aid center just wanted to receive the supplies they were allowed to take, then leave without any more interaction than necessary. Shade genuinely seemed kind and interested in them as people, even if he was only being polite. With returning to any of Lightspeed's bases being out of the question, that one connection with Shade was all Josie had to grasp for, tenuous as it was.

Before stepping out the door of the armory, Josie had powered the GPS unit up and by the time they reached the weeds, it had acquired the satellites that allowed it to pinpoint their location. She'd already used the device to plot a route between their current location and their destination. That route was displayed as a highlighted path on the display.

"We'll stay in the woods for about a half mile, then rejoin the road," Josie said in a low voice. "From there, it's approximately sixty miles."

"Approximately?" Lamar asked. "You have a GPS unit. Can you not be more exact?"

Josie cut him a look, not that he could see it. "You know, fear turns you into a real bitch, Lamar. I could be more precise if I had an address or exact coordinates, but all I have is some vague reference to a roadhouse in a particular town. Forgive me if that's not precise enough for you."

Lamar ignored her insult. "So, you don't even know where we're really going? What are we supposed to do when we get to the town?"

"Then stay here!" Josie hissed. "No one wants to listen to you whining for days on end."

Even Brendan was getting tired of Lamar being so high maintenance. "We ask around when we get there, dude. Surely someone will tell us how to find the roadhouse. How many functioning ones can there be?"

"Of course, the locals might shoot us on sight because we're strangers," Yana pointed out.

"You're not helping," Josie snapped. "Let's get moving. And this is your last chance, Lamar. Staying or going?"

"Going."

Wishing his decision had gone the other way so she'd be done with him, Josie sighed and stood up. "Then let's go."

Dragging their heavy rolling cases behind them, they waded through the weeds, briars tearing at their clothing and burrs collecting on their pants. It was rough going with their rolling cases not designed to be pulled over such uneven terrain. Shortly, they emerged on a back street that cut through a row of small houses with aluminum siding, tiny front porches, and fenced yards.

"I've never seen anyone coming or going from these houses," said Brendan. "I believe they're empty."

"They are," Yana confirmed. "Security kept an eye on them as part of their area study. Whoever lived in them before the collapse didn't have the resources to continue staying in this location. They packed up and cleared out long before Lightspeed ever set up the distribution center."

That the houses were empty didn't make the team any less paranoid about being exposed and in the open. There were noises in the night that made their minds race, their hearts skip a beat, and their blood freeze in their veins. The scampering of a small animal through dried leaves *could* also have been human footsteps; the sound of wind on a distant mountaintop could also have been the murmur of voices talking quietly; the rattling of a loose piece of siding on a dilapidated home could also have been someone sneaking out a door to pursue them. There was a time when imagination was helpful and a time when imagination worked against you.

The team eventually hit the main street through the area and continued walking for an hour, barely speaking at all, urgency driving them forward as if marauders were hot on their heels. Only after that first hour of frantic walking did they think they'd come far enough that they could slow to a more comfortable pace. Even so, it was still another hour before they felt like they'd gone far enough that they could stop and take a much-needed rest break.

"Ten minutes," Josie announced, setting a timer on her watch.

Yana watched her friend with amusement. "God forbid one of us rest for *eleven* minutes."

They had reached an empty section of highway, or at least a section that seemed empty from where they stood. In the faint moonlight they could see a mobile home dealership ahead and to the left, the inventory of homes arranged in neat rows. To the right was a convenience store, long ago looted and all its windows broken out. An automotive repair shop occupied the squat cinderblock building next door, the parking lot filled with cars that would probably never be driven again. The fuel-filler doors stood open on many of them, a reminder of those times in the early days of the collapse when one could still find fuel in the tanks of sitting vehicles.

The team had stayed in shape and physically active while the aid distribution center was open and handing out supplies. Their days had been long but satisfying, and they'd frequently worked to the point of exhaustion. In the weeks since Lightspeed died and his grid collapsed, they'd mostly sat around waiting for the rescue that never came. They'd grown out of shape and unused to physically demanding days. As a result, their legs and feet were already tired from walking. Their backs protested against their heavy packs, their arms and shoulders tired of dragging the heavy rolling cases along behind them, and their feet ached and complained.

"I'm starting to think that pulling a trailer behind me for sixty miles might be a bad idea," Lamar said. "This is going to be a *very* long trip."

"You're as technology dependent as I am," said Brendan. "You abandon that stuff on the road and you're going to hate yourself later."

"No one said anything about leaving it," Lamar said. "I'm just complaining."

Brendan glanced at him. "Yeah, you do a lot of that."

"What's that supposed to mean?"

Brendan couldn't hold in a laugh. "It's self-explanatory, dude. Ask anyone. It's practically your brand."

Josie got to her feet and sighed. "If you've got the wind to argue, you've got the wind to walk. Let's get moving."

"Thanks a lot, guys," Yana grumbled. "I really could have used a few more minutes. I wanted to take the full eleven."

"Ten," Josie reminded her.

"I know. I was teasing."

They walked in silence for a while before Josie spoke. "Listen, I know we bicker like siblings sometimes, but we have to get through this together. Once we find a place to land, you're all free to do whatever you want to do. We can stay together or split up—it really doesn't matter to me. But until we get where we're going, we *need* each other. There's strength in numbers, both physically and emotionally. Don't forget that we worked together for months as a team and we kicked ass. We were a well-oiled machine. Don't let the last couple of weeks destroy what we accomplished. If this is the end of our time together, let's go out on a high note."

"We're not talking about a few bad weeks at work," Lamar argued. "Our whole world blew up."

"Our whole world blew up a year and a half ago," Josie said. "Lightspeed lifted each of us out of the dust, pulled us into his little bubble, and we forgot how hard it was to live in the real world every day. We forgot about the fear and uncertainty that everyone else is living with. Now we're back in the shit too and that's just the way it is. So, for the next sixty miles, we have to buckle down and deal with it."

Lamar wasn't done griping. "You're not the boss anymore. You were the team leader back at the aid center and that's history now. If that life is done, so is your rank. We're all equals now, so don't be laying down the pep talks and inspiration bullshit. I'm not falling for it."

Josie was nonplussed by Lamar's attitude. "First, you're the one who keeps pointing out that I'm the team leader, which we all know is your way of avoiding having to decide anything for yourself. Second, we'll only be equals when you stop whining like a toddler, because no one else is doing that. We'll be equal when you grow a pair and tough it out like the rest of us are doing. Until then, you probably stand a stronger chance of surviving if you sit back and let the grown-ups make the important decisions."

Everyone was shocked into silence. Josie could be a hardass, but she rarely cut that close to the bone. No matter how stressful and tense things got, she usually tried to keep a cool head. Her reprimands had always seemed surgical, intended to make Lamar rise to the occasion. Perhaps Josie felt a stronger speech was warranted in this case. Either way, Lamar fell silent and didn't speak to them again until the next day.

7

Town

CLAY GEORGE WALKED STIFFLY from his bedroom and headed straight for the woodstove. The house was cold but would warm quickly once he got a fire going. He'd shut off all the rooms he didn't use and blocked off the upstairs with hanging quilts to keep the heat from rising to the second floor. When he reached the living room, Clay saw that his uncle Tim was asleep in the recliner near the wood stove. At least he *thought* he was asleep. Tim was in his late seventies and looked like every sleep could be the final one.

"It wouldn't be so damn cold in here if you'd added a log to the fire. You're sitting right beside the stove."

Tim didn't move. His eyes were closed and his mouth gaped open.

Clay gave his uncle a second look. "You alive?"

This time Tim jerked awake, slightly disoriented. Eventually his eyes came to focus on Clay. He drew a sleeve across his face to wipe off some drool. "You say something?"

"I asked if you were alive. At your age, it's a relevant question. I've seen corpses that looked better."

Tim scowled and pointed at his crotch. "I got your relevant question right here, nephew."

"What's that? A soggy adult diaper?" Clay teased.

Tim pulled in the footrest of the recliner. He yawned and rubbed his eyes. "Ain't no diapers here, kid. I always preferred those skimpy mankini drawers. The women love them."

Clay looked doubtful. "Is that right?"

Tim struggled to his feet and stretched, his old joints cracking like a handful of pretzel sticks. "Damn straight. When I was living in Tampa back in the seventies and eighties, I used to wear a Speedo to the beach, so I had a good tan. When I came out of the bathroom in that bikini underwear—"

Clay held up a hand. "You can stop right there. I didn't want to hear this story the first two hundred times you told it. I sure don't want to hear it again."

Tim clapped his wrinkled hands together. "Boom! It was like those women had been struck by lightning. Panties dropping everywhere." Tim did a little disco-era dance move.

"Just because women were speechless did not mean they were in awe of your physique. Maybe they were just shocked at the audacity of your choice in undergarments."

Tim ignored him, smacking his hands together again. "Boom, I tell you. Boom!" Laughing to himself, he danced off toward the front door.

Clay eased himself down to the ground beside the wood stove. He was in his sixties now and active but getting up and down from the floor wasn't as easy as it had once been. "Hey," he called out to Tim, "where you going?"

"To see a man about a dog."

"Can you start peeing off the back porch instead? Miss Castle gets upset when you use the front porch."

"The only time Miss Castle gets upset is when she misses the show." Ignoring Clay, Tim headed for the front porch.

Clay opened the door on his wood stove and used the poker to stir the ashes. Enough red coals glowed that he'd only need to add kindling to get the fire going. He shut the door, then opened the bottom door of the stove to remove the ash pan. He got up and headed for the back door so they could dump the ashes in the garden.

It was only by sheer misfortune that Clay ended up with Tim living in his house. Tim lived in Florida, in some fancy senior community with lots of women that he described as "hot to trot." He'd flown north a year and a half ago to visit family and pay his respects to some of their departed relatives. That was when the terror attacks shut down the country and Tim got stuck staying with Clay. Now Clay wasn't sure if he or Tim would live long enough to see things go back to the old idea of normal.

Clay dumped the pan of ashes over the garden fence, catching some in his mouth as a gust of wind blew them back in his face. Keeping the fire going required so much work it was nearly a full-time job. It almost made Clay wish that he had been visiting Tim in Florida when the attacks happened. At least it wouldn't take so much work to stay warm. He could imagine it would have been quite the adventure with Tim always trying to set him up with one of the "hot to trot" resident cougars.

Clay stopped on the back porch and loaded the empty ash pan with split kindling. He let himself back into the house and returned to the wood stove where Tim was pacing the floor.

"Can you hurry up with that fire?" he complained. "I'm freezing my ass off here."

"If you'd added a log last night, it would have been plenty warm in here this morning." Clay removed the kindling from the ash pan and distributed it over the glowing coals. He replaced the ash pan beneath the iron grate, leaving the bottom door cracked until the kindling caught flame.

"By the way, Miss Castle says hi," said Tim.

Clay lowered his head and shook it. "Don't tell me you talked to Miss Castle."

Tim shook his head. "Nah, I only waved, but not with my hand."

Clay looked up at Tim to see if he was serious. Tim gave him a lascivious wink.

"There's a special place in Hell for people like you, Tim. I don't even know what to say to you sometimes."

Tim shrugged innocently. "I don't know where I'm going when I die. Heaven don't want me and hell is afraid I'll take over."

Clay stood up and added some larger sticks to the fire. As the flames grew, he looked at his uncle and shook his head. "I'm glad you woke up with so much piss and vinegar this morning. I've got a long list of jobs for you today."

"I'm a frail old man," Tim whined. "Not fit for doing anything but sitting by the fire all day."

"Nonsense. You're not frail, just crotchety and half crazy."

Tim laughed. "Flattery will get you everywhere. Feed me and I'll give you a day of work."

Clay added a larger log to the fire and decided it should keep for a while. "Fine, let's go to the kitchen."

"Now you're talking." Tim rubbed his hands together eagerly.

They headed for the kitchen and Tim planted himself at the kitchen table. Clay opened his pantry, which was nearly half full of packaged MREs. Clay scrolled through a couple, naming the options, then picking one for himself.

"I'll have the huevos rancheros," Tim said. "And can I get a cup of coffee? Ideally, I'll take it delivered by some hot young fifty-year-old with too much lipstick and too little clothing."

Clay rolled his eyes. "These MREs have instant coffee packets in them, but you'll need to heat up some water on the stove."

"It'll take a kettle three days to boil on that little fire of yours."

"Then you build the fire tomorrow, Grizzly Adams. You're lucky I put up with your complaining."

Tim grinned. "I make up for it with my charm and wit."

They ate, making small talk and discussing the list of chores that needed done over the course of the day. Frequently, Clay threw out ideas that Tim thought were ridiculous. When Clay insisted those harebrained schemes were worth trying, Tim would throw his hands up in the air and surrender.

"You're the engineer," he'd always say.

It was true, after all. Clay *was* an engineer. He had been scheduled to retire just a few months after the terror attacks collapsed the nation. Had he worked through until his retirement, he planned on selling his house in Virginia and moving further south to enjoy warmer weather. Tim had suggested his nephew come to Florida so they could be roomies, but Clay had made it clear he had no intention of living near Tim. He'd spent his entire career in the coal industry, working in dirt, mud, and coal dust. He wanted his retirement to be warm and sandy instead. Since the collapse, it was just dark, gloomy, and boring.

When they were done eating, Clay shoved their MRE wrappers into the wood stove. He insisted that none of their food trash go outside because he didn't want to take a chance on anyone learning that they had resources, and Clay *had* resources. Engineers spent their careers studying worst-case scenarios and Clay had done the same throughout his life. He lived through the energy crisis of the Seventies, nuclear war scares, and Y2K. He'd done the drills where students hid under their desks. There'd even been a sign on the door to his school advertising that the building could also be used as a "fallout shelter, which forced his mother to explain what that meant.

As a result of a childhood spent beneath the shadow of doom and gloom, Clay was a closet prepper. Every month, like clockwork, he bought something to further his preparedness and increase his chances of survival if something bad were to happen. Every month he bought a case of MREs or freeze-dried meals and stuck them away in a closet. At the time, he didn't know if he would ever need them, but he understood it was better to play it safe. That was the engineer speaking and in this case his inner engineer had been correct.

"Let's hit the garden first," Clay said. "It's looking a little needy."

Situated on one of the back streets in the town, Clay's home was on a slight hill. Like many of the homes on the street it came with a garage that had been cut into the hillside. The walls and roof were concrete. The original garage doors had been wooden and hinged on the sides so that they swung open into the street. They were missing when Clay bought the home and he had them replaced with a high quality, insulated garage door. There were no windows in the structure and the only other entrance was a walk-in door also situated against the street. Clay had upgraded that to a secure steel door at the same time as the garage door was installed.

Clay and Tim stepped onto the front porch and looked around to make sure there were no strangers in sight. There weren't many people remaining in this neighborhood anymore. Some had moved off since the collapse while others had died under various circumstances. A few had simply disappeared and Clay had no idea whether they were living or dead. On his end of the street the only homes that were still occupied were his house, Miss Castle's house, and the Stanley home a few doors down.

Clay grasped the narrow black handrail and climbed down the concrete steps, then down the narrow sidewalk to the street. Once they reached the garage, he tugged a key ring from a retractable lanyard on his belt and used two keys to unlock the door, one for the deadbolt and one for the handle. He stepped inside, then closed the door behind Tim.

At this time of year, with it getting dark early, Clay preferred to do his gardening during the day. That way any light escaping out the door didn't attract as much attention. Clay had gone to great lengths to make sure the room was light-tight, so he didn't open the door after dark unless it was an emergency. That was because for sixteen hours a day, his garage was as bright, warm, and humid as a Mexican resort.

Rows of full-spectrum LED lights hung from the ceiling, their power cords coming from a set of wooden shelves that held batteries, an inverter, and a charge controller. The solar panels that powered the setup were concealed behind a privacy fence in Clay's backyard. It wasn't a large enough system to power his entire house, but it powered a few circuits and kept the indoor garden functioning. Like Clay's food supply, the gardening setup was something he had built out over time, with small purchases when extra cash was available.

To thrive throughout the year, the garden didn't just need power and light. It also needed heat and water. Because the structure was two-thirds underground, it was well insulated by the earth and held heat well. Clay had originally installed a woodstove when he first came upon the idea of using the garage as an emergency garden. Later, to cut down on the labor required to keep two woodstoves going, he built a waste oil burner.

The waste oil burner had been a welding project and was constructed primarily of scrap metal. The key components were a heavy brake drum and a scrap air compressor tank, into which he had cut a door. Nearby, a ten-gallon tank fed oil through a filter and drip fed it into the burner assembly. Clay had enough gas cans of waste oil to fuel the stove for months. He collected oil from deep fryers and abandoned vehicles on the fringes of town. Being the considerate person that he was, if he drained oil from a vehicle, he replaced the drain plug when he was done and left a note inside indicating that the oil was gone. When and if the world ever got back to normal, the owner of the vehicle might wonder where the oil had gone, but they would appreciate knowing they needed to refill it before they cranked the vehicle.

Water came from a series of eighteen blue barrels lined up inside the perimeter walls of the garage. They were fed by the gutters on the front porch, through an underground pipe. The barrels held more water than Clay really needed to keep on hand since it rained frequently enough to refill the barrels, but they served another purpose in the subterranean garden. Clay's waste oil burner was wrapped in copper tubing and plumbed into the barrels. This system heated the water in the barrels, causing them to act as radiators, which evened out the temperature in the space.

Being an engineer, Clay originally designed the system to circulate the water via a thermo-siphoning effect. Not satisfied with the effectiveness of that, he eventually installed the type of low voltage pump that was used to circulate the water in commercial fire sprinkler systems. Yes, it was another component that could break, and it did draw some power from his solar system, but it also improved the consistency of the heat in the room.

The room was divided according to the maturity of the plants. One area held the more delicate plants that were still small. Another area held taller plants that were in their vegetative state. There was even an area where Clay could shut off the light to trigger flowering in plants like tomatoes. Bagged potting soil was stacked high in one part of the room and a table was set up for planting seeds. While Tim bitched about having to plant seeds, he didn't have Clay's knowledge of gardening. It was one of the few jobs Tim could do without damaging anything. Clay was particular about his plants and had no interest in allowing some buffoon like his uncle to destroy them.

"So, what you want me to do today?" Tim's tone was that of a child who had resigned himself to being forced into some task he had no interest in doing.

"Why do you always have to say it like that?" Clay asked. "You're always complaining when you have to do some work. I don't hear any complaining when I put a plate of vegetables in front of you."

"You're too sensitive. It must be an engineer thing. I spent my life working *manly* jobs with guys who busted each other's balls all day long. There wasn't any room for pouting."

"I'm not pouting, and you were a used car salesman for your entire career. I'm not sure you can say that's any more manly than being an engineer. I wore a hard hat and stained coveralls at my job. You wore polyester suits and white shoes."

Tim waved him off. "You were in an office all day punching a calculator."

"I was a coal mining engineer. I was running around mine sites, trying not to get killed by heavy equipment or run over by haul trucks. I had the manlier job of the two."

"You need my help or not?" Tim grumped, changing the subject. "I offered my help and all I'm getting is a bunch of lip."

Clay sighed and took a calming breath. "There's a packet of seeds over there for Brussels sprouts. Put a wet paper towel down on a plate, then spread the seeds out on a paper towel. Put another paper towel on top of it, then sandwich another plate on top of that. Put it on the warming shelf near the oil stove when you're done. They'll stay there until they sprout."

Tim frowned in disgust. "Brussels sprouts? That the food of manly engineers?"

Clay shrugged. "Maybe it is. How about you plant them and quit your whining?"

"Brussels sprouts," Tim muttered, wandering off to the potting bench. "I don't know who the hell he thinks he is eating Brussels sprouts. You know what I'd like? A grouper sandwich. Grow me a grouper sandwich and then we can talk."

8

"WHERE DID you get this rabbit jerky?" Pete asked. "Did you make it yourself? It's good."

Charlie tore off a bite and chewed. "I got it from Shade."

Pete stopped mid-chew and grimaced. "You got this from Shade?"

"That's what I said. Everybody knows he makes the best jerky around. They sell it at the roadhouse as fast as he can make it."

"It's what he makes it *from* that concerns me," Pete said. He held a piece up in front of his face and studied it as if the scrap of dehydrated muscle might reveal to him from which mammal it originated.

Charlie huffed. "I told you it was rabbit. Shade *told* me it was rabbit. He ought to know."

"Yeah, well, my dad told me that Shade would make jerky out of anything that stood still long enough—buzzard, blue heron, cat, weasel, possum, raccoon or even groundhog."

"If Shade can make a chunk of buzzard meat taste this good then more power to him," Charlie replied with a mouthful of jerky. "I'd eat it until I split open."

Pete stared doubtfully at the chunk of meat in his hand before ultimately surrendering and shoving it into his mouth. He supposed Charlie was right. Regardless of what critter it was made from, it sure was tasty.

"How do you want to go this time?" Pete asked.

They were on their way to Nana and Pops' old house on the far end of town. To keep Pops happy, they checked on it at least once a week just to make sure nothing was wrong. The boys didn't mind. They'd go inside, check all the rooms, and make sure no windows were broken. After that, they'd wander around the yard and confirm that none of the outbuildings had been broken into.

"Let's take the back street on the north side of town. We haven't been through there in a while."

"Works for me," Pete said. "I like that street. There are some cool old houses."

"Bet you could get a good deal on one of them right now."

Pete laughed. "No doubt. You could probably just walk in and claim one if someone hasn't beat you to it."

The pair turned off Main Street at the farmers market and followed a paved road through an industrial park toward the northern periphery of town. As the road left the industrial park it narrowed to a residential street and they entered an older part of town. They followed that street past a halfway house and the old farm supply. Several blocks away the empty jail rose into the sky toward the middle of town. The building had not fared well in the apocalypse. Nearly all of its windows had been shot out by people who held a grudge for having been forced to spend a night there back in the days when law and order existed. Pete found it funny how people could blame a building for their own bad decisions.

Continuing up the back street, they passed a trailer court and Pete pointed to one of the mobile homes. "My gym teacher lived in that one. I wonder if he's still alive?"

"What's his name?"

"Coach Asshole."

Charlie grinned. "You sound more like your dad every day."

"Thanks." Pete wanted to be like his dad.

"But seriously, I must've had his brother at my school. I had a different Coach Asshole for gym *and* study hall."

They continued riding, sharing stories of the teachers they had both liked and despised back when school had been a regular part of their lives. When they came to the next intersection, they paused. A right turn would take them toward Becky's house while going straight would take them past Ian's.

"Which way?" Charlie asked. "I picked at the last intersection. It's your turn now."

After considering for a moment, Pete pointed to the right. "How about we go up toward Becky's house, then take a left on the last street before her house."

Charlie furrowed his brow. "I don't remember that street."

"I don't think we've taken it before. It's a dead end and we usually stick to the through streets. It might be a nice change of scenery."

"Anyone still living back in there?"

Pete shrugged. "No idea. I don't recall hearing anyone talk about it."

"You say it's a dead end?"

"If you're in a car it is. On horses you can cut across a driveway or yard."

Charlie swept a hand in the direction Pete had indicated. "Lead the way, boss man."

They rode north a short distance, passing some of the town's older brick homes. Before they reached the enormous house that Becky lived in, they turned left up a gradually ascending street that followed the slope of the hill. Many of the homes here were older also, dating to the early and middle twentieth century. There was one sprawling Victorian and a few brick ranches. There were white cottages with black shutters and wraparound porches. Some had aluminum awnings over each window. It had been a nice neighborhood at one time, desirable because there was none of the through-traffic that a lot of other streets experienced. Now the yards were overgrown and many of the mature shade trees had been hacked up for firewood. Non-burnable garbage was piled in yards, some of the stacks large enough to fill an entire garbage truck on their own.

One of the things that Pete wanted to point out to Charlie was that many of these homes had garages sunk back into the earth. While it wasn't a unique feature in some towns, there weren't many such garages in their town, and that made them interesting. Some of them were constructed of cut stone laid by Greek masons, while others were brick with metal or shingled roofs. Some were even solid concrete with flat concrete roofs.

"You see those garages?" Pete asked. "I always thought those were kind of neat."

"They're a little small. You are not fitting a big Cadillac or a lifted pickup truck in there."

"I guess not, but you could sure fit a horse and that's all we've got to drive around."

Charlie sniffed the air. "There must be somebody alive back in here. You can smell smoke."

"There." Pete pointed at a house ahead and to the left. "They have smoke coming out of their chimney. That one too. I guess the neighborhood isn't empty."

"You see that one there?" Charlie tipped his head toward a neat little cottage with aluminum siding and green awnings over the windows. "You can tell that one is empty. No smoke and no trash."

Pete curled his nose. "Speaking of garbage, it smells like somebody is burning some down the street."

Charlie pointed. "Look at the black smoke. It could be somebody burning a tire. It smells oily."

Pete took up his reins and nudged his horse in that direction.

Charlie followed him. "What are you going to do? Write them a ticket?"

"I'm just curious. I don't care what they burn." Pete crested a rise in the street and stopped. "It's coming from one of those little garages I showed you. You think it's on fire?"

"No, you need glasses. Look closer. There's a little chimney coming out of the garage. You see it?"

Pete said, "I see it now."

They continued down the street toward the small garage, wondering why it was puffing black smoke like a locomotive. On this far end of the street, close to the point where it came to a dead end, the houses were further apart. Of the few houses there were, only a handful appeared to be occupied, as evidenced by the trash piles and smoking chimneys. Pete didn't know anyone who lived back in this neighborhood, and he had no idea who might be living in these houses. He certainly didn't know who owned the garage that currently had their attention.

Charlie was also aware that the people living there might have no connection whatsoever with the people who *used* to live there. Even the valley they called home was like that. Pete and Charlie lived in a stranger's abandoned house. Randi and Gary both lived in homes they had taken over because the previous owners had died. Pete had heard his dad talk about this often. When the lights came back on, it was going to be difficult to know who the true owner of such homes would be. Records were lost. People were lost.

"Do you think someone's living in that garage?" Pete asked.

"No idea."

They were getting closer by the minute and were perhaps only fifty feet away. The street was silent except for the clop of their horses' hooves on the cracking pavement. Pete swung his rifle off his back and around to the front of his body. He chambered a round and let it rest across the front of his saddle.

"You see something to be concerned about?" Charlie asked.

Pete shook his head. "No, but my gut is going off like an alarm clock. This neighborhood is starting to give me the creeps."

"That's good enough for me." Charlie brought his own rifle around and charged it. He left his safety on, but had his thumb resting on it, ready to flip it off if he needed to.

For as much as their interest was drawn to the garage and the chimney puffing like a smokestack, Pete and Charlie were both experienced enough to understand the dangers of getting tunnel vision. To become too fixated on the garage was the same as wearing blinders. There were other houses around them and the circumstances within each of those homes was unknown to them. There could be people watching them in the same way they had once sat in the shadows and watched strangers pass through the valley. Just because town had been quiet for a while didn't mean it would remain that way. Time spent out in the world was always time exposed to risk.

The two young men stopped just outside the garage but didn't say anything to each other. They stared at the building, listening for anything that might explain the churning smoke. The structure didn't appear to have any windows—not in the thin strip of wall exposed above the overgrown yard, not in the roll-up door, and not in the smaller hinged door beside it.

Pete looked at Charlie and tapped his ear. He heard something now. Charlie nodded; he heard it too. Inside the building, two men were arguing, their voices muffled.

"You think someone has a prisoner in there?" Pete asked in a low voice.

"Could just be men arguing." Charlie gestured to the road ahead of them. "Maybe we should get going and report it back to your dad. Let him and Hugh figure it out."

As interested as Pete was in understanding what was going on here, he knew Charlie was right. Just as he was about to agree, the side door to the garage flew open. An old man stalked out, his attention directed toward someone still inside the building.

"I don't know how anyone ever worked with you, Clay. You're a slave driver. I'm family and you treat me this way? I can't imagine how you were with people you didn't give a shit about."

Whoever was inside was fired up too. "Go change your panties, Tim! Better yet, take a nap, you old geezer!"

The old man slammed the door shut, took a step, then turned to see Charlie and Pete on their horses just feet away from him. He clapped a hand up to his chest, grabbed his heart, and staggered backward. He made a strangled cry somewhere between a curse and a prayer, then fell back against the door.

Pete slipped off his horse and was at the man's side in a half-dozen steps. "Are you all right?"

"No, I'm not all right you fop-headed hillbilly! I just fell and busted my ass."

Pete reached for the old man just as the door flew open again. A slightly younger old man stood there with an upraised pistol in his hand, aimed right into Pete's face.

"Drop that gun!" Charlie barked, his rifle aimed at the old man on the sidewalk. He could see the pistol aimed at his best friend, but the old man was the only one of the two he had a clear shot at. "Don't make me shoot that old bastard."

"Do it," Clay said. "Please! You'd be doing me a favor. You'd be doing the *world* a favor."

"Hey now!" the old man protested. "That's no way to treat your elders."

Pete held his hands up in front of him, showing they were empty. "I was just helping him up. He got startled when he saw us and fell down."

"I won't ask again," Charlie said. "Lower your gun or I kill the mouthy old man."

Pete made eye contact with Clay. "He'll do it. I swear he'll do it."

"Lower your gun, Clay," Tim snarled. "I refuse to die in this cold-assed hellhole. My body deserves to rot in the Florida heat."

"You're about to lose any say in the matter," Charlie said.

Tim looked skyward. "I always thought I'd be shot by a jealous husband. This isn't how I'm supposed to go out."

"Lower your gun, mister," Pete begged. "We were just riding by and noticed the smoke coming out of your garage. We didn't come to cause you any trouble. We're just riding across town to check on my grandparents' house."

"I'm done talking about this," Charlie said. "I'm shooting the old man on three. One..."

"Dammit!" Tim groaned. "I think I just pissed my pants."

Clay blew out a frustrated breath, lowered his gun, and holstered it. Charlie responded by lowering his rifle. Pete and Tim exchanged a relieved glance, then Tim waved his hands.

"Somebody help me up off this sidewalk. I'm freezing my ass off."

"Guess you should have worn those adult diapers after all," Clay teased.

"Don't look at me," Charlie said. "You can rot there for all I care."

Tim shot Pete an imploring look. Pete in turn looked to Clay for permission. He didn't want his gesture to be misinterpreted as hostile and lead to another armed standoff.

Clay crossed his arms over his chest. "I'm with the kid on the horse. I ain't helping him. My uncle is the most cantankerous old man I've ever met. I don't care if you help him or not."

Used to helping his grandfather, Pete grabbed Tim by the bicep and helped him up.

"Thanks, kid," Tim said once he was on his feet. He dusted off the seat of his now soggy tracksuit. "As for the rest of you, you two can kiss my wrinkled old ass."

Clay looked at Charlie. "I guess if you really want to shoot him, who am I to step in the way of fate? Go for it."

Tim stuck up a middle finger and aimed it at Clay. "If you weren't family, you'd be getting a knuckle sandwich instead of a one-fingered salute."

Clay rolled his eyes. "If *you* weren't family, I'd have fertilized my garden with your corpse eighteen months ago."

Charlie shifted in his saddle. "Let's go, Pete. These guys are making my head hurt and we have shit to do."

"One second." Pete turned his attention to Clay. "I don't recognize you guys. Do you two ever come to the roadhouse in town?"

Clay shook his head. "I don't recall there being anything like that in town. When did that happen?"

"My dad opened it a while back. After the collapse, not before. They serve food, beer, liquor, and sell some goods that people need. They don't take money, people barter for what they want."

"We don't get out much," said Clay.

"We don't get out at *all!*" Tim said, making clear it was Clay's fault.

He put his hands on his hips. "And let me get this straight—there's a functioning bar in this town?"

Pete nodded. "Yeah, they've got live music most nights."

"If you can call someone playing a banjo *music*," Charlie piped in.

"I'm telling Lloyd you said that," Pete said.

Charlie ignored him.

Tim perked up. "So does this bar have chicks?"

"As in women or poultry?" asked Charlie. "Because depending on the day, they might have either or both."

"As in broads," Tim clarified.

Clay groaned. "Oh Lord. No one says that anymore."

"They do have broads," Charlie replied. "And that's exactly how you should ask for them. I suggest you go straight to the bar, ask for a lady named Randi, and then ask her if this is where you can find some broads."

Tim leered. "Is this Randi hot to trot?"

"That's another question you'll have to ask her," Charlie said. "I'm not even sure I know what the hell that means."

Tim cocked an eyebrow. "Randi a looker?"

Pete frowned at Charlie. "You're going to get this man killed on his very first visit to the roadhouse."

"Killed?" Tim swallowed hard.

"You go to the bar asking about broads," Pete explained, "my guess is Randi will pin your hand to the bar with a knife then use a broken beer bottle to cut out your tongue."

Tim chuckled nervously until he saw that Pete was not laughing. "Seriously?"

Pete shrugged. "If not your tongue, something you'd probably miss just as much."

"Thanks for the warning." Tim turned his attention to Charlie. "As for you, kid, I'm going to keep my eye on you. You're one twisted son of a—"

Tim didn't finish the sentence because Pete lunged forward and clamped a hand over Tim's mouth. Startled by the move, Clay dropped his hand to his gun but didn't draw it. Charlie had not raised his rifle, but he had tightened his grip on it. Pete knew he could whip it up and kill someone in a fraction of a second.

"You don't ever call my friend what you were about to call him," Pete warned. "He lost his mom and that's about as sore as a sore spot gets. You understand?"

Tim bobbed his head and Pete let him go.

"I'm sorry, kid." He gave Charlie a sheepish look. "I didn't mean anything by it. I just got a foul mouth."

"You get a pass since you didn't know," Charlie said. "But only one, because you know better now."

Pete wondered if the old man knew just how close he'd come to being killed. These were times when deeply offending someone led to a punch in the nose, but the consequences of this insult would have run much deeper.

"We need to get going." Pete climbed on his horse. "You guys should come by the roadhouse sometime. It's a good place to network and learn what's going on in the community. Come on, Charlie."

The two of them rode off down the street, Charlie turning in the saddle to keep his eye on Tim. Pete took a left through the yard of an abandoned house and they kept riding until they lost sight of the two men standing by the garage.

9

Route 460
    Tazewell County, Virginia

WHEN THE SKY began to lighten with the approach of day, Josie and her people crashed in an abandoned factory that had once built mining machinery. Despite the emerging sun, the temperature remained cold and there was nowhere but the concrete floor to stretch out and sleep. None of them had any outdoors experience so they hadn't thought to bring backpacking mattresses to insulate them from the cold ground. Even with thick sleeping bags, the cold concrete wicked the heat from their bodies.

They each laid awake and shivering for much of the day, trapped in that unpleasant comatose state where one was too tired to move, but unable to find the peace of sleep. Their thoughts tumbled like rocks in a cement mixer, their worst fears emerging to taunt them, a waking nightmare that wouldn't quit. After several hours, Brendan finally climbed out of his sleeping bag in frustration and stood. One by one, they all followed suit. They were frozen to the core and no one felt rested.

"If we can't sleep, we might as well be walking," Brendan said.

"I don't feel like I'll ever be warm again," Lamar groaned. "I don't think I've ever been more miserable."

"If the world ever gets back to normal, I'm moving somewhere tropical and never suffering through cold weather again," said Yana. "Why would anyone ever live here? Why would anyone ever be okay with being cold? It's just...dumb."

"The sooner we get walking, the sooner we'll start to thaw out," Josie said.

Brendan yawned. "Promises, promises. Not sure I'll thaw out until summer."

"The sun is directly overhead," Lamar said. "This is probably as warm as it's going to get today."

"Always a ray of sunshine," Yana said sarcastically.

"Just preaching fact," Lamar said. "The truth is the truth."

They spent ten minutes answering the call of nature, eating energy bars, and drinking water so cold it made their teeth hurt. Once they were all squared away, they geared up and headed out.

Brendan winced as he pulled his rolling case out the front door of the building. "Pulling this case was bad enough last night, but I'm feeling it today. I've worked muscles I don't remember ever using before."

"My back hurts too," Lamar said. "I feel like I been twisted like a wet dishrag. I'm ready to kick the damn thing in a ditch and leave it behind."

"We've been through this, Lamar. That would be short-sighted," Josie cautioned. "The gear in those cases will provide the only advantage we have over most people stuck out here in the wilds of America. We have communication capabilities and access to data that other people would kill for."

"Or maybe even pay for," Yana added.

Josie nodded. "Even if that payment is in the form of providing a safe roof over our heads."

"We went from handing out aid to needing aid ourselves," Brendan mused. "How quickly the tides change."

"Indeed," Josie agreed.

They walked across the trash-littered parking lot to the four-lane highway and turned left. While they all knew it was safer to travel a less visible route, those heavy plastic cases with their tiny wheels were only suited for hard surfaces. There was no way they could pull them through grass or down trails for any distance. Having to travel an exposed route was the tradeoff they made for being able to take their most valuable possessions with them.

Lamar's already negative attitude was made even worse by poor sleep. It was no time at all before the complaining began. "You keep talking like all this equipment is the golden ticket that's going to let us to buy our way into a community, but I'm not sure where that confidence comes from. I remember this Shade dude you're talking about. He looked like some giant hillbilly off a tv show or something. Like a professional wrestler or a villain in some *Wrong Turn* movie. What makes you think he's going to be impressed with computing power? Hell, he might not even know what a computer is."

Josie frowned at Lamar's characterization of Shade as a neanderthal. "I find your attitude to be elitist, classist, and snobby. You obviously didn't talk to him, Lamar. Shade not only has a commanding physical presence, he's intelligent and well read."

"Sounds like someone has a crush," Brendan teased.

"I have a feeling that it's *you* who would be crushed if Shade heard how you were talking about him," Josie fired back.

"Gonna send your boyfriend after me?"

Josie winked at Brendan. "He could snap you like a twig."

"I talked to Shade a lot," said Yana. "He spoke extensively about the group he was part of and how this roadhouse was the hub of it. It sounded unique among the survivor stories I've heard. I'm interested to see what we find."

"It sounds like a longshot to me," Lamar said. "I'm not being critical because I agree this seems to be the *only* option available to us right now. I'm just saying that a degree of skepticism is warranted. I won't believe anything Shade said until I see it. No offense, but he might just be a dude who was talking up some chick he met."

Josie's mouth tightened. "I'll excuse you for characterizing me as 'some chick' for the moment, but I do have a bit more information about the place we're headed if you're interested in hearing it."

Brendan gestured at the empty road ahead of them. "I don't know about Lamar, but I'm interested. What else do we have to do to pass the time? Talk! Tell us a story, Mommy."

Yana nodded. "Please do."

"Well, unless Lamar has some objection to me continuing," Josie eyed him, "Shade told me that the man who opened and runs the roadhouse is named Jim Powell. I took the liberty of running his name through some of the databases we have access to as part of the Lightspeed organization."

"Recently or a while back?" Brendan asked.

"This was back when the aid center was open," Josie confirmed. "When the wireless grid was still up and running."

"Did you get any hits on him?" Lamar was pushing his rolling cart ahead of him now like a beer delivery man pushing a dolly of Bud into a corner store.

Josie cocked her head to the side and nodded. "Some interesting ones, actually. He's listed in state and federal databases going all the way back to the Nineties because he worked for a state agency here in Virginia. They required background checks and fingerprinting as a condition of employment. From everything I saw, it looked like Jim was a choirboy up until the apocalypse. After the attacks, Jim Powell apparently rubbed some people the wrong way."

Brendan held up a hand. "Okay, wait a minute. I have to ask, who in the United States was still maintaining databases *after* the collapse? I mean besides the Lightspeed organization. I can't believe you were able to find public records that had been updated with post-collapse information."

"Oh, these weren't public records." Josie held up fingers as she rattled off the entities. "Homeland Security, the CIA, the NSA, the FBI, the military, and even the IRS continued to update their databases in some form. Mostly they were trying to monitor insurgent activity since there were forces resistant to the acting government's plans."

"The plan to trade land and mineral rights to foreign governments in exchange for aid?" Brendan asked.

Yana shrugged. "That wasn't a plan, it was a *scheme*. It was corrupt officials hoping to sell off land and mineral rights to improve their own personal circumstances."

Josie held up a hand. "Don't get me sidetracked. That's a whole other debate."

"Back to Jim Powell," Lamar said. "Are you saying he was in these databases?"

"Yes, he was. There was no mention of Shade, but Jim Powell was mentioned in several instances. He was characterized as an insurgent."

Brendan laughed. "Walter Lightspeed was too, so that's not exactly a bad thing. It just means Jim Powell didn't agree with those corrupt bureaucrats who ran the government in the aftermath of the collapse."

"Exactly." Josie nodded. "I read one report that said someone in the government made an inside deal to give away some power plants to foreign entities if they could get them running again. United Nations Peacekeepers were sent in to provide security for this operation. This was also around the time that the Comfort Camp initiative was launched, where people could move into aid camps if they surrendered all their weapons."

"I remember," Lamar said. "That wasn't popular."

"Well, it was unpopular enough with Jim Powell that he blasted a mountainside into a local river, damming it up. The lake that formed behind the dam flooded one of the power plants that the government had given away. As the water was rising, a battle ensued and some NATO troops were killed. Shortly after that, the local comfort camps were closed, which made Jim Powell very unpopular with the locals who'd been interested in moving into them. It also made him unpopular with the government since the whole incident was an embarrassment to them."

"That's kind of a badass move," Yana said. "I have to give him props for that."

"Soon after that, a kill order was issued for Jim Powell."

Lamar let out a low whistle. "Shit! Sounds like he pissed off the wrong people."

"I'm sure he did anger a lot of people," Josie said, "but in this case, it was the wrong *person*. The initial kill order was issued by a rogue operator who'd been stationed at the power plant. Jim Powell's attack killed his team and he held a grudge. Of his own volition, he scattered thousands of flyers over the area where Jim Powell lived, putting a price on his head. There are no details as to what happened as a result, but the guy who put out the hit disappeared and the whole operation was only uncovered after his death."

"I had no idea things were that crazy out here," Brendan said. "And that's just one man in one community raising all that hell."

"You said that was the *initial* kill order," Yana said. "There were more?"

Josie nodded. "The next one was more formal. A man named Browning worked for one of the private military contracting firms that were running national security before Lightspeed took over. Apparently, there were still some people out there who viewed Jim Powell as an insurgent threat because of the whole power plant incident. Browning assigned a specialist to take Jim Powell out. He hired a contractor named Conor Maguire. Sound familiar?"

Brendan raised a brow. "Conor Maguire? The hired gun on Lightspeed's security detail?"

"Oh, he was more than a hired gun," Josie said. "He and his people were part of Lightspeed's inner circle."

"Well, as far as I know, Conor Maguire is still ticking and so is Jim Powell," said Lamar. "Any idea what happened there? Why wasn't Jim Powell killed?"

"According to the records, Maguire made contact with Jim Powell and determined that he wasn't a threat. Maguire ended up killing Browning instead, then the whole network of contractors supporting the old government collapsed because of Lightspeeed's soft coup."

Josie threw a hand up. "It's apparently a small world, but a very complex one with lots of moving pieces."

"I never met Conor Maguire," said Brendan. "I heard they called him the Mad Mick."

"I was in several meetings with him," Yana said. "To speak with him, you'd never believe the stories people tell. He was charming and quite funny. His daughter, on the other hand, was a bit of a loose cannon. Not one I'd care to have a scuffle with."

"I feel like I'm in *Star Wars*," Lamar said. "All this intrigue between rebels and a shadowy, evil empire."

"It resonated in *Star Wars* because it's a story as old as time," Yana said. "It's the stuff of myths and legends."

"Yeah, well the movie I'm trapped in right now feels more like *Revenge of The Nerds*," Brendan quipped. "All laptop and no lightsaber."

"Then I hope we nerds triumph this time and reach our destination safely," Josie said.

10

Outside of St. Paul, Virginia

SINCE MOVING into the valley with Jim and his people, Hugh had taken to patrolling the perimeter of their community like some range rider of the old west. Sometimes one of the others would ride with him, but most often he rode by himself, just as he preferred it. Not only did it give him time to think, but he was also more attuned to his surroundings when he wasn't distracted by conversation. He was more prone to picking up signs, to noticing changes in the land, or detecting movement in the far distance. Jim was probably the only one who got that. He also understood that the void of silence didn't demand to be filled with conversation.

Sometimes Hugh rode horseback, patrolling the frequently traveled roads and trails that led into town. While he didn't always engage with the people he met along the road, he kept an eye out for anyone who triggered his gut. Most people were armed, so the presence of weapons alone wasn't concerning. It was more of a feeling, a sense honed through a lifetime of being around dangerous people and in dangerous places. It could be a look in their eye, their body language, or simply a vibe that Hugh picked up like a beagle scenting on a rabbit.

Regardless of what Hugh decided about the people he met on the road, he didn't engage with them unless they made a move first. His self-appointed mission was recon and intel gathering. If Jim's mission was to monitor the roadhouse, Hugh's was to monitor the fringes of their community, the boundaries of their area of operation. He made notes on what he saw in a little book he carried in his pocket. When it benefitted him to do so, he used an old iPhone to snap pictures of the things he saw so he could share them with Jim later.

On this occasion, Hugh was on an overnight recon outing, checking out the small town of St. Paul, where Ed had his brewery before Jim brought him to the roadhouse. Despite its tiny size, the town had always been a crossroads of sorts. The railroad track passed through there, as did the Clinch River. The town sat at the intersection between rural farmland and mineral-rich coalfields. Enough people passed through that Hugh liked to keep an eye on the town. He'd cultivated a few sources there that he checked in with once a month or so, trading them ammunition or other goods for keeping him abreast of local goings-on.

Near a place called Buzzard's Roost, Hugh left his horse with a farmer he knew and continued on foot. He preferred visiting St. Paul in this manner in order to draw less attention himself. The town had always held some attraction to outlaws and had become such a place again in the collapse. Although good people still formed the core of the community, there were enough shady types to make it advisable to keep a low profile.

Hugh traversed the land by field and trail, moving northwest of the highway. As usual, his plan was to handrail the main road until he got closer to town, then he'd follow Castle Run Creek to where it intercepted the Clinch River. He'd continue along the Clinch into town, track down his contacts there, then make camp for the night. He'd hike out in the morning, retrieve his horse, and ideally be back at the roadhouse by dark.

Hugh was never more in his element than when he was on foot in the woods. Whether it was the hardwood forests of central Appalachia or the rainforest of Central America, Hugh felt at home walking silently though the woods. He'd learned at a very young age the importance of foot placement and it came natural to him now. He didn't have to look for sticks, leaves, or anything that would make a noise underfoot. His subconscious was so attuned to this environment that Hugh took in his surroundings automatically, processing it with the efficiency of a predator born and raised in this environment.

Hugh's brain analyzed the sights, sounds, and smells of the woods in a manner that was almost automatic. His senses provided data that streamed through his brain like lines of code through a computer. When something unfamiliar or out of place appeared, Hugh didn't immediately recognize it. His body froze of its own accord, like an animal, while he tried to figure out which of his senses had been triggered.

The only sound in the silent winter forest was that of his own breathing, which he did his best to still as he focused on his hearing. When his ears provided no information, Hugh began scanning more intently with his eyes. First, the forest ahead of him, then the more distant areas visible through the trees ahead. That was when he spotted movement in a high meadow on a distant ridge. Something was moving in his direction.

Hugh slowly raised his rifle and switched his low power scope to the full 6x magnification. With the sling stretched taut around his support arm, he glassed the figure, assuming it might be a deer or cow since the bottom half was obscured by the high grass of the hayfield. No, it was human. The figure was approximately eight hundred yards ahead and appeared to be a man with a pack. Assuming he kept to his bearing and Hugh kept to his, they'd likely cross paths.

That in itself wasn't of concern. Passing people on foot was the norm these days and most of them carried packs and guns. Encountering people in the woods, however, was different than meeting them on the road. People traveling the woods were often more skittish. They were quicker to suspect that the people they encountered meant them harm. It was something about the isolation and the fact they were so far from assistance of any sort. Screams for help in the woods rarely reached human ears.

Hugh wasn't worried. He assumed the man was a hunter or some local taking a shortcut. He wouldn't take evasive action to avoid him. To do so in these steep hills would only add time and distance to his already long hike. He might take cover and let the man pass without an encounter. If the man was indeed a local, Hugh saw no reason to bring attention to himself as a stranger skulking around the woods outside of the town. It was easier on all fronts just to avoid an encounter entirely.

He resumed his stealthy trek down the trail. He was able to monitor the man's progress for about five more minutes before the terrain blocked his view. At that point, figuring he had less than fifteen minutes before they ran into each other, Hugh began looking for a good place to conceal himself. There was a large diameter poplar that had blown down a short distance off the trail, the bark peeling away in sheets. It was tempting to take cover there but the thick carpet of leaves between the tree and trail would make it impossible to hide his path. Anyone attuned to reading the forest would spot the disturbed leaves and understand immediately that the path had been left by a human.

To his right was the mouth of a gulley that deepened as it continued down the slope. Millenia of rainfall and runoff had carried away the leaves and topsoil, exposing the rocks that lined the sides and bottom of the wash. Recent rains had left a disturbed path that would hide his steps. Deciding it was his best option, Hugh set off in that direction, taking care to only place his feet on hard surfaces that would hide his boot prints. Because the gulley deepened gradually as it left the trail, Hugh had to go around fifty yards before the ravine was deep enough that he could find a decent spot to hide out.

Once he was satisfied, Hugh sat down on a pile of crumbling yellow limestone, the rock cool beneath him. He took off his pack and flattened himself to where he could see up the winding path of the ravine toward the trail. From there he should be able to see the man pass by, then he'd make his way back to the trail and continue on his way. Part of him wondered why he was going to this much trouble to avoid meeting someone on this remote trail. Another part of his brain reminded him that the best fights were those one avoided.

Hugh settled in for the wait, making himself comfortable and slowing his breathing. He figured the guy should pass his position within fifteen minutes comfortably unless he stopped for a break on the trail. When the man hadn't gone past in thirty minutes, Hugh frowned. He should have passed by now. These ridgetops were narrow, and the only trail followed the peak. It would be highly unusual for someone to venture off through the woods. That is, unless he was doing exactly what Hugh was doing.

For a moment Hugh wondered if the man might have spotted him, just as he had spotted the man coming toward him, although that seemed unlikely. For one, that man had been walking through a sunny meadow in plain sight. Hugh had been in deep woods, in shadow, and presumably should have been more difficult to spot. Hugh understood that *difficult* to spot didn't mean *impossible* to spot. Perhaps he *had* been seen.

Hugh got up and stood there with his rifle at a low ready. He turned his head, trying to catch even the faintest hint of a disturbance amidst the natural sounds of the forest. He must have stood there for five minutes but he picked up nothing. Finally, he shouldered his pack and picked his way up the ravine. He chose his steps carefully, not wanting to make a sound. He avoided loose rock, twigs, and crackling leaves from habit as much as from intent.

When he regained the trail, he turned a full circle, his rifle at a low ready position, but he didn't see anything unexpected. Deciding he'd wasted enough time, Hugh started walking. He'd only made it three steps when he heard someone clear their throat behind him. Hugh spun, rifle up. His barrel stopped center mass on an old man standing approximately twenty feet from him.

The old man was wearing a pack and had a rifle slung over his shoulder. He slowly raised a lean brown rabbit into the air. "You eat rabbit?" His voice was gravelly, as if he hadn't spoken in days.

"Where the hell did you come from?" Hugh asked.

The old man gave a low laugh. "Son, you ain't the only one knows how to move around in the woods."

Hugh lowered his rifle. The old man didn't appear concerned about Hugh and wasn't behaving in a threatening manner. To continue aiming a rifle at him just seemed rude.

Feeling almost embarrassed, as if he'd been caught doing something he shouldn't have been, Hugh said, "I had no bad intentions toward you. I saw you coming and thought I'd lay low off the trail until you passed. Sometimes that's easiest."

The man nodded once. "I suspected as much. If I'd suspected ill intentions, we wouldn't be having this conversation."

Hugh cocked an eyebrow at that. If he was reading the comment right, the old man had a pretty high opinion of his abilities. It was a reminder to Hugh that he shouldn't be taken in or fooled by appearances. Older didn't mean feeble and it certainly didn't mean a man wasn't dangerous. It reminded Hugh of that proverb about fearing the old man in the land where men die young.

Curious, Hugh said, "I do enjoy rabbit."

The old man grinned, revealing a few missing teeth. "Good. Let's strike up a fire then."

11

Highway 460
  Tazewell County, Virginia

"My feet feel like they've been beat with a hammer," Lamar griped.

For once, none of them rolled their eyes at his complaining. All of them were learning the hard way that there was a big difference between working on their feet all day and using those same feet to cover miles of paved road. They wore boots, but they'd been more concerned with style than comfort when they'd selected them from the offerings Lightspeed had available in his stores. Now they found that fit and function were significantly more important than appearance.

"I'll never look at socks the same again," Yana added. "What the hell was I thinking when I bought socks because they were cute? They're thin as tissue paper. I had to throw yesterday's pair away when I took them off. They were nothing but a bloody rag full of holes."

"We can chalk it up as a learning experience," Josie said. "As long as we survive it."

Lamar looked uncertain. "Outcome undetermined."

It was midday. They'd abandoned their plan to travel only at night, finding it too slow when it was hard to see where they were going. Though they had lights they could use, wearing those headlamps felt the same as wearing beacons on their heads announcing their presence. And if they were being completely honest, the night was somewhat terrifying. Not being able to see what was going on around them left everyone in a constant state of anxiety. Every bump in the night felt like the prelude to attack.

Of course, traveling during the day meant being visible even without the beacons on their heads. It also meant more random encounters with locals and other travelers. The cases they pulled along with them rumbled and roared as the plastic tires rolled over pavement and gravel. Despite the durable nature of the cases, Josie had begun to wonder if those wheels would hold up for this journey. While the cases were meant for hard use, she couldn't imagine they were designed for these conditions.

It was due to the roar of their rolling cases that they didn't hear the approaching bicyclists until they whooshed past them. The half-dozen cyclists were in a tight pack but split at the last minute when they came upon Josie's people, passing to either side of them with an uncomfortably close margin. It was an intentionally intimidating move.

'What the hell?" Brendan cried out, one of the cyclists passing so close that he brushed his elbow.

"Assholes!" Lamar shouted, assuming the cyclists would keep going.

They didn't, whipping their bikes around to block both lanes of the road as they skidded to a stop. The riders were four boys and two girls. Josie saw them as boys rather than men because they appeared to be younger than sixteen, but it was hard to tell sometimes. People wore their age differently these days. Everyone's skin was darker from being outside more and bathing less, and many had gaunt cheeks from poor diets without enough protein.

They rode mountain bikes they'd outfitted with baskets and small pouches. They didn't seem to be the kinds of bikes one would travel long distances with, designed more for errands and local travel. Josie noted with concern that several of the riders had long, intimidating knives on their hips and all of them carried baseball bats slung over their shoulders like rifles. If they had guns, they kept them concealed.

Josie's people trailed to a stop. They tipped their rolling cases up and let them stand on their own. Yana leaned on hers casually, waiting to see where this went. The cyclist at the center of the pack was a boy with dirty blond hair that stuck out from a combination of being windblown and poorly cut. He squinted as he spoke, an affectation he might have picked up from a movie or video game. He might have thought it made him look older or tougher, yet it wasn't working.

"Where y'all headed?" he asked.

Lamar snapped. "None of your damn—"

"I'll handle this." Josie held up a hand in Lamar's direction. "We're on our way to Russell County to stay with a friend."

"That's a long walk," the boy replied. "What you dragging along in those suitcases?"

Josie smiled. "That's none of your concern, young man." Her tone came off a little more patronizing than she'd intended, which she didn't realize until it was too late.

It rubbed the young man the wrong way. His face darkened and he got off his bike, letting it drop to the ground. His companions had looked entertained a moment ago, waiting to see where this went. Now they were dead serious, as if they'd been simultaneously offended by Josie's condescension.

The young man swung the bat off his shoulder, staring a hole through Josie with intense eyes. "You know, I've been on my own for a year and a half now. The one thing I swore I'd never let anyone do to me again was talk to me like I was a kid. Now, I'll be damned if you haven't gone and done it. That just pisses me off."

Josie held both hands up toward the boy, as if her gesture might help maintain the distance that separated them. "I meant nothing by it. We just want to be left alone to continue our journey in peace. Your business is none of my concern. Mine is none of yours."

One of the girls suddenly dismounted, dropping her bike too. "If you're on this road it's our business. We live here and you're just some strangers passing through. We don't know you and we don't owe you shit."

"The thing about strangers," Yana said, straightening up from where she'd been leaning on her rolling case, "is that it's easy to underestimate them. It's easy to assume you can hurt them and steal from them because you've done it to others in the past. That may not always be the case."

The blond-haired boy kept walking toward Josie, adjusting his grip on the bat, his intentions clear. Josie's head was about to be used as a baseball.

"Stop!" she demanded.

The boy drew the bat back like he was leaning into a pitch, then all hell broke loose. In what felt like slow motion, Josie drew her handgun without even taking her eyes off the boy. She took aim, seeing in his eyes that he had no intention of stopping. He was going to beat her, rob her, and maybe even kill her.

Josie fired twice, double tapping him in the manner she'd been trained to do when someone was charging her from a close distance. The boy fell at her feet, his bat rolling across the asphalt. Chaos erupted around them. One girl screamed and drew her bat while the second pedaled off. The other boys unslung their own bats and charged Josie's people. Yana drew her weapon and fired, striking a boy rushing toward her with a bat raised over his head.

Paralyzed by panic, Lamar fell over backward. A boy was only steps away, bat raised over his head like an ax. On the ground, Lamar threw his arms up, attempting to shield his face and head against imminent attack. Josie swung in his direction and fired, dropping Lamar's attacker. The boy fell and screamed, clutching his side.

Brendan was also paralyzed for a moment but quickly became unstuck at the thought of taking a bat to the head. He drew his weapon, firing nearly half the magazine into the boy charging him with a bat.

The one girl who'd remained behind to fight dropped her bat and crouched over the first boy to die. She drew his knife from his sheath and pointed it in Josie's direction, grimacing. "You bitch!"

"Don't," Josie said in a low voice. "Put it down and go! Please!"

The girl took another step, uncomfortably close now. Afraid that Josie couldn't make herself take the shot, Yana did it for her, shooting the girl in the head and dropping her. Yana immediately spun and took aim at the one remaining cyclist, the girl pedaling furiously away from them. Before Yana could take the shot, Josie placed a hand on her arm and forced it down.

"No, this was bad enough. I can't watch you shoot a fleeing child in the back."

"That fleeing child might have parents or friends who'll chase us down tonight and kill us for what we've done. Letting her escape could be a fatal mistake."

"Then we'll have to do our best to not let that happen," Josie said calmly.

Yana blew out a breath and holstered her firearm, watching the girl disappear into the distance. "Just so you know, I would have taken no pleasure in that. I don't like to kill, but I don't want to die either."

Josie turned away, trying her best not to look at the carnage around her. Even though she didn't want to see any of it, her eyes were drawn to the one injured boy who was still alive. He was crying, his breath a wheezing rattle. "Do we need to...finish...him?"

Her question was directed to anyone who might have an answer —her companions, herself, even God.

"He'll die on his own." Lamar gulped. "His lungs are filling with blood. He doesn't need any more help from us."

Josie turned away from the dying boy and found Brendan sitting on one of the bikes.

He looked up eagerly. "We can use these bikes. They're a little beat up, but with a few mods we could pull our rolling cases like trailers. We could cover a lot more ground."

Josie turned around and looked at Yana, trying to block the dying boy's sounds from her ears. "There's your answer. If we use the bikes, we'll be long gone before that girl returns with anyone."

Yana didn't look convinced. "Let's hope so."

12

Outside of St. Paul, Virginia

"MY NAME IS HUGH." He stuck out a hand.

"Garnet," the man replied, sticking out the rabbit-less hand to shake.

Hugh found a forked stick and used it like a rake to clear dried leaves for a fire, then began gathering small pieces of wood for a cookfire. While he worked, Garnet made a slice in the rabbit's back and turned it inside out, like a man stripping off a glove. In less than a minute he had the rabbit skinned, gutted, and ready to cook.

While Hugh got a fire going, the man removed a flexible cutting board from his pack and quartered the rabbit. To a scorched and well-used frying pan, he added a scoop of bacon grease from an old mayonnaise jar.

"I growed up on rabbit," Garnet said.

"Me too," said Hugh.

"Had a lot of Himalayan rabbit too. You ever eat those?"

Hugh furrowed his brow. "Himalayan?"

Garnet nodded. "Found *him a layin'* in the road on the way home from school."

Garnet cackled and Hugh laughed along with him.

"Yeah, I guess I had a few of those too."

Once they had a small bed of coals, Garnet balanced the skillet on a few rocks the appropriate distance above the coals. When the grease sizzled, he prodded the chunks of rabbit with the blade of a knife, turning them occasionally.

"What you into on this fine day?" Garnet asked.

The question sounded more conversational than nosey, so Hugh answered it. "Well, my friends back in town have had trouble in the past from situations that snuck up on them. Foreigners, outsiders, and government people showing up to put all kinds of rules in place. We decided it might be better if we had advance warning in the future. So, I get out every few weeks and visit the surrounding communities just to make sure everything is as normal as it can be, considering the times we live in."

Garnet pulled the skillet off the coals and balanced it on a single flat rock. "Dig in. I assume you got some kind of eating utensil?"

Hugh retrieved a spork from his shirt pocket. He forked up a chunk of rabbit and held it aloft while it cooled, smoke wafting off it into the cool morning air. They ate in a silence that was neither uncomfortable nor awkward. It was the quiet of two men accustomed to the silence of the woods and who understood each other in some rudimentary way.

After the frying pan cooled, Garnet wiped it clean with a wadded-up piece of newspaper. He tucked it into his pack and buckled the flap closed.

Hugh stood and brushed the seat of his pants off. "Guess I should be getting on my way."

Garnet regarded him seriously, still sitting on the ground. "They aren't."

Hugh cocked an eyebrow. The comment seemed disjointed and out of place. "What's that?"

"Things *aren't* as normal as they can be."

Hugh started to wonder if Garnet might be slightly off, one of those people who'd spent too much time alone during the collapse. "You referring to anything in particular or is that just a general statement to the condition of things?"

Garnet got to his feet, spry for a man who had to be in his seventies. "I saw something in St. Paul. A train."

"A moving train?"

Garnet frowned. "What would be the point of me telling you about some rusting train that's been sitting on the tracks for a year and a half?"

"I guess none," Hugh admitted.

"What I'm trying to tell you is that I saw a train passing through just before dark last night. A diesel train with maybe twenty cars attached."

"Military?"

Garnet shook his head. "I don't think so. Didn't look like anything official to me, based on what I saw."

"What exactly did you see?"

"Men on the rear platforms of some of the cars. They were drinking bottles of beer and holding rifles."

"You get a look at the rifles?" Hugh knew that sometimes the weapons a group carried could tell you something about them.

Garnet nodded. "AK-47s."

"You sure?"

Garnet cocked an eyebrow. "Son, I handled hundreds of them in Southeast Asia. I can spot an AK from a mile off and it was a lot closer than that. I was camped by the river and the train passed within fifty feet of me. Besides, these AKs were a lot easier to make out than some of the ones I used to see in the jungle."

"Why do you say that?"

"These were gold-plated."

13

The Reset Roadhouse

JIM HEADED TOWARD THE BAR, noticing that Riley Blackwood was merrily drinking away at the tab he'd successfully prepaid with his haul of confiscated pocketknives. Riley waved his arms in an animated fashion as he spoke, and Becky nodded agreeably as she wiped the bar. Randi was engaged in a conversation with a woman Jim didn't recognize, which was a little unusual for this time of year. The colder months of the year usually only brought locals into the roadhouse since no one wanted to be out moving around in the cold weather unless they had to. When Jim thought back through all the strangers who had appeared at the roadhouse since it opened, he was aware that it rarely meant anything good. Strangers normally brought trouble or bad news, and he wasn't in the mood for either. As much as he didn't *want* to, he *needed* to drop in on the conversation and see what was going on.

By the time Jim reached the bar, Becky had abandoned Riley's story and joined Randi's conversation. Jim wasn't sure if that was a testament to Riley being boring or Randi being interesting. Despite

Randi serving as the manager of the roadhouse, not much got past Becky. The bar was her domain and nothing happened there without her knowing about it. She was also a naturally nosy person, which she didn't deny at all.

"Can you repeat that?" Becky asked, cocking her head toward the stranger as if she'd had trouble hearing her. That wasn't likely, however. Becky had supersonic hearing.

Jim leaned against the bar and studied the stranger. Now that he was seeing her up close, he was certain he didn't recognize her. She also didn't look like the women he was accustomed to seeing around the community. After a year and a half without power, most people had adapted their grooming standard to the conditions. Men wore beards of varying lengths and women wore hairstyles that were more manageable in a world without curling irons, blow dryers, and hair care products. Sometimes hair dyes were available, but most people let their hair go to their natural color, not interested in the maintenance required to keep their roots done.

This woman looked a little more polished and put together. Her hair was styled, and her skin didn't have that weathered tan look that most people now had as a result of more frequent sun exposure. She also wore some jewelry which was uncommon these days out of concern that it might attract the wrong kind of attention and lead to being robbed. Her clothes were cleaner, a little less worn, and even her hiking boots appeared newer than Jim was used to seeing.

The stranger leaned forward over the bar and repeated herself at Becky's request. "I said my name is Josie and I'm here looking for Shade. Do you know who I'm talking about?"

Becky grinned, put down her towel, and stepped closer to the bar. "That's exactly what I thought you said."

Like a bat targeting through echolocation, Josie's voice allowed Becky to precisely home in on her. Becky lashed out and grabbed Josie by the hair, slamming her face into the bar. With her other hand, she pounded on the back of Josie's head with solid hammer fists. Josie screamed and tried to pull herself out of Becky's grasp, but Becky was strong. She'd already pulled Josie halfway across the bar and was still pummeling her. If Becky managed to get her across the bar and into the floor, there was no telling how bad this would get.

"Help!" Josie screamed, her legs kicking in the air.

Jim grabbed Becky's hands, trying to prevent her from snatching Josie's hair from her head. "Becky! Let her go!"

Becky showed no signs of letting up, continuing to swing wildly with her free hand and nearly punching Jim in the face.

"Stop it!" Jim ordered to no avail.

Randi grabbed Becky around the waist. "Dammit, Becky! Stop until we hear her out!"

Red-faced and puffing like a steam engine, Becky stopped fighting. She released Josie's hair, though only after shoving her face into the bar top one more time. Josie reeled backwards when she was released, one hand on her scalp and the other holding her throbbing nose. She almost went down, but Jim got an arm around her and helped her onto a stool.

Only then did he turn his attention to Becky. He pounded his fist on the bar. "What the hell was that about, Becky? I heard the conversation. She did nothing to provoke you."

"She's after my man," Becky snarled. "Nobody ever comes in here asking for Shade. This one's a tramp! I can hear it in her voice."

Josie reeled again, almost going over. Jim grabbed hold of her arm and steadied her. "I beg your pardon! I'm not after your man!" Josie smoothed her hair down and straightened an earring. "My name is Josie and I ran one of Lightspeed's aid centers. Shade came in there several times and mentioned this place. He said my people and I should stop by if we were in the area."

"So, you thought you'd just sashay in here and steal my man?" Becky shrieked. "I knew you were a tramp."

Josie looked appalled. "I thought nothing of the sort! Shade was proud of what you all had here and he bragged about it. I was interested because I hadn't heard of anything else like it in the region."

This revelation did nothing to calm Becky down. "Sounds like I need to kick Shade's ass too. He's got some nerve inviting some random bitch to stop by the bar where his girlfriend works."

Josie's mouth dropped open at Becky's words. "I am *not* some random bitch, and I repeat, I am *not* after your man. Our distribution center was at the National Guard armory about sixty miles from here. Shade was up there several times with his horse-drawn wagon to pick up supplies, which he said he was delivering here."

"Well, why aren't you back there handing out aid?" Becky demanded. "Surely you have better things to do than coming down here to troll for men."

Josie rolled her eyes. "I'm not trolling for men."

"Trollop!" Becky yelled. "Whore!"

Josie looked to Jim for help.

"Are those distribution centers still open?" Jim asked.

Josie sighed and shook her head. "No. Once the wireless grid collapsed, we were informed by radio that the Lightspeed organization had collapsed along with it. There was no continuity of leadership and no plan in place for rescuing the various teams working in the field around the country. We've been abandoned."

14

The Reset Roadhouse

"Who is *we*?" Jim asked.

Josie took a deep breath and let it out, trying to calm herself after being flailed by Becky. "My coworkers Yana, Lamar, and Brendan. We were the only Lightspeed employees onsite aside from the security team, and they abandoned us too. Everyone else was a local volunteer."

"Where are your friends now?" Jim asked.

"Who cares!" Becky growled.

Jim sighed. "Becky, how about you wait on customers while I try to figure out what's going on here? You're not helping matters."

Becky frowned. "That sounded an awful lot like an order, Jim."

"Putting aside the fact that I *am* your boss, consider it a request made with utter respect and adoration."

Becky folded her arms across her chest. "Asshole."

"Becky, I promise if Josie says anything that requires hair-pulling or face-slapping you'll be the first to know."

Becky stalked off, mumbling to herself.

Randi shook her head. "We're going to have to keep an eye on her tonight. She's a little *volatile*."

"I'll say," Josie whispered.

"I heard that!" Becky shouted. "Don't make me come back down there!"

Jim tugged on his ear. "She has supersonic hearing, Josie. You've been warned. Now about those people of yours?"

"They're waiting outside," Josie said. "We thought one person coming inside to scope things out might not draw as much attention."

"Which works until Becky decides to break bad on you," Jim said. "How long have you guys been on the road?"

"Several days," Josie said. "We're about frozen. We weren't really supplied or trained for trekking cross-country. It was terrifying."

"Why don't you get your people?" Jim suggested. "You can stow your gear in the back, warm up, and have a hot meal while we talk. Sound okay?"

Despite her watering eyes and a red welt on the side of her face, Josie appeared relieved. "That sounds amazing. Will Shade be back here at some point? I'm sure he'll be surprised we actually took him up on his invite."

Jim shot a look in Becky's direction. She was casually sharpening a butcher knife halfway down the bar. "Let's not worry about Shade right now. I'm sure he'll be back shortly. My name is Jim. As you may have picked up, the one who tried to kill you is Becky and the one who tried to save your ass is Randi. The drunk dude over there who watched the show with such amusement is Riley."

Riley smiled and waved in a friendly manner.

"How many are there in your group?" Josie asked.

Jim blew out a breath and looked uncertain. "God, I couldn't tell you. It depends on the day of the week. Let's get your people inside and we can talk about that while you're eating."

"Be right back." Josie hurried toward the main door of the roadhouse.

"That was interesting," Randi said. "I wonder why they're here?"

Jim shrugged. "I don't know, but I plan to mine them for information. They're bound to know things we don't. They've had a vastly different picture of the last few months than we had. Besides, Shade is a pretty good judge of character. I don't think he'd have extended the invitation to them if he didn't feel it was merited. Of course, I'm sure he never really expected them to show up, either."

Randi cringed. "Well, if he knows what's good for him, he better not seem too excited about seeing Josie and her friends. Becky might not be able to *see* Josie, but she can still kill her. And if she starts shooting or swinging a knife, there will be some collateral damage, and I don't want to be part of it."

Jim and Randi were still talking when Josie came back through the front door, her entourage following behind her. Besides a backpack, each of them was pulling a rolling hardcase along behind them. Jim headed over to intercept them, leaving Randi at the bar. He pointed at a large round table near one of the woodstoves. "Grab a seat over there. It's warm and next to the kitchen."

"Warm sounds delightful," Yana gushed. "I can't remember the last time I was warm."

Jim led them toward the table and showed them a spot along the wall where they could stow their gear. "You guys pull those cases all the way from the armory?"

"Yes," Josie replied. "Every damn inch of the way. We were able to ride bicycles for the last half of the journey, but even that was difficult."

"I hope what's in those cases was worth the effort," said Jim.

Josie didn't offer to explain what the cases carried, instead artfully changing the subject with a sweep of her hand. "This is my team."

Introductions were made and Jim shook hands with each of them. He couldn't help but notice that every hand he shook was ice cold. He'd been there himself many times and that bone-deep cold was not a feeling he enjoyed. "You guys warm up by the stove. I'm going to run into the kitchen a second."

Jim returned a moment later with a tray of steaming mugs, warm slices of homemade bread, and fresh butter. He wasn't the most coordinated server, so it took him a second to awkwardly transfer his serving tray to the table. "Help yourself to the bread. It was made fresh this morning and it's amazing. The mugs are a local herbal tea with honey. It's our main hot beverage here since coffee and tea are not in steady supply."

The new arrivals didn't have to be asked twice. They flew toward the tray with such urgency that Jim stepped back involuntarily, almost afraid of being trampled.

Josie offered an apologetic smile as she cupped a warm mug between her hands, her face hovering in the rising steam. "I'm sorry if we appear desperate. We didn't have anything to eat today, or yesterday for that matter."

"Was there no food left at the distribution center?"

"There was," Josie admitted. "But to save weight, we brought freeze-dried backpacking meals instead of MREs. We weren't thinking clearly. The MREs had chemical packets that would have warmed them. The freeze-dried meals required a fire for boiling water and we were too scared to build one."

Jim offered a faint smile, having walked many hungry miles himself. "That sucks. Running on no calories is exhausting."

"Tell us about it," Lamar said with his mouth full of bread.

"You don't have rifles?" Jim asked, suddenly noticing the absence of long guns.

Josie lifted the tail of her jacket to expose her holstered handgun. "Lightspeed had a protocol for everything. People with our duty assignment were issued handguns with the instruction they were only to be carried in an emergency. We had a security team at the armory who was responsible for maintaining order, preventing theft, and keeping the rest of us safe. So, in theory we shouldn't have *needed* rifles."

"You said something at the bar about your security team ditching you?"

"The assholes abandoned us," Brendan spat. He had long curly hair and a dark beard, reminding Jim of a young Don Henley of the Eagles.

"They didn't feel like I was doing enough to get us rescued," said

Josie. "I did everything I knew to do, but apparently it wasn't enough for some people."

Jim caught Lamar shooting Josie a look, as if he might have agreed with that assessment.

"The problem was that the collapse of the Lightspeed organization stranded thousands of teams around the country and most of them are in the same boat as us," Josie went on. "We lost military support and our ability to request helicopter transport. None of our official liaisons in the military are answering our calls."

"Meanwhile, we were left as sitting ducks," Lamar said, unable to keep his mouth shut any longer. "Locals were attacking the armory every day, and it was only a matter of time before they got in. Security did their best to keep them at bay, but everyone was stressed out and fighting. Then we got up a few days ago and there was no one left guarding the place. Locals were pounding on the door of the building and we were on our own."

"It was terrifying. We left that night," Josie added. "We had no choice."

"Leave or die." Brendan gulped. "That's what it felt like."

"You guys had power here, right?" asked Yana. "When the wireless grid was up?"

"Until the repeater exploded," Jim said bitterly. "We have a lot of questions and few answers. One of our people is a radio operator and he gets some information from the outside world, but it's hard to know what to believe."

"People were working against Walter Lightspeed on all levels," Brendan said. "It's sad. Every time he made any progress, someone sabotaged him. It just didn't make sense to us how people could be so hungry for their own nation to fail."

"Was it our people who took him out?" Jim asked. "We haven't heard."

Yana shrugged. "Much of the resistance was foreign funded but there were also Americans working with them on all levels. People in the military, the old government, and even people within the Lightspeed organization. We don't know who ended up killing him, but there was a Chinese missile attack on Camp David and that was his last known location. It's likely that's how he died. His death wasn't just a loss for the United States, it's a loss for everyone on the planet. His tech would have changed the world forever."

"The level of global intrigue is dizzying." Josie sighed. "It's impossible to know or trust what's going on at the national and international level now."

Jim grew disgusted. "We kind of had things figured out here on a local level until Lightspeed threw us for a loop by turning the lights on. Now that it's all collapsed *again*, we're going back to doing things the way we were before we ever heard of him. We're doubling down on building our own community and our own lives back without concern for what the rest of the country and the world is doing. It's all we have. All we can do."

Josie had thought about this moment throughout the journey from the armory to the roadhouse. She knew it was risky, but she didn't feel like she had any choice. Her gut told her she could trust Shade and now it was telling her she could trust Jim. What she was about to reveal could put her people in danger if she was wrong. She tipped her head toward their stack of gear piled against the wall.

"Jim, I have a satellite phone and a solar charger. I was able to call around to some of the other teams scattered around the US. I'm still in contact with them, for what it's worth. A very lucky few made it back to DC, but most were abandoned like us. They're stranded in unfamiliar territory with no prospect of rescue. We all agreed our only hope was to find some local group we might be able to integrate with until...things improve or something changes."

"Hence your visit here," Jim summarized.

Josie nodded, wiping her hands on her pants. "We're not here looking for a handout, I assure you. Shade made this place sound interesting and appealing compared to what was going on in some of the other local communities. I thought if there was any place where we might be able to contribute and find a temporary home, this might be it."

"Staying at the armory was a death sentence," Yana threw in.

"A slow one," Lamar growled.

Jim pointed at Lamar. "I'm not picking on you, but it doesn't look like you guys were prepared for being outdoors."

Lamar gave a mournful shake of his head. "We weren't. That was never supposed to happen. All our clothes and gear were picked with the idea that we would be working under shelter most of the time. It was physical work, but we had industrial generators to help with heating and cooling. It wasn't as plush as an office job on Lightspeed's yacht or at the command center, but it wasn't like fieldwork either."

"We had it much better than the crews installing the repeaters," Yana explained. She was a short woman with dark hair and an accent that belied a Middle Eastern origin. "Most of the people manning distribution centers were young professionals from the Washington, DC and Northern Virginia area. We worked for government agencies, data companies, and Internet startups before the collapse."

"We met the installation crew that raised our local repeater," Jim said. "In fact, they tasked me with handing out the converters, which is a story in itself. But I saw how hard those guys worked. We delivered them dinner one night so we could pick their brain about national events."

Josie smiled. "I'm sure they appreciated that."

One of Gary's daughters appeared at the table with a much larger tray. She placed glasses on the table, a pitcher of water, and a cutting board containing slices of smoked venison sausage and local cheeses. Brendan started to reach for the cutting board, but Josie smacked him on the back of the hand.

"Jim, do you have a place we could wash up? We really should wash our hands before we eat. We should have done it before eating the bread, but we were all too hungry to think about it."

"I understand." Jim pointed to the far wall. "There are a couple of sinks there that drain into the creek outside. Toilet facilities are outside. A couple of people live here in the roadhouse, so we have showers also. Both the sinks and showers have hot water, generated by all these woodstoves. If you want showers, there's a sign-up sheet for those. There's a lot of demand because we allow local residents to use them too."

Lamar groaned. "A warm shower would be amazing, but I need food more." He headed off across the room toward one of the sinks.

The rest of the group fell in with him and they talked between themselves as they wove through the tables of guests.

"Are you going to let them crash here?" Ian asked, wandering up to the table. "Randi just filled me on who they were. Sounds like asking Becky to put them up at her house is out of the question."

Jim cracked up. "That's a fair assumption." He leaned back in his chair, staring across the room at their guests. "I'm inclined to let them stay here until we come up with a plan for them. They're poorly equipped for running around on their own out there in their world and I'm sure there's a lot of information in their heads that we could use. They were tapped into a network that I can barely imagine."

"You think they have a long-term future with us?"

"I don't know what their particular skills are, but they have to be smart and able to think on their feet," Jim said. "I can't imagine Lightspeed would've had them running a distribution center if they weren't."

Once the newcomers returned from washing their hands, Jim introduced Ian and the two of them watched the group eat with interest. It was evident that these were polished people, with excellent manners, and accustomed to all the rules of decorum that governed eating in social settings. The struggle was real though. They were obviously ravenous, and it was all they could do to not shove fistfuls of food into their faces and eat like starving wolves.

Jim filled their glasses from the pitcher. They might be laser focused on the food at the moment, but they would need to drink eventually. While Jim was pouring water, a server came from the kitchen and placed four large bowls of chili on the table.

Jim said, "If any of you are picky eaters, vegetarians, or have dietary restrictions, I apologize in advance. We were able to expand our menu when the power was on, but now we're back to more humble offerings. We fix one dish a day and serve it until it's gone.

We offer a few side dishes, like smoked sausage, bread, and cheeses. That's about it."

While Josie's group looked like the kind of crowd that placed complicated Starbucks orders every day back in the old world, they didn't ask any questions about the food that was put in front of them today. They took hold of the spoons they were given and dug in with gusto. From the looks on their faces, the food was even better than they had imagined.

Jim retook his seat and scooted up to the table. "I'll be honest with you folks, I'm very intrigued by the story you have to tell. I'm sure you have information that we've not had access to, and I'd like to hear what you have to say. I know you're hungry and exhausted, so I'm not going to badger you with questions now—except for one. Would you guys like to be my guests at the Reset Roadhouse for a few days?"

Everyone looked up from their bowls, exchanging glances between themselves, Jim, and Ian.

"Are you serious? Is that a possibility?" Josie asked.

"We're out of private rooms, but the building itself is warm and safe. We have cots that you can set up here in the main room after closing at night. You can move them as close to the fire as you want. We try to keep the fires burning all night, so the building doesn't get cold. The damn place takes forever to heat if the fires go out."

"There are several people living here now," said Ian. "I live in the back and there's Ed, the guy in charge of making the beer and liquor. There's also a kid named Conway that you'll see running around here. He's a little rough and unfiltered, but he grows on you."

Yana, who'd been eating her chili with a little more dignity than the rest of the group, placed her spoon firmly on the table. She wiped her mouth and looked Jim in the eye. "I'm very appreciative of your offer of hospitality. I'm pretty sure that all of us are in agreement that we would like to take you up on your offer. Can I ask what happens once you have the information that you're seeking? Are you going to throw us out then? I'm alone in America. I have nobody looking for me and nowhere to go. I need a safe place to live and friends to give me a reason to want to live. I understand I may be getting a little ahead of myself, but is there any opportunity for me to build a future here?"

Jim appreciated Yana's directness. She apparently understood that Jim was trying to be polite by not badgering them with questions, but she also wanted to make her position clear. She wasn't looking for a stop along the way to somewhere else. She was looking for a future and a place to put down roots. Whatever Shade had told them about the roadhouse and their community had made these people feel like this would be a safe place to come. For people with very few options, this had been the most appealing one.

It wasn't exactly rare for Jim to smile. He frequently did it in conversation and when laughing with his friends and family. However, it *was* rare for him to smile when having a conversation with strangers. He didn't feel any need to put people at ease or charm them. In this case, he wanted to acknowledge Yana's inquiry, to show her that he appreciated her directness and that she was safe here.

Breaking out that rare smile, Jim said, "It's not easy to live here under the present conditions, but I suspect it's not easy to live anywhere right now. The opportunities you seek are available here, but some work will be required. My friends and I've made a strong effort to stabilize our local community, and this roadhouse stands as a monument to that. There have been a lot of bumps along the way, and I suspect there will be a few more before life returns to normal."

"By bumps, he means violence," Ian interjected. "There've been a lot of people along the way who were determined to see Jim fail. Some even tried to kill him but obviously they haven't succeeded."

Jim laughed. "From what I've heard, I'm about as popular as Walter Lightspeed was. I don't have the brains or the technical abilities he had, but I've been just as unpopular at times. There's some old adage about sticking your head out and making it easier to chop off. There's a lot of truth there."

Josie gestured at Yana. "If Yana, and maybe others, wanted to stay longer, are there accommodations available in the local community? Empty houses or people needing roommates?"

"There are plenty of houses," Ian said. "Some of them are better suited to a world without power than others. The best ones have functional chimneys and small rooms that can easily be heated."

"We don't have any idea how many houses are available right now. We had a better idea a couple months ago, but we lost a lot more people after Lightspeed's grid went down," Jim said.

Brendan nodded grimly. "It's not just here. Suicide has been rampant everywhere."

"Thankfully, it seems to be tapering off," said Jim. "However, we suspect there are a lot of houses containing dead people we don't know about. To be honest, things have been so busy since the collapse that I don't really know who's alive in this community unless I've run across them. The roadhouse and the valley where I live are pretty much the boundaries of my world these days. Outside of those two places and the road in between them, I don't get out much."

"That's probably safest," said Josie. "One out of ten, don't recommend travel right now."

Ian and Jim both wore radios to monitor any situation around the roadhouse that might demand their attention. Conway, their rooftop hillbilly, was pulling sentry duty on top of the building and was tasked with giving them advance warning of any threats that might show up outside.

"Shade's back," Conway announced over the radio. *"I guess he's going to want help stacking firewood."*

"We'll be right there," Jim replied.

Josie tipped up her bowl of chili and drained the liquid, then spooned the last few chunks of meat and vegetables into her mouth. "I'll help."

"You need us too?" Lamar asked.

Josie held up a hand. "You guys finish your food. You can come out when you're done and see if there's still more wood to stack."

"You all take your time," said Jim. "There's plenty of work to do around here so it's not like you're missing your only opportunity."

Jim, Ian, and Josie headed across the floor of the roadhouse and toward the back door. Randi had also heard the radio transmission and she caught Jim's eye when he looked in her direction. She pointed at Becky, cringed, and fanned herself to indicate that Becky was still hot over the idea that Josie was here to take her man.

The woodpile was outside on the loading dock, which required they walk past the bar as they headed for the door.

Becky must've recognized Jim's steps. "I heard on the radio that Shade got back with a load of wood," she called out. "That bitch with you?"

"No," Jim lied. "Ian and I are going outside to help Shade with the firewood."

Becky cackled. "Liar! I can smell her. I hope she drops a log on her foot."

Jim shot Josie an apologetic look. "I'm sorry. You try to raise them right and this is how they turn out."

"I can hear you!" Becky said over the murmur of the crowd. "I hope you drop a log on your foot too!"

"Can you chill out?" Jim growled.

Becky ignored him. "You send Shade in here. We need to talk."

15

The Reset Roadhouse

SHADE'S HORSE-DRAWN wagon was not like the fancy doctor buggies that were commonly seen in modern parades. It was a plain, sturdy design that would have been the equivalent of a Kenworth semi in the late 1800s, used to move freight, haul lumber, and deliver crops to the market. On this occasion it was stacked high with firewood, and the massive horses that pulled it stood stomping and shifting in their harnesses. Two solar powered lights illuminated the loading dock area.

Spotting Pete and Charlie seated on a stack of pallets, Shade said, "You boys unload those chainsaws first." His voice was resonant and booming, loud even at its lowest setting.

Jim had taken several battery-operated chainsaws in on trade at the roadhouse. He'd been lucky to get them as they were one of their most sought-after items in the community. The heavy-duty batteries that powered the saws could be charged by solar and a couple of them could run the saws long enough to fill Shade's wagon with fire-wood. Jim and Shade both owned large gas-powered chainsaws, but they weren't getting much use these days. Occasionally someone would walk into the roadhouse with an unopened container of premixed fuel they wanted to barter, but those instances were becoming fewer and fewer.

Shade's uncle Nooner jumped down from the front of the wagon, staggering a little when he hit the ground. He reached back inside and pulled an empty beer growler and empty moonshine jar from beneath the seat. He'd drop them off at the bar to be washed and refilled. It was well past noon and Nooner was well past drunk, but from everything Jim had seen, the old man continued to do good work in that state. And even though logic should have dictated that he not operate a vehicle in such a condition, Nooner frequently drove his multifuel tractor when he had consumed more alcohol than the tractor itself. Fortunately for everyone in the community, the tractor was slow and the roads were not crowded.

Shade hopped down and was stretching his back when an unfamiliar face stepped from the shadows. Shade narrowed his eyes and stared at Josie for a moment. "Where do I know you from?" He wasn't as much talking to Josie as he was talking to himself. He was prone to thinking out loud while he gathered his thoughts.

She took another step and the beam of the solar lights fully illuminated her.

Shade snapped his fingers. "You worked at that aid distribution center. Am I right?"

"That's right. I'm Josie. I hope I'm not putting you on the spot, but you told me a lot about this place and said we should check it out if we ever had the time."

Shade nodded slowly. "Josie...yeah, that's right. I remember telling you that but when the grid collapsed, I assumed you folks went back to wherever you came from. What are you still doing around these parts?"

Josie nervously clasped her hands together, one foot tapping against the ground. "Lightspeed's aid network collapsed when his grid went down, but we weren't recalled to base. In fact, it all collapsed so quickly that my people and I were left stranded at the armory. Our security team abandoned us a few days ago, disappearing in the middle of the night without so much as a word. Once they were gone, it wasn't safe for us to remain there. We...we didn't know where else to go."

Shade looked at Jim a bit apologetically. "I hope I haven't put you on the spot here, buddy. When I extended the invitation to them, I had no idea it was going shake out like this. I was just being conversational."

"We can leave if it's a problem," said Josie.

"Nonsense," Jim told Josie. "You're not going anywhere. And Shade, it's fine, man. I would've done exactly the same thing in your situation. I'm feeding her people now and we're going to put them up at the roadhouse for a few days. I'd like to hear what they have to ay and it will give them an opportunity to see what we're about."

"Drinking," Nooner slurred. "We're about drinking."

Ian, Pete, and Charlie cracked up at Nooner's comment.

"Not all of us," Shade boomed. "Fortunately, you and Lloyd don't set the tone for the whole community. It would be a hell of a place if you did."

Nooner grinned. "It sure would. A hell of a *fun* place."

"I didn't mean that as a compliment," Shade clarified.

The comment rolled off Nooner's back. Like Lloyd, criticism of his alcohol consumption went totally ignored.

"Well, like I was telling Josie," said Jim, "if they decide they want to stay, we can help them find a place to settle down. We can always use more smart people in the community."

"That's the damn truth," said Shade. "If dumb asses were donuts this place would be a Krispy Kreme." Shade winked at Pete and Charlie, both of whom were laughing so hard their eyes were watering.

"I hope you can charm Becky as well as you charm those boys," Jim quipped. "You got some fences to mend inside the building."

Shade looked confused. "What do you mean?"

"Josie asked for you at the bar when she came in. That didn't go over so well."

Shade winced, fully understanding what Jim was implying. "Becky get a hold of her?"

"By the hair," Jim said. "She got in a few good licks before we separated them."

Josie cringed. "She did."

Shade offered Josie a sincere look. "I'm awful sorry about that. Becky gets a mite jealous. I'm her first serious boyfriend and she seems intent on making sure I'm the last."

"No harm done," Josie said with a nervous smile. "I'm sure my hair will grow back eventually, and the bruises will heal."

Shade cringed. "I'll take care of this. It's happened before and I'm sure this won't be the last time. If it's any consolation, Josie, she's not killed anyone yet—at least not over me." He didn't clarify under what circumstances Becky *had* killed people. That was a story for another night.

Jim jabbed a thumb toward the side door of the roadhouse. "You get on in there and talk to Becky. We'll get this firewood unloaded."

Shade headed in that direction, pausing to pat Josie on the shoulder as he passed. "Good to see you again, Josie. I'm anxious to hear what you all have gone through since I saw you last."

Nooner checked his wrist like he was looking for a watch, even though he had never worn one in his life. "You guys need my help? It looks like I'm about to miss happy hour."

Jim grinned. "You look like you've been happy all damn day."

Nooner wasn't sheepish about his condition. He owned it. "Reckon I have."

Jim couldn't help but laugh at him. "Well, you get on in there too. We got this."

Once Nooner left, Josie clapped her hands and rubbed them together. "Okay, I'm ready. Someone show me what to do."

Ian pointed at the wagonload of wood and then at the stack leaning against the wall beneath the covered loading dock. "We take that and we put it there."

"I can do that," Josie said eagerly, grabbing several pieces of firewood, stacking them in her arms, then carrying them to the stack against the wall. "It seems you all have quite the cast of characters here."

"Oh, you haven't seen the half of them," Ian laughed. "There's Lloyd, and he's in a category of his own. Then most of these folks have families and they're full of feisty characters too. Not to mention some of the more colorful townsfolk. It's quite the assortment."

"It's quite the circus," Pete corrected.

"Of course it is." Charlie pointed at Pete. "That's why we have so many monkeys."

Pete got Charlie in a headlock, making all sorts of halfhearted threats.

"If you have the energy to fight, you have the energy to unload this alone," Jim said.

Pete quickly released Charlie and began filling his arms with wood again. "No, we appreciate the help."

Jim patted Pete on the back. "I thought you'd see it that way."

With all of them working, unloading the wagon didn't take any more than twenty minutes. They were warm, but not sweating on the cold evening. When they were done, Pete and Charlie excused themselves to get some of the venison chili.

"You guys must go through a lot of wood," Josie commented, pulling her coat back on. "I assume you're cutting stuff that's easy to get to?"

"We mostly cut trees that fall in storms or dead trees on the perimeter of town. We cut firewood nearly every day. Most of what we cut goes here, but we also cut some for people in the community who don't have the means to cut it themselves."

"That's nice of you."

Jim shrugged. He had a hard time accepting that he did anything just to be nice. Giving away firewood might have been benevolent, but it was also strategic. Keeping people comfortable made the community more stable.

"This community was a disjointed mess after the collapse. The whole country was. We come together a little tighter every day as the bad apples are weeded out. There are a lot more people doing things for the good of the community now than there were a year or even a couple months ago. Everyone is realizing we have to work together to survive. It took me a while to figure that out too."

"Shade talked about that. I didn't get the full extent of it until now. I haven't heard of many people doing what you folks are doing. Sadly, there's more fighting than cooperation."

Jim frowned. "That's not surprising but it's sad to hear."

They went back inside and the sound of the door caught Shade's attention. He was standing behind the bar with his arm around Becky. He raised his free hand and beckoned them over.

"Hell no," Josie said. "I'm not going within reach of that crazy woman."

"We won't let anything happen to you," Jim promised.

Josie hung back a little, letting Ian and Jim take the lead.

Once they reached the bar, Becky sniffed the air. "I smell that your new friend is with you."

"I'm here," Josie said. "I'm keeping my distance for now."

"What are you drinking?" Becky asked.

Josie pointed at herself. "Me?"

"Yes," Becky sighed. "What would you like to drink? Would you care for an alcoholic beverage?"

Josie looked around the bar. "What do you have?"

"We have a couple of different beers made here at the roadhouse," Jim explained. "We also sell a couple of different liquors, but most of them are the same liquor just in different bottles."

Josie looked confused. "I don't get it."

Becky spoke very slowly, as if she were trying to explain something to a turtle. "We distill liquor here at the roadhouse. Most of it is the same damn liquor out of the same damn still, but we store it in whatever old liquor bottles we can find. If we put it in a bourbon bottle, we call it bourbon. If we put it in an Irish whiskey bottle, we call it whiskey. If we put it in a vodka bottle—"

"You call it vodka," Josie finished. "Are you sure you're ready to be nice to me? Maybe you just want to make me a drink so you can spit in it?"

Becky offered a wicked grin. "I admit I'm capable of that, though I suspect both my boss and my boyfriend would be very angry at me if I did. Besides, Shade explained to me that this was all a misunderstanding."

"I also tried to explain that to you," Josie said. "You were more interested in killing me than in listening."

Becky threw her arms out. "Because who would listen to a man-stealing hoochie mama? That's what I thought you were at the time."

"I guess that makes sense," said Josie. "Then how about a bourbon?"

"Bourbon it is." Becky slipped from beneath Shade's arm, turned to the shelves of liquor, and ran her fingertips down the braille labels she had placed there. When she found the bourbon, she unscrewed the cap and poured a measure into a glass, then slid it across the bar.

Josie stepped forward and picked up the glass. She took a sip. "Not bad. I take it you're visually impaired, Becky. How do you know how much to pour?"

"I pour with my finger in the glass," Becky explained. "When my finger gets wet, I stop pouring. I try not to use the same finger I pick my nose with, if I can remember."

Josie froze and stared down at her glass. Shade started snickering.

Becky's face split into an evil grin. "Did I get her? Did I gross her out?"

"You did, doll baby," Shade said. He chuckled and the sound of his laughter was as deeply resonant as the snoring of a Rottweiler.

"She's teasing," Jim assured Josie. "She pours by counting."

Josie stared at the glass in her hand, then downed it in a single swallow.

16

The Reset Roadhouse

JOSIE THANKED Becky for the drink, returned the glass, then excused herself from the bar to rejoin her group. Jim stuck around to speak to Shade for a moment.

"See anything interesting today?" Jim asked.

Jim probably asked that question fifty times a day, always curious what people ran into as they moved about the community. It was impossible for him and his people to be everywhere and see everything. Maintaining a global picture of his community required the eyes and ears of the people who came through the roadhouse every day. They were his intelligence gathering machine and the very reason he opened the roadhouse to begin with.

Shade took a sip from the glass of liquor Becky had poured for him. It was the clear liquor they called tequila, even though it was just straight clear moonshine in a tequila bottle. Lloyd had once tried to replicate mezcal by adding a worm, but all he could find was a nightcrawler and he said it wasn't the same.

"Nothing in particular. I cut up a fallen oak today on one of the side streets. Nooner and I talked to some skittish old man who lived in a big white Victorian house. He didn't have a lot to say, but he didn't seem to hear all that well, either."

"I know that house," Jim said. "It belongs to a man named Blevins who used to teach history at the high school. I figured he'd been dead for twenty or thirty years."

Shade shook his head. "He ain't dead but he might be within shouting distance of it."

From out of nowhere, a loud rebel yell split the air. Jim didn't even have to look around to see who it was. "Speaking of shouting," he muttered.

Lloyd had just strolled through the main door with this band in tow. He had a guitar, bass, and fiddle player who backed him up while he rotated through an assortment of instruments. The members of his band were at least twenty years younger than him and less experienced at playing in public. They cringed at Lloyd's boisterous entrance, ducked their heads, and made a beeline for the stage. Lloyd headed for the bar.

He elbowed his way through the crowd and leaned on the counter, nodding at Jim and Shade. "Howdy, boys. Glad you got to see me today."

"I feel like the Lord has truly blessed me," Shade said.

"Speaking of someone who's blessed, where's that woman of mine?" Lloyd asked, craning his head around. He cupped his hands around his mouth and shouted, "Randi! Get your ass over here and bring me a damn drink!"

Jim gave his friend a pitying look. "Boy, you ain't never gonna learn."

From across the roadhouse, Randi heard Lloyd and headed toward him with her arms folded across her chest. The crowd parted for her, all of them falling silent at her icy passage. She had that look on her face that the frequent patrons of the roadhouse had come to fear. No one wanted to be on the receiving end of it. Only Lloyd seemed oblivious to it and that was at his own peril.

Randi came up behind Lloyd and smacked his hat off his head.

"You better have a damn good reason for calling my name like I'm a coon dog! Haven't you learned anything about how to talk to a woman?"

Lloyd picked up his hat, mashed it back on his head, and stared at Randi with a smug expression. "I see those lips moving but all I hear is blah blah blah. Are you gonna bring me a drink or not?"

Up and down the bar, throughout the roadhouse, everyone who heard Lloyd's comment let out a long, low "ooooooh". Jim got up from his seat at the bar and moved down two seats, wanting to be well clear of any violence that might be about to take place. Shade, standing safely behind the bar, slid down to where Jim now sat. If Lloyd was about to get the thrashing he deserved, no one wanted to be collateral damage.

Despite the building tension in the room, Randi did not lose her cool. She calmly raised a finger in the air and stared daggers at Lloyd. "One."

Suddenly Lloyd began to look concerned. He raised both hands in the air. "Now, Randi, I was only joking. It was just part of my big entrance, and you know I like to tease you. I didn't mean any disrespect. I'm a showman and that's all part of the show."

Randi raised a second finger into the air. "Two."

Lloyd's eyes went even wider. All bluster and bravado were gone from him. He seemed on the verge of trembling. "Now, honey, baby, we don't want to make a scene in front of all these nice people."

"Ain't no nice people here!" someone in the crowd shouted.

"Beat him like he beats that banjo!" yelled another.

"Don't show him no mercy," Nooner piped in. "He never shows us any when he's playing the banjer."

Lloyd looked at Nooner in surprise. "Et tu, Nooner? You turning on me too? I thought us drunks had to stick together."

Nooner raised his glass. "She's the one serving the liquor around here. All you serve up is misery."

Lloyd turned back to Randi in a panic. He saw that third finger began to rise and he dropped down to his knees, clasped his hands together, and began pleading. "Oh, my most beautiful and precious flower. I am so sorry if I offended you with my rambunctious display of affection. If I say stupid things, it's because all the blood is rushing into my heart when I am in your presence and it leaves my brain empty as a rusty bucket. I beg your forgiveness, though I know I'm not worthy." He lowered his eyes to stare at the floor, waiting to receive his punishment.

Randi raised that third finger, then lashed out with that same hand and grabbed Lloyd by the collar. She hauled him up and drew back her fist like she was going to punch him. There was a gasp from the crowd and Lloyd crunched his eyes shut, waiting for the blow he knew full well he deserved. To everyone's surprise, instead of knocking Lloyd's head off his shoulders, Randi pulled him up into a long, passionate kiss.

When she broke it off, she gently shoved Lloyd onto a stool. "Let this be a learning experience for you."

Lloyd swooned, waving his arms around in the air, face flushed. The bar erupted in cheers and clapping as people shouted Randi's name. She threw her arms up in the air, accepting the accolades like someone who'd just scored a touchdown. Those close to Lloyd shoved and jeered at him, smacking him on the back.

Lloyd winked at Jim, then leaned over and spoke in a low voice. "I showed her, didn't I?"

"You want me to get her back here to make sure she's clear on that?" Jim asked.

Lloyd quickly held up a hand. "Noooo, she's got work to do and I need to get on stage. When she calms down, have her bring me a triple of that blackberry moonshine."

Jim shot him a doubtful look. "*If* she calms down."

"She eventually does. My charm wins out."

Lloyd took off, weaving his way through the crowd toward the stage. People called his name and cheered. Even those who weren't fans of traditional mountain music still found Lloyd entertaining. He was a natural comedian who made fun of himself, Jim, and Randi with equal fervor. When he reached the stage, Lloyd placed himself front and center with the same aplomb as he entered the roadhouse itself. It was showtime.

Since he played there every night, Lloyd already had an assortment of instrument cases piled on the stage. He selected a battered instrument case and pulled out a century old open-back banjo. He walked to the front of the stage, turned on his microphone, and gave the banjo a powerful strum. When he first began playing the roadhouse, the sets had been all acoustic with Lloyd simply singing at high volume and thrashing his banjo like it owed him money. Someone eventually came up with a portable sound system that operated off batteries and could be recharged by solar power during the day. People still joked about how much better Lloyd sounded when they couldn't hear him as well.

Lloyd unleashed another rebel yell then leaned into the microphone. "Ladies and gentlemen, we're going to start tonight's set out with a little tune called 'Rabbit Up A Gum Stump.' This one is sure to put lead in your pencil."

Lloyd counted off, then jumped into the tune with the frenetic vigor of someone whose life depended on the energy they brought to the stage. People clapped and shouted and for a moment everyone was able to forget the conditions they were living under.

"I'm going to go talk to our guests," Jim told Shade. "Hand me one of those bottles of blackberry liquor and some glasses, please."

Shade placed a tray on the bar and filled it with the items Jim requested. Jim was not as comfortable as the serving staff with balancing a loaded tray, so he held it close to his chest and very carefully made his way through the crowded bar. He already knew that if someone knocked it from his hands, he was grabbing the precious bottle of liquor and letting the rest of it fall. It was important to plan for emergencies.

Jim breathed easier when he reached the table at the back of the roadhouse. He set the tray down and presented the bottle of blackberry moonshine with the formality of a fancy waiter showing diners a bottle of the house's finest wine. "Would anyone care for a drink?"

Yana squinted and tried to read the label.

Jim chuckled. "There's no point doing that. We use whatever bottles are available for bottling liquor. It's becoming a running joke around here. This is blackberry moonshine and it's one of my favorites. Lloyd, the guy playing banjo on the stage right now, is one of my oldest friends in the world. We make this from his grandfather's recipe."

While Josie's people might have been hesitant to try homemade liquor back in their old lives, they were different people now. Their work at the distribution center had exposed them to what people who were not living under Lightspeed's protective wing were going through. They had also experienced what it was like when that protection was withdrawn and how it felt to be on the road, vulnerable to the threats presented by man and nature. Jim imagined they understood a bit more about the fragility of life now and the importance of building bonds with people when their lives might depend on them.

Jim opened the bottle and poured two fingers of the dark purple liquor into each glass. As he handed them out, everyone sniffed the glasses and appeared pleasantly surprised by how inviting the aroma was.

Jim raised his glass in a toast. "To your future, whether with us or elsewhere."

They clinked their glasses, and Jim took a seat at the table while everyone sipped. He watched their faces as they sampled the liquor.

"That's good, but you can tell it has a kick to it," Lamar said. "That's the kind of liquor that sneaks up on you."

Jim gave a knowing nod. "Indeed, it is. There are many in this room who have fallen victim to that very thing."

Josie pointed to the bulletin board on the nearby wall. "What's the story on that?"

Jim hardly knew where to even begin. "That thing has evolved over time. Originally it was a way for people to find something specific they needed, like a particular medicine or glasses that might work for them. Almost immediately, people began putting up notes about lost people they were trying to find or particular services they needed someone to perform."

"We noticed the missing people," Brendan said. "There's lots of them."

"It's heartbreaking," said Yana. "It's difficult to comprehend the depth of suffering, of loss, represented by all those scraps of paper."

Jim stared at the wall and the thousands of scraps of paper stuck there. "It's hard to know when to take any of that stuff down. Mostly we just leave it. The one exception is when we find notes posted by people whom we know have died. Whatever they were posting about, we consider the matter resolved at that point."

"That's sad," Josie said.

"It's a sad world if you spend much time thinking about it," said Jim. "You're safer not dwelling on it. Suffering is a bottomless pit."

Lamar gestured at the board. "How can you *not* think about it? Especially when it's there staring you in the face every single day."

Jim averted his eyes from the board and faced Lamar. "If you spend too much time thinking about the loss and sadness around you, you'll be crushed beneath it. You'll lose hope. People without hope have no reason to keep going. They make bad decisions and risk their lives over dumb shit because their lives don't matter to them anymore. I believe most of the people in this room are still alive because they found their own way to kindle that flame of hope. They found something in their lives to be happy about and enjoy."

"That sounds like a very difficult thing to do," said Josie.

"It is. Everyone has to find their own path. It's different for each of us, but somehow we do have to find a way to muddle through the destruction and devastation. By now, most of us have learned that there are things that trigger us personally. For me, it's thinking about the world my children will inherit and how different their lives will be from the one I had. If I spend too much time dwelling on that, I risk falling into a hole I might not be able to climb back out of. Instead, I have to think about what I can teach my children about this situation. If there's a teachable moment here, I want it to be that they need to find a way to keep going when the world is falling apart around them."

"That's admirable," Yana said. "And difficult."

"It's *essential*." Jim spread out his hands. "When the power went out the last time, we had to open a mass grave to deal with all the suicides. When you have people who have survived a year of this shit, then you have to bury seventy of them in a single day because they couldn't face one...more...day, it shows you how crucial hope is. The loss of it is fatal."

17

The Valley

AFTER THE ROADHOUSE closed that night, the group returning to the valley rode in darkness, not requiring headlamps to stay pointed in the right direction. Their horses had made the trip so many times that they needed no input from their riders. They knew all the turns, knew when to leave the road for a muddy trail, and when to cross the river to knock a few miles off the trip.

When the group reached Jim's house, he turned off while everyone else continued down the trail that led through the field to Randi's house, then eventually on to Gary's. They said their goodbyes in the casual manner of people who saw each other every day. Once they were gone, Jim rode into the barn, clicked on his headlamp, and wearily dismounted.

No matter how many times he made this ride, the smell of smoke from his woodstove and the glow of solar-powered lights from the cozy interior of his home warmed his heart. Jim could never forget how he'd longed for this place on that terrifying walk home from Richmond in the early days of the collapse, wondering if he'd ever see it again. Wondering if his family would be alive when he got here. He'd never take returning home for granted again. A safe return after leaving home was never promised.

Jim settled his horse in for the night, picked up his pack and rifle, then headed for the house. Ariel heard him coming up the steps. She peeked out the window to make sure it was him, then slung open the door, and stood there with her hand on her hip.

"About time you got home!"

She always cracked Jim up. She was eight feet of attitude in a body half that size. "I got here as fast as I could, Ariel. Daddy has a job these days, it's just different than the job I used to have."

Ariel stepped out of the way so Jim could come inside, then she closed the door behind him and locked it. After riding home in the cool night air, Jim stood for a moment basking in the heat of the warm room. It was glorious.

"Lloyd says it isn't really a job and that you don't do anything," Ariel said. "He says you just ride around on your high horse and boss everybody around. He said the only reason people come to the roadhouse is to hear him play."

Jim dropped his pack and placed his rifle on the rack that had become a permanent fixture in the home's entryway. He sat down on a stool and began unlacing his boots. "You shouldn't listen to Lloyd. He drinks too much and thinks too little."

"*I* think he's funny," she announced, as if her word was the final authority on the matter.

"Of course you do." Jim removed one boot, dropped it on the floor, and began unlacing the other. "His favorite pastime is picking on your daddy. Come to think of it, what's *your* favorite pastime?"

"Picking on my daddy." Ariel giggled and ran off.

"Now I understand the attraction," Jim muttered.

He hung up his coat and followed Ariel into the living room. He stood over the woodstove, holding his hands in the heat that rose from it. Ariel had resumed her seat on the hardwood floor where she and Ellen were working a jigsaw puzzle on a scrap of plywood. Without cable and internet, jigsaw puzzles were in favor again and families traded them back and forth when they were done with them.

"It's nice to have our house back," Jim said, looking around the tidy room. "I'd forgotten what that was like."

Jim's parents had moved in with Ellen before Jim had even made his way back from Richmond. Ellen had requested their assistance, afraid that she'd be unable to protect her home and children without some help. Those early days had been chaotic, confusing, and rife with random danger.

As much as they didn't want to abandon their home, Nana and Pops couldn't refuse Ellen's request. They moved in with a truck and trailer load of possessions, cramming them into Jim's already cramped house. On top of that, people like Lloyd, Hugh, and Charlie had stayed with them at various times since the collapse. Now Nana and Pops were in their own house a mile up the road and had taken all their belongings with them. In order to provide Nana and Pops with a home that didn't require much work, Pete and Charlie had moved out of Buddy's old house and relocated to a previously abandoned home near Randi. For the first time since the collapse, Jim's home was just him, Ellen, and Ariel.

Ellen's face grew somber. "Doesn't seem like our old home with Pete gone."

"He's close enough you could probably yell and he'd hear you," said Jim.

Ellen shook her head. "Yeah, but you see him at the roadhouse every day."

"He comes to see you guys every day, doesn't he?"

Ellen shrugged. "I guess."

Jim didn't know what to say to that, nor did he know what to do to fix it. It just *was*. He tried to change the subject. "What did you guys do today?"

"We're still deep cleaning, one room at a time," Ellen said. "I went and saw Nana and Pops. They were doing fine."

"Yeah, Pete and Charlie gave me a report when they showed up at the roadhouse."

"By the way, I fed Pete and Charlie when they got back to the valley this evening. They said they'd already eaten at the roadhouse, but they're at that age where they can't eat enough. I swear, seven meals a day wouldn't fill them up."

"Fortunately, they like to hunt and trap," Jim said. "People who eat that much need a steady supply of food."

"Tell me about it." Ellen faced her daughter. "I think I'm done with the puzzle for now, Ariel. I want to talk to your daddy for a while. You want to keep working on this or put it up for now?"

Ariel pressed a finger to her temple and cocked her head while she considered the matter. "We can put it up. I'm going to watch a movie on my tablet."

"You've seen all those movies a million times," Jim teased.

"So? I've seen you a million times too." Ariel giggled at herself, then prissed off to get her tablet off the charger.

Jim's home didn't have a fancy off-grid system. He'd wanted one but never had the kind of money required to install one. Instead, he'd picked up a few solar panels one at a time and used them to charge an array of boat batteries. That was enough to allow them to run some low voltage lights, charge some electronics, and run the microwave. Combine that with a gravity-fed water system to feed to the toilets and faucets and they had a fairly decent setup compared to most.

"The boys were filling me in on the happenings at the roadhouse today. They said some new people showed up." Ellen got up from the floor and placed the puzzle on a table along the wall. Before Jim could respond to her previous comment, she asked, "Are you hungry? Can I get you anything?"

Finally warming up a bit, Jim left the woodstove and followed Ellen to the kitchen. "I could really use a cup of coffee. Something to perk me up a little so I'm not crashing in fifteen minutes."

"We don't have any real coffee, but we have some instant that you brought from the roadhouse."

"Yeah." Jim was disappointed. "I was excited about that stuff when those people first brought it in. They said it came out of an old camper they found in the woods. It's probably ten or twenty years old. I'm not sure I could tell the difference between a spoon of dirt and a spoon of that coffee."

"Is that a yes?"

Jim sighed. "Yeah, I'll take it. It's better than nothing, but just barely."

"You want anything to eat or just the coffee?"

Jim leaned onto the counter. "What is there?"

Jim had recently swapped out their regular refrigerator for a slightly smaller RV refrigerator. They'd never been able to run their old one as much as they wanted because it was a power hog and consumed too much of their limited electricity production. This more efficient camper model was easier to power with their solar setup, especially during the shorter days of winter when they produced less power.

Jim ended up going with a sandwich of homemade bread, homemade peanut butter, and honey. The peanut butter was the result of the gardening experiment from the summer. Peanuts were a huge agricultural crop in Virginia, but no one locally had any experience in growing them. This had always been tobacco and cattle country, while peanuts were raised farther east.

The process was simple enough, they discovered. A raw, uncooked peanut still in the shell was stuck in the ground and the plant grew from that. To everyone's surprise, the sack of peanuts originally destined for someone's squirrel feeder in the pre-collapse days grew an entire field of peanuts. While it was a simple, low maintenance plant to grow, harvesting it was not nearly as easy. The peanuts themselves grew underground so the trick was to pull the plant without leaving the peanuts behind in the ground.

Since they had none of the specialized equipment required to harvest peanuts, Jim and his people had to improvise. They used pitchforks to loosen the soil around the base of each plant, then carefully pulled them. Though it worked well enough, it was labor-intensive. After they were picked, the plants were rinsed off to remove any dirt, then dried in the sun. After a certain period of time, the peanuts were picked from the dried plants and stored in sealed buckets until they were used. Despite the work required to grow the crop, it was nice to have another protein source.

"Like I said, when the boys were by here earlier, they said some strangers showed up at the roadhouse today," said Ellen. "What's the story on that?"

Between bites, Jim updated Ellen on the new guests, including Becky trying to snatch Josie's soul from her body.

Ellen giggled. "She's feisty."

"Randi might be the manager, but when Becky is behind that bar, she runs the show. She runs the crowd."

"What are the new people going to do?" Ellen asked. "Are they going to live here or continue on their way?"

"They want to stay for a while. At least some of them do. They said this was the only stable community they knew of in the region and it's not like they have a lot of options."

"That's got to suck," Ellen said. "Being abandoned while you're out here doing a good thing."

"It's not like Lightspeed abandoned them. He was also trying to do a good thing and got killed for his troubles."

After mulling this over for a moment, Ellen said, "I want to go into town with you tomorrow."

For most of their marriage, Ellen had been the more sociable of the two. She genuinely liked people. Jim...didn't. Since the collapse, she'd fallen into the groove of gardening, working on projects with other families in the valley, and taking care of her family. Jim, the one who hated people to legendary proportions, was the one who ended up working with the public nearly every day. Fate was a cruel thing sometimes.

"Sure. You're welcome to come. How long has it been since you went in? I can't even remember."

"A couple of weeks. I've got some items we don't need any longer and I want to deliver them to the store."

"I can always do that if you don't want to make the trip."

"No, I *want* to make the trip. I feel like I need a change of scenery. I'm getting mopey."

Jim studied his wife. "Everything okay?"

Ellen nodded. "I guess so. Once your parents moved out, it took a while to get things back in order. The house was in chaos for over a year and a half. Now I have things back under control, but it all seems different. It's like the whole process of restoring order caused me to relive all the things that led to the disorder. Does that make sense? It's too much to deal with right now and I need a project to distract me."

Jim finished his sandwich and drained the last of his coffee. "I'm sure you'll find something. There's no shortage of projects that need done. Will we be taking Ariel?"

Ellen shook her head. "Nana has been asking her to come up and spend the day with her. I'll leave her in their capable hands."

18

The Reset Roadhouse

THOSE WHO WORKED at the roadhouse trickled out of the valley at different times in the morning. Because of that, Jim and Ellen were able to make a rare trip to town alone after they dropped Ariel off with Nana and Pops. From there, they took the shortcut that crossed the river into town near the abandoned superstore. This was the way most of their group rode to town unless there was snow or ice. No one wanted to cross the river if its banks were even more slippery and dangerous than usual.

Jim noticed that Ellen was smiling to herself as they rode to the field. "What are you smiling at? The beautiful day?"

"Nah, but it *is* a beautiful day. I was just thinking about the future I imagined when we got married. Did you ever think there would be a day when it was normal for us to ride horses into town?"

Now Jim was smiling too. "You know, it's funny but when I was a kid people rode horses into town all the time. It was nothing unusual to see farm boys playing football on the high school lawn with their horses tied to trees. There was a burger and ice cream joint called the

Tastee Freeze and you saw them tied up outside there too. I guess I assumed those days were gone forever."

"You got it backward. Horses made a comeback while the ice cream shop and the high school fell by the wayside."

"It's interesting to consider that," Jim said. "It's easy to have this warm, golden memory of what the hometown of your childhood was like. Sometimes we remember it as being better than it actually was. Then, when you reach a certain point in life, you start to miss those days. You long for simpler times. Now we've had those simpler times thrust upon us and it's not what we expected."

"Yeah, I don't think this is a world anyone would've predicted. I would have been fine with going back to the 1970s. Instead, we skipped all the way back to the 1870s."

Judging by the position of the sun, it was around 10:30 when they reached the roadhouse. The building was cozy warm since the woodstoves had been tended all night. Jim and Ellen migrated to the nearest one and took a moment to thaw out. The kitchen crew was already hard at work concocting whatever dishes would be served that day. One of Randi's daughters was working in the store, hanging clothes up on display racks.

Ed, the brewer and distiller, was working with an apprentice in his section of the building. Ed said he kept his workspace roped off to prevent contamination, but Jim knew it was to prevent Lloyd and Nooner from guzzling the product. Lloyd had once worked with Ed, but that arrangement had eventually gone south for obvious reasons. In the interest of diplomacy, Ed had framed Lloyd's firing as a promotion. He told Lloyd he'd been raised to the level of Master Taster rather than admitting he'd fired him because he couldn't keep his hands out of the cookie jar.

Ian appeared as if materializing from thin air. "How goes it?"

"Where did you come from?" Ellen asked, startled by his sudden appearance.

He shrugged innocently. "I was in the back."

"How were things last night?" Jim tipped his head toward the back table where Josie's people were engrossed in deep conversation. "I see our guests are still alive."

"They were well behaved and appear to be exactly who they say they are. While it pays to be cautious, I saw nothing that concerned me."

"Yeah, I didn't get a sketchy vibe from them yesterday," Jim said. "But it makes sense that any new arrivals in the community should be met with skepticism until we feel comfortable with them."

"How can you possibly control that?" Ellen asked. "The town is open, with several roads going in and out. Would you stop people from moving in if they just showed up one day and you got a weird vibe from them?"

Jim thought a moment. "I don't think we're at the point of gating off the town, like we did our valley at one point. We've not seen anything recently to merit that level of caution, but it's always an option if we have to. We can't take our safety for granted."

"Town is small enough that it's easier to monitor now," Ian added. "We only have a fraction of the people we had in the early months of the disaster and it's not because Jim killed them all." He winked at Ellen.

Jim rolled his eyes. People were constantly busting his balls for having a heavy trigger finger. He had not started out that way but had developed that trait over time. When his impatience was mixed with a short tolerance for idiots and criminals, that was what tended to happen. Jim was working on a smartass response to Ian's comment when Josie approached.

Jim was preparing to introduce Ellen, when Josie beat him to it, shoving out her hand and smiling broadly. "I'm Josie."

"I'm Ellen." She pointed at Jim. "I'm married to this guy."

"Nice to meet you," Josie said. "I've only met one significant other since I got here and it went poorly. Thank you for not punching me in the face."

Ellen giggled. "I heard about that and I'm sorry. I swear we're not all violent." She cut Jim a sideways glance. "Well, maybe some of us."

Josie laughed. "All things considered, it could've been worse. We encountered people on the road who wanted to kill us before any introductions were even made."

"We got one of those," Ian said, elbowing Jim. "He's trying to do better."

"Noted." Josie pointed at the table where her people were sitting. "Jim, when you have some time, we have some ideas we wanted to discuss with you. Just some thoughts. We don't want to step on any toes, but we have some ideas that might genuinely help you and the people in your community. All of you are welcome to join us if you want."

Jim cringed inwardly at the mention of helpful suggestions, especially when accompanied by the warning that they didn't wish to step on any toes. In his experience, meetings that began with disclaimers never amounted to anything good. People who warned that they didn't want to step on toes usually planned to gleefully stomp them flat.

Jim was willing to give Josie the benefit of the doubt because her team came in with a level of expertise and experience that didn't exist in his community. They had seen and heard things beyond what anyone else locally had. They were seeing his world through a fresh set of eyes, and it was indeed possible that their suggestions would be more helpful than annoying. He would be nice to them, and he would listen because they were the best source of intelligence now available to him. Best of all, they had simply walked right through the door and offered themselves up.

Jim, Ian, and Ellen followed Josie to the table she'd pointed out. Everyone was introduced and Jim's people pulled up chairs.

"How was your night at the roadhouse?" Jim asked.

"Relaxing," said Yana. "It's the first time I felt safe in weeks."

"Same here," Lamar added. "I slept like a baby. A very warm baby."

"Most of us did," Josie said. "Even Brendan, and he rarely sleeps."

Brendan sighed. "It's not that I don't sleep at all, I just don't sleep much. My mind doesn't shut down easily and I get a lot of ideas at night. I've learned to sleep with a notepad beside my bed so I can write them down. At least that way I can go back to sleep without obsessing about them." He held up a notepad full of scribbles to illustrate his point.

Jim gestured at the legal pad. "There's a lot of notes on there. Are those all from last night?"

Brendan looked sheepish. "Uh, yeah. I start with a fresh page each night and then I date it. It keeps things nice and orderly."

Jim looked at Josie. "Are these some of the helpful suggestions you mentioned?"

She smiled awkwardly. "Only part of them. Those notes inspired a lot of conversation over our herb tea this morning."

"Then let's hear it." From the corner of his eye, Jim noticed Ian and Ellen both watching him nervously. They knew how *receptive* he was to suggestions and were obviously concerned this wouldn't go well. Jim had to admit that he was concerned about that too.

"Would you like to start?" Josie asked Brendan. "You're the one who got the ball rolling this morning."

"Sure! In my old life, I was a social media marketing expert," Brendan began. "Obviously, there's not much call for that skill in our current circumstance, so Walter Lightspeed got me involved in the logistics of distribution centers. Josie managed the aid distribution facility, but my role was in communicating with other distribution centers and with Lightspeed's central command. It was a lot like being a juggler, except I was juggling information instead of tennis balls or bowling pins."

Brendan swept an arm toward the bulletin board. "There's a lot of information there, but it takes a lot to digest it all. We all spent hours sucked into that board yesterday and I don't know that we even scratched the surface of what's there."

"It's accumulated over a year and a half," Jim explained. "People are even still adding to it."

"There are things that could be done to organize the information and make it easier for people to process," said Brendan. "Before the collapse, advertisers learned there were a lot of moments in the day where they could capture the consumers' eye outside of television commercials and newspaper ads. Think about the video screens at the gas pump, on billboards, and in restrooms. I mean, you obviously know what's on that board, Jim, but I saw grassroots business startups advertising their services. There are missing people and others who are searching for specific items they need. All of it's mixed together in one big jumble."

Jim nodded. "People are coming around to the fact that this is a new world with the new economy. They're starting businesses and providing services to their neighbors. Money isn't of much use, but there's plenty of barter going on."

"I noticed that you had some electricity here," Brendan said. "Obviously that's not Lightspeed's power any longer."

"Sadly not," Jim replied. "It's what we were using to power the place before Lightspeed came along."

"With a little work and a little of that electricity, we could install a Wi-Fi network in here that would push the information on this bulletin board to tablets placed on tables and at the bar, Jim. It could be as simple as using an old phone to photograph every scrap of paper on this wall, then broadcasting that slideshow to monitors mounted on the wall. As far as people selling goods and services, you could certainly advertise all that for free now, but it could potentially be a source of revenue down the road. Imagine people paying you to have their goods and services displayed to the patrons of the roadhouse."

Jim leaned back in his chair and folded his arms over his chest. He wasn't exactly skeptical of what he was hearing, but he lived in a very practical world. His concerns were very basic at the moment, as were those of most people. In his mind, his community was more interested in food, water, clothing, and shelter than in marketing schemes with flashy displays.

As if reading his mind, Josie added, "It could also be a way to spread news and information more efficiently. Shade mentioned that you had an amateur radio operator in the community."

"That would be my friend Hugh," Jim said. "He's out in the field right now, performing a security function."

"Has Hugh managed to pick up any information about what's going on in America and the world?" she asked. "Have local people been interesting in hearing news of the outside world?"

"Yeah," Jim admitted. "We don't always know what to trust, though. Some of what we hear is outrageous."

Lamar raised a hand. "Trust me, dude, the truth is outrageous right now. Nothing is too wild to be off the table."

Ellen winced. "That's disappointing."

"I agree. There's nothing comfortable about it," Yana said. "It's hard to imagine the country coming back from this. Lightspeed could have done it, but he was sabotaged from all sides. The last shreds of our surviving government couldn't stand to see an outsider succeed. They'd rather watch it all burn to the ground than give credit to someone who isn't part of their system."

"So back to the Wi-Fi," Jim said. "What exactly are you suggesting we could do with news?"

"Stream it to devices here in the roadhouse," said Brendan. "Not individual phones, yet, but to the same tablets and monitors I was talking about earlier. Not only would it be a community service, people might frequent the place just to learn what's going on in the world."

Jim laughed. "We serve booze. That's enough of a reason for most people to frequent the place."

Josie's people looked downcast, taking Jim's comments as a sign he wasn't interested. Noticing their reaction, he softened.

"I'm not shooting you down. Our experience of the last year and a half has probably been different than yours. There have been a lot of ups and downs, with most of it being downs. A degree of skepticism is warranted."

"There are other things we can help with," Yana suggested.

Jim held up a hand. "Listen, you guys don't have to give me a sales pitch. You're welcome to come stay in our community as long as you can be self-sufficient. I appreciate the skills you bring to the table, but you don't have to pay your way in."

Yana ignored Jim's comment and kept going. "There's another

thing from our discussion this morning that seems important to bring up. This is a time when every person and every skill is critical. From what I can see, it doesn't appear that you have a grasp on who's here in your community. You know about the people you pass on the street and the people who frequent the roadhouse, but out of the total population of your community, how many people does that represent?"

Jim, Ellen, and Ian exchanged glances.

Jim shrugged. "We don't know really."

Yana smiled as if Jim's admission proved her point. "That's because you need to conduct a census. Our group was trained in logistics, inventory, and outreach. That's how we ran the distribution center. What is a census but reaching out to the community and conducting an inventory of human assets?"

19

The Reset Roadhouse

LATER THAT DAY, Jim was working with Ian to redo some of the wiring on their solar power system when Hugh came rolling in with an older man. Jim was up on a ladder and he stared for long moment, thinking he recognized the man with Hugh, but he couldn't be certain in the low light.

"Hugh!" Jim called.

When Hugh and his companion started in his direction, Jim climbed down the stepladder and wiped his hands on his pants.

The man with Hugh was possessed of a nervous, frenetic energy that was almost contagious, making Jim feel anxious even before he spoke to him. His posture was rigid and he craned his head with bird-like movements, taking in the interior of the building. He was hyper-aware and one finger nervously tapped his thigh as he walked. Jim hoped the man's state was from being in the unfamiliar setting of the roadhouse and not because he had some concerning news to deliver. If Hugh wasn't with the man, Jim might have dropped his hand to the butt of his handgun just in case the man's nerves were the precursor to an attack.

Only when the man was closer did Jim recognize him. Suddenly the anxiety emanating from the man like heat from a furnace made sense. Jim knew this man, or at least knew *of* him, and in that knowing he understood the man was most likely not a threat. The unease the man was experiencing was an old condition, pre-existing both the roadhouse and the collapse itself. In fact, his unsettled state had accompanied the man for as long as Jim knew, a persistent demon refusing to be exorcised.

Hugh had probably planned on making an introduction, but Jim beat him to the punch, sticking out a hand. "If I remember correctly, your name is Garnet, right?"

Hugh looked surprised at Jim's greeting.

Garnet's face cut to an uncomfortable smile, like Jim was someone he should have recognized. "Uh, that's right. Garnet Dillon." His brow furrowed a bit. "Can't say as I recall you. Do we know each other?"

Jim shook his head. "We've never been introduced but I went to school with your daughter, Winnie."

Garnet nodded thoughtfully. He flipped open the tab on a shirt pocket, pulling out his makings, and deftly began rolling a cigarette. For a moment, Jim wondered if he'd made a mistake by invoking the name of Garnet's daughter. So many people had died or otherwise been lost since the collapse that it could be delicate territory. Most family trees were now as broken and tangled as a forest after a hurricane.

When Garnet finished his cigarette, he stuck it in his lip, lit it with a butane lighter, and sucked in a calming inhalation of unfiltered smoke. "Yeah, Winnie is my girl. I hope she's okay. She moved down to Arkansas a few years back. Has a family down there. When things first went to hell, I thought about trying to walk down there, but I'm sure she's got enough on her plate already. She doesn't need saddled with my troubles too."

Hugh's expression revealed that he had no clue what was going on between Jim and Garnet. He wasn't familiar with this history they were discussing. It was totally unrelated to the business that brought Hugh and Garnet together in the woods outside of St. Paul.

"Winnie and I were never close friends," said Jim. "But our class was small. Everyone knew each other. She and I were together from first grade on."

What Jim didn't say was that part of knowing Winnie was being aware that what Garnet referred to when he said he didn't walk to Arkansas because he didn't want to saddle his daughter with his "troubles." Everyone who had lived in the community long enough probably knew the nature of those troubles Garnet mentioned. The consensus was that Garnet was a good, though troubled, man.

Jim noticed that Garnet wore the threadbare Vietnam Veteran cap that he was always seen in when he was out walking around. Supposedly, Vietnam was where all his problems began, but Jim didn't know for certain. His own experience with the trauma of violence and the stress of armed conflict was that it didn't always *create* emotional disorders from thin air, though it could. In some people it simply exacerbated underlying issues. Jim didn't know which of those applied to Garnet. Had he always had those troubles lurking in the deep waters of his mind and Vietnam only stirred the silt off them?

"I sort of remember you from those days," Garnet said. "Hugh said your name was Jim, but I didn't realize you were the same Jim who'd gone to school with my girl."

"I haven't seen you around town in a while, Garnet. I didn't know you were still here."

In the days before the collapse, Jim saw Garnet on a regular basis. Anyone who drove the local roads would have. He was always walking somewhere. Sometimes it was with a destination in mind. Other times it seemed simply an exercise in trying to exhaust his demons, as if they'd get tired and give up if he just kept moving long enough.

"Yeah, I'm still around. You know where I live?" Garnet asked.

"Out on Route 71, right?"

Garnet nodded. "The house I grew up in. I raised my family there but now it's just me. It's a little off the road so most people don't notice it. I don't come into town as much as I used to. Ain't much call for it."

Jim knew where Garnet lived because it was on the same road his parents lived on. He'd passed Garnet on that road a lot before the collapse. Several times Jim had stopped and asked Garnet if he needed a ride when the weather was particularly nasty or if he saw Garnet carrying several bags of groceries, but he never took Jim's offer. He'd politely defer, saying it wasn't very far, and the walk would do him good.

Although Jim could be oblivious sometimes, he was aware enough to understand when a man was punishing himself. Garnet didn't take those rides from Jim because he *wanted* to suffer. Garnet wasn't the first person to cause himself pain in hopes it might drown out the torment coming from his own mind. It was like the self-flagellation of those in a religious order or a teen girl cutting herself. It was the act of making the outside hurt more than the inside.

"You have kids, Jim?" Garnet asked.

"I do. I came into this mess with two, but I sort-of have three now. I have a son named Pete and a daughter named Ariel. Then there's Charlie, and he's kind of a shared responsibility. My wife and I are helping raise him, as well as the bartender over there, Randi. Hugh here is also playing a big part in his upbringing. Charlie's mother was a friend of mine, and she was killed in the early days of this disaster. I promised her I'd take care of Charlie and we've done our best."

Garnet took a drag off his cigarette and nodded. "In some ways this mess has made us better people. Taking in that boy to raise is the way people used to do things before the government started meddling in everyone's business. We were better people back then. We didn't need so many rules and laws telling us how to act and what to do."

Jim pondered that. "I'm not sure all of us are becoming better people again, Garnet, but one thing is for damn sure—there are a lot fewer of us."

Garnet shrugged. "I ain't so sure that's a bad thing."

"How are you getting along? You doing okay?" Jim's concern was genuine. Garnet had never had it good even when times were better.

Garnet picked up on Jim's underlying question. "I ran out of medication early on, if that's what you're wondering about. I went through a pretty intense withdrawal. All that shit warned there could be serious side effects if you quit taking it suddenly and they weren't kidding. My head was all over the place for months. I could probably find more medication now that so many people have died, but I reckon I'm used to living without it."

"That had to have been miserable," Jim said.

Jim had never been a counselor, but he had worked at a mental health agency long enough to know that it wasn't easy for someone with Garnet's issues to live without medication. Jim hadn't forgotten what he found when finally reached his old office after walking home from Richmond. There were dead outside the main doors and dead in the parking lots. People had killed themselves when they found the offices closed, preferring death over the prospect of slowly being swallowed by the blackness of their declining mental health.

Garnet sighed. "My demons have outlived my family, Jim. I know them well. I wouldn't call them comforting, but we talk each day. Their presence reminds me I'm still alive."

"Let's sit down." Jim pointed to a nearby table. As they headed in that direction, Jim asked, "What are you doing for food and water?"

Garnet settled into a seat. "Water ain't no problem. There's a spring back in there that feeds the house. We grew up hard when I was a boy and I learned to feed myself when I was young. I eat a lot of things most people won't fool with—muskrats, possums, and even those big old creek rats if I get hungry enough. There are times things have been lean, but I ain't starved yet."

"I might cook rats if I was on my own," Jim said. "I doubt my wife and kids would go for that."

"Your kids get hungry enough and your wife would change her

tune. I can still remember the look on my momma's face when she saw us cold and hungry. It was the look of shame and torment that I'll never forget. That's why boys like me did so well in the Army. I got to wear shoes year-round, I ate every day, and they gave me a damn fine gun to shoot. Kids like me could get sent to the shittiest places the world had to offer and stay tour after tour. Hell, if the war hadn't ended, I'd probably still be there. In some ways it was the best life I've ever had. The problems didn't start until I got home."

"Which problems? PTSD?" Jim was pretty sure that he knew what Garnet meant, but he didn't want to assume.

Garnet pointed at his head, then jabbed his finger into the side of his skull, perhaps a little too hard. It was like he was trying to drill a hole with the tip of that dirty finger. "The problems in there. They didn't have a name for it then, but things were never the same after I got home."

Jim started to ask another question but hesitated. "Have you eaten today?"

"Hugh and I shared a rabbit yesterday, but we ain't et today."

Hugh nodded. "That's how we met, after playing a little hide and seek in the woods." His expression said that was a story for another time.

Silent up until that point, Ian asked, "Would you like me to grab something from the kitchen?"

"That would be great," Jim said. "Could you grab one of the meat and cheese appetizers and a bowl of stew for each of them?"

Ian headed off toward the kitchen.

Garnet lowered his voice. "I ain't got no money to pay for anything."

Jim shook his head. "We don't take money."

"Ain't got no other way to pay either."

Jim held up a hand. "You paid already. You paid in Vietnam and every day since."

Garnet didn't have a response for that, but he seemed to understand that what Jim was saying was true. He leaned back in his chair and relaxed some, taking another long drag off his cigarette.

Seeing an opening, Hugh jumped in. "So, I had no idea you two were acquainted, but I met this gentleman on one of my recon passes down in the St. Paul direction. He has an interesting story to tell. Interesting enough that I wanted you to hear it in person."

Garnet leaned forward and rested his elbows on the table, cigarette hanging off his lip. "I met your buddy there snooping and pooping around the woods. That's what we used to call a recon op back in Vietnam. When he told me what he was doing, I read between the lines. I spent enough time in combat to know when someone is running recon. I took a chance and told him what I'd seen. He apparently thought it was something you'd be interested in."

Ian returned to the table carrying a wooden cutting board with a selection of homemade sausages and local cheeses. One of the servers followed behind with a tray holding two bowls of stew, a couple of spoons, napkins, and two glasses of water.

Jim was desperately curious to know what Garnet had seen but wanted to allow the man to enjoy his food. Garnet stared at the meal, looking ravenous but uncertain. Jim patiently explained what each item was and held off on his questions while Garnet sampled the food. Despite his meager diet and the fact he hadn't eaten today, Garnet didn't eat like a starving man. He ate with the caution of someone uncertain about introducing new foods into a limited diet.

Finally, Jim could stand it no longer. "So, what did you see, Garnet?"

Garnet stuffed a slice of sausage in his mouth, chewed with his eyes closed, and said, "That's good stuff. Anyway, if you know anything about me, you know I walk a lot, right?"

Jim nodded.

"That's my therapy. Back when I actually had *real* therapy, my therapist didn't approve of all my walking. He said it was an addiction and I was overdoing it. Pair of shoes lasted me about a month before my feet poked plum out the bottom. Well, I said the right things and told him that I cut back on my walking, but I didn't. What I wanted to tell him was that he was *not* inside my head and didn't know what it was like in there. If he did, he'd probably be running instead of walking."

"Did you see something on one of your walks?" Jim asked, trying to keep the conversation pointed in the right direction. He noticed Hugh was nodding.

"Sometimes I go far. I take a pack with a sleeping bag and I stay gone for days, even weeks at a time in the warmer weather. The other day I was in the western end of the county, near the town of St. Paul. I was camping on the river. Do you know where I'm talking about?"

Jim did. Back in the days before staying alive was exercise enough, Jim would go trail running alongside the river. He'd taken his kids there to hike, fish, and play in the river. "It's beautiful there. I've been there many times."

"There aren't many fish left unless you get outside of town. The locals cleaned out everything that was easy to get to, but there's still pockets of big smallmouth in some places. Don't ask me where because I won't tell you." Garnet grinned, indicating this was *partially* a joke, but only partially.

Jim understood. Fishing holes were sacred. "I can't say as I blame you."

"The railroad tracks go along the river, just like they do in town. I made my camp beneath a rock overhang. I can't even imagine how long people have camped under that same rock to fish. Tens of thousands of years at least. The roof and back wall are scorched and blackened from thousands of campfires. It's a weird feeling sitting there at night staring at the fire and thinking of how many people have done exactly that same thing."

"You saw something there?" Jim was used to pulling information out of storytellers. It was an art and not always a quick one.

"A train. I saw a train. First one I've seen since things went to hell." Garnet ate a piece of cheese and chewed, letting Jim process his words. "That stew is good."

"There's more where that came from if you want a second bowl."

"That's very kind. I think I would."

"I'll get it." Hugh hopped up before Jim could protest. "You need to hear this."

Garnet didn't say anything for a moment, focusing on his food. Occasionally, he jerked his head up and scanned the room in a paranoid fashion. Other times he would tilt his head to one side or the other, as if catching movement there. Jim suspected that Garnet lived in a constant state of hallucinating and that was what he was responding to. Still, it didn't invalidate any information the man passed on. For most people like Garnet, hallucinations were more of a distraction than their primary source of sensory input.

When Hugh returned to the table, Jim tried to get the conversation moving again. "Tell me more about the train, Garnet. You might not know this, but both NATO and China had been struggling to gain a foothold in America since the collapse. Unfortunately, they've been getting help from the crooked politicians they have in their pockets."

"I didn't know that," Garnet said. "I don't hear much. Don't talk to people very much."

Jim could understand that. If he himself didn't have a family and friends to worry about, that might be his life too. A true hermit, silent and wandering. "I ain't much of a people person either, Garnet. The only reason I opened this business was because bars are a good place to hear what's going on in your community. We had to find a way to start gathering intelligence because we were tired of being blindsided."

Garnet mulled this over as he chewed. "I saw one of them. The people on the train, that is."

"That right?" Jim asked.

"He wasn't Chinese and wasn't wearing a NATO uniform neither."

"Could you tell anything about them? If they weren't Chinese or NATO, who were they?"

Hugh spoke up. "When I met Garnet in the woods, he told me that he saw some of them smoking on the rear platforms of the train cars as they rolled by. He said they had shiny AK-47s. *Gold-plated* AKs, if you get what I'm saying."

Jim knew exactly what he was saying. As far as Jim knew, gold-plated weapons were associated with gangs and cartels. If either of those were operating in the area, that was a concern. "Did he show you where he saw the train?" Jim asked Hugh.

"I checked it out and we walked the tracks for a bit. I found an empty pack of Lucky Strikes with Mexican packaging and a busted Topo Chico bottle. That's not exactly proof, but it does support his story."

Jim let out a long breath. "That's a lot to process. Where do we go from here? Any suggestions?"

Hugh and Garnet exchanged a glance, appearing as if they might have discussed this among themselves on the way back to town.

"We track them," Garnet said. "If you want to know what they're up to, that is. More snoop'n'poop."

"We have to know," said Hugh. "They're in our area of operations now. We have no choice."

"Obviously you can track them," Jim said. "They don't have any option but to go where the railroad tracks go. But how do you intend to catch them?

"We discussed that too," Hugh replied. "Only short stretches of the tracks are unobstructed. The railroad track is just like the roadways. Since no one has been maintaining them, they're frequently blocked by fallen trees, boulders, and mudslides. They won't be able to go very far without stopping and getting their hands dirty."

"That's true," Jim agreed. "I also heard there's a missing trestle at Honaker. Apparently drunk people like to set things on fire and watch them burn. Who knew?"

"We could burn a few more trestles and probably keep them out of the region for good," Garnet suggested. "I'm not sure what they're after but I doubt they're interested in having to rebuild two dozen bridges just to pay us a visit."

"It's too early for that," Jim offered. "We need to learn a little more about them first."

Hugh looked uncertain. "Letting them get a foot in the door might be dangerous. I worked around cartels in Central America back in the Eighties. They take off like kudzu if they get their roots in the ground."

"Noted," Jim said. "Can you ride a horse, Garnet?"

Garnet looked uncertain for a moment. "It's been a while, but I can try. Animals seem to take to me just fine. People not so much."

That comment made Jim smile. "I know all about that. I'm not very popular with two-legged animals either."

20

The Reset Roadhouse

"I'm going to divide you into teams," Jim announced, pacing between tables.

They were in the roadhouse, seated around the large woodstove made from a home heating oil tank. The door came off an old boiler and the tank was lined with a layer of firebrick. It held logs up to three feet long and radiated a soothing heat. It was early in the day and the roadhouse was not yet open for business. With the days growing shorter, everything had to be done earlier in the day. Daylight was too precious a commodity to waste.

"Hugh, I want you with Yana and Josie. This will be a good opportunity to familiarize our new arrivals with the town." He spotted Ellen in the group. "How about you take Brendan and Lamar? Pete and Charlie, you two work as a team. Ian and Conway, I'll put you guys together. Does everyone have flyers?"

Some raised their stacks of hand-drawn flyers. Others pointed to stacks of crude signs heaped onto the table. The posters advertised an informational meeting Jim would be holding at the roadhouse to discuss forming a community leadership council. The other purpose of the meeting—one Jim felt a slight apprehension about—was his self-appointment to a leadership role in the community. Although he had not yet figured out what he was going to call that role, it was an important decision. The wrong title could sour people on the whole idea of Jim being in charge, if their personal opinions of him hadn't done that for them already.

"Things have been relatively calm, but that doesn't mean they'll stay that way. Little Caesars Pizza had a saying back in the day that they kept their pizzas hot and ready. Keep your weapons the same way. The rest of you know this, but I say that as a reminder to our new guests. When bad things happen, they usually happen quickly and without warning."

All of Josie's people met his eye, which Jim took as an acknowledgment that his warning had hit home.

"Since you'll be showing Josie, Yana, Brendan, and Lamar around town, make sure you point out things of interest or importance. Show them the common landmarks we refer to and the frequently used streets. Make sure they know where the courthouse is and the farmers market."

"I'm guessing we need to explain the landmarks that aren't even there anymore," Pete commented with a smirk on his face.

"What's that supposed to mean?" Jim asked, genuinely confused.

Charlie finished the thought. "You guys still tell people to turn at the old drive-in movie theater and that place has been gone for more than thirty years. Same with Pizza Hut."

"You use the wrong names for *all* the schools," Pete added.

Ellen giggled at the truth of it.

Jim smiled. "You tell them whatever information you think will be helpful to them."

"Oh, we got a lot of that," Charlie said.

"Be safe," Jim warned. "I'll see you when you get back."

Everyone got up, pulled on their coats, and gathered their gear.

Pete and Charlie left out the back door to collect their horses from the roadhouse corral. They'd be ranging farther than the rest of the team, hitting the outlying neighborhoods on the fringes of town. Everyone else would be heading down Main Street with one group placing posters north of Main Street and the other to the south. Pete and Charlie were already riding down the road by the time the rest of the group made it outside.

"It's nice to be able to walk outside without feeling afraid," Josie commented, basking in the light of the sunny day. "Since the collapse of Lightspeed's network, we've been trapped inside the distribution center. Our walk here was our first foray outside in weeks and it wasn't exactly relaxing. I'd almost forgotten what it was like to take a casual walk down the street."

"It hasn't always been that relaxing here," Ellen replied, her face clouding at the memory of what life in the community has sometimes been like since the collapse. "There's been a lot of violence. People tried to kill Jim several times and even targeted our family."

Yana gasped. "That's horrible!"

"Things are very strange right now," Hugh said. "In some ways, the situation is the bleakest it's been since the collapse. The prospect of an actual recovery becomes more distant every day. Yet in other ways, this is the *safest* we've been since the terror attacks took place over a year and a half ago. I don't want to jinx us, but it's almost like we're getting closer to whatever our new normal is going to be."

Lamar uttered a sarcastic laugh. "Not sure it'll ever feel right to use the word 'normal' again."

They turned onto Main Street in the direction that led deeper into town. They passed an abandoned fast-food restaurant, all the windows broken out and the interior a jumble of destruction. Alongside it was a gas station and convenience store in much the same condition. Both buildings had been looted in the early months of the disaster when the town was more chaotic and crime was rampant. The same fate had befallen a drug store a short distance further. Any place with the potential to have drugs or medications had been a target nearly as soon as the lights went out. Drug addicts were among the most desperate criminals, intent on taking advantage of every situation, and more concerned about feeding their cravings than finding food.

"So, this is your town," Josie said, taking in the destruction.

"Obviously it wasn't always this way," Ellen said. "And it's not the center of town. The whole place has grown since I was a kid. At least it had been growing up until the collapse. I guess that was the peak of things." She fell silent, her comment throwing her into a spiral, the awareness that she'd seen the town at its zenith, a peak it might never reach again.

"The 2010 census showed the town having around 3500 people and the county having a population a little under thirty thousand. Any idea how many of those remain?" Lamar asked.

Hugh grinned. "Obviously, someone did their research. You do a background check on us after you met Shade?"

Lamar didn't answer immediately but looked at Josie as if seeking permission. They'd disclosed to Jim and Ellen that they had access to what remained of the internet via satellite modems, but that was the extent of it. No one else knew.

Noticing the look that passed between Lamar and Josie, Hugh asked, "What's that about? Some kind of proprietary Lightspeed secret?"

"Not exactly," Josie replied. "There is something we haven't told everyone yet. We mentioned it to Jim but I'm guessing he hasn't had an opportunity to discuss it with you yet. You'll have to excuse our caution, but we wanted to make sure we were welcome here before we disclosed too much information about ourselves."

"Jim wanted to tell you yesterday, Hugh, but got all sidetracked when you came in with that old man," Ellen explained.

"Garnet," Hugh said. "Yeah, Jim was a little rattled by what he had to say. It was concerning."

"My team and I have laptops with satellite access," said Josie. "Just like satellite phones, the satellite modems still work. Over the last month and a half, some of Lightspeed's servers have gone dark. I assume that's because the data centers housing those servers lost power. Some of Lightspeed's cloud is mirrored and backed up to foreign severs, which means we can still access it. We can also access the global Internet through foreign servers. Unless our access gets blocked somewhere along the line, we can still reach the world, for what it's worth."

"Fascinating," Hugh said, sounding a bit like Mister Spock from the old *Star Trek* series. "I have an amateur radio set up back at my place in the valley. I can perform some data functions, but I could never afford the latest and greatest equipment. A lot of it is outdated and has limited my capabilities."

"We can access a great deal of public information," Josie said. "It all depends on what was mirrored to foreign data centers. So much internet traffic was managed by American servers that the loss of power here has had a global impact. We were able to do a little research on your region, though. A 'background check' so to speak."

Yana had been lost in staring at the wrecked drug store they passed but rejoined the conversation. "Obviously, we would like to limit the number of people who know that we have outside communication. Even though our laptops require biometric access, people might steal them thinking they can use them. Even if it wasn't anything that drastic, it's likely that people would hound us, wanting to know if we could find their lost relatives or arrange a rescue for them. We experienced that at the armory and it was overwhelming. It should be obvious we can't arrange rescues since we can't even arrange our own."

"I agree that it would be wise to limit who has access to that information," Hugh said.

Ellen cleared her throat. "Back to your original question about how many people remain in our community. Jim always told us to expect a death toll of somewhere around ninety percent by the time we're one year into the disaster. He based that number on some reports he read."

"The EMP studies?" Josie guessed.

"Yeah, something like that," Ellen said. "Rural people fared better than most, but we were still hit hard. We don't have any numbers to back that up, though."

"As we mentioned, once we lost power a second time, we got hit with a wave of suicides," said Hugh. "I don't know how many, but we've found close to fifty so far just here in town. There's probably more we don't even know about."

"That's all the more reason you need a detailed census," Brendan said. "We mentioned this to Jim and Ellen already. Every resource is critical right now, particularly human ones. You might have people living here in your midst who could be a tremendous help if you only knew they were out there."

"As long as you're realistic enough to understand that not every person out there is a resource," Hugh said. "There are also thieves, greedy bastards, power mongers, psychos, and just plain assholes. God knows we killed a stack of them already, but more keep showing up. It's like one of those video games where the bad guys endlessly regenerate."

Hugh noted that Josie and her team appeared a little disturbed at this revelation, though they tried to hide it. He knew Josie and her people had run into trouble during their escape from the armory, but he assumed they'd mostly been sheltered from the graphic carnage required to survive an apocalypse. He imagined the coming months were going to be difficult for them as they adjusted to the reality of life outside the Lightspeed bubble.

"Don't let Hugh scare you. Things have been quiet for the last month." Ellen looked around her town with a sad expression. "People are always somber going into winter, even though Virginia winters are shorter than some. You dump the suicides and loss of power on top of seasonal depression and you have all the makings of a very dark winter."

"Then we need to reframe this." The optimistic, team leader in Josie rose to the surface. "Maybe in his meeting with the public, Jim should reframe this as the winter of discovery. The winter of *reunifica-*

tion. This could be the one where we find the lost—the *hidden*—and bring everyone together."

Ellen and Hugh shared a skeptical look. They both understood that things were never that easy. While goals, ideals, and optimism were important, so was tempering them with a healthy dose of practicality.

21

The Reset Roadhouse

THE NEXT DAY, everyone in the Reset Roadhouse family was present to help prepare for the community meeting. Jim anticipated a larger than normal crowd, which meant they needed all hands on deck. Ed and his apprentice brewer had worked for several days to make sure plenty of beer and liquor would be available. The kitchen staff had put in extra work as well. When Lightspeed gave them power, they developed a more elaborate menu, but once Lightspeed's grid imploded, the staff immediately scaled back to the simpler menu they'd had when the roadhouse first opened. In honor of the big meeting, they had prepped for several appetizers that could be thrown together in a hurry. They'd also assembled a menu of dinner options that could be served without a lot of work. Without electric appliances at their fingertips, simplicity was the key to keeping the kitchen running efficiently when they were slammed.

Hugh was running security, and he'd coached his people on what to look out for. He had security staff working all the doors, wandering the floor, and perched up high so they could watch the crowd from above. It was his job to be aware of potential threats the minute they stepped into the building and to help keep a lid on the proceedings should they get too heated. Those were his primary objectives. His secondary objective was to keep Jim from killing anyone if tempers flared. Jim had already agreed a public killing would be counterproductive to the purpose of the meeting.

As usual, Lloyd saw himself holding a pivotal role in the event. It didn't matter what event was being held, he treated *all* events as if they were merely showcases for his greatness. In his mind, he was always the headliner and whoever was holding the meeting was some low-rent side act—the appetizer to his main course. In preparation for the event, Lloyd had taught his band some new songs, including a couple of bluegrass covers of classic Eighties metal songs.

"Those will bring down the house," Lloyd assured his uncertain bandmates. "You guys are too young to understand this, but when I start banging out AC/DC on the banjo, the place is going to go mad. 'Back In Black', baby." He held up a devil's horn sign with his hand and pretended to bang his head.

"Are you sure the world is ready for you?" Jim asked when he caught sight of Lloyd's head-banging.

Lloyd puffed himself up. "They better be because Lloyd waits for no man. I'm pulling out all the stops. I don't amplify my banjo, but if I did, I'd be turning it all the way up to eleven tonight."

Jim let out a long "oooooooohhhh" as if this was the most exciting thing he had heard all day. There might have been a little sarcasm intended.

"That's right." Lloyd scowled. "You should be impressed."

Randi was hard at work readying the bar and her staff for the night. She had even broken into their precious supply of disposable drinkware. She wanted to have some on hand so they wouldn't run out of clean glasses if the bar got too busy. As much as they longed for one every day, they didn't have a commercial dishwasher that could clean and sanitize a rack of glasses in a matter of minutes. Instead, they had a washtub of water with a little bleach added that simmered on a woodstove most of the day. Whoever was handy and had a few minutes to spare would jump in and scrub glasses when the washtub filled up.

Randi had been inspired to come up with some new cocktails for the event. Someone had brought in a couple of tubs of powdered Gatorade mix that had hardened into something resembling pink concrete. She mixed the fruit flavored powder into a cooler with some moonshine and fruit cocktail to create an apocalyptic jungle juice. She'd also managed to secure a dozen boxes of Jell-O and had whipped up a variety of Jell-O shots in disposable plastic medicine cups from the hospital. Even the people who rarely drank were anxious to try out the Jello shots for the novelty of something new. The idea of Jello shots transported everyone back to a simpler time in their lives.

Months ago, Randi's daughters had launched their own cannabis business specifically to sell treats at the roadhouse. Anticipating a big crowd, they whipped up special infused treats for the night. Their items always sold well, so they wanted to have extra muffins, brownies, cookies, and lollipops on hand for the meeting. Jim hoped the crowd would indulge heartily in those treats. He saw nothing wrong with having a roomful of extra mellow and agreeable people while he was addressing them.

As the afternoon leaned toward evening the roadhouse began to fill with people and the atmosphere grew electric. It was the first organized meeting of any kind to take place since the wireless grid went down. The townspeople seemed genuinely happy to see each other. Those who'd endured it all and had the backbone to stick around to see how this story ended were excited to see others who possessed the same grit. They needed this sense of community now more than ever and it was easy to forget that beneath the burden of daily tasks. They'd gone from being a region, to being a community, to being a town, and perhaps now they were simply a tribe. The survivors. Those too stubborn to die.

The buzz of conversation filled the room as Jim made his way to the bar. "I might need a shot before I hit the stage."

"Need some liquid courage?" Becky asked.

Jim shook his head. "Something to keep me chill so I don't blow a fuse and cuss out the town."

Becky cackled. "I wasn't there, but I hear you've done that before."

"He has! It was a beautiful moment," Randi said, coming down the bar with a tray and placing it in front of Jim. "Here, have a Jello shot. They're all lime, which is why I found so many unopened boxes of it. No one eats lime."

Jim didn't like lime Jello either, but it didn't stop him from slurping down two, then filling a cup with Randi's jungle juice concoction. He stood. "Wish me luck!"

"To hell with luck," Randi said. "Just try to be nice."

With the booze already warming his belly and taking the edge off, Jim headed toward the stage. Lloyd was warming the crowd up, and he was plenty warm himself. He'd sampled a few of Randi's Jello shots before they were available to the public and had a tall glass of moonshine mixed with branch water sitting on a conveniently placed table. As Lloyd often said, some musicians needed sheet music stands, others needed drink stands.

Currently, Lloyd had a cigar in his mouth and was playing a barn-burner version of "Foggy Mountain Breakdown." Lloyd wasn't particularly a fan of the song, but it never failed to get the crowd tapping their toes and clapping. When the song ended, Lloyd removed his fedora and waved it in the air, cigar pinched between his teeth.

While Lloyd was taking a bow, Jim climbed onto the stage and pulled a microphone from a stand. "Let's hear it for Lloyd and the Misguided Youth."

Jim couldn't wander far with the microphone tethered to a battery-powered PA system, but even with its limitations, this beat the hell out of having to yell to be heard. The clapping audience cheered even louder, shouting Lloyd's name, and unleashing loud hillbilly cries into the air.

When Lloyd straightened up from his bow, he frowned at Jim. "Just when I was getting them warmed up, you step in to take over the stage. Trying to steal my spotlight!"

"That was always the plan. You knew that."

"Doesn't mean I like it," Lloyd complained. "Up here harshing my mellow."

Jim rolled his eyes. "I'm sure your mellow will come back with a few more Jello shots."

Lloyd didn't argue with that. "Will you require musical accompaniment?"

Jim looked around the stage. "Why, do you know any musicians?"

"Hardy har har, I'll just visit the bar," Lloyd sang. "Asshole."

Jim swept his arm toward Lloyd as he exited the stage. "Let's have another hand for Lloyd. His biscuit isn't done in the middle, but he tries with what limited faculties he has."

Lloyd gave Jim the finger as he wove his way through the crowd.

"That reminds me," Jim said. "How do you know if a banjo player is playing out of key?"

Someone in the crowd shouted, "His fingers are moving!"

Jim pointed at the man. "That's it! How about this one? What do baseballs and banjo players have in common? Anyone?"

When there were no responses, Jim said, "Everyone cheers when you hit them with a bat."

The crowd erupted in laughter. All except for Lloyd, who was booing from the bar.

"I've been called worse by better men," Lloyd fired back.

Jim shrugged. "Sorry if I pushed your buttons, I was looking for 'mute'."

Again, the crowd broke into laughter, but this time Jim held up a hand. "Okay, that's enough of that. We have things to talk about, and I appreciate all you coming out tonight."

The crowd began to settle, the mood of the room changing to something more serious. Servers still wove in and out of the tables, delivering drinks and food. In the back of the room, Ian washed glasses while Pete and Charlie added wood to the various stoves. Shade was on overwatch from an elevated catwalk at the back of the room. The smell of burning tobacco, roasting meat, and wood smoke hung in the air.

Jim gestured toward the bar. "I'm sure you've heard this from your servers already, but there's a good menu tonight. Lots of food and drink specials, so ask about those if you're interested. If you're just here about the meeting, that's fine too."

Jim grew more serious. He didn't have any prepared notes, but he'd spent a lot of time thinking about what he wanted to say and how he wanted to say it. It wouldn't be like any speech he'd delivered to the people of his town before. Certainly, he didn't plan to curse or threaten any of them this time unless things went really, really south.

"It's an understatement to say that the last year and a half has been challenging to all of us. We thought that first year was the worst of the dark ages and that the future would bring relief. There were numerous false starts, signs that help was coming, but our government failed us. The foreign governments that drained our aid coffers for decades failed us. At times, sadly, we failed each other. And when Walter Lightspeed promised to turn the power back on, we were all skeptical until he did it. Even when the lights began working again some of us remained skeptical, while others went all in and assumed normality was just around the corner. Obviously, it wasn't. We are further from recovery now than we've ever been. Thanks to some new arrivals in our community, we have a clearer picture of what's been happening at the federal and international level, and it doesn't paint a pretty picture."

Jim went on to introduce Brendan, Lamar, Josie, and Yana. He kept it brief, but explained they were Lightspeed employees abandoned in the region when Lightspeed's recovery network collapsed. He went on to summarize some of the things he'd learned from them about how Lightspeed died and how his organization died with him. From his vantage point on stage, Jim could see the impact this news had on people. He had their full attention, which made him wish he had better news to deliver. It seemed cruel to tell these already beaten people there was no hope around the corner, but what else could he do? They needed to know the truth. They *deserved* to know. Acceptance of the reality of their situation was essential to moving forward.

"One of the things that came out of my discussion with the newcomers," Jim continued, "is that we need a clearer picture of our community now that there are fewer of us. How many of you know people who aren't here at the roadhouse tonight?"

Hands went up around the room.

"How many of you know people that you haven't seen since Lightspeed's grid collapsed?"

More hands shot up.

"We don't know if those people are alive or dead, do we?"

People shook their heads or looked at the floor ashamed, as if it was a failure on their part that they hadn't been more diligent in checking on their neighbors.

"How many of you are aware of people who are alive and getting by, but never come into town?"

Some hands went down, fewer this time.

"That's the last test question. I promise," Jim said. "The point is that every living person in our community is potentially a resource to us now and we need to be aware of those resources. Some of these people you mentioned might need things that we have available. They might have skills that would be useful to other people. However, before we can understand how to better utilize the members of our community, we need to do a census and find out just what we're dealing with. How many of us are there? We need to know."

Jim let that idea sink in for a moment before he continued.

"That's only part of what we need to talk about tonight. If we're going to tighten our ranks and try to work together as a community, it might be time we have a leader. For as much as I've fought against the idea...I'm ready to assume that role if no one has any compelling argument against it. I assure you it's not something I've sought out. Any of you who know me know I've done everything in my power to try and avoid being responsible for other people, but my friends, people I respect, tell me it's time."

Jim braced himself for the protests and outcry. Looking around the room and meeting the eye of those closest to him—Ellen, Hugh, Randi, Lloyd, Gary, Shade—Jim saw they were holding their breath just as he was, waiting to see how the public reacted to the statements he'd just made. Before this moment, nearly everything Jim had proposed to the community had been rejected by some element, often vocally and with violence. There were always those who hated him based on actions he'd taken since the world collapsed. Perhaps he represented something they feared or hated. Or perhaps he represented some aspect of themselves that they were afraid to acknowledge.

This time was different. This time Jim's proposal was met with utter silence from those in attendance. Alone, while that wasn't a signal of complete acceptance of his proposal, it wasn't outright rejection either. Then to Jim's complete and utter surprise, someone began clapping.

Jim searched for the person who initiated it and saw it was Cookie. He of all people had wanted this to happen for some time. He'd specifically asked Jim to take a leadership role in the community before and Jim had refused. The timing wasn't right then, but it appeared to be now. The clapping spread throughout the room. Jim's jaw practically hit the ground as the room resounded with the sound of people applauding the idea of him assuming a leadership role in the community. He couldn't have been more shocked.

Maybe Jim should have stopped the applause sooner. Should have raised a hand, thanked them for the sentiment, and continued with what he had to say, but he was too stunned. This was a significant turning point. Even though the entire community wasn't present in the room, even though there might still be some naysayers and haters out there in the town, this moment was an indication that a majority of people had come to see something beneficial in the way Jim Powell thought and acted. Had they come to see that Jim Powell was right about a lot of things after all? It was a hell of a world.

Finally, Jim snapped out of it and signaled that he had more to say. "I genuinely appreciate that outpouring of confidence. I'm not even sure what to say about it. When my friends and I were talking about this decision, someone said that the people who want to lead are the least suited for the job. As I've said, I never wanted this. I wanted to stay in my valley, take care of my family, and be left the hell alone. But if you don't go to meet the world, it comes to meet you, and that's exactly what happened to us. What I've done here, what I've *become*, is what had to happen to help my friends and family survive and thrive in this environment. It has not been perfect, but I'd bet those closest to me would agree that we've fared better than most. I hope I can help the rest of you to improve your situation in that same way."

Some people started clapping again, but Jim held his hands up for them to stop. "You all have to quit doing that because it's freaking me the hell out. I'm not used to all this acceptance. I appreciate you all signaling your support but we're good now. I get the point."

The applause turned into laughter. Jim sucked in a deep breath and blew it out. Even with the liquor, this moment had made him more anxious than he'd expected. He felt better now. The support the audience was offering buoyed his spirits. It was the polar opposite of most of his experiences speaking to the community.

"I can't do this without a team. I've been known to be a little rash sometimes. You might've heard stories."

Hugh, Lloyd, and Randi all broke into bouts of conspicuous coughing that brought more laughter from the crowd.

"Sounds like I got an amen on that," said Jim. "As I was saying, I need an advisory council. I'm thinking maybe a dozen people to start with who represent different interests of the community. I need someone who can speak about building infrastructure, like water and sewer. Someone who is familiar with the livestock situation. Someone who knows a lot of the elderly folks who are still alive. Someone with a medical background."

"Can we nominate people?" someone in the crowd called out.

"I *need* you to," Jim answered. "This may come a shock to some of you, but I'm not really a people person."

"Noooooooooooooo," Lloyd said, the words oozing sarcastically from his mouth.

"Oh, that reminds me, you know why a banjo player and herpes are alike?" Jim asked.

"Why?" Pete shouted.

"Because you can't get rid of them." Jim winked at his son. "But seriously, if you have someone you think would be good on the council, or you think *you* might be good in that capacity, leave your name at the bar or speak to me afterward."

The patrons in the bar began speaking between themselves, sharing ideas of who they might suggest for the council. Some were presenting a case to their friends and family as to why they would be perfect for the job themselves.

"One more thing," Jim said into the microphone. "We need volunteers for conducting the census I was talking about earlier. A census is a lot of work in the best of times and these certainly aren't the best of times. It would be a good way to meet new people and grow your personal network. It might be a way to connect with people you can help or with someone who can help you. Because we all have so much to do just to survive, I anticipate that we'll only be working on the census for a few hours a day for now. If you're interested in volunteering, show up here tomorrow morning. You'll be working in teams so we can keep it as safe as possible. Any questions?"

Not a hand went up, which made Jim grin.

"That's good. Now get back to drinking and stuffing your faces." Jim pointed at Lloyd. "The stage is yours, Banjo Boy. Bring on the noise."

22

The Reset Roadhouse

THE BANJO MUSIC resumed and Jim wandered through the crowd, shaking hands and speaking with people. He was almost lightheaded from the unexpected show of support. It had utterly disoriented him. He was relieved when he saw Pete flagging him down from the back of the room. He and Charlie were standing alongside two men Jim didn't recognize and it gave him just the excuse he needed to escape the crowd.

"I'd like you to meet my dad," Pete said when Jim reached them. "Dad, this is Tim and Clay. You remember me telling you about Charlie and I meeting them on the back street when we were going to Pops' house that day?"

"Yeah, I do," Jim said cooly, sticking out his hand.

"I'm Tim," the older man said, taking Jim's hand. He had the aggressive handshake of an eager car salesman. "Clay here is my nephew."

"Clay," Jim said, taking the nephew's hand and shaking.

"I guess the boys told you how we met," Clay said. "It was a little tense there for a minute. We kind of got off to a bad start."

"Sounded that way," said Jim. "I don't know if you could tell from my demeanor onstage, but I'm kind of a blunt and plainspoken man."

"I picked up on that," Clay said with an amused grin.

"Good," Jim, returning the grin with a smile that didn't reach his eyes. "Then understand that if you ever point a gun at either of these boys again, I'll kill you before the day is out and you'll die crying. Are we clear?"

Clay's grin faded and he swallowed hard. He could read the warning in Jim's eyes and knew he wasn't joking. As he usually did, Hugh arrived from nowhere just in time. He stepped forward to intervene, sticking his hand out to Clay.

"My name is Hugh. I try to keep Jim in his lane when I can, but it's not the easiest job. What did you say your names were?"

Clay introduced himself and Tim.

Hugh shook Tim's hand, then returned his attention to Clay. "Are you a family man, Clay?"

"Uh, no," Clay said, a little unsettled by the easy way Jim handed out that threat. "Never found the right woman, I guess."

"I get that. Story of my life too. The reason I was asking is that people can get touchy about their family, even when your reaction might have been reasonable under the circumstances. I'm sure you can understand that, so don't let Jim's warning scare you away from the roadhouse. Like Jim said, he's plainspoken."

"I guess so," Clay said, his voice high and throat tight. Despite Hugh's assurances, Clay looked sorry he'd let Tim talk him into visiting the roadhouse.

Trying to salvage the situation, Pete said, "Dad, you should talk to Clay about what he's doing at his house. If you don't scare him away from the roadhouse permanently, he might be someone good to know."

Jim smiled, or at least offered his most friendly grimace, which was sometimes the best he could manage. His smile was a constant source of amusement to his friends and family. "Sorry if I got us off to an awkward start, Clay, I just had to get that out of the way. So, what is it that you're doing at your home that so impressed these boys?"

Clay looked uncomfortable with the question. He'd tried so hard to keep his project secret that he didn't like the idea of talking about it. Yet he understood that by coming here he had already accepted that he was at least willing to entertain the idea. Maybe, like Jim, he'd reached the point where he was beginning to understand that no man was an island. Beyond that, he was tired of having no one but Tim and the old lady next door to talk to. He needed some mental stimulation and they sure as hell weren't providing any. He took a deep breath, let it out slowly, and dove in.

"I have a pretty decent indoor growing operation. Back before the collapse, I grew starter plants there every year for my garden. Since I'm an engineer and a little paranoid, I had all the equipment on hand to run the operation off-grid should the need ever arise. Obviously, it did."

Hugh gestured at Jim. "He and I have talked about this a lot. We've experimented with it on a small scale, but we haven't really had the time to make a serious go of it. We'd love to have a few of those set-ups scattered around the community that could produce fresh vegetables throughout the year."

"And starter plants for summer," Jim added. "Having that head start gets us to harvest quicker and should give a higher yield."

"Heat and light are the key," Clay said. He looked around the roadhouse. "If this place was mine, I'd have a little something on the roof right now. Obviously, the days are shorter, but a greenhouse could catch enough light to keep some varieties of plants going all year."

"Wouldn't they freeze this time of year?" Jim said.

Clay shrugged. "You're producing a ton of heat in this building. Do you heat it at night?"

Jim nodded. "Takes too long to heat up the next day if we don't."

"Then you could vent some of that heat into a greenhouse and keep it warm enough, assuming you designed it specifically for this situation. You'd have to experiment and see what would grow, but anything you produce is better than nothing."

"That's what we've been thinking," Hugh said. "We've also discussed building some indoor community gardens if we find the right space. Get everyone to work together to take care of it."

"A basement," Clay said. "Someplace with dirt banked up against the outside walls to hold in heat from a few stoves."

"Wood is so labor intensive," Jim said. "That's part of what's been holding us back. It's ridiculous how much time is spent just trying to heat spaces."

"I heat my growing operation with oil," Clay said. "I built a home-made waste oil burner and it produces an insane amount of heat. I drain oil out of disabled vehicles, old hydraulics, deep fryers, whatever I can find. It drips into a burner and you control the rate with a valve. It's stupid simple."

Jim and Hugh exchanged a glance.

"That's definitely something we'd like to learn more about," said Jim. "I've seen commercial waste oil heaters in garages, but I've never explored how to build my own."

"The lighting is the issue," Clay said. "You have to come up with decent grow lights that don't require too much power, then you need solar panels, batteries, and a few other simple things. I know where to source most of this. I believe we could make it work if you wanted to."

Jim looked away and scanned the crowd. "Could you work with my friend Cookie on that? He's here somewhere and I could introduce you guys. He lives here in town and he's tapped into the local resources."

Clay cut Jim a wry look. "I'd be glad to work with Cookie, especially since he hasn't threatened my life tonight. If he can help me find some spaces that might work, I can design systems specific to them. Then we'll need to source materials and conduct a few experiments to make sure our components will do what we require of them."

Jim offered a sheepish look. "I'm not going to apologize for threatening you. It was just business we had to get out of the way."

"You have a different way of doing business than I do," Clay said.

"Indeed, he does," Hugh agreed. "But his method is strangely suited for the world we find ourselves in. The audience's reaction to Jim's announcement is proof of that. A year ago, they thought he was crazy."

"And now they think he's not?" Clay concluded.

Hugh shook his head. "No, they still think he's crazy, but I guess they understand that crazy is what the situation calls for."

Jim frowned at Hugh, then turned his attention to Tim, ready to change the direction of the conversation. "So, your nephew is an engineer. Do you bring any special skills to the table, Tim?

The skinny old man hitched his khaki pants and grinned, rocking back and forth on his feet. "The ladies seem to think so."

Pete and Charlie cracked up. Tim winked at the boys. Jim and Hugh rolled their eyes while Clay cringed.

"Where you from, Tim?" Jim asked.

Tim beamed. "Florida—the Sunshine State—and I wish to God I was back there right now. I feel like I'm stranded in the Arctic."

"A little Florida would be nice about now," Jim laughed.

"Tim considers himself to be quite the ladies' man." Clay winced. "He'll gladly tell you all about it, whether you want to hear it or not."

"Hey, it's not just *my* opinion—it's the consensus of a long line of satisfied ladies." Tim raised arms in the air and rotated his hips in a slow grind.

Charlie clapped his hand over his mouth. "I just threw up a little."

Jim looked like he was close to doing the same. "Well, this ain't Florida and times have changed. Proceed with caution."

"Caution ain't how I roll, Jim. Besides, it's not like I have to do anything. All I have to do is walk in the room and women go wild."

Jim cocked a doubtful eyebrow. "Is that right?"

"Do they throw down their bingo cards and chase you on their little scooters?" Pete asked.

Charlie cracked up. "With those big, long menthol cigarettes hanging out of their mouths?"

"And bright red lipstick!" Pete added.

The idea was just as funny to Clay, Jim, and Hugh as it had been to the boys. They all started laughing.

Tim didn't find it as amusing. He ignored them, his confidence not swayed at all by their jabs. "Well, gents, I'm heading for the bar to wet my whistle. What do you recommend, Jim?"

"I recommend the Jello shots, but not the cannabis-infused lollipops unless you want to end up in the woods out back trying to call Bigfoot."

Tim nodded curtly. "Noted."

"I recommend you stay away from the bartenders," Hugh threw in. "You get too fresh with either of those ladies and your night will go downhill fast."

"I like the feisty ones," Tim said, rubbing his hands together.

Jim pointed at Becky. "That one is feisty, but not nearly as feisty as her boyfriend. He's about eight feet tall, strong as an ox, and could probably kill you with a single punch. The shorter one is Randi and she's twice as mean as her boyfriend is. She'd kill you herself and laugh at you while you were dying."

Tim's eyes lit up. "Nice! I like a challenge."

"Do you like walking home with your organs dragging along behind you?" Hugh asked. "Because that's a real possibility if you mess with either of those two."

Finally, Tim seemed to be getting the message. Perhaps it was the idea of being disemboweled that got through to him. "If those two are off-limits, you have any recommendations? Who's fair game? Any widow women who might be hot to trot?"

Hugh choked back a snort at the expression. Pete and Charlie didn't give him a pass. They looked at each other and cracked up again.

"Hot to trot?" Charlie mouthed.

Jim scanned the room, stopping on an old lady with a glass of homemade wine in her hand. She appeared to be around Tim's age, even though Jim wasn't sure he'd characterize her as "hot to trot." She'd been more sophisticated in better times, but hadn't everyone? She looked tired and a little haggard these days. Her hair was neat, but not styled or colored. Her clothes reflected the times, intended more for comfort and utility than fashion.

"That lady right there." Jim pointed her out. "Her name is Vera. That's where you should start."

Tim licked his fingers and slicked down his eyebrows. "Vera, huh? I'm on it."

They all watched him go, a pep in his step.

"That one hot to trot?" Clay asked with a giggle.

Jim shook his head. "Vera worked in the courthouse and she was rude as hell every time I went in there. I don't know what her problem was, but she had one. I hope Tim annoys the shit out of her. Call it payback."

"Could I get a few minutes of your time, Clay?" Hugh asked. "I'd like to pick your engineer brain about a few things. I can also introduce you to Cookie while we're talking."

Clay nodded, probably glad to exit his conversation with Jim. "Sure. Can I get a drink first?"

"By all means." Hugh gestured toward the bar. "After you."

23

The Reset Roadhouse

AFTER A LATE NIGHT at the roadhouse, Jim and Ellen were back there before opening the next morning. Ariel came with them this time, wanting to play with some of the other children who accompanied their parents to work. The day ahead promised to be a busy one for both of them. Jim had a list of suggested councilmembers he intended to pore through when he had the time. The people who had expressed an interest in working on the census were also supposed to meet at the roadhouse that morning to receive their assignments and be placed on teams.

Perhaps most important of all, they were launching a recon operation to follow up on Hugh's previous mission. Going on the assumption that the train Garnet reported could only travel so far before hitting blocked tracks, Hugh and Garnet would attempt to catch up with it to see what they might be able to learn about its purpose. Charlie would be going with them. Randi wasn't happy about him being included. She didn't like Charlie being exposed to danger and refused to admit that he'd become a capable young man.

Ellen had finally accepted that the roadhouse served an important function in their tribe's wellbeing, though she'd stayed away from town for most of the last year because of all the bad memories. At one point it had seemed as if the entire town was ready to string her husband up, which tended to leave a sour taste in one's mouth. After that, she'd been content to stay in the valley and limit her interactions to friends and family. Only now was she beginning to get over it and seek the company of people outside her tribe in the valley.

When Ellen came to town the other day to help put up flyers about last night's meeting, she found that she enjoyed getting out and interacting with people again. She ran into friends she had known forever, but she also met new people and enjoyed having conversations with them about silly, random things. So much of their lives for the last year and a half had been focused on survival that there hadn't been a lot of time for casual, relaxed interaction with people. It was something Ellen had craved without even knowing she missed it.

As soon as they entered the roadhouse, Ellen made a beeline for the back of the building. Josie and her people were already sitting at a table, making plans for the day.

"Hi, Ellen," said Yana. "We're just having a strategy session."

"You mind being the ringmaster this morning?" Josie asked. "We have all the logistical stuff worked out and even made up some notebooks to log census data into, but people tend to zone out when an unfamiliar face is throwing a lot of information at them. We need somebody familiar and local. Our experience shows that audiences are more receptive to that."

"I'd be glad to," Ellen said.

Brendan raised a yellow legal pad in the air. "We had twenty-seven people sign up last night to help with the census."

Ellen did the math in her head. "Between those folks, you guys, and the volunteers from our crew, that should give us nearly forty people."

"That's impressive," said Yana.

"Yes, but the sad part is that those forty might account for half the town," Ellen said. "It would be really unfortunate if all we had to do to conduct a census was stand outside and count each other."

"That would still be helpful, Ellen, because then you'd at least have concrete data. I think you'll learn a lot about the current state of your town by getting out and visiting everyone," Josie said. "While all life is precious, some might argue that it's even more precious when seventy-five percent of your town is gone."

"I'm anxious to see who those survivors are," Brendan said. "Not to brag but assessing strengths and matching them to needs is one of my superpowers. Hopefully, it's one of the ways I can help out as a new resident."

"I hope we can all find a place here," Yana said. "Being among your people is the first time I've felt safe since Lightspeed died. It's terrifying feeling like there's no safe place for you to go. I hated it."

"I can't imagine feeling like that," Ellen said. "Even when things were at their worst in the valley where Jim and I live—even when neighbors were turning on neighbors—my home usually felt safe. The one time it didn't, we had another option on the property that served as a fallback position."

"An underground bunker?" Lamar teased.

"Almost," Ellen said. "A cave that my husband turned into a bunker. It was damp and unpleasant, but we never had to worry about anyone breaking in or setting the house on fire."

"A cave?" Brendan echoed. "That sounds fascinating. I'd love to see it sometime. I have this obsession with unique and repurposed dwellings."

"Jim would love to show it to you," Ellen said. "He loves talking about that place and how he built it. I don't think he's even been in there in months. He'd probably get a kick out of giving a tour."

"I'll mention it to him." Brendan made a note on his legal pad.

Ian approached the table. "Is this where the glee club is meeting?"

Ellen laughed. "Yeah, that's us, Ian. Pull up a chair."

Ian pointed toward the front door. "I would, but there's a horde gathering at the gates. The rest of your bean counters are here, and you might want to corral them before they wander off."

Brendan looked at his watch. "They're early."

Ellen held up her wrist and shook it, pointing out the lack of watch. "You are in the Appalachian Apocalypse Time Zone now. They are right on time."

Brendan laughed and scooted his chair back. "Then let's get to it."

Outside, it was a beautiful morning. It was cold but felt like the kind of day that might hit the low fifties later. Everyone was dressed for the weather and looked excited to have something new to do. Ellen felt the same.

"Good morning, everyone," she said, louder than she normally talked. "I'm glad to see you all here this morning and I can't wait to get started."

24

Route 71

JIM'S COUNTY was more geographically diverse than some of its neighbors. To the north side of the county were the mineral-rich lands that produced coal and natural gas. To the south were the steep, ancient mountains that were covered by dense national forest. On the western end, the county transitioned to rocky, rolling pastures that were home to cattle farms. Route 71 was the road from town that led in a westerly direction, passing by Nana and Pops' home, and a short distance further, to Garnet's.

Hugh wore his full loadout with his rifle slung around his neck. He had connected two backpacks together by clipping a carabiner to the carry handles. They straddled his horse's back and were lashed to the saddle so they wouldn't slide off. Those improvised saddlebags carried enough food and gear to support both he and Garnet. When planning for this outing, Hugh and Jim had assumed that Garnet would have nothing to bring to the table other than the information he carried in his head. With that in mind, Hugh made sure he packed a sleeping bag and tarp for Garnet, as well as weapons and extra ammunition.

Since Garnet fought in the Vietnam War, Hugh assumed he was familiar with the M-16 platform. Hugh set up an AR for him with basic iron sights. There was no complicated optic, laser, or anything beyond what Garnet would have run into in the jungle in the late 1960s. Even if Garnet hadn't touched this type of weapon since then, Hugh knew it would come back to him. Operating the rifle that your life depended on wasn't the kind of thing you forgot.

Charlie rode at Hugh's side. His participation in this mission had been a spontaneous thing that came up at the roadhouse between Hugh and Jim. The group would pass within a few miles of Charlie's grandmother's house. He'd been living there after the collapse when he'd lost both his father and grandmother. Both Jim and Hugh assumed that Charlie might like to visit his father's grave and see what had become of the farm where he had so many fond memories. It didn't hurt, either, that Charlie was capable with a rifle and had no compunction against using one to take a life.

Despite the cool morning, Garnet was waiting for them on his porch. He was kicked back in an old 1970s kitchen chair, his boots propped on a warped wooden railing. He smoked a cigarette that had nearly burned down to his fingers. Two marsupial carcasses, the meat darkened from exposure to the cold air, hung from strings above the porch rail. Chunks of flesh were missing, cleanly sliced off in a size appropriate to the skillet.

Garnet stood at their arrival and flicked the butt of his cigarette out into the yard. "I'll be right back."

Charlie stared at the cigarette butt smoldering among a sea of others that had landed in roughly the same spot. "How many butts you reckon been tossed off that porch?"

Hugh shrugged. "A good many."

Garnet returned shortly with his worn backpack over his shoulders. He locked the door by slipping a padlock through a hasp, then came down the three steps to the yard. Each wide stair tread was supported on the ends but not in the middle. They sagged so deeply beneath Garnet's boots that Charlie was fully expecting them to break, but they didn't.

"Got everything you need?" Hugh asked.

"I reckon I do. I don't need much. I'm used to making do without things." Garnet stopped in front of the spare horse Hugh had brought for him. He regarded it for a moment, as if trying to determine how best to proceed in getting on top of the thing. He looked at Charlie as if noticing him for the first time. "Who's the young feller?"

"That's Charlie," Hugh said. "He had family in the direction we're headed. His daddy is buried down that way and he wants to pay his respects."

Garnet nodded at Charlie as if that was all the explanation he needed.

Hugh held up the reins to the extra horse. "I'll hold the reins until you get on."

Charlie added, "She's a calm girl. She won't give you any trouble."

Despite his age and apparent hesitation, Garnet swung onto the horse with no problem. He took the reins from Hugh and sat the animal like he had been doing it his whole life. Hugh was pleased that mounting the horse had been easy for Garnet. That was a positive sign. Hugh reached down and unhooked the sling of a spare AR from his saddle horn, then held it out toward Garnet. "I assume you know how to run one of these things."

Garnet took it and looked the weapon over. "It's been a while, but I remember the basics. It's close to what I carried in Nam."

"That's what I assumed. The mag is full, but the chamber is empty."

"I can fix that." Garnet efficiently chambered a round and dropped the sling around his neck.

"You comfortable with a handgun?" Hugh asked.

"I'm rusty as a gate hinge but I was a fair shot in my day. I was issued a Colt 1911 in the service."

"Just as I expected." Hugh reached into one of the packs behind his saddle and extracted a well-worn Springfield Armory 1911 in a kydex holster.

The holster was a paddle-style, worn outside the hip with a molded plastic "paddle" that slid inside the waistband to hold it in place. Garnet stared at the holster as if it were missing vital parts. "How the hell do you work this thing? They ain't no belt loop."

Hugh rode his horse around to Garnet's right side. He explained how to wear the holster and made sure that Garnet got it positioned properly. "I've got more magazines for both those weapons when you need them. I also brought food and gear for the both of us."

Garnet looked uncomfortable with that. "You all didn't need to do that. You done fed me yesterday and I ain't used to people going out of their way for me."

"Just consider it payment for being my guide."

Garnet wasn't convinced. "I don't want to be beholden to anyone. I only told you about the train because I had a bad feeling about what I saw and wanted to make sure someone else knew about it."

"You're not beholden to anyone," Hugh assured him. "Let's hit the trail and enjoy the day. We have an adventure ahead of us."

With a low, uncomfortable laugh, Garnet muttered, "Every day is an adventure for me and the boys."

Hugh looked toward the house with confusion. "The boys? I didn't realize there was anyone else in the house since you locked it behind you."

Garnet laughed again. "The boys ain't in there, son. They're in here." He tapped the side of his head. "They don't ever stay behind."

25

Route 71

"YOU A LOCAL BOY, HUGH?" asked Garnet.

They'd ridden in near silence for over an hour. It hadn't been an uncomfortable silence, simply a period in time that required no words. They were three men at home in the world, taking in the country around them. Three men as much a part of the outdoors as the crows that called to them from dead powerlines, as the rabbits that jumped from weedy ditches, and as the deer appearing as brown whisps in distant fields. They were creatures risen from the world and comfortable in the fact that they would settle and die upon it at some time not of their choosing, whether that time was decades in the future or whether that time was today.

The smell of woodsmoke floated on the cool air, puffing from the chimneys of sporadic homes set back from the road. Most of the houses were low-slung Sixties and Seventies ranches made fully or partially of brick. Some were two-story farmhouses with barns in the yard. Occasionally a mobile home sat in a slash of land at the end of a steep driveway.

"I grew up on the other end of the county," Hugh said. "A place called River Mountain."

"I know of it." Garnet let his reins drop while he reached into his pocket for the tin that held his cigarette makings. The horse knew what to do without any input from him. He held the tin up and tapped it with a finger. "I growed some 'baccer last year. Got plenty if you need any."

Hugh patted his pocket. "Thanks, but I have my own. I grew a patch too."

"I enjoyed tending it," Garnet said. "Took me back to when I was a boy."

Hugh smiled at the memory. "Same here. I grew up working 'baccer for my daddy and not getting paid a red cent for doing it. Other times I'd work it for neighboring farms. Work all day and they'd give you five dollars like they were giving you something."

"Ain't that the truth of it," Garnet sang out. "Ain't nobody cheaper than a farmer." He pulled a partial, flattened roll of toilet paper from his pocket and held it up. "Ran out of rolling papers but this works. The cheap stuff is best. Tried some of that fancy scented toilet paper one time when I didn't have anything else and it give me the dry heaves. It was like puking up a gas station air freshener."

Charlie's eyes went wide, clearly repulsed by the idea of smoking toilet paper. He cut a look at Hugh, afraid to say anything for fear of offending Garnet.

Hugh said, "Nothing new about that, Charlie. In a pinch, that's how we rolled dope in high school."

"Did the same in 'Nam." Garnet stuck the finished cigarette in his lips and tucked the tin away. He lit the cigarette with a butane lighter, took a draw, then took his reins back up. "Were you a military man, Hugh?"

"Not really."

Garnet burst out laughing "Not really? Son, the Army don't allow you to join halfway, as far as I know."

"I was never in the military," Hugh clarified. "However, I was a military contractor at one time."

"Iraq?" Garnet asked.

"Central America. A war that wasn't a war unless you were there fighting in it. If you were, you didn't have any doubt it was a war."

Charlie was watching Hugh now. While he and Pete frequently speculated on Hugh's past, Hugh never said much. Even the occasional drink didn't loosen his tongue. If he was talking now, there was something about this old man that brought it out of him.

Garnet asked, "So how did a boy from River Mountain end up in the jungle, in a war that wasn't a war?"

Hugh shifted in his saddle and stared off toward Clinch Mountain in the distance. The wooded, irregular humps, softened by millennia, looked like a dragon's spine from some fairytale. "I guess you'd call it a desire for adventure dampened by a lack of opportunity."

"Sounds like a lot of young men I knew," Garnet said. "Me included."

"I tried community college when I got out of high school, but it seemed pointless. The goal I was working toward was dry as dust, but I didn't know what else to do. Jim Powell and I were already friends at that point. He and I used to work together at a local radio station, working evenings and weekends."

"Jim from the roadhouse?"

"That same one. He was a couple of years younger than me, but we were both addicted to *Soldier Of Fortune* magazine. Ever hear of it?"

"Can't say as I have." Garnet hit his cigarette. "Never was a big reader and didn't have the money for magazines."

"I never heard of it either," said Charlie.

"The magazine billed itself as the journal of the professional adventurer or some shit like that. It was full of stories about mercenaries, wars going on around the world, and first-person accounts of famous battles. It was exciting stuff for a couple of hillbilly kids stuck in the mountains."

"Especially with no internet." Charlie shuddered. "That must have been horrible."

Hugh shrugged. "For one, we didn't know any better. For two, magazines *were* our internet. The best part of SOF was the ads, though."

Charlie crinkled his face. "I never read ads."

"Like for guns and stuff?" Garnet asked.

"Not those kinds of ads. The classified ads in the back of the magazine. That's where the good stuff was. There were ads for hit men and bodyguards. Ads for A-Teams."

"Like the show?" Garnet said. "I used to watch that one. Mr. T was a badass."

"I think the show was inspired by those ads," Hugh said. "A lot of guys came back from Vietnam with nothing at home to hold their interest. They'd become adrenaline junkies fighting in the jungle and didn't want to give up the adventure. Some of them formed A-Teams and others advertised that they'd do any job—no questions asked— for the right price."

Charlie's eyes widened. "For real?"

"Some of them definitely were. People went to jail for hiring hit men out of that magazine and paying them to kill people."

"Shit," Charlie breathed. "Sounds crazy."

"The crazy part is that I saw this one ad that was a little bigger than the rest. The people who ran it obviously had the money to splurge on one of the bigger box ads instead of the little classified ones. The ad featured a drawing of this badass looking guy posing with a rifle. Below the guy it said, 'Seeking adventure? High pay and exotic locations. Call now.' There was a phone number at the bottom."

"You didn't call that damn number, did you?" Garnet asked.

Hugh pulled one of his own pre-rolled cigarettes from his pocket and lit it with a Zippo. "Not at first, but I must have read that ad fifty times before Jim came into work. Not sure what the pull was. It was a simple ad and the words didn't explain a whole lot. There was just something about it that hit me. It's like that ad was put out there specifically for me to see. Like it was speaking to me personally. Then I showed Jim the ad and he talked me into calling them."

"What happened?" Charlie was eating the story up. He'd never heard it before since Hugh rarely talked about his past. No one but Jim really knew much about him and Jim kept secrets well.

Hugh took another drag off his cigarette and attempted to recall the memory in detail. "This guy answered the phone and he says the name of the company."

"What was the name?" Charlie asked.

"I'll redact that from my retelling of events. Let's just say it was a major security contracting company that a lot of people in the Eighties would have heard of."

Charlie scowled. "Ah man."

"I told the guy on the phone that I was looking at his ad in SOF and that it sounded like something that might appeal to me. He asked if I was prior military and I tell him no, then I ask him if that rules me out. He explains that it doesn't, but that they have a training program I'll have to go through if I don't have a military background."

"What was the job?" Charlie asked.

"I asked the man that same question and he told me that they were an international security contracting firm and they provided support and training to developing nations."

"What the heck does that mean?" Charlie asked.

"Your buddy here was a mercenary," Garnet breathed, exhaling a lungful of smoke.

"Basically." Hugh expounded. "Mostly I was training locals on the same things the company trained me on. Often that training was conducted in the field, during operations, with live fire—often in conjunction with American Special Forces and spooks."

Charlie frowned. "Spooks?"

"CIA," Garnet clarified.

"Were you in gunfights?" Charlie asked.

"A lot of them."

"Who were you shooting at?" asked Charlie. "Terrorists?"

Hugh shook his head. "In those days it was communists."

"The enemy of the mercenary is whoever the man with the checkbook tells you to kill," said Garnet. "In my case, it was Uncle Sam pointing the finger."

"It was Uncle Sam in my case too," Hugh said. "But there were other men in the middle, put there to hide the money trail and keep the public guessing."

Charlie didn't appear to understand a lot of what was being said between the lines. Hugh and Garnet knew a world in which he was unfamiliar, despite all his experiences since the collapse.

"I served four tours in 'Nam," Garnet said. "My friends thought I was crazy for that, but I had it better in Vietnam than I did here at home. I wasn't in any hurry to come back to being poor. You want to hear something *crazy*?"

Hugh cocked an eyebrow. Considering Garnet's life and mental health history it was bound to be something interesting. "I'm all ears."

"For years, I wasn't even sure if I even came home at all. I wondered if I died out there in the jungle like so many of my friends did and my spirit didn't get the memo. You live too far removed from the world of men and that shit happens. It messes with your head."

Hugh mulled over Garnet's words, trying to figure out the best response, but Charlie spoke up before he did.

"Maybe you should visit the roadhouse more often," he suggested. "Sometimes being around other people pulls you out of your head."

Hugh offered Charlie a smile. "That was sound, mature advice."

"Being around people helps me when the memories get to be too much," Charlie admitted. "When I can't quit thinking about losing my family."

Garnet had smoked his cigarette down to a nub. He took one last drag, then crushed the cherry between two spit-moistened fingers. He let the butt drop to the ground. "Might try that. Kept to myself for a year and a half now. Between isolation and coming off my meds, I get a little out there sometimes, boys."

Garnet let out an uncomfortably loud laugh and Hugh had to wonder if the "boys" Garnet was referring to were him and Pete, or if he was referring to the demons he said followed him everywhere.

26

The Reset Roadhouse

JIM SAT at the bar with Lloyd while Randi prepared the bar for the day ahead. Jim had the sheet where people had either signed up to be on his advisory council or had been thrown under the bus by a friend. He was recopying the list in his own handwriting because that somehow made it easier to process.

"I'm surprised you didn't go off on that little field trip with Hugh and Charlie," Randi commented, lining up several partially empty liquor bottles on the bar and removing the caps.

She'd refill them all—whether they were vodka, tequila, bourbon, or scotch—from the same gallon jug that sat nearby. Unless someone was lucky enough to come across a bottle of pre-collapse liquor, the labels on the bottle were nothing more than an inside joke. Liquor was liquor these days. Drunk was drunk.

"I thought about it and part of me wanted to go, but I'm trying to learn to delegate some things. If I'm going to take responsibility for this community, I'm going to have to let some things go. There are plenty of capable people in our circle."

"About damn time you realized that," Lloyd piped in.

Jim cut his eyes at his oldest friend. "Don't get too excited, Banjo Boy. No one's talking about you."

"*Everyone* should be talking about me," Lloyd countered. "I'm not just capable, I'm practically a superhero compared to some of the dullards around this place.

"It's too early for this!" Randi groaned. "Can you all save the arguing for the dinner crowd? They get a kick out of it. Me? Not so much."

Jim and Lloyd scowled at Randi in unison, looking like a matched pair of disgruntled gargoyles perched atop a medieval cathedral.

"Don't start pouting or I'll give you something to pout about!" she snapped, placing a funnel in the mouth of one of the bottles.

Jim returned to the list in front of him. "I'm not sure what to call this council I'm looking to build. I sure as hell don't want to call it a town council. Even the idea of that leaves a bad taste in my mouth."

"Council of Elders," Lloyd suggested. "Since you're old as dirt."

"He doesn't know the age of the people on that list," Randi said. "Some of them might be younger than him."

"Everyone is younger than him."

"We're the same age," Jim replied.

Randi giggled. "Yeah, old."

Lloyd stiffened. "Listen, Granny, you—"

Randi jabbed a finger at Lloyd. "Choose your next words carefully."

Lloyd froze, bit his lips, then looked down at the bar. "Oh nothing."

"That's what I thought," Randi huffed.

Jim tried some alternatives, seeing how they sounded when said aloud. "Advisory Council, Tribal Council, Community Council..."

"How about Citizens' Council?" Randi suggested. "There's nothing in the name to imply that anyone is above anyone else."

"You can't use Advisory Council because you rarely take advice," Lloyd said.

Jim snarled. "You rarely offer any worth taking." He returned his attention to Randi. "But yeah, I like the idea of Citizens' Council too. Now I just have to pick who's going to be on it."

"You having elections?" Lloyd asked.

Jim frowned. "No, these aren't elected offices. It's simply a group of people I can bounce ideas off of to make sure I keep this place pointed in the right direction. I'm not wasting time on elections."

"No one expressed an interest in elections," Randi reminded Lloyd. "When Jim proposed running the town like an extension of the roadhouse, people seemed excited."

"You need a uniform," said Lloyd. "Like Fidel Castro or something. You could grow your beard out."

"Not happening," Jim said. "No uniform."

"Can I wear one?" Lloyd asked.

"No one is stopping you," Randi said. "Knock yourself out."

"Court jester, maybe," Jim suggested.

Lloyd mumbled, "Asshole."

"How many people you picking?" Randi asked.

Jim shrugged. "Maybe five or six off this list. Then Hugh, Shade, Gary and you, Randi, if you're interested."

Lloyd looked offended. "Not me?"

"I'm sure you have court jester duties to attend to. Sobriety is also a condition of being on the committee, at least for part of the day."

Now Lloyd was even more offended. "You threw that one in just for me, didn't you?"

"Maybe."

"Cookie, too," Jim said. "He's on this list. I've got a few others in mind. I just need to speak to them first. They're people I'm pretty sure I'd be on the same page with."

"Good idea." Lloyd nodded. "I'd hate for the first meeting to go south and you kill everyone for pissing you off."

"*You're* pissing me off right now," Jim said. "Dwell on that for a moment."

Lloyd abruptly slid off his stool and stood up. "I need to go practice with the band."

"Oh, that's long overdue," Jim called after him. "I hope it works this time."

Lloyd raised a middle finger and kept moving.

"So, when is this council of yours meeting?" Randi asked, re-capping the bottles she'd just filled.

"Only when I need them. Pointless meetings are a scourge on humanity. I hated them back when we used to work together. There's too many people out there who hold meetings just because they like to listen to themselves talk. I used to set a timer on my phone that sounded like a ringtone. When I got trapped in a meeting, I'd set it off and claim I had an emergency call I needed to take, then I'd never go back into the meeting."

"You were indeed a master at avoiding meetings."

"I didn't mind the work, just the meetings. Waste of time most days, so we won't recreate that useless practice in our new council. We'll get together when I need them, or they have an issue. Then and only then."

"Yes sir!" Randi said, throwing him a salute.

"Was I on my soapbox?"

Randi held two fingers together in the air, like she was pinching something between them. "Just a *little* bit."

"Noted." Jim got up. "I'm heading into town to meet with that Clay guy. I want to see his indoor garden."

Randi giggled. "That uncle of his is something else."

"Tim?"

Randi nodded. "Yeah, he's a master of bad jokes, sexual innuendo, and low-quality flirting."

Jim winced. "I'm surprised you didn't kill him, then."

"Kill him? I loved it. Until he came along, I didn't realize there was a critical member of the bar crowd that we were missing. Now he's here and that position is filled."

"Who's that? What were we missing?"

"A dirty old man." Randi cackled with delight.

27

Western End Of The County

"This where you grew up, Charlie?"

They'd turned off Route 58 a couple of miles before they hit St. Paul and were riding a stretch of paved two-lane road. There was a dense concentration of homes toward the intersection, but those thinned out quickly. After a mile or two, they were into farmland with more barns than houses.

"No, but my grandparents had a farm on this road, and I spent a lot of time here. We passed the house I grew up in on Route 71. I could see it from the road."

"You didn't want to stop?" Garnet asked.

"Nah, it's close enough to town that I can go there often enough. I've only been here to my grandparents' place a couple of times since I moved to the valley. It's a long ride with a lot of memories I'd rather not relive. It messes me up for a few days after a visit."

Garnet coughed and spat. "You asked about my demons earlier. One way I've described them is the feeling like you're not just haunted by your past, but by your present too."

Charlie swallowed and made eye contact with Garnet. "That hits home in a way it didn't when you were explaining it earlier."

Garnet nodded in acknowledgement. "It's accurate."

"My mom's parents lived on this road," said Charlie. "After my grandfather died, my dad did a lot of things around the house to help Granny out. After the terror attacks, Dad was worried about her being down here all alone. In the end, we decided it was safer for us to come live with her. She had land and livestock. We lived in a subdivision with a tiny yard. Didn't even have a woodstove or running water."

"That was a good call," Garnet said.

"Mom was still in Richmond, as far as we knew. She got stuck up there on a work trip with Jim. We didn't know when or if she'd make it back. Dad struggled with what to do, but finally we packed up and moved in with Granny. We left Mom a note that she could find us over here if she made it home. We hoped she'd find it, but we had no way of knowing. We never imagined she'd walk home. Hell, if it hadn't been for Jim and Gary, I'm not sure she would have. She might have decided to just stick around Richmond until things got back to normal. I can't imagine what that would have been like."

Hugh shifted in his saddle and adjusted his rifle sling. "Staying in Richmond would have been a bad time."

Charlie sighed. "She might have been better off. The mom who came back to me wasn't the one who left. That trip home changed her."

"How?" Garnet asked. "If you don't mind me asking."

"They had some kind of falling out on the way home, a disagreement about what to do, and they ended up splitting into two groups. Instead of going with Jim, Gary, and Randi, my mom went with another woman they worked with. It was the wrong call. I don't know all the details, but that other woman got killed on the way home by some psycho. He took Mom prisoner and she ended up having to kill him."

"She still loved you," Hugh reminded him. "She proved that up until the second she left this world."

"I know that," said Charlie. "I don't know how to describe what she became, but it's like she lost the ability to be human."

"Can I say something?" Garnet asked.

Charlie shrugged. "Of course."

"I can't speak for your mother because I didn't know her and don't know what she went through. However, I do know a bit about trauma."

When Charlie didn't say anything, Garnet continued. "There's been times in my life that the demons pulled me to their side of the fence. There's a lot of things that can cause that to happen. Too few people to talk to; no way to make sense of the things you went through; too much pain and suffering in your head for you to make logical decisions any longer. You're right that you lose your ability to feel human and do human things."

"What's that like?" Charlie asked. "I know what it was like for me, but what was it like for her?" The way he asked that question made clear he wasn't sure he was ready for the answer.

Garnet picked up on his hesitation. "You sure you want to know?"

"No. I *need* to know, even if I might not *want* to know."

Garnet blew out a breath and stared ahead. The world was silent except for the noise of their horses' hooves and the creak of saddle leather. "The world loses color. For me, blues and greens go first. Nothing left but gray, black, red, sometimes yellow. It's like someone takes a knife to the world and scrapes off everything that means something to you. You don't always feel sad as much as you feel *empty*. Some days you ain't even sure you're still alive. I've stuck my own hand to the stove just to check. I've stuck a knife into my leg just to see if I could feel it."

"How can you not know if you're alive or not? I ain't doubting you, I'm just struggling to understand."

Garnet thought a moment before responding. "It's easy to forget you're alive when the things that surround you most often aren't human and the things that made you feel human are gone."

"So, there's a chance my mom could have come back from it if she'd lived longer?"

"It's different for everyone, son, but quite possibly. I have spells where I lose months at a time to the darkness. Thankfully, there's enough good days thrown in to keep me on this side of the dirt."

Charlie was pondering this when he raised his hand and pointed at a gate a short distance ahead of them. "That's Granny's house up there."

When they reached the driveway, Charlie got off his horse and stood at the gate for a long time. He was facing away from the other men, away from the road, yet made no effort to unlock the chain securing the gate. Both Garnet and Hugh assumed Charlie was overwhelmed with emotion at seeing his Granny's house again, but it was more than that. Finally, he turned around and faced Garnet.

"I don't know how I feel about what you said. Part of me is happy to know there was hope she might have come back if she'd lived long enough. Another part of me is sad she didn't live long enough to see that day."

Garnet leaned over, spat, then dug around in his shirt pocket for his cigarette makings. "Well, I didn't know your mother, but I can tell you how I'd feel if my daughter was in your place and I was looking down on the situation from above."

Charlie pulled the gate key out of his pocket and after some difficulty, worked it into the rusty padlock. "How's that?"

"I'd rather my girl be happy knowing that some of me was still alive inside there as to think I was all gone and nothing remained of the person she loved."

The sound of Charlie pulling the gate chain loose was the loudest thing they'd heard in hours. He shoved on the gate and it swung wide, squealing in protest. "That's good to know, Garnet. Thank you for telling me that."

Charlie returned to his horse and Hugh handed the reins back to him.

"You want us to come with you?" he asked.

"Nah, I'll be fine," said Charlie.

"Head on a swivel then. You don't know who might have moved in since the last time you were here."

"I'll keep an eye out." Charlie mounted his horse, clucked his tongue, and walked it through the gate.

Hugh watched Charlie ride off. Garnet swung off his horse, tied it to the woven wire fence, and sat down in what remained of the gravel driveway. He opened his tin of makings and set about the delicate work of rolling his next smoke.

Hugh dismounted and led his horse over to graze the overgrown ditch line. He dropped the reins, knowing the horse wouldn't go anywhere with a face full of high grass. He lit one of his own pre-rolled cigarettes and studied the countryside around them. "Your words helped that boy in a way that mine wouldn't have. I appreciate you speaking to what you know. I don't reckon it's easy."

"Hell of a lot of easier to talk about it than live through it most days."

"I imagine that's a fact."

28

Town

Although the census takers carried handguns, they decided it was less threatening to approach houses without rifles. No one liked to open their door to armed strangers. Conway, Ian, and a few other people designated as security were hanging back with rifles in case they were needed. The plan was that the census team would work together, staying in relatively close proximity to each other as they worked their way through neighborhoods. That way there would be backup if things went south.

Much as Ellen had expected, the homes closest to the roadhouse and Main Street were mostly a known quantity. She or others collecting census data already had an idea which houses were occupied and which weren't. They knew which homes had been emptied by the owner's death, whether through murder, illness, or by their own hand. They knew which houses were empty due to the unexplained disappearance of their owners. Then there were the houses that were too damaged through looting, vandalism, or decay to be lived in.

As for the occupied homes, it was hard to keep one's presence hidden when everyone needed to burn wood to stay warm. Properly seasoned wood didn't smoke much, but people were burning everything with a BTU in it to try and survive. It was nothing to see black smoke puffing out of a chimney as people burned magazines, plastic soda bottles, broken furniture, and garbage to survive. They shredded couch cushions and burned chunks of the foam rubber padding. They used axes and bolt cutters to break tires into burnable chunks. Some tried burning books but found the dense material didn't burn well unless single pages were slowly fed onto a bed of hot coals.

On colder days, black smoke hung over the town like a menacing, toxic fog. The smell of burning plastic was everywhere but no one had time to worry about the effects of what they were breathing in. Freezing to death was a real, immediate possibility. Cancer from the toxic fumes they were inhaling might never come to pass and if it did, it would be years down the road.

Twenty miles outside of town people had old coal mines and exposed coal seams they could use for fuel if they could get the heavy coal to their homes. It wasn't unusual to see people chipping away at rock cuts along the highway, trying to fill buckets and sacks with the rich black mineral. Shade had once explored the idea of hauling loads of coal to town to sell by the sack, but it wasn't a viable business model since they were depending on horses and wagons for transportation.

"I feel like a dork," Pete said, holding up a clipboard Brendan had issued him. "I've never marched around with a clipboard in my entire life."

Lamar jabbed a thumb over his shoulder, pointing to the backpack he was wearing. "Anyone can wear a backpack, but a clipboard lends a man authority. You can go anywhere with a clipboard and no one questions you."

"It's true," said Brendan. "One of a hacker's greatest tools isn't computer skills, it's social engineering skills. No need to spend hours breaking into a computer network with brute force when you can show up with a clipboard, say you're a repairman there on an air conditioning call, and access a server from right inside the building."

Ellen giggled. "You're right about a clipboard lending authority. Jim told me that one of his most important work skills was the ability to look busy even if he wasn't. He said you should always carry a clipboard or a manila file folder full of papers, even if they were blank."

Pete studied his clipboard and the stack of papers attached to it. Each member of the census team had been issued the exact same packet before they left the roadhouse and had the contents explained to them. "How did you manage to print all these satellite photos of the town? These look straight from Google Earth."

In fact, they *were* straight from an American GIS, or Geographic Information System, mirrored to servers in Europe. Brendan had downloaded them via the satellite modem on his laptop and printed them from a laser printer Jim found for him. While several folks knew Josie's people had satellite modems and could access the internet through other nations, it was still considered to be sensitive information.

In order to preserve the secret, Josie fielded the question. "We downloaded the entire region to portable hard drives while we still had access to Lightspeed's network. It was part of our back-up plan in case we ever had to hit the road. We thought this information would come in handy if we had to find a new home, and it did. The maps helped get us here and to find safe places to crash along the way."

"Before we left the roadhouse, you mentioned we should make special notes on the maps of anything interesting," said Pete. "What's going to be done with that information?"

"We're building a database," Brendan replied. "Once the census is complete, the idea is that we'll catalog resources that might help us survive as a group."

"Food? Supplies? Stuff like that?" Pete asked. "I'm not sure how much of that is left after all this time. People have been rogueing their way through empty houses ever since the collapse. Empty houses were considered fair game."

"I supposed they will continue to be fair game," Ellen said. "No one is proposing that every empty house become communal property. Not that I've heard, anyway."

"That idea wouldn't go over well." Pete shook his head. "There are people at the farmer's market whose businesses are built on selling items they salvage from empty homes. You can buy windows, doors, hardware, woodstoves, and stove pipe. People are having to reuse and adapt."

"As I see it, the idea is to catalog resources that might be useful on a community level as you guys start working together more," Yana proposed. "Like noting that a home has an old greenhouse frame in the backyard or an old trailer that could be converted to another use. Another home might have a large pile of pipe that could be useful for a water project or camper that could be modified for a particular use."

"Gotcha," Pete said. "I understand now."

They split into smaller groups after they turned down a side street and started hitting houses there. Most of the homes in the neighborhood were built in the late Forties up until the early Seventies. They were smaller cottages and ranch houses, most of them occupied by older folks prior to the collapse. They spent two hours working their way through that neighborhood before heading back onto Main Street. Some of the census workers worked the homes along that section of Main Street while others turned down the next side street. Ellen, Ian, and Pete stuck close to Josie and her people, all of them getting to know one another while they worked.

"What's that?" Yana asked.

Ellen looked in the direction that Yana was pointing. "The industrial park?"

"Yes, those buildings."

"That was an information park," Ellen said. "The county built a new industrial park specifically to attract technology businesses to the area."

"I only see two buildings," said Landon. "Admittedly, they are large buildings but there's only two of them."

"They were only able to recruit two companies," Ellen said. "It never materialized into what they imagined. Local businesses hoped the employees would live here in town, but there's not enough here to attract or keep young people. Most of them chose to live in bigger towns with more things to do and you can't blame them for that."

"You can't make a community be something it's not," Ian said. "No matter how much money you spend."

"So, what were the two companies?" Yana asked. "Anyone we might have heard of?"

"One was a software company. The other stored backup data for a major defense contractor that worked with the government. They had a data storage contract, and this was supposed to be their safe, redundant storage location since it was situated away from Washington."

Brendan nodded. "Interesting. Have you all been through those buildings?"

"There were people living in the software company headquarters for a while, but they took off before the first winter hit," Pete answered. "I guess it was getting too cold in there and they didn't know how to heat the place. They pretty much trashed it."

"What about the other building? The defense contractor?" Josie asked.

Ellen smiled. "No one has been able to get in there and plenty of people have tried. It's become a running joke around town."

"Can't you just break a window out or something?" Yana asked.

"No windows," Ellen said. "And the doors aren't like anything we've ever seen before. No one has been able to get through them."

"What about the roof?" asked Brendan. "Sometimes those buildings have a roof hatch for maintenance. Maybe it could be pried open."

Ellen glanced at the distant building. "It's a fairly tall building and we haven't been able to come up with a ladder that would get us up there. Then there's some kind of razor wire around the top. No one wants to be up that high, balanced on a ladder, wrestling with razor wire. Eventually people decided to leave it alone, figuring there wasn't anything in there worth risking their lives for."

Overhearing the conversation, Ian said, "How did I miss all this? I assumed that building had been ransacked already. I had no idea that no one could get in it."

Ellen shrugged. "I don't know. I guess it never came up when you were around."

Ian stared at the building. "I'm pretty sure I can get in there. I've got a few tricks up my sleeve."

29

St. Paul, Virginia

IT WAS DUSK WHEN HUGH, Charlie, and Garnet finally reached St. Paul, a little town along the Clinch River in Wise County. It was the same town where Ed's brewery had once been located before Ed and all his equipment had been moved to the roadhouse.

"This town was once like the wild west," Garnet mused. "It was the closest liquor store back in my day. Drunks hung out under the bridge as you came into town. They practically had their own city there on the river and they'd stay there until it got too cold to sleep outside."

"Really?" Charlie loved a good story about degenerates.

Garnet nodded, then pointed toward a section of town, visible as they rode around a bend in the road. "That there was called the Western Front. It was a street packed with bars and whorehouses. Railroad tracks ran behind it. If a man got killed in a fight, they'd drag his body onto the tracks so a train would run over it and hide the cause of death. Happened quite often from what my daddy told me."

Charlie looked disappointed. "I never got to hear those kinds of stories when I was growing up. My granny was the storyteller of the family and most of her stories wove back around to the bible one way or the other. I like hearing about the old days, but not *that* old."

Garnet chuckled. "Well, I reckon there were some lessons about right and wrong being learned there on the Western Front. Probably gave the local pastors plenty to preach about come Sunday."

"Not to change the subject, but you're the guide here, Garnet," said Hugh. "We should probably start looking for a camp for the night."

"Safer to get a little farther out of town. Let's turn right up here. This road follows along the tracks for a good bit. Once the houses thin out, there are some places to camp that should be safe enough."

"We'll still run a watch tonight," Hugh said. "I sleep better knowing someone is awake and keeping an eye out."

Garnet shook his head at a memory. "I haven't sat a watch since I was in the Army."

"I ain't a fan," Charlie said. "Gets a little lonely at night.

Garnet tapped his head. "Not if you got a headful of haints. Then you always got company."

Charlie glanced at him. "What exactly do you mean by that?"

It would have been too personal, too sensitive a question for an older person to ask. Most adults knew better than to go poking around in someone's personal darkness. Even though Charlie was like an adult in many ways now, there were situations in which he still lacked experience and maturity. This was one of them. Garnet, however, wasn't sensitive about it. He appreciated the boy's candor and they'd broken the ice already when they were discussing Charlie's mom.

"You don't have to answer if you don't want," Charlie said.

Garnet shook his head. "Nah, it's okay. I wish more people had asked over the years. Life might not have been so lonely, and I might not have been so misunderstood. People were always scared of me, like I could snap and kill everyone within arm's reach. I might be crazy but I ain't blind. I know when people are avoiding me."

They reached the intersection and turned right. A long abandoned old drive-in restaurant called the Frosty Bossie sat on the shoulder of the road, the paint faded and every window broken.

"I had many milkshakes from that place," Hugh commented.

"As did I." Garnet returned his attention to Charlie. "You ever hear people talking about having demons, boy?"

"I heard my granny talk about demons a lot. She said playing with the Ouija board could open the door for them to take over your body and possess you."

"These are a different kind of demon and they damn sure didn't come from no kid's game."

"Granny said it wasn't a game."

"Nevertheless," Garnet continued, "I'd venture to say these aren't exactly the same kind of demons your granny was talking about. I'm not possessed. Tormented might be a better word. Plagued is another fine choice."

"Where did these demons come from?" Charlie asked.

"I've asked myself that same thing a million times. Was I born with them and they always lived inside me somewhere, just waiting for the right time to show themselves? Did they come from something I saw or did during the war? I don't know and they ain't saying." He laughed a little too loud at that last sentence.

"You can get demons from seeing stuff?" asked Charlie.

"Some people can," Hugh said. "The mind is a strange thing. Some people experience violence and are unchanged by it. Others are never the same again. I might have told you before that you should be careful what you watch because you can't unsee something once you've seen it."

"You *have* told me that. I didn't understand it at first, but I've come to know what it means." Charlie regarded Hugh, a man he looked up to more than anyone else in his life. "You have demons, Hugh?"

Hugh thought it over a long moment before answering. "No. I have no idea why, either. Some of the shit I've seen and done in my life...I damn sure earned a few demons. I try not to think about it too much. It's not like I'm missing out by not having them."

"If you knew why some of us have demons and some don't, you'd be a rich man, Hugh. The world would beat a path to your door." Garnet looked over at Charlie. "What about you, son? Any demons took root in there yet?"

Unlike Charlie, Garnet had no compunction against asking prying and uncomfortable questions.

They rode for a good minute while Charlie considered this, the only sounds those of the horses' hooves on asphalt, the creak of a saddle, or the occasional rattle of a bridle.

"I don't believe I do," Charlie answered at length. "You ever go into an empty auditorium or an empty church? With no people there, it's just a big empty room that don't quite feel right."

Garnet pulled his tin of cigarette makings out and popped the lid open. Talking made him smoke. So did thinking. "I can picture that."

"That's what it's been like in my head ever since my family died. When my dad and granny died, my mom was all I had left. She died trying to get me to Jim's valley because she told me I'd be safe there. Safer than with her. I have been safe, but I've been *different* too. I feel like a hollow log some days. I'm starting to wonder if some of those demons you talk about might be an improvement over the emptiness. Over the nothingness."

"I'd argue that the emptiness is better," Garnet countered. "At least you can think and have a moment to yourself. There are so many voices in my head I can't even put a thought together some days. They're always mumbling and whispering in there. Other times they shout and scream. Sometimes they're taunting and other times they're angry with me. You can't plug your ears against it when the voices are *inside*. While I'd be glad to trade with you, I wouldn't wish it on you for nothing."

Hugh looked at Charlie with concern in his eyes. "Maybe we can refill that emptiness, Charlie. Rebuild things one experience at a time."

"I hope so. I really do."

They set up camp at a clearing on a silty riverbank. Charred logs, partially consumed by previous campfires, indicated the spot had been used recently.

Garnet dismounted with a groan and tied his horse off to a nearby tree. "I'm going to feel that in the morning. I can walk for weeks without getting sore, but I used some muscles today that are a bit rusty."

Charlie stared at the campsite with a somber expression. "My dad said he used to camp along this river as a kid. They didn't have tents, so they stretched out blankets by the fire and hoped it didn't rain. Makes me wonder how many people have camped here over the years."

Hugh scoured the riverbank for driftwood, tossing it toward the circle of blackened rocks that served as a fire pit. "These riverbanks have held forts, villages, and Native American encampments for centuries. The Cherokee called this river the Pellissippi."

Garnet moved around the campsite, gathering handfuls of dry leaves from around the base of trees. He dumped them into the firepit and topped them off with twigs he broke into short lengths. When he had a pile about a foot high, he used a butane lighter to light a birthday candle. He used that candle to light a fresh hand-rolled cigarette, then placed the burning candle in the nest of leaves.

"These river leaves hold a lot of moisture," he explained to Charlie. Sometimes it takes a little bit of work to get a fire going with them, but in the summer all the smoke helps keep the bugs off. While I don't expect we'll have that problem this time of year, you never know."

The flames spread slowly through the gritty leaves, dense smoke rising from the small fire. Soon the twigs were crackling and Garnet added more sticks. By the time Hugh returned with an armful of wood, Garnet had a blaze going.

Hugh held his hands out to warm his fingers over the fire. "It's a lot easier to run a watch at night with a fire to keep you company."

"Like I mentioned, I haven't had to keep watch over people since Vietnam," said Garnet, "and we couldn't have a fire then. Sometimes even the glow of a cigarette was enough to give you away. The Viet Cong were like ghosts in those jungles. You wouldn't see them coming until your throat was already slit and you were bleeding out in the dirt."

Charlie's eyes went wide. "That sounds terrifying."

"It was. I was barely older than you. Too young to really know what I was signing up for. You see, boys my age had all grown up listening to stories from World War II veterans. They filled our heads with all these exploits and adventures that we wanted to experience too. The only problem was that the world was different by the time we came around."

Charlie took a seat on a nearby log. "How so?"

"Politicians had decided that war needed more rules. The problem is that war is one of those situations where rules rarely fit. We were sent there to win a war but were not allowed to do so. There were times we weren't allowed to shoot back and other times when men followed us around taking notes on everything we did. It was frustrating."

Hugh lit up a cigarette. "I never got a taste of that kind of war. I was in a secret war in a place we were not supposed to be, so we got less scrutiny. I understand the later wars in Iraq and Afghanistan were even worse than Vietnam. War doesn't seem to be about winning anymore. It's about moving public money into private hands. It's money laundering in plain sight."

Charlie was silent for a moment, processing this. He was still young and uninformed about many topics. "Are we at war now? I've been wondering for a while. With all the killing and destruction, I wasn't sure."

Hugh and Garnet exchanged a glance, uncertain of how to respond to the complex question.

Finally, Garnet spoke up. "I think the world is at war with us."

Charlie looked confused. "Even our allies? What did we do to them?"

Garnet shook his head. With a sweep of his arm, he gestured at the trees, the sky, and the countryside around them. "Not that world —this world. The *natural* world. I don't know what we did to piss it off, but it's been raining hell down upon us each and every day."

30

"I can't believe you never heard us talking about this building," Jim said, incredulous.

Ian threw his hands up. "I can't either, but there's a lot of buildings in town I haven't asked about. I had no reason to. Has this one become the holy grail because you can't get in it? Like a door in the attic that no one has a key to?"

Jim laughed. "Maybe a little. Hugh was probably the most interested because he suspected they might have powerful backup batteries because of all the computer equipment. When this place was operational, they were obsessed with keeping the power on. The building is connected to the electrical grid at multiple points. If the town lost power, this building kept it unless the entire region was out."

"So, Hugh wanted the batteries for solar setups?" Ian asked.

Jim nodded. "That was the plan and it's why I brought Clay along this morning. If we find any battery backups, he can tell us if they might be helpful or not. Hugh is going to be sorry he missed this. He loves a good breaching operation."

"We could always wait until he gets back."

Jim did a double-take. "No way! I barely got any sleep last night. Ever since you said you thought you could get in here, it's been all I could think about. I was ready to try it yesterday."

"I didn't have the equipment I needed yesterday," Ian said. "Which is why I didn't get much sleep either. I had to go back to my old house and grab a few things I didn't bring bring with me when I moved into the roadhouse."

"Like what?" Clay asked.

"Like you'll see momentarily," Ian said with an air of showman-ship. "But first, this operation requires proper attire." He reached into a shirt pocket, removed a black eye patch, and stretched it onto his head. That was followed by cheap felt pirate hat.

Jim blinked. "What. The. Hell?"

Ian laughed. "You'll have to excuse me here. Presentation is important but you'll soon see that the costume is entirely appropriate to the task at hand."

Jim rode straight there from the valley that morning, but Ian and Clay caught a ride to the building from Shade. Shade had also deliv-ered a sprawling pile of gear from Ian's house, much of which was packed into boxes, duffel bags, or wrapped in tarps. Jim had no idea what he was looking at.

Ian grew animated and waved his arms around as he spoke, looking not so much like a pirate as a drunk employee at a cheesy seafood restaurant. "When Ellen pointed out the building yesterday and explained the challenges you guys faced in trying to get in, I immediately realized it was because you weren't thinking like pirates."

Clay cocked a brow. "Hence the wardrobe change?"

"Indeed." Ian hurried over to his pile of gear and removed a tarp from a heavy object about three feet long.

Jim frowned. "Is that—?"

"A cannon!" Ian said with pride. "My dad and I made it when I was a kid. He was a machinist by trade. Worked in a plant making gears most of his career but this was his passion."

"Cannons?" Clay asked, genuinely intrigued.

"Not only cannons," Ian explained. "Implements of destruction, improvised weapons, and the type of stuff you'd see in James Bond movies. He had a socket wrench that fired .22 rounds. He made a cane gun. He had cigarette lighters that would fire bullets when you went to strike them. If you held them wrong, you could shoot yourself by accident. He made knives out of nearly anything that could be hardened and sharpened."

"Which explains your fascination with stabby things," Jim said.

Ian nodded. "Yes, I was doing that from an early age except I didn't have his skill level or eye for precision. He truly had a mechanical engineer's mind while I'm just a hack with a knack for making stabby things."

Jim scratched his head and stared at the cannon. "Ian, while I appreciate your enthusiasm—even the costume—I can't imagine there's anyway that little thing is going to blast a hole in this building."

Ian wagged his finger at Jim. "You are *not* thinking like a pirate, sir. We're not trying to sink this building. We're trying to breach it."

Jim furrowed his brow, watching doubtfully as Ian unzipped a duffel bag and dumped the contents onto the ground. It took Jim a minute to understand that what looked like a tangled mass of giant fishhooks was actually a pile of homemade grappling hooks. Now he was intrigued.

Ian rubbed his hands together. "First, we're going to blast one of these hooks overtop that razor wire and pull it down."

"Okay..." Jim's tone sounded like he was humoring a dangerously insane man.

"Not as difficult as you might think," said Ian. "I'm a little punchy from working most of the night, but I'm pretty sure I've got it figured out."

Ian placed the cannon on its heavy wooden base, then draped two hefty sandbags across the top of it. He eyeballed it several times from different angles until deciding it was aimed properly. When he was done, he cut off about eight inches of green string and threaded it through a small hole in the top of the cannon. "Cannon fuse!"

Jim cocked an eyebrow. "You just happened to have that laying around?"

"Yep," Ian replied. "Back when we had an internet, you could buy it online by the foot. I kept some around in case I wanted to fire the cannon... or something."

Jim smiled. "I can only imagine."

With the fuse in place, Ian pulled a plastic bottle of black powder from another bag and dumped a portion into the barrel.

Clay watched with concern. "I'm assuming you must have premeasured that quantity, right? Did you calculate the charge based on the particulars of that cannon and the properties of that black powder?"

Ian frowned as if that was the most absurd thing he'd heard all morning. "Certainly not! This is art, Clay, not science."

Clay wasn't convinced. "No, I'm pretty sure it's science."

Ian rolled his one visible eye. "You sure know how to take the fun out of something, Clay. How about you just roll with it for now?"

Clay still looked concerned. "If that thing blows up like a bomb, pieces of us will be rolling everywhere."

"Speaking of getting blown up, how long will that fuse give us?" Jim asked.

"This is the one foot per minute variety. I *think* it is anyway. It's been a few years. We might have more time, but we might have less."

Jim winked at Clay. "Clearly, it's the run like hell variety of fuse."

Clay took a step back. "Clearly."

Ian used a length of sawed-off mop handle to compact the powder, then used a pair of scissors to trim a piece of kitchen sponge to the approximate size of the cannon bore. This was inserted into the barrel, then firmly seated with the broomstick.

Ian grabbed one of the grappling hooks and held it up. "I had to modify the shaft of the grappling hooks to make them fit the bore better. We want it tight enough to shoot accurately but not so tight it jams and explodes."

Clay frowned. "No, we don't want that."

Ian clipped a length of small diameter chain to an eye welded onto the shaft of the hook. He took the end of a stout rope and tied that onto the small chain. "Can one of you stretch this rope out straight behind the cannon?"

Jim took the coil of rope and began uncoiling it, stretching it into a straight line. "You sure this is enough?"

Ian shook his head. "No, I'm not sure about anything."

"This might have been one of those situations where consulting an engineer could have come in handy," Clay pointed out. "Shame there aren't any engineers around."

Ian snickered. "There you go sucking the fun out of things again."

Jim returned from uncoiling the rope. "What else you need?"

Ian tipped his head toward Jim's horse. "Take that horse and get clear."

Ian flicked a lighter and Jim didn't have to be told twice. He hopped on his horse and rode a safe distance away, while Ian and Clay took cover in a nearby ditch. Ian wanted to stay close enough to see how close the hook got in case he needed to adjust the load or the aim for a second shot. Clay wanted no part of Ian's guesswork and kitchen sink science. He flattened out in the ditch and covered his head like they were about to be carpet bombed.

The explosion was surprisingly loud and created a magnificent cloud of smoke that instantaneously obscured the cannon. True to Ian's backyard ballistics, the grappling hook shot into the air, began to lose momentum, then arced onto the roof of the building. It cleared the razor wire by about twenty feet before dropping neatly onto the roof.

Ian jumped up and shouted with victory. Jim couldn't see the grappling hook land, but he suspected it had to have gone well based on the cheering.

"Is it safe?" Clay mumbled, still face-down in the dirt.

"Hell yeah, it's safe! I nailed it! Who's your daddy now, Mr. Engineer!" Ian climbed out of the ditch and performed an awkward victory dance as he returned to the cannon. The rope he'd attached to the hook now hung down the side of the building with perhaps thirty extra feet of slack stretched out on the ground.

"Impressive," Jim said, riding up on his horse.

Ian was grinning ear to ear. "Hell, I even impressed myself. I assumed it might take a few shots to dial it in, but I nailed it on the first go." He picked up the slack rope and held it toward Jim. "Tie this off to your saddle horn and start pulling. It should pull the razor wire free of the building."

Jim took the rope. "Are you sure it'll be that easy?"

"I glassed it yesterday. The wire is only attached to the vertical posts with hog rings."

"What are hog rings?" Clay asked.

"Little bits of wire that you clamp closed with special pliers," Jim said. "You can easily pry them open, or in this case pull them open."

"Go slow and be careful," Ian warned. "You don't want the wire stretching, then springing loose, and coming down on you and your horse. We don't have to pull it entirely off the building, we just need to create an opening."

"Then what?" Clay asked. "We climb the building like Spider-Man?":

Ian didn't miss a beat. "Basically, but I'll explain that once we have an opening in the wire."

Jim and Clay shared a look of concern and amusement, then Jim did as Ian instructed. He kept his head turned as his horse pulled the rope, constantly watching the loops of concertina to make sure the wire wasn't going to break loose and fly in their direction. Ian's rope dragged over the coiled loops of wire atop the building until the grappling hook snagged onto the razor wire. Jim tugged carefully, not wanting to dislodge the hook, but it held fast.

He nudged his horse as the rope tightened, then there was a sound like a spring popping as the first of the hog clips snapped loose and sailed through the air. The horse continued to pull, and the wire began to snap more hog ties, pulling free like a zipper being unzipped. The rings whistled through the air, pinging when they hit asphalt, concrete, and parked vehicles.

"Whoa!" Ian called, signaling Jim. "That's enough."

Jim released the rope, dismounted, and tied his horse off to a nearby guardrail. "You think you can get past that wire now?"

Ian was already unpacking another grappling hook from his pile of gear. "As long as I can hook onto something. I've got an extension ladder that will get me twenty feet into the air. That should only leave me having to climb about twenty feet of rope, then I'll be on the roof."

"You're assuming you can gain entry through the roof?" asked Clay.

"I am. I worked in construction for several years. Roofs are rarely as hardened as walls, doors, and windows. Plus, I've got a big bag of wicked breeching tools over there," Ian said. "The one that rattles."

"All your bags rattle," Jim noted.

"True that. Either way, when I get to the roof, I'll pull that bag up behind me and I'll get in. Trust me on that."

"I have all the faith in the world," Jim said. He caught Clay looking at him like he was crazy, but Jim shrugged. "Why not? He's already gotten us farther than we've gotten in a year and a half."

Minutes later, Ian flawlessly dropped another grappling hook onto the roof of the building, just as he'd done earlier. When he tugged on this hook, it snagged securely onto the parapet wall and didn't come loose even when they tugged on it with all their body weight.

"Seems secure," said Clay. "Then again, I'm not the one trusting my life to it."

"I still don't get how you're going to climb that, Ian," Jim said. "You're really going to hop off a ladder, then scramble up the side of that building like some superhero?"

Ian dumped out another bag. "Sort of. I'm going to *jumar* up it using these ascenders."

"Of course you are," Clay said. "What the hell is a jumar?"

"To jumar is to climb using an ascender," Ian explained, holding up a shiny metal device about the size of a cell phone. "It's a climbing technique you can use on a tree, a mountain, or a telephone pole. You slip one of these devices onto a rope and they slide up freely, but then they lock down tightly when you put weight on them. By shifting your weight from one device to the other, you can slide your way up the rope. I've done it many times."

"When and why?" Jim asked.

Ian cut him an enigmatic look. "Various reasons. Nothing I care to get into at the moment."

Jim shook his head. "I love you, man, but I'm glad you don't have family here. When you fall off that building, we'll all be broke up about your death, but at least you won't leave behind a grieving widow and children."

Ian ignored Jim's sarcasm, raising the aluminum ladder Shade had delivered that morning and extending it up the wall. Just as he'd expected, it only went about halfway up.

"Wish me luck!"

"I'm praying it's a quick death if you fall," Clay muttered. "I don't want to have to shoot you if it's not."

Ian ignored the comment and scrambled up the ladder with surprising grace for a man of his size. When he reached the highest safe step on the ladder, he locked his ascenders onto the rope. He was already wearing a climbing harness, which he fastened to one of the ascenders with a carabiner and a short tether. Below the ascenders, nylon webbing with foot loops hung free. Ian threaded a boot into each loop, then transferred his weight onto the rope.

"Crazy bastard," Jim said, watching from the ground with Clay. "There's no way in hell I'd do that."

The rope spun and twisted, and Jim waited for the worst to happen, but it didn't. The hook didn't come loose from the roof, nor did the ascenders fail and zipline Ian straight into the ground. The rope didn't break without warning and send him into freefall. Everything was working just as Ian had promised.

Ian shifted his weight to the lowest of the ascenders so he could freely slide the uppermost one to a higher point on the rope. When that ascender slid as far as he could reach, he transferred his weight to the foot loop attached to that device, then slid the second ascender up the rope until it collided with the first one. By repeating these same steps over and over, shifting his weight from one ascender to the other, he climbed until he was halfway between the ladder and the roofline. A dozen more steps and he was nearly within reach of the roof. A few more steps and Ian plopped a big arm over the parapet wall at the edge of the roof. He'd done it.

"Woohoo!" he yelled, dragging his body over the wall and collapsing onto the roof.

On the ground, Clay and Jim finally found their breath again.

"I can't believe what I just watched," Clay said. "I expected crazy, but this was a step beyond."

Ian unclipped from the rope and yelled down, "Tie that bag with the breaching tools to the rope, then step clear! You damn sure don't want that bag dropping on your head if I lose my grip."

Jim understood the full gravity of that comment once he moved the bag. He peered in and saw bolt cutters, a fireman's Pulaski, a Halligan tool, and several other prying and banging implements. Indeed, that bag landing on someone's head from any distance would ruin their day. He clipped the bag to the rope as instructed, then stepped clear and signaled to Ian that the bag was ready to haul.

Ian pulled the bag up hand over hand and made good progress for about the first twenty feet. Soon, it was clear that the weight of the load was taking its toll. By the time Ian finally got the bag to the roof, he was bellowing curses and working a lot slower.

"What now?" Jim asked. "You hauling us up next?"

Ian wheezed a laugh, shaking his arms out. "No, hopefully I'll be meeting you at the front door shortly."

Ian wiped the sweat from his forehead, then dragged his bag of tools to the raised roof hatch. Most commercial buildings had these to allow for maintenance of the roof or any equipment installed there, such as HVAC systems. The roof was constructed with a ballast system utilizing a rubber membrane covered with tiny white stone. The roof hatch stood proud of the stone, with a latched steel cover protecting it. Ian knew from experience that it would be locked from the inside. He also knew that these openings were rarely as substantial as an exterior door.

He studied the hatch for a moment before selecting the Halligan tool from the bag. Designed by a firefighter, the device was allegedly based on a burglar tool that proved particularly good for breaking into buildings. It was like a heavy crowbar with a few extra tricks up its sleeve.

Instead of attacking the roof hatch on the latch side, Ian went for the hinges, noting that the welds there looked vulnerable. He found it amazing how many expensive things had shoddy welds. Indeed, this hatch looked finely crafted in all aspects until the point where the hinges were attached to the lid. Those looked like a four-year-old kid welded them on with a coat hanger and a car battery.

Ian found a tiny gap he was able to exploit with the Halligan tool. After a few attempts, he was able to create enough room to slip the entire end of the tool into the gap. He applied all his weight to the bar and was reward with a satisfying *sproingggg* as the weld cracked loose. Ian gleefully set in on the second weld and was pleased when it broke loose just as quickly.

He then flipped his tool around and used it to pry up on the roof hatch. The latch holding the lid shut was engineered to resist prying when it was applied near the latch. However, it wasn't designed to stop someone from removing the hatch cover if they lifted from the hinge side. The whole cover gave way and Ian let it drop onto the white stone with a thud.

Giddy from a lack of sleep, he wanted to cheer again, but there was no one close enough to hear his cry of victory. He focused his attention on the roof opening, knowing there should be a ladder mounted inside that would deliver him down to the uppermost story of the building. He lifted one leg to place on the ladder and froze.

The sun penetrating the hatch opening cast a stark square of light on the floor below. A man stepped into that square of light, a rifle upraised and pointed directly at Ian.

"Not another step," the man growled.

31

The Data Center

Ian slowly raised his hands. "Easy there, friend."

This was the last thing Ian had expected. He'd thought he would be descending a ladder into an empty building, so his handgun was holstered, and his rifle was slung around his back. This guy had the drop on him and there was no way he was turning the tables. Sure, he might be able to shove himself backward and clear of the roof opening before the guy got off a shot, but he was scared to risk it. The guy wasn't just pointing his rifle at him—he was sighting through an optic and had his finger on the trigger. One twitch and the guy could put a round in him.

"Who the hell are you?" the man snarled. "Did you just try to blow my door open with a bomb?"

"It wasn't a bomb. It was a cannon. A small one."

"A cannon? Is that why you're wearing an eye patch and a stupid pirate hat? What the hell kind of town is this?"

Ian cringed. He wasn't just scared now, he was slightly embarrassed. "I can take them off."

"I suggest you remain still."

Ian sighed. "We weren't trying to blast the door down. We used the cannon to get a rope up onto the roof so we could climb the wall. We thought the building was empty and we wanted to see what was in here."

"*I'm* in here, and I can guarantee you don't want to see me."

Ian cleared his throat. "Then how does this end? Now that I've seen you."

"Well, I could kill you and throw your body off the roof. That might send a clear and distinct message to your friends and neighbors that I want to be left the hell alone."

Ian shrugged but kept his hands in the air. "You *could* do that, but it would be the end of any peace and privacy you've enjoyed. If I know my friends, they would spend their remaining days trying to root you out of here like some stubborn gopher. They'd eventually succeed. They're persistent like that."

"Then you tell me how this ends."

"You might as well talk to my friends now that we know you're here. I'm the only one on the roof so you can keep a gun on me and address them from up here. I promise not to try anything. I didn't wake up with the intention of dying today and that hasn't changed."

The armed man cursed at his misfortune before finally arriving at a decision. "I'm coming up. You stay where I can see you."

"I won't move until you tell me to."

In a flash, the man transitioned from his rifle to a handgun and started up the ladder. When he neared the top, he ordered Ian to back away. Ian did as he was told, stepping back from the roof hatch, his hands still in the air. The man climbed from the opening and switched back to his rifle, his eyes never leaving Ian.

The man gestured at Ian with his rifle. "With one finger, you lower that rifle to the ground, then do the same with your pistol. Any sudden moves and I'll drop you without a second thought. Are we clear?"

"Crystal." Moving slowly, Ian did as he was told. He used the sling to lower his rifle to the roof deck, then placed his handgun alongside it. When those tasks were complete, both hands went back into the air, and he stepped away from the weapons.

"Now turn around and put your hands behind your head. I'm securing you for my safety."

As much as Ian disliked the idea of being restrained, he wasn't particularly fond of being shot either, so he complied. A flex cuff was secured around one wrist, then that arm was bent down behind his back. A strong hand grasped his other wrist, twisted it down behind his back, and secured it to the other. As the icing on the cake, the man placed the barrel of his rifle against the back of Ian's head.

"I don't want to kill you, but I don't know how well your people shoot. I want them to think twice about capping me while we're having a friendly discussion."

On the ground, Jim and Clay were not-so-patiently standing back, waiting expectantly for a door to open somewhere. Because their attention was focused elsewhere, they didn't immediately notice the man appear at the railing using Ian as a human shield.

"Morning, gents!" the man bellowed. "This belong to you?"

Jim's head snapped up and his hand dropped to his holster. He had kept his hands free while he helped Ian onto the roof in case he had to provide some kind of emergency assistance, so he wasn't carrying his rifle. He cursed himself for getting too comfortable. He drew his handgun and leveled it on the stranger. Even as he did so, he knew this probably wasn't a shot he could make. It was sixty or seventy feet, at an odd angle, with Ian blocking much of the man's silhouette. Sure, he'd hit something, but it was more likely to be Ian than the stranger.

"I've got a gun to your buddy's head. I suggest you lower your weapons." The man spoke in a casual tone. He wasn't scared and didn't seem the least bit nervous about his predicament. "The odds of you killing me before I kill him are pretty low."

"Who are you?" Jim demanded.

He had always suspected there might be people living in town right under their noses that had somehow gone undetected. Clay, the man at his side, was a perfect example of that. He expected the census would uncover even more. But finding this man living in this highly visible building in the center of town came as a shock to him.

"I guess it was inevitable," the man said. "I'm actually surprised I got away with it this long."

Accepting that he couldn't shoot his way out of the situation, Jim lowered and holstered his handgun. "Let's try this again. My name is Jim Powell and I live in this community. The man to my left is Clay and that's my buddy Ian up on the roof with you."

"You can call me Wrong Way."

"I'm guessing that's a nickname?" said Jim.

"That would be correct. The result of an unfortunate navigational incident when I was in the Marines. It's funny how one dumb mistake can haunt you for the entirety of your career."

"You had the choice of giving us any name to call you and that's the one you went with?" Jim replied. "Clearly, it's grown on you. Can I ask what you're doing here?"

"Well, I had a late night, and I was still asleep when I heard this explosion outside my door. Your man here says it was a cannon. I was on my way to the roof to check it out when I heard someone prying at the hatch. Imagine my shock when the hatch lid gets torn off and this bozo pokes his head in. He's lucky to still be wearing it."

"If it's any consolation, I was just as shocked," Ian said. "We thought this building was empty because no one has been able to get in it."

"Not until today," said Wrong Way.

"Under different circumstances, I might take that as a compliment. A testament to my skills," Ian replied. "It loses some of its grandeur when delivered at gunpoint, though."

Wrong Way looked at each of them in turn. "If I lower my gun, does everyone promise to behave?"

When everyone agreed to do so, Wrong Way holstered his handgun, but left Ian restrained and kept one hand on his shoulder.

"Can I ask how long you've been in that building?" Jim asked.

"Since the beginning. Or maybe you'd call it 'the end'. I'm not sure which is more fitting."

"You've been in there a year and a half?" Jim asked, astonished.

"I have."

"You've not been out at all?"

"Oh, I've been out. I slipped out the back door and wandered around town several times. I even visited that roadhouse across town and drank some of that lousy rotgut they sell."

Jim frowned. "Hey, that's *my* roadhouse and we do the best we can."

"No offense intended. Either way, I kept my outings short and had minimal interaction with people. I didn't want to attract any attention and have people start asking questions."

Jim was still in shock. "How did you survive? Eat and drink?"

"And heat this place?" Clay asked. "It's the smoke from fires that draws attention and gives people away."

"I haven't seen any smoke from this building," Ian said. "By the way, now that we're all friendly, you think you can loosen these cuffs? They're a little uncomfortable."

"We're not that friendly yet. You just hang tight."

"Did you have supplies? And what made you choose this building in the middle of town?" Jim had a lot of questions.

"I didn't choose this building. I didn't even choose this town. This data center is owned by an international defense contractor. I was hired in DC and this is where I was stationed. The building isn't ever supposed to be empty, so even when they evacuated, I stayed behind, assuming it would be a short-term thing."

"Was the building set up for that?" Jim asked. "I mean in terms of supplies?"

"It's no secret that the company contracted with the government to provide data storage outside of the Northern Virginia area. The idea was that it would be safe in case there was a nuclear attack in Washington. There were all kinds of stipulations not just around the operation of this facility, but around the construction too. The operations protocols specified that at least one of the security staff would remain in place even if an extended power outage occurred. That's the job I signed on for and sufficient provisions were put in place for that contingency."

"How did you stay warm?" Clay asked.

"I didn't. Not only would a fire give me away, there's no way to have one inside this building. I spent a lot of time in a sleeping bag, wearing thick layers of clothing. Fortunately, we're not in Minnesota or something. The weather here is generally mild enough to survive without heat, even though it's not very comfortable."

"I have a lot of questions," Jim said. "I'm not going to ask them though, because I feel like they might seem intrusive at this point. I don't want you to get all paranoid and think that we're interested in stealing your provisions or something. I assure you that's not what this is about."

Wrong Way nodded. "Yeah. I told you about all I'm going to tell you for now."

"So how does this end?" Ian asked. "I'm hoping you aren't going to throw me off the side of this building."

"No, I don't think so. Here's what I have in mind. I'm going to blindfold you and walk you through this building, then I'm going to shove you out a random door. Your friends can find you and cut you loose."

"We appreciate that," Jim said. "We'll wait right here. You have my word."

A few minutes later Ian came stumbling around the side of the building, looking a little sheepish at having been taken prisoner. His hands were still cuffed behind his back. "Sorry, guys. That wasn't how I expected it to go. I thought the worst was behind me when I broke that hatch open. Little did I know."

Jim patted him on the back. "No big deal. You're safe and that's what matters."

"I guess we got an answer to the big question too," Clay said. "We know what's in the building now."

"Yeah, and it's something we don't want to mess with," Ian summarized.

There was a thump as Ian's grappling hook was dropped from the roof to the ground, startling the men.

"Excuse the lack of warning, but I'm a little pissed off I have to put this razor wire back in place," Wrong Way called from the roof. "If I leave it hanging, some other dumbass might try this trick. I hate fooling with this stuff." He pulled on thick gloves and began hauling the razor wire back into place, using special pliers to snap new hog rings onto the wire.

"We wouldn't have screwed up your wire if we knew you were in there. We would've knocked on the door first," Jim called.

"Somehow, I didn't think it would be very smart of me to hang a sign on the building advertising my presence. I was hoping this place was fortified enough that I could lay low until this whole thing blew over. Speaking of which, if I can ask a favor, is it possible that you can keep your mouth shut and not tell anyone else I'm here? I don't want to have to do this every day."

"I'll make you a deal," said Jim. "We promise to keep this information contained to a small group if you come by the roadhouse sometime so we can talk. I don't know if you have access to any information or not, but there's no indication this collapse is going to blow over anytime soon. If that's what you're waiting on, I'm afraid you're going to be sorely disappointed."

32

St. Paul, Virginia

WHEN MORNING BROKE, Charlie was on watch at the riverside campsite. He'd allowed the fire to burn down to embers as the sky lightened, pink with the coming of day. He kicked some sandy soil atop the remains of the smoldering fire and spoke aloud to wake the other men. Charlie had learned there were certain men you didn't wake by touching or shaking them. It was safer to stand out of range and speak to them in a calm voice, hoping they weren't startled.

While Hugh and Garnet stretched and stirred, Charlie filtered water from the river and filled all their bottles. They drank it cold with biscuits Hugh had brought from the roadhouse, topped with ham and homemade cheese. They saddled their horses, packed their gear, and rode out of camp. The railroad tracks continued to follow the river, arcing away from the road and cutting through expansive cattle farms.

"Anyone know who owns this land?" Hugh asked.

"No idea," Garnet replied. "I've walked this stretch of river many times and never seen a soul. It's a big farm that runs up against other big farms. You see a few houses, cross a couple of roads, but for the most part it stays this way until you reach the town of Honaker on the other end of the county."

"If the train stayed on these tracks they wouldn't make it past Honaker," Charlie said.

Garnet cocked an eyebrow. "Why not?"

"There's an old wooden trestle just outside of town and they say some drunks burned it down. They were quite proud of themselves from what I heard. Those old creosote timbers made one hell of a bonfire." Charlie shook his head at the notion.

"The drunk man has many great notions that seem less so in the light of sobriety," Garnet said.

"I can attest to that myself." Hugh placed his hand over his heart as if offering testimony. "These days I drink less for that very reason."

They rode along the railroad tracks for the next two hours, not seeing anyone or anything of concern. Once, they heard the barking of dogs in the distance but never saw one. Another time, they heard a gunshot echoing over the rolling hills, although it wasn't close enough to be of concern. A coyote zipped by them with a squirrel in its mouth. Deer bedded in the high grass flushed like quail and bounded off at their approach.

Hugh and Garnet did most of the talking, swapping stories about their experiences living the way of the gun in foreign lands. Charlie asked questions but mostly he just listened, trying to remember the stories to share with Pete when he got back home. The two of them always got a thrill out of learning a new story about the adults around them.

Hugh was in the lead when he reigned his horse to a halt. "Whoa." He stuck out an arm to indicate that the others should stop too.

"What is it?" Charlie asked.

Hugh had observed that Charlie was quick to ask what was going on, while Garnet was more likely to go silent and hypervigilant. Charlie wanted to be told what was happening while Garnet tried to ascertain it for himself. It was a difference in experience levels, a difference in the frame of reference of a young man versus that of an old man.

"Trash." Garnet pointed to a green garbage bag that had burst open in the high grass beside the tracks. "Had to have come from the train. Ain't nobody in their right mind going to haul a bag of trash all the way out here to dump it."

Hugh slid off his horse and handed the reins over to Charlie. "You guys keep a lookout."

Garnet didn't have to be told. As soon as Hugh began to dismount, Garnet swung his horse around to keep watch in the direction from which they'd come. Charlie alternated his attention between the tracks ahead of them and what Hugh was doing down in the weeds. Again, it was an issue of experience. Garnet, the more experienced man, knew his role in this situation. He'd let Hugh investigate while he covered his back. The less experienced Charlie struggled between performing his duty and satisfying his curiosity.

Hugh was already wearing gloves to protect his hands, but he unsheathed his knife and used the blade to explore the contents of the bag. He pulled several items out and laid them in the grass. When he was done, he picked up several of the bottles and returned to the horses. He held them up for Charlie and Garnet to examine.

"Corona beer," Charlie commented in a disappointed tone. "What's the big deal? I saw that stuff in every Mexican restaurant I've ever been to."

"Not in this bottle you haven't." Hugh handed one to Charlie and the other to Garnet.

"Are you thinking this is the Mexican label?" Garnet asked. "I don't drink Corona, but I'd assume the American bottles are in English. This one is in Spanish."

"It would be consistent with the theory that Jim and I bounced around," Hugh said.

"Wait, there's a theory?" Charlie asked. "No one told me about any theory. I thought we were just running recon." He handed the empty beer bottle back to Hugh.

Hugh tossed the bottle back into the pile of trash at the base of the tracks. "Garnet said that the men he saw on the trains looked like they were carrying gold-plated AK-47s. Sometimes you'll find those guns in America, but they're most prevalent among the cartels. If you put this beer with those guns, that's more data supporting our theory."

Charlie was incredulous. "Your theory is that these people running the train might be part of a cartel?" He didn't know much about cartels, but the idea that they might be operating here where he lived, this far from the border, was hard to fathom.

"Well, you know we've had issues with the United Nations being here since shortly after the terror attacks. That didn't go over so well because they were trying to disarm everyone."

"I remember," Charlie said.

"There have also been issues with the Chinese attempting a soft invasion," said Hugh. "I've picked up chatter about it on my radios. Josie and her people confirmed it."

"I don't know much about what's been going on outside of our town," Garnet said. "Most of my conversations are with people that aren't even real, as far as I know. If all this is true about the Chinese and there really are cartel soldiers on the train, it sounds like we're fixing to be overrun with all manner of unfriendly people."

Hugh spat a fleck of tobacco from the tip of his tongue. "That might be inevitable. America is bleeding and the predators are like sharks, sensing blood in the water. It's what they do and it's hard to blame them. America does the same with its enemies."

"Well, if it's inevitable, what are we even doing here? What's the point of tracking the train?" said Charlie. "I enjoy a good adventure as much as the next guy, but what do we gain by finding it?"

"Intelligence," Hugh replied. "We might have fared well so far but there's no way our community has the ability to take on Chinese operators. Unless we're forced into the situation, that would be suicide. Cartel soldiers aren't as highly trained, if they're trained at all. While we might fare better with them, it depends on numbers. If it's an isolated unit, we might be able to take them out. If they have the ability to rapidly call in support, it's hard to say."

Charlie spat. "Dude, you're seriously depressing me. Just when I think we've found the bottom, more shit comes along. Where does it end?"

"All of us need a proactive mindset, Charlie. Don't give in to the doom. We have to accept that there will *always* be threats, and our best chance of survival comes from learning as much about those threats as we can. Knowing the enemy allows us to build a better defense or arrive at strategy for dealing with that threat. There might be things we can do to delay or deter an invasion of our community."

"By ourselves?" Charlie grumbled.

"Ideally, we could hope that there is somebody out there somewhere preparing a larger scale defense. Someone with a plan of how to take America back. Yet we can't depend on that. We have to wake up each day prepared to protect our little square of land as best we can."

"Was this Lightspeed character planning to defend America against foreign invaders?" asked Garnet. "Did he have a plan for that?"

"Yeah, and there's a good chance that's what got him killed," Hugh said.

33

Finney Community

R.J. Hawkins lived in the northern part of the county, in a community called Finney. He lived in a $500 mobile home with shag carpet, bouncy floors, and a leaky roof. One of the windows was broken and covered with a sheet of plastic held in place by duct tape. Rebel flag bath towels purchased for a dollar each at the flea market served as curtains. The home was on a half-acre lot that was perhaps one of the least desirable pieces of real estate in the entire county. He paid twenty-five dollars a month to rent a chunk of land that no one in their right mind would care to live on.

The community's trash dumpsters were located right beside R.J.'s trailer and filled his home with the aroma of hot garbage on warm summer days. Before the collapse, he'd been awakened at all hours by people dumping their trash, tossing in empty beer bottles, or disposing of animal carcasses. Then there were the rats brought in by the garbage. R.J. thought about moving every day but was too poor to be picky. He owned the roof over his head and no one could take that away from him. He was appreciative of that.

The railroad tracks passed immediately behind R.J.'s trailer, only adding to the desirability of the property. Anyone who had ever lived beside a railroad track knew you'd eventually become accustomed to the sound of passing trains with their loud whistles and clattering wheels. It was a little tougher to get used to when those trains passed so close that they shook the home and startled you from sleep nearly every night. In the years immediately before the collapse, there were fewer trains because of the slowdown in coal mining. While fewer trains meant better sleep, the slowdown in mining also put R.J. out of a job.

R.J. had fared better than most during the apocalypse, which was a combination of resourcefulness and low expectations. He'd grown up poor and unfortunately managed to stay close to his roots. He got a coal mining job when he graduated from high school, but it lasted less than a year before the government quit renewing mining permits and the industry slumped yet again. R.J. bought an old pickup truck with his first paycheck and his mobile home with his second, then there were no more checks. A very helpful president said that R.J. would be able to get a green energy job instead of working with coal. R.J. had never heard of any such jobs in his region, nor had anyone else he'd inquired of. He eventually figured out "green jobs" was presidential code for "eat shit, hillbilly."

The community of Finney was remote enough that there was not a lot of hunting pressure on the wild game. R.J. ate regularly through a combination of traps, trot lines, and hunting. His close-knit community of less than a dozen families all helped each other out. No one let any food go to waste. If there was extra food left after a meal, there was always a neighbor who appreciated a full plate. They all helped each other out with firewood, repairs, and gardening when the season allowed it.

R.J.'s closest neighbor was a widow named Margaret who had worked at the local sewing factory until the so-called Free Trade Agreements sent those same factories south of the border for cheaper labor. Margaret had lived in Finney her entire life, on the same plot of land on which she was born. When she married her husband, they dragged in a new mobile home and her mother moved in with them. The old tarpaper shack she'd been raised in was still standing and they'd used it for storage up until Margaret's husband died. After that, she was afraid to go inside for fear of rats and snakes.

Though forty-five years separated them, R.J. and Margaret helped each other out during the collapse. R.J. was a decent shot but had little idea how to prepare some of the traditional Appalachian game that he brought home. Margaret was no stranger to cooking possum, raccoon, groundhog, deer, and bear. From the nearby river, R.J. harvested bass, muskie, red eye, chunky bluegill, smallmouth bass, and even the occasional garfish. Along the riverbank, he shot turkey, duck, geese, grouse, and even a blue heron when times were lean.

"Damn, that's good."

It was midday and R.J. was sitting on Margaret's porch with a plate in his lap. Margaret cut him a look.

"Excuse my language," R.J. apologized. "It's just that it's good and I'm hungry."

Margaret harrumphed. "People these days don't know hungry. Times were lean when I was a kid and there weren't any government handouts then. You couldn't go to the welfare and sign up for food stamps. I remember times we ate a whole month off a sack of potatoes. There was eleven of us kids and my mother gave each of us a boiled egg to take to school for lunch. If times were hard, that egg was all we got that day."

R.J. had shot a small doe that morning and Margaret had cooked up the backstrap in some bacon grease. R.J. thought it might have been the finest meal of his entire life, even though it was nothing more than the meat, fried potatoes, and some home-canned green beans.

"Well, if people these days don't know hunger, someone needs to tell my belly because it feels pretty darn hungry," R.J. teased.

"You just hush that smart mouth and enjoy your food, boy."

R.J. laughed. Such was the nature of their relationship. They teased each other back and forth all day, and neither was sure how they would have made it through this event without the other. They kept each other's spirits up and that was perhaps even more valuable than a hot meal.

Margaret was slicing a bite off her backstrap when she paused and looked up, a confused look on her face. "You hear that?"

"You chewing? Darn right I heard it. I thought there was a moose behind the house." R.J. winked at her playfully.

Margaret shook her head rapidly. "I ain't playing, R.J. I swear to the good Lord I hear a train."

R.J. frowned. "I think you gone soft in the noggin', old woman. It's been a long time since we had a train come through here."

"If you'd quit flapping those jaws and use your ears for holding up more than your hat, you might hear it too."

R.J. set down his knife and fork, leaned back in his chair, and raised his cupped hands to his ears. He was making an exaggerated effort at listening just to irritate Margaret and that was when he heard it. His eyes went wide. "Shit! There *is* a train!"

Margaret wagged a finger at him. "That'll be enough of that nasty talk. I've warned you. You ain't too big for me to take a switch to. If your mama was here, she'd probably step back and tell me to go right to it."

R.J. was too distracted to apologize for his crude language. He hurriedly set his plate down on the flimsy outdoor table and hopped off the porch.

"Where you going off to in such a hurry?" Margaret called.

"I'm grabbing my rifle. If that *is* a train, we don't know who's on it."

By now R.J. was certain that Margaret was right. There was a train coming and there was only one place it could go—right behind his mobile home and right through the center of their tiny community. He would be less concerned if he thought the train would keep moving. Obviously, he would be interested in who was on it and where they were going, but the desire to arm himself would be less urgent. He *knew* the train would stop. It would have to, because the track was blocked less than a quarter mile from his trailer and it was utterly impassable.

Heavy rains last summer had loosened the ground and the high winds that followed had toppled trees onto the tracks. Not just one or two small trees but perhaps two dozen large poplars collectively weighing many tons. A slow-moving train might have been able to push a single tree from the track but there was no way they were plowing through this wall of timber. If the people on the train wanted to keep going, they would have to stop and clear the tracks.

R.J. wondered if they had chainsaws. He couldn't imagine actually having a working chainsaw and the fuel to run it these days. He didn't, nor did he know anyone who did. People gathered firewood with bow saws and axes. One neighbor had pulled an antique two-man saw off the side of his barn and put it into use, finding it still cut surprisingly well.

R.J. shoved through the front door of his trailer and into the warm interior. He grabbed his beat-up lever-action hunting rifle and went back outside, jogging across the street to Margaret's house. Whatever was happening, he felt like they should process it together. As odd a pairing as they might be, they had gotten this far as a team, and it had worked for them.

Starting up the steps to Margaret's porch, R.J. paused. The approaching train was even louder now. Along the road, he could see other neighbors had heard it as well. They were coming out onto their porches and standing in their driveways, trying to make sense of what they were hearing.

"Maybe we should go inside?" R.J. suggested.

Margaret scoffed. "I've talked to a few people passing by on the road and they said it was dangerous in town and in the big cities, but we haven't seen any of that here. There's no reason for anybody to come back in here and start trouble. What have we got that anybody would want? We're just a little speck on the map. We ain't worth bothering with."

"They're going to be bothering with us in a little bit. That track is blocked and they're going to be coming to a stop whether they want to or not. Our little speck on the map is fixing to get company."

Margaret began eating with urgency, unwilling to abandon a plate with food remaining on it. "Then you best be finishing your meal before company comes."

"You could finish yours in the house. It would be safer in case there's trouble."

Margaret shot a fiery glance at R.J. "The only trouble about to happen is from you trying to tell me what to do! Besides, I already said I ain't going anywhere and I don't chew my cabbage twice."

R.J. rolled his eyes. He had dealt with Margaret's stubbornness before and knew there was no changing her mind once it was made up. He leaned his rifle against the porch rail and sat down. He hurriedly cut the rest of his backstrap into bite-sized pieces and began shoving them in his mouth. The meat had already gotten cold in the short span of time it had taken him to retrieve his rifle. R.J. was a little resentful of his meal being disturbed but it couldn't be helped. He'd feel much more comfortable greeting strangers with a rifle in his hand than a fork.

As they finished their meal, the sound of the train grew louder. It was not moving as quickly as it would have during normal times. Obviously, whoever was driving this train understood there was a chance they might come upon blocked tracks at any moment. R.J. imagined that across the nation there had to have been thousands or hundreds of thousands of places where the tracks were similarly blocked with trees, landslides, or other obstructions.

The train came around the bend, moving perhaps fifteen miles per hour. The windows of the locomotive were closed, making it difficult to see who was operating it. The entire train was little more than two dozen cars. There were shipping containers, a tanker, and a flatbed car that held a small bulldozer and several ATVs. Multiple cabooses brought up the rear and the platforms to the front and back of each were crowded with men smoking cigarettes, slung weapons prominently on display.

"That's why I wanted to take cover," R.J. said. "Them boys ain't here to play. You see those rifles?"

"I saw them, but a man would have to be a fool to *not* carry a rifle these days. A gun don't mean nothing."

"Well, a person might also be a fool if they don't show some caution when armed strangers show up on their doorstep."

Margaret frowned at R.J. "I appreciate that you're trying to keep me safe, but I was having babies before you even *were* a baby. I'm going to do whatever I take a notion to do and there ain't nobody going to stop me. Are we clear?"

R.J. hung his head. "Yes, ma'am."

"Alrighty then." Margaret stood up, stretched her back, and hitched her pants up nearly to her chest. She'd always dressed like a man since she worked like one, and most days she wore the same thing—a well-worn barn coat, oversized jeans, and green rubber farm boots. "Let's go."

"Where we going?" R.J. was exasperated. It was bad enough remaining out there in the open when armed strangers showed up. Now they were going to go chasing after them?

Margaret replied as if it was the most natural thing in the world. "We're going to say howdy. It's the friendly thing to do."

34

Finney Community

THE HIGH-PITCHED SQUEAL of train brakes filled the air as Margaret and R.J. walked down the gravel road that ran parallel to the tracks. Several families were out in their yards, trying to decide what they should do. Some were armed, following R.J.'s instincts, but Margaret's decision to stroll right into the unknown without a care in the world was contagious. People fell in behind her like she was the Pied Piper. It was a testament to her role in this tiny mountain community. She was without question their matriarch.

The short train had stopped just ahead of the downed trees, so it didn't take long for the contingent of locals to catch up with the rear of the train. Men bearing AK-47s crowded out onto the rear platform of the caboose, not raising their weapons, yet not averting them either. While there was nothing friendly about their demeanor, they were not outright threatening. Nothing in their actions told the locals that they should turn on their heels and go home.

R.J. almost wished he'd left his rifle back at the house now. He was vastly outgunned and wouldn't have a chance if this interaction turned hostile. "You sure about this, Margaret? Seems safer to wait this out at home."

She flicked a hand at him. "Boy, if you only do the things in life that you're sure about, you won't do a hell of a lot."

That was news to R.J.. He didn't yet know enough about life to have that much perspective on it, so he'd have to take Margaret's word for it. She'd given him a lot of advice and hadn't steered him wrong yet. "Reckon I'll follow your lead then."

"Reckon you will," she confirmed, as if that had never been in question.

As Margaret and her neighbors closed in on the train, the men in the caboose began dropping to the ground. They tossed away beer and soft drink bottles. Some lit cigarettes. Though they didn't raise their weapons, they weren't exactly waving and greeting the residents of the community. Finally, the last man exited the caboose, cut through the gang of armed men, and headed toward the parade of locals.

The man from the train wore a felt cowboy hat, shiny boots, and a Western sport coat. He looked like a rancher at a cattle auction, complete with a large, engraved belt buckle. Unlike the band of armed men who'd come to stand behind him on the road, this guy was smiling and appeared friendly. He almost reminded R.J. of a lost delivery driver sheepishly coming to ask directions.

He was forty feet away when he stopped, deciding that was a polite distance from which to greet the locals. He took off his hat and tipped his head. "Good day, friends." His English was flavored with a Mexican accent.

Margaret stopped when he spoke, which halted the entire procession following her. "Afternoon!" She spoke to the man like he was someone she'd seen at the grocery store her entire life—a genuine, grandmotherly warmth, dripping with country charm. "It's been a while since we've seen a train in these parts."

The man replaced his hat and smiled. "I can tell that from the state of the tracks. Sadly, much of your nation is in this same condition from what I've seen and heard."

Margaret separated herself from the group and stepped forward, hand extended. "Honey, my name is Margaret and I ain't used to talking to people across distances like this. I don't see or hear like I used to."

The man walked forward to meet her, extending his hand. "Of course. I understand. My name is Santos and it's nice to meet you, Margaret."

Margaret waved a hand behind her. "These are my neighbors, or what's left of them anyway. They're a bit on the skittish side considering how things have been since the lights went out. We don't get much company back in here, so people tend to err on the side of being standoffish." She cut an accusatory look at her neighbors, as if disappointed in their rude behavior.

"I don't blame them for that, Margaret. In times like these it's only natural to be suspicious of strangers. I'm sure you folks haven't seen a train in over a year, then here I come driving into your little village. I'm sure that's alarming."

Margaret chuckled. "Maybe to some people, but I'm the nosy sort. Considering all that's going on in the country, what are you doing riding around on a train anyway? I'm sorry for being rude, and I don't mean to badger you, but I have a ton of questions. We don't get much news back in these parts and what we do get is already months old by the time it reaches us."

Santos looked past Margaret and raised a finger in the air as he ticked off the number of people standing behind her in the street. "Is this everyone in your village?"

Margaret laughed. "We don't use the word village around here. We call it a community, and this is most everyone. There are a couple who can't get out of their house for health reasons." Suddenly growing suspicious of his question, she added, "Why do you ask?"

"Don't be alarmed, Margaret. I'd love to answer your questions but maybe we can do so over a meal. If you can give me about ten minutes, my men will set up tables right here in the street. We have hot soup, fresh bread, and lemonade. Would any of you be interested in a hot meal?" Santos spoke loud enough that even those farthest back in the crowd could hear him.

"What's the catch?" R.J. asked. "Is it going to cost us anything?"

Santos offered a compassionate smile. "There's no catch, young man. It's just a small thing we do for people as we pass through their villages." He winked at Margaret. "I mean *communities*."

Margaret covered her mouth and giggled. "I don't know about the rest of these folks, but I'm in. I'd love a meal I didn't have to cook myself and I can't remember the last time I had fresh bread or lemonade."

"We just ate," R.J. whispered.

Margaret shushed him and hissed, "I ain't turning down a meal."

"Excellent." Santos turned, cupped his hands around his mouth, and called to his men in Spanish.

About half of the men jumped into action, handing plastic folding tables out of the caboose and carrying them down to the street. When Santos turned back around, Margaret was offering him a coy smile.

"You aren't a Virginian now, are you?"

Santos winked at Margaret and wagged a finger in her direction. "You are a sharp one. I can see who runs the show around here."

"Is that Spanish I hear?" It wasn't that Margaret was an expert on languages. Spanish might have been the only foreign language she had ever heard in person in her entire life and that was at Mexican restaurants.

"I will explain everything in due time, Margaret."

Just down the street, the armed men had wasted no time setting up plastic tables and filling them with food. There were two vats of steaming soup with one man standing by, ready to serve. Another was slicing bread from homemade loaves. There were Styrofoam cups and plastic spoons for the soup. Someone was pouring lemonade from a pitcher into smaller Styrofoam cups. Even in the open air, the smell of the soup was intoxicating. Santos smiled and gestured that they head for the tables.

Margaret didn't have to be told twice. She hitched her pants, elbowed R.J., and marched right by Santos toward the table of food. Like sheep, the two dozen or so residents of the community fell in behind her. Some of them nodded warmly at Santos and mumbled their thanks. Others avoided his gaze entirely, as if making eye contact might somehow obligate them to be in his debt.

"You sure they ain't going to poison us?" R.J. whispered to Margaret as they walked.

"What would be the point of that?"

R.J. shrugged. "They could rob us."

Margaret looked at him like he was an idiot. "Boy, they have a train and food enough that they can afford to give it away to strangers for free. What could they possibly need from us?"

"I reckon you might have a point there."

Careful to avoid any sudden moves that might be interpreted as aggression, R.J. slung his rifle over his shoulder so he'd have both hands free for eating. Besides, he was horribly outgunned, and his rifle did nothing but make him stand out as a potential target. If any shooting broke out, he'd certainly be one of the first to be killed.

Despite their extended deprivation, the people of the community moved through the line politely. Everyone took a cup of soup and a slice of bread, then their lemonade. Though there were no chairs, empty tables had been placed in the street so that Margaret and her neighbors would have a place to set things while they ate. Some politely spooned their soup into their mouths while others hungrily drank from the cups, liquid running from both sides of their mouths.

As they finished, some of them in less than a minute, Santos directed them to return to the serving line for seconds. Soon after that, he climbed up the gravel shoulder of the railroad tracks, just high enough that he could see everyone in attendance.

"For those of you who might not have heard, my name is Santos. As you people might say, my associates and I are 'not from around these parts'. In fact, as some of you have speculated, we're not even from America. We are neighbors from south of the border who've come to render aid in whatever way we can."

Santos gave a moment for that information to settle in and then he continued.

"For the past year and a half, the people of Mexico have watched in shock and horror as no one came to help you." He held an apologetic hand in the air. "No, excuse me, that's not entirely true. People *did* come to help, but only if there was something in it for them. NATO sent aid workers. Did any of you see them?"

A few hands went up.

"Through a partnership with corrupt politicians, NATO had a plan to deliver aid to the people of America, but it was contingent on everyone turning in their weapons and we all know that is not the American way. In fact, it made absolutely no sense when conditions were so unsafe. Eventually, this effort was abandoned and forces within the old government began working with military contracting companies to form new regional governments and a new system of law enforcement. This too was aimed at the eventual goal of disarming the population. Did any of you ever meet a regional sheriff?"

Again, a few hands went up.

"There was one came through here a few times," said Margaret. "Haven't seen him in a while. Something happen to those folks?"

"Walter Lightspeed is what happened to those folks. Sources within the Mexican government tell us that corrupt politicians in league with China were selling off United States farmland and mineral rights in exchange for living in luxury during the apocalypse. I don't know if that's all true, but that's what I was told."

"Speaking of what we were told," R.J. said. "We were told this Walter Lightspeed guy was going to turn the lights back on and that never happened here. Town got power but it never reached us. Don't know whatever became of it."

Santos grew somber. "Sadly, Walter Lightspeed is dead and his technology died with him. In the battle between Chinese interests and Walter Lightspeed, China eventually won out. In fact, they have soldiers and military contractors on the American mainland right now and they are slowly working their way west. They're trying to remain lowkey to avoid international pressure, but Chinese forces are systematically eliminating pockets of resistance here in America. Do I need to explain to you what that means?"

"Yes. What exactly does that mean?" Margaret asked. "I get the gist of what you're saying, but how serious is it?"

Santos folded his arms across his chest. "China is going to work their way across America and kill everyone who gets in the way. Their goal is that there will never again be an America. This country and the people living here will fall under Chinese rule if they succeed."

R.J.'s voice rose in pitch. "How far off are they?"

"The last I heard, there are units of Chinese military contractors as close as Richmond, Virginia. What's that, a little over three hundred miles?"

There was a murmur from those in attendance as they discussed this news among themselves. The idea that there were Chinese aggressors in their own state and heading their way was almost too much to comprehend. On the other hand, with all that had happened to them already, maybe this was simply par for the course. Santos watched without expression as the sidebar conversations grew frantic. Their fear would work to his benefit.

"Can I ask you a question?" Santos said, speaking loudly to be heard over the tumult.

The crowd gradually grew silent.

Santos pointed at the crowd with both hands. "If you folks had to choose a partner moving forward, someone to help you restore your nation and find a way back to normal life, who would you choose? Would you prefer to partner with China, or would you prefer to partner with your neighbor to the south? With Mexico?"

Santos let this sink in. There was more discussion among the people in attendance, but it was not as heated as the panic of a few moments ago, which he took as a good sign. It meant that his proposal was not a point of contention. They were considering his words.

"I ain't quite sure why you're asking us, Mr. Santos," Margaret said. "We're countryfolk and most of us are older. We don't have anything of value and we wouldn't be much good in a fight. Hell, some days I get winded just walking to the outhouse."

Santos offered Margaret a warm smile. "I don't need you as soldiers. The people I work for have plenty of soldiers. What I need is your support, although I might need a little help today."

"What do you mean by support?" R.J. asked.

Santos grew serious. "I sincerely think this is a situation in which *all* Americans will eventually be forced to choose sides. If you choose us over the Chinese, we will protect you to the best of our ability. If you choose *not* to support us, then you will be on your own in your fight against the Chinese. I don't mean that in an unkind way. That is simply the reality of the situation."

"So, we support you over the Chinese and you protect us?" Margaret asked.

"It's more than that. You support us and we will support you by providing aid and doing our best to drive China from American soil." Santos turned toward his men and gave a nod.

A half-dozen men walked to a boxcar and opened the door. Half climbed inside while the other half remained on the ground. There was clattering from the boxcar and then the sound of heavy wheels rolling. A pallet jack appeared in the door carrying a pallet stacked high with boxes.

"I apologize for this meager offering, but we have a lot of stops to make and we weren't sure how communities such as yours would respond to our offer. I can assure you that if you do lend us your support, future deliveries will be regular and larger."

"You mean that's for us?" Margaret asked.

Santos nodded. "It *can* be."

"What's the catch?" R.J. asked.

"There's no catch, but there are conditions. For now, help us clear the railroad tracks. My men have chainsaws, winches, and a bulldozer, but it helps to have people tossing brush to the side. When the track is clear, we will leave aid boxes with each of you. The boxes contain rice, beans, powdered milk, powdered eggs, salt, flour, lard, a small first aid kit, batteries, cigarette lighters, and a few other helpful items. As I said, there will be more to come later, as long as certain conditions are met."

The members of Margaret's community stood there taking this all in. They were silent for so long that Santos almost thought they were going to reject his offer.

Finally, Margaret hitched her pants and began rolling her sleeves. She glanced back over her shoulder at her neighbors. "I reckon I'm gonna be pitching some wood. Anyone who wants goods off that pallet best be doing the same."

Santos was delighted and a broad grin spread across his face. "You've made a wise choice. A *wise* choice."

35

The Reset Roadhouse

A PART of Jim longed to be out on the trail with Hugh, Charlie, and Garnet. He had struggled with the idea of whether he should go with them or stay in town, but ultimately his sense of responsibility won out. If he was going to help protect the people of town and organize them into a community of survivors, he needed to be available and keep that effort headed in the right direction. Though it was a tough lesson for Jim to accept, if he was going to be an effective leader, he was going to have to delegate. That had always been a struggle for him. He was usually of the mindset that it was easier to do things himself than to explain how he wanted them done, but that didn't teach people anything. It didn't help people learn to succeed and thrive. Jim was finally understanding that if he was going to improve his community, he had to do some self-improvement too. It was a bitter pill.

It was for that reason that he found himself sitting at a table in the back of the roadhouse with Clay, Shade, Josie, and her people. Pete was with him, along with Hank Rose, the fish farmer who joined them in the valley after his home was burned down and his friends killed. He'd been working to build a trout farm in the valley, and Jim was interested in seeing if he could do something similar in town that the townspeople could maintain. Clay was involved because he was resourceful and creative in addition to being an engineer.

In Jim's old job as a project manager for a state mental health agency, he'd frequently dealt with architects and engineers. He often found both professions to have tunnel vision. Despite being capable of designing entire buildings, they often lacked the ability to see the big picture. It wasn't that they were incompetent as much as they sometimes designed things that were unnecessarily complicated to build and difficult to maintain in the long term.

Jim blamed this shortcoming on the fact that many people in those fields had never gotten their hands dirty on a jobsite, and they knew little about the materials they used in their designs. That attitude didn't win him any friends in construction meetings back in the day. Despite the way he'd berated engineers in the past, Jim had often wished for the skills of an engineer during the collapse when his talents as a hillbilly Jack-of-all-trades fell short. Now that he finally had an engineer on his team, he had to remember to be nice so he wouldn't drive the guy off. He couldn't throw out engineer jokes as loosely as he threw out banjo jokes or he might piss the guy off.

"I'd like to look at creating some type of fuel for combustion engines," Clay posed.

The group was brainstorming about things that could be done to improve life in the community.

Jim pointed his thumb back over his shoulder at Ed and his apprentices, who were working like mad scientists to distill the next run of booze for the roadhouse. "People have been suggesting we make fuel for some time, but all my research shows it's not that easy. In the past, alcohol was mixed with gasoline to make it go farther. Everything I've read says that pure moonshine isn't a reliable source of fuel."

Clay shook his head. "I have no interest in running cars. What we should be running is a generator for a couple of hours a day. Your friend Shade mentioned his uncle had a working tractor you used to haul some heavy loads."

"Uncle Nooner," Shade said. "And in case you haven't noticed, he earned his name because he's drunk by noon every day. You'd never know it, though. He still manages to put in a full day of work."

"Unlike Lloyd," Jim said. "Who is also drinking by noon most days."

"I like Lloyd," Josie said. "He's quite the character."

Jim scowled. "That's one way to put it."

"The challenge will be finding the right size of generator," Clay continued. "We need one that can be hauled on a trailer but is of a sufficient wattage to do what I have in mind."

"What is it you have in mind?" asked Yana.

Clay sat up in his seat and rested his elbows on the table, leaning into the conversation. "Admittedly, I've been a hermit since this whole event took place. I spent a lot of time thinking about things I would do if I had the manpower. I didn't realize we had this kind of organized labor pool available or I would have spoken up sooner. There are things we can do that would make life much more convenient. It's not going to be instant, but even baby steps help."

"That's true," said Jim. "Even baby steps have a profound psychological effect. Small elements that bring comfort and convenience go a long way. We've all seen that in action. That brief period where we had working electricity was like a magical time."

"I'd like to get some water flowing through town," Clay said. "For now, the easiest way would be to power a small pump, pressurize a few lines at a time, and install some frost-free hydrants around town. We probably can't get running water to every house yet because too many pipes froze and broke last year, but it would be a start. We could run it a couple of hours a day and let the public know the schedule. That would provide clean water for people and reduce the burden of hauling it."

"Hopefully we'll know how many people you have soon," Lamar said. "The census should provide that data when we're done. Knowing how many people there are and where they live could help you plan infrastructure projects like this. You'd obviously want to position water spigots where they'd benefit the most people."

"Using a fuel-powered pump would only be an interim measure," Clay continued. "Long-term, there's no sense in using fuel to pump water when the water plant is on a moving river. I should be able to design some type of micro-hydroelectric system that will harness the water power to drive pumps continually."

Hank held up a finger. "Jim said you were also interested in raising fish in town?"

Clay turned in his seat, angling his body toward Hank. "I have a pretty successful indoor growing operation at my place. We talked about replicating it in a couple of different places in town. I suggested the roof of the roadhouse would be a good place because it's heated already. There might be other buildings in town that would be suitable for both indoor gardens and aquaculture. I recall seeing setups on the internet where dirty water from the fish provides nutrients to the plants."

"I mostly know about raising trout," Hank said. "They don't do very well in closed systems. They need cold, moving water to thrive."

"Some experimentation will be required," Clay cautioned. "It would be nice if we could find a local farmer with a pond containing a lot of catfish. We should ask around. Catfish might be a good place to start."

Josie gestured at the community message board in the roadhouse. "Maybe put a note up there asking if anyone knows of a good source for catfish."

"We still hope to make that bulletin board electronic soon," Brendan added. "Paper is so...twentieth century."

"That's an even older system," Lamar said. "Leaving messages on a wall is like caveman shit."

"How about you two guys work with Cookie," Jim said to Hank and Clay. "He couldn't be here this morning, but he knows the town, the resources, and nearly everyone who could be of help to you. He can find the manpower you need to make these things happen."

"Excellent," Clay said. "You mind if Hank and I go off and talk for a while? There's no use interrupting you guys while we talk fish and gardens. Was there anything else you needed from me right now?"

Jim shook his head. "Food production is primary. Once we get a handle on that, we can start looking at generators and running water. For now, I'm most concerned about people staying warm this winter and getting enough to eat."

Clay and Hank excused themselves, taking a table a short distance away so they could continue their conversation without disrupting the meeting.

"While we were making census visits, your wife said that the townspeople actually have a community herd of animals?" Josie said. "She said you keep them on the football field."

Jim cringed a little. "That was something I mentioned to them over a year ago in a not very polite manner, yes. They took my suggestion and carried it out. Before that, people were butchering stray livestock at random and most of the meat was going to waste. Now they butcher on a schedule and people can line up to receive meat. It's worked well, but we really need to get the animals off the football field. There's no grass left which means we have to bring the feed to them and that's labor intensive."

"I'll see what I can figure out about that." Yana wrote a note on her clipboard. "Who's in charge of that operation?"

"That's Cookie again," Jim said. "Have you met him yet?"

Yana smiled. "Briefly. He's a nice guy. Very enthusiastic."

"We're going to spend the afternoon working on the census," Josie said. "Your wife and Ian have teams out knocking on doors today. They're getting close to finishing up all the areas we designated as being part of your community. Anything else you'd like us working on, Jim? We're here to help in any way we can."

Jim pondered for a moment. "There is one thing, but I'd like to discuss it with you in private once we're finished here."

After five more minutes of housekeeping, the meeting broke off, and Jim pulled Josie to the side. "You know we found a guy living in the data center, right?"

Josie's eyes went wide. "I heard! I can't believe he managed to stay hidden so long."

"Yeah, me neither. I think he might be an asset to the community, not to mention the fact that there could be resources in the building, such as batteries, which would prove useful for some of the projects we discussed. He seems to take his obligation to his employer strongly. I don't think he'll abandon his post unless we can provide him an update on the status of his employer."

Josie blew out a breath. "This reminds me of those stories where people found Japanese soldiers on deserted islands in the Pacific decades after World War II was over. They thought we were still at war."

"Exactly. I'd like to find out if there's still a basis for his loyalty or if he's like one of those lost soldiers."

"So, you'd like us to research the company online and see what became of them?"

Jim nodded. "They're a multinational defense contractor with offices around the world. Someone has to know something."

"I'll see what I can find out."

Jim offered a rare smile. "Thank you. I'm glad you guys found your way here and I hope you'll stay, at least for now. You're a tremendous resource."

"Thank you for that," Josie said. "It's good to be appreciated. We don't want to be a burden."

"You're not. I assure you."

"Knowing that makes us want to stay."

"I've got Ian working on finding you guys a home," Jim said. "Hopefully you won't be piled up here in the roadhouse much longer."

Josie looked around the room. "It's not that bad, really. It's warm and safe. Those are things I'll never underestimate again."

36

MARGARET HAD BEEN DRAGGING brush for nearly an hour, resting as she needed to. While she'd worked hard her entire life, and she was no stranger to breaking a sweat, this kind of work had been a lot easier fifty years ago. She removed her gloves and was using her shirt-tail to mop sweat from her brow when Santos approached.

"Somehow I'm not surprised to see you outworking your neighbors," he said.

"That ain't saying much, Mr. Santos. We're an older community. Ain't many young people want to stick around a place like this. There's nothing for them to do and they don't get any signal for their little phones."

"The young are different these days. It's the same where I'm from. They want different things than I wanted when I was their age. Theirs is a different world."

"I'm glad I lived when I did. Times were hard but we appreciated what little we had. I think that makes it easier to accept the way life is now." Margaret flashed a weary smile.

"Perhaps I can help with that. Can I speak to you in my office for a moment?"

"Your office? You have an office on the train?"

Santos offered a patient smile. "Just because I'm out in the field doesn't mean the work stops, Margaret. My bosses have certain expectations that continue even when I'm thousands of miles from home."

"Reckon I can even get up there?" Margaret looked doubtful. The bank leading up to the tracks was steep, then there was the boarding ladder on the platform to deal with.

"We have a step that will make it easy for you and obviously I'll be glad to assist."

"You're quite the gentleman, Mr. Santos. Let's go."

"Where are you headed?" R.J. asked, staggering in their direction with a long branch dragging behind him.

Margaret gestured toward the train with a crooked finger. "I'm going to speak to Mr. Santos on the train."

R.J. paused, looking from Margaret to Santos.

Sensing his uncertainty, Santos walked over to R.J., patted him on the shoulder, and smiled warmly. "I assure you that she'll be completely safe. I appreciate the way you're concerned for her well-being. Caring for the older folks in our communities is a trait that's been lost to time. You're a good man for keeping those traditions alive."

R.J. wasn't even sure how to respond to that, so he nodded awkwardly and mumbled, "Thank you." He was still concerned about Margaret getting on the train with these men, but Santos left him no way to intervene without seeming rude. He didn't dare say anything that would result in Santos leaving without giving them the supplies he'd promised.

True to his word, Santos helped Margaret up the bank to the tracks and one of his men placed a plastic milk crate on the ground to help her board the train. Once she was safely aboard, Santos led Margaret back through the train toward the car that held his office and sleeping quarters. Margaret had not been aboard a lot of trains in her life and she took in her surroundings with interest. The rearmost cars appeared to house most of the men. One was set up for dining, with a kitchen and booths. Cases of food, drinks, and paper goods were stacked along the walls and in every spare corner.

Two cars were lined with bunk beds, with showers and toilets at each end. Those cars seemed particularly untidy to Margaret because the beds were unmade and laundry hung drying from lines stretched along the ceiling. Stoves in each car provided heat. Margaret also noticed that all the cars could do with a good deep cleaning—at least some air freshener—since they reeked of so many people staying in such tight quarters. After passing through several cars, they reached the last one before the train turned to boxcars and a tanker.

"This is my quarters. Please excuse any clutter. We made no provisions for maid service on this expedition."

Santos gave a small laugh, but Margaret had already suspected there was no one cleaning up behind these men. That made sense. It probably wouldn't have been safe for a woman to make this trip just to keep the rooms clean. Santos and his men were being nice to her and her neighbors, but Margaret was no fool. Men were men and she knew how they might behave when away from home for long spells.

"Please have a seat." Santos gestured toward a wooden chair opposite a neat metal desk. "Would you care for some coffee?"

Margaret's eyes went wide. "Why, I'd love some! I can't tell you the last time I had a cup."

Santos walked to a coffee pot and poured some into a large Styrofoam cup, which he handed over to Margaret. He took a seat at his desk while she inhaled the aroma of the hot coffee.

"That smells delightful. Is it Maxwell House?" she cooed.

Santos smiled patiently. "No, it's a special blend I pick up back home. I grind the beans myself."

She tested it with her tongue and found it cool enough that she could take a small sip. Even if she burned her tongue the smell was so alluring that she couldn't resist. She smacked her lips with pleasure. "So, what is it you need from me, Mr. Santos?"

Santos leaned forward conspiratorially. "Margaret, I sense you are something of a matriarch here in your community. People respect you and follow your leadership. Am I right?"

Margaret was pleased that Santos sensed the way people deferred to her. He was right. Their community might not be much more than a wide spot in the road, but she did run things around there. If someone wanted to rent the community center for a party, it was *her* they had to come to. If they wanted to know who to vote for in the next election, they asked her. If the road went unplowed after a winter storm, it was Margaret who called the highway department and demanded something be done.

"You might say that people have a certain level of respect for me," she conceded. "I am responsible for a few things around here. If the county has questions about matters of interest to me and my neighbors, I'm the one they come ask. Everyone knows who runs the show around here."

Santos winked. "I could tell that instantly, Margaret. It was evident who was in charge the minute I stepped foot off this train. You asked what I needed, but it's more of a question of what we can do for each other. My employer relies heavily on the goodwill of the people in the communities where we operate. We secure their goodwill, and their loyalty, by helping each other. It's a two-way street."

"You scratch my back and I scratch yours?"

"Exactly," Santos oozed.

"You want me to be your eyes and ears, don't you?"

Santos wagged a finger. "Not much gets by you, does it?"

Margaret grinned. "I'd like to think I'm pretty sharp."

"My employers have learned that small towns are better than cities for keeping track of what's going on in an area. Cities are too crowded and chaotic. Something can be happening on one side of a city and the people on the other side know nothing about it. Small towns aren't like that. Word travels. People such as yourself probably know everything that goes on around here."

Margaret looked at him directly. "I ain't one to gossip, but I do hear things."

"That's exactly what I'm looking for. I need someone who can let me know what's going on around here. I don't need chit-chat and rumors. I don't have time for that. What I need is someone who will let me know when they see something with their own two eyes." Santos pointed to his own eyes with two splayed fingers.

"What kind of things exactly?"

Santos reached in his desk and removed a device, which he placed on the desk in front of Margaret.

"What's that? A cell phone?" she asked. "Honey, those ain't never worked around here, even when the power was on."

"This is a satellite phone. It will work just about everywhere."

"What am I supposed to do with it?"

"If the Chinese or any other foreign forces show up in your community, I want to know. If any armed soldiers of any kind show up here, I want to know. If anyone comes through asking about this train, I want to know. I'm handing out hundreds of these phones on this one trip, so obviously I can't be bothered with every little thing. This is not a request line. This isn't a way for you to call and put in a shopping list for my next trip. Is that understood?"

Margaret nodded seriously. "I get what you're saying, but I'm not too good with electronics. Is that thing easy to work?"

"I'll leave clear instructions. They'll be in a special box that we'll deliver to your house if you agree to take the phone."

"You can depend on me, Mr. Santos. I take my responsibilities very seriously." In her eyes, the fate of her community's aid deliveries rested entirely on her shoulders now. If she failed, there would be no more trains, no more boxes, and no more pallets of goods.

Santos pointed to a nearby suitcase. "The instructions will be in that suitcase, along with a solar charger that will allow you to keep the phone charged. There's also a few special items in there just for you, because of your willingness to help us. There are extra rechargeable batteries you can use around the house, along with a solar charger for them. There's a flashlight, a solar lantern, some antibiotics, some coffee, and a few other tokens of our appreciation."

"I appreciate that, but I'm not sure I want my neighbors to see me getting special treatment."

"They won't," Santos assured her. "Most of them are still working to clear the tracks. You show me which house is yours and I'll have one of my men leave these items at your back door. No one will see."

Margaret processed this. "Not being pushy, but how often are you going to have people through here? People are going to wonder when they might be getting more supplies in the future."

Santos sat back in his chair, crossed his legs, and tapped a finger on the desk. "That depends on several variables. It depends on the willingness of other people along the tracks to cooperate with our endeavor. It depends on any resistance we meet. On a practical level, it depends on how much work is involved in clearing the tracks. We might encounter places where the tracks must be rebuilt or replaced in order to continue, and my small team is not equipped to do that. But certainly, once we have the tracks clear, trains will come through on a routine basis."

"I'll do what I can, Mr. Santos."

Santos stared directly at Margaret. "Do you have any reservations about the fact I'm not American?"

Margaret thought for a long moment about how to word her response. "We're a tiny community. During the last election cycle, there was a man came through here wanting me to vote for him for the local Board of Supervisors. He wasn't from my preferred party, but you know what? He was the only one who thought I was important enough to ask. He was the only person who showed me the respect of coming to my house and asking for my vote, so I voted for him. I feel the same way about your arrival here. You're the first person to come by here and show us any respect. You're the first person to bring us any food or offer us any hope. For that reason alone, you have my vote."

Santos smiled and extended his hand across his desk. Margaret took it and the two of them shook hands.

"To a new friendship, Margaret."

37

The Data Center

JIM TIED his horse off to the flagpole where a tattered Old Glory still presided over the matted lawn of the data center. He marched over to the main entrance to the building and banged his fist on thick, bullet-resistant glass. He wasn't sure if the sound would penetrate the deep recesses of the building, so he added in a few solid kicks too. If that didn't work, he planned to fire off a few rounds from his handgun until Wrong Way showed himself.

He caught a flash of movement inside the lobby as a figure emerged from the edge of his peripheral vision. Wrong Way stepped into view bearing a rifle and full loadout. Despite the fact that contact had already been established when they tried to break into the building, Wrong Way wasn't taking the visit lightly. He still seemed to think Jim was there to lay siege to his building.

When Wrong Way saw it was Jim, he jabbed a thumb upward and yelled, "Outside!"

Jim could barely make out the words through the thick door but got the message. Wrong Way wasn't unlocking the door for anyone.

Yet again, Jim would be addressed from high above, as if he was meeting with Julius Caesar. He rolled his eyes, backed out of the entrance alcove, and glanced at the rooftop with shielded eyes. A couple of minutes later, Wrong Way appeared at the edge of the roof.

"Just because we met one time doesn't mean I'm ready to open the door to you," said Wrong Way.

"I get that, but I've got info you might be interested in."

"A likely story."

Jim shrugged. "Yeah. This one is true. I understand part of your hesitation at leaving your post is because you feel you have a contractual obligation to satisfy."

"That's correct."

"I understand that sense of duty. I respect it, but I have some information on your employer."

"Of course you do."

Jim looked at the ground and tilted his head from side to side. Looking up was making his neck ache. "We have people on our team now who recently worked for Walter Lightspeed."

"Who's that?"

Jim groaned. This was like trying to update Rip Van Winkle on everything he'd missed while he'd been asleep. "That's a long story in itself. Let's just say for now that these people who have come to live at my roadhouse have access to information the rest of us don't have. *Current* information. One of them has contacts within the company you once worked for. When America fell, your employer made their Saudi Arabian office the new base of operations. All American data centers were scrubbed in anticipation of a foreign invasion, most likely from China. The information was mirrored to data centers in other countries, the location of which was not disclosed."

Wrong Way barked a laugh. "Anyone could say that, man. *Anyone.* You've got some massive cojones to just show up here, feed me some line of shit, and expect that I'm going to take it as gospel. That ain't happening."

Jim had expected this reaction. "I'm going to reach into my jacket."

Wrong Way took a step backward. He had his rifle held across his chest and he tightened his grip on it. "Go slow."

Jim reached into his jacket and pulled out Josie's satellite phone.

"What's that?"

"It's a satellite phone."

"Sure it is. How do I know that's not some old Nokia you yanked out of your kitchen junk drawer?"

"I have a number for the new headquarters. You can make the call yourself and confirm what I'm telling you. This is going to require a little trust for both of us. You've got to trust me enough to take the phone and I've got to trust that you'll give it back. Can we agree to do that and behave nicely?"

It took Wrong Way a long time to make his decision. Long enough that Jim grew concerned he wasn't going to go for it. Long enough that Jim could have taught himself to knit and then gone on to actually knit a sweater. Finally, he got his answer.

"Leave the phone in front of the door and back away. I'll open the door and make the call in front of you. Leave your weapons on the ground. We'll go from there."

"Works for me." Jim stretched his sore neck again. He wasn't exactly pleased about setting his guns down, but he was taking a leap of faith here. He headed for the front door and carefully placed the priceless phone on the ground. Beneath it, he tucked a sheet of paper Josie had printed off the internet.

It was an internal directory of phone numbers for the company that had once owned this data center. Jim hoped there was someone on that list who could verify the story he had just relayed to Wrong Way. He backed away from the door, placed his weapons on the ground, and waited.

A few minutes later, Wrong Way appeared at the door, unlocked it with a series of keys, and opened it. He slid out enough to pick up the phone and the sheet of paper beneath it.

While Wrong Way scanned the directory, Jim said, "You'd have saved yourself a lot of running if you'd have just opened the door when I was banging on it a few minutes ago."

Wrong Way ignored him. He studied the phone in his hand, then powered it up. He seemed familiar with the device and asked no questions, not that Jim could have answered them anyway.

Wrong Way selected a number from the sheet, punched it in the phone, then held it to his ear. Someone on the other end must have answered because Wrong Way gave his full legal name, a number of some kind, and asked to be routed to a particular department. Jim listened with interest.

Wrong Way cocked his head when someone at the requested extension answered the phone. "Yes sir, it's really me and I'm still on the job. The facility remains secure. I managed to stay undetected until recently."

He paused as the person on the other end spoke, then replied, "One of the locals provided me with this phone. He's telling me that the data center has been wiped and the data moved offshore. He suggested I call to confirm that."

Wrong Way's face clouded as he received the answer Jim suspected he'd get. He'd been telling the truth a few minutes ago when he explained the situation to Wrong Way. The security contractor hadn't wanted to believe it, even though a part of him might have suspected that it was possible.

"Yes sir, I understand. Yes, I appreciate that. Good luck to you too, sir."

Wrong Way ended the call and looked like he wanted to throw the phone.

"No!" Jim said. "Don't throw that phone!"

Wrong Way sucked in a deep breath, then tossed the phone to Jim, who panicked for a second before catching it in both hands. When Jim recovered, he found Wrong Way leaning back against the wall, rubbing his temples with his fingers.

"You were right, man. They said they scrubbed everything over a year ago. I've been guarding empty servers." He repeated it again slowly for his own benefit. "I've...been guarding...empty servers...for over a year." He slid down the wall until he was in a sitting position.

Still about ten feet away and uncertain of what else to do, Jim sat down on the sidewalk where he was standing. "You have family?"

"I've got a brother. He and his family live in Arkansas. My parents died years ago."

"You were in the military, weren't you?"

Wrong Way bumped his shoulders in a shrug. "Yeah."

"So, this can't be the first time you did something pointless, right?"

Wrong Way gave a sarcastic chuckle. "That's the damn truth."

"How about you lock this place up and we go get a beer?" Jim suggested.

Wrong Way gave Jim a wary look. "I'm not going without a weapon."

Jim laughed. "Hell, man, we *encourage* weapons. We even sell them at the roadhouse for the poor saps that show up without one. Lock that place up and let's go."

Wrong Way managed to stand up. "I could use a shot of liquor. You guys sell Jim Beam at your roadhouse?"

Jim grinned and patted Wrong Way on the shoulder. "We've got every bottle of liquor you can imagine. I'll just leave it at that."

38

AFTER A DAY of riding the tracks through open fields, Hugh, Charlie, and Garnet camped in the woods near a stream. Again, they kept a watch, but this time they slept cold, without a fire. The next morning, they were up early, their sleeping bags frosted over.

"This is more fun in summer," Charlie complained, rubbing his gloved hands together. They were too cold to even saddle his horse properly.

"It'll warm up shortly," Garnet pointed out. "The sun will top that rise soon and warm your face like a kiss from a pretty girl."

Charlie blushed. "If you say so."

Hugh cupped his hands around his mouth, warming them with his breath. "We're just a couple of miles from Finney. The tracks go right through the middle of the community. Unless that place has turned into a ghost town, they'll have seen something."

"Never been there," Charlie said.

"Ain't much to see." Hugh shrugged. "It's a wide spot in the road that refuses to dry up. Average age of the people living there is probably seventy years old."

Garnet winked. "That might be where you find a kiss from a pretty girl, Charlie."

Charlie blanched, then choked. "Sometimes my imagination is too good. I just made myself vomit."

Garnet laughed, then mounted up, swinging into the saddle like he was halfway getting the hang of it. "Might have to get me one of these things. Me and the boys have decided we like it better than walking."

Charlie shot Garnet a concerned look. Even though he understood the old man better now, he still wasn't entirely comfortable with the idea that the guy toted an entire entourage around inside his head.

"I might be able to help you with that," Hugh said. "Remind me when we get back to town. There are people who own horses who can't take care of them properly. They want to trade them off, but they're afraid people might buy them just to eat them. I'm sure they taste fine, but it seems like a waste of a good horse to me."

Garnet looked pleased at that. "I'll remind you."

They covered the miles to the Finney community without much conversation. They were dressed for the weather, but a man didn't generate much body heat sitting on a horse. True to Garnet's promise, they did get some relief once the sun broke over the rounded knolls of the surrounding hills. It promised a warm day but was certainly taking its sweet time delivering.

"Smell that?" Garnet asked.

Hugh nodded. "Wood smoke, probably from stoves. Finney is just around that bend up there."

"You reckon anyone will be out moving around this morning?" Charlie asked. "I'm assuming you're going to want to ask someone about the train, which means we have to *find* someone first."

"We'll find someone," Hugh assured him. "It's a tiny little place. Riding a horse through there is like riding one through someone's living room. They'll make an appearance."

Charlie looked concerned. "As long as they don't show up shoot-ing. I wouldn't take kindly to someone riding through *my* living room."

Once they were in sight of it, Charlie noted that Finney looked like some of the old coal and lumber camps he had passed through over the years. It was little more than a tiny cluster of cookie-cutter houses placed along a remote stretch of road. Some of the tiny homes had fallen in on themselves over the years and been replaced by mobile homes of varying sizes. Those old work camps had been built to provide employee housing for people working in the timber or coal industry. Charlie didn't know if the houses at Finney were built for that same purpose, or if they just had the misfortune of resem-bling some of the region's least desirable housing. Smoke rolled from the chimneys of several houses and mobile homes.

Charlie reined his horse to a stop and sniffed the air. "That smoke smells funny."

"Some of those are coal fires." Hugh pointed to a distant chimney where black smoke roiled like it was pouring from the exhaust of a diesel engine. "That's what it looks like when you get a coal fire going in the morning."

"Best heat there ever was," Garnet said. "I grew up with it. Put out so much heat you didn't even have to insulate your house if you had a coal stove. Couldn't let that fire go out, though, or things in the house would freeze solid."

While they sat there discussing the merits of coal fires, the back door of a nearby mobile home flew open. It was opened with such urgency that the men all shifted in their saddles and raised their weapons. The man who flew out the door wasn't responding to their presence. In fact, he hadn't seen them at all because he was so invested in yanking down the front of his long underwear. He stopped at the railing and let fly with a stream of urine, closing his eyes as he relished in the bliss of the close call. As the job neared completion, the man opened his eyes again, sucking in his breath when he saw he had an audience, all of them pointing weapons in his direction.

"Poor planning to bring a Johnson to a gun fight," Garnet mused.

The man covered himself, then raised his hands. He was fully aware that if they were intent on killing him, he wouldn't be able to make it back to the safety of his mobile home before he was mowed down.

Hugh lowered his rifle, then gestured for Charlie and Garnet to do the same. "Sir, we're sorry we startled you. You did the same to us when you came flying out that door."

The man lowered his hands. "A feller has to piss!" He was doing his best to reclaim his dignity and appear outraged, while only wearing long underwear, boots, and an orange hat with fuzzy ear flaps.

"That he does," Garnet agreed.

"Mind if we ask you a couple of questions?" Hugh asked.

The man shivered. "Mind if I put some damn clothes on first? I didn't come out dressed for bullshitting." His tone was snappy, a mix of embarrassment and nerves.

Hugh held up a hand. "Take your time. We'll meet you around front."

The man started back into his trailer, prepared to close the door behind him, then he paused. "Questions about what? What the hell you people want?"

"We want to ask you about a train," Hugh replied.

The man hesitated only a second before slamming the door behind him.

"He didn't seem shocked at the idea of a train, did he?" Charlie remarked.

"Nope," Garnet said. "He could have told us that he hadn't seen any train and slammed the door, but he didn't."

"I'm going to ride around front and talk to the man," Hugh said. "Why don't you two hang back a little just in case he comes out with a bad attitude."

"Copy that," Garnet said. "We got your back."

Ten minutes later, Hugh was waiting near the guy's front porch when he came out more appropriately dressed for the weather. He man carried a rifle but didn't hold it like he was prepared to use it. It seemed more like an accessory he was accustomed to taking with him when he left the house.

"Expecting trouble?" Hugh asked.

"Expecting to go deer hunting since you already made me go and get dressed," the man said resentfully.

"Sorry about that," Hugh said. "Let's start over. My name is Hugh and I'm from River Mountain. It ain't all that far from here so there ain't no need to be on edge. We're practically neighbors."

"Where's your buddies?"

"They're hanging back in case you planned on coming out here and blowing my head off."

The man screwed his head around but didn't spot Garnet and Charlie. "Ain't no call for that...yet."

"What's your name?"

"R.J."

"You didn't seem all that surprised when I asked you about a train, R.J."

"I saw a train. That ain't a secret, as far as I know."

Hugh shifted in his saddle. Sitting his horse, he was about the same height as the man standing on his porch. He considered dismounting to appear less threatening, but decided it was better to remain on the same level as the man for now. "What can you tell me about it?"

"Mexicans," R.J. said. "Hell, maybe thirty of them. I didn't count."

"They stopped here?"

"Stopped and fed us. They had chainsaws, four wheelers, and even a dozer. Got us to help them clear the tracks so they could keep going. Gave each household a box of supplies for helping out."

"They carrying fancy rifles?" Hugh asked.

"Some of them were gold. Ain't never seen nothing like it. I asked them what that was all about, but they just looked at me. Didn't say nothing."

"Did they say anything at all?"

"The guy in charge did. He did all the talking. He's the one that told us they'd hand out supplies if we helped them clear the tracks. He also told us some other stuff."

Hugh cocked an eyebrow. "Like what?"

R.J. glared. "Hell, Mister, they was a lot. He talked about the Chinese invading us and the politicians screwing us over, which ain't news if you ask me. Then he said they'd come back with more supplies in the future. He talked to Margaret the most. She probably knows more about it than I do."

"Where can I find her?"

R.J. looked across the street, noting the smoke pouring from her chimney. "Across the street. She's up, judging by that smoke."

"Will you introduce us, so Margaret doesn't get startled the way we startled you?"

R.J. mulled this over for a minute. "How about I go talk to her and get her to come out here? Will that work?"

"Works for me." Hugh spoke into his radio. "Why don't you boys come on around and join us?"

Charlie and Garnet walked their horses around the trailer while Hugh dismounted. R.J. clambered down his rickety porch steps and stalked across the road to Margaret's house where he tapped politely on the door.

Margaret opened the door, then looked slightly alarmed when she noticed Hugh in the street. R.J. explained what he wanted while gesturing several times at Hugh, then at Garnet and Charlie. Finally, Margaret shut the door and R.J. jogged back in Hugh's direction.

"She'll be out in a minute."

"You're welcome to go on hunting if we're holding you up," Hugh offered.

"Reckon I'll stick around so Margaret feels comfortable, if it's all the same to you."

Hugh shrugged. "Ain't no crust off my pie."

After an awkward moment of Hugh standing in the street asking R.J. more questions he didn't want to answer, Margaret's door opened and she ambled out onto the porch. Hugh instantly felt like he knew this woman from the way she was dressed. As someone who'd grown up not far from this community, he'd met many women who dressed like men, spoke like men, and worked like men their entire lives. It didn't mean that they weren't feminine. It was more a testament to the fact that the rural, hard-scrabble life required so much physical labor that the entire family had to pitch in to make it happen. Living here had never been easy, even in the best of times. When this woman had grown up, just as when Hugh was younger, it was nothing to see entire families out working fields. They'd be barefoot in the soil, from the oldest to the youngest, each with a hoe, a bucket of seed corn, or a damp bundle of tobacco seedlings.

"What can I do you for?" Margaret growled in the customary greeting of rural people of a certain age. "R.J. said you wanted to talk to me."

Hugh offered his warmest smile, which was about as awkward as Jim's. Both of them looked like they were wincing in pain when they attempted it. "Margaret, my name is Hugh. I'm originally from River Mountain."

Margaret grinned. "Local boy."

"Indeed I am. Went to school at Honaker. My mom worked at the sewing factory and my dad was a farmer."

Margaret huffed. "Sounds like me. What was your mommy's name?"

Hugh told her and Margaret gave a knowing nod.

"I worked with your mother for years. Knew her well. Didn't recognize you as the little feller who was always bouncing up and down in the car window when your daddy came to pick her up." She winked.

"I've grown." Another awkward smile.

"But yeah, there was a train through here yesterday. They asked for our help clearing the tracks. Paid us with a bowl of soup and some fresh bread. Worked my ass off and I'm feeling it today."

Hugh's innate lie detector had been honed during his years of working as a military contractor. Walking into villages in the jungle, elders and spokesmen would swear one thing while CIA assets provided intel that told a different story. Years of this taught Hugh how to read someone and he could tell instantly that Margaret was not telling him the entire story. Certainly, what she was saying *might* be true, but there was more that she wasn't admitting to.

"Anything you can tell me about them?" Hugh persisted. "Where they Americans? NATO? Some foreign aid operation?" Hugh had a suspicion of who they might be, so this question was intended as a test.

"They were Mexican gentlemen according to the man in charge. I didn't speak to anyone else, but they all appeared to be Mexican as far as I could tell."

"How many men were there?"

Margaret shrugged. "Maybe two dozen."

"Any women or children?"

"Nah, just men as far as I saw." Margaret put her hands on her hips. "Why all the questions? Is there something I need to be concerned about?"

Hugh had already decided he wasn't going to relay any of his suspicions since he didn't have any real data to support those theories. "I'm living over there in town now and we've had a lot of problems since the lights went out with people who said they were there to help us. In most cases it turned out to be the opposite. There are a lot of rumors right now about Chinese soldiers working their way across the country and taking out any communities where they meet resistance."

"These men definitely weren't Chinese," Margaret said.

"Even so, there has to be a reason they came here. That's why I'm asking questions. I'm not implying they have bad intentions, but it pays to know who's in your neighborhood. Wouldn't you agree?"

"Well..."

"Have you ever had a drug dealer move into your community?"

Margaret huffed a laugh that was like a tight bark. "Those people don't last long around here. We run them off."

"Exactly. It doesn't take much of a bad influence to throw off the whole balance of a community."

"So, you think these fellows should be run off if they come back?"

Hugh shook his head. "Not at all. I'd simply like to have a conversation with them. Ask them a few questions."

Margaret looked doubtful. "The boss man was friendly enough, but I ain't sure they were the kind of men who take to being questioned."

"That's good to know. I appreciate your time, Margaret." Hugh touched the brim of his hat. "You have a good day now."

Hugh returned to Charlie and Garnet and took his horse.

"How'd it go?" Charlie asked, mounting up.

"That sweet old granny is lying her ass off."

Garnet laughed so loud that Hugh and Charlie both turned in their saddles to look at him.

"Something I said?" Hugh asked.

"Not you." Garnet pointed at his head. "The boys."

39

"THERE'S a lot you left out of that story," R.J. pointed out as they watched Hugh leave.

Margaret frowned at R.J. "Boy, you've got a soft heart but a hard head. Sometimes there's more to people than you see at first glance."

R.J. blanched at the comment, though he was used to Margaret's tough love. "He seemed okay to me."

"I ain't saying there was anything wrong with him. I ain't saying that at all. What I'm saying is that it's never wise to show *all* your cards to someone. A better question is why *would* I tell him those Mexicans gave us a load of supplies. What if he decided he wanted to steal them from us? What if he came back tonight with more men and they robbed us? For all we know, those boys right there might have been following this train for days, robbing everyone they hand out supplies to."

"So, I shouldn't have told him they gave us supplies?"

Margaret's mouth fell open. "You didn't tell him that, did you?"

"Nobody ever said anything about keeping it quiet."

"Ain't nobody telling you to breathe, either, but you're doing it right now! Sometimes you have to think, boy." She rapped him on the side of the head with her knuckles.

R.J. flinched. "Jesus, Margaret!"

"Maybe that'll learn you. Next time think before you talk."

R.J. rubbed his head. "He said he was from River Mountain."

Margaret shook her head in disappointment. "I can say I'm Elizabeth Taylor but that don't make it true. I swear, boy, if you want to stay alive, you're going to have to be a little more suspicious of people. If you share *any* information, there should be a reason behind it. Nothing is free in this world."

"Geez, I never knew you were so...conniving. You seem like such a sweet old lady."

Margaret cut her eyes at him. "Watch your tongue, boy. You're getting awful close to being a smartass. I'm *calculating* is what I am. A tiny community like this can be a den of vipers at times. You don't get to my age without learning how to deal with people."

"Reckon I do need to study up on that some more. I always been one to take people at their word until they give me a reason not to."

Margaret sighed and patted R.J. on the shoulder, thinking perhaps she'd been too hard on him. "You don't need to study on it. Just pay attention and learn from what's happening right in front of your very own eyes. Now I've got work to get back to. You keep an eye out and make sure those boys keep riding. I'll talk to you later."

"Yes, ma'am." R.J. hung his head and walked back toward his trailer.

Margaret watched him go, shaking her head in disappointment. She wasn't sure if his ignorance came from being naïve or from being a man. She'd always felt like men had no idea how the world worked. They didn't question peoples' motives in the same way that women did. Men seemed shocked when a close friend backstabbed them, while women almost expected it and were always on the lookout for it. Their naivete made Margaret wonder how men survived at all when they were so poorly equipped to function in society. More importantly, why the hell were they in charge of so many things?

Margaret ambled back to her house, shutting the gate on her chain-link fence behind her. She climbed her creaky steps, went inside, and locked the front door behind her, something she'd never done before the collapse. She dropped heavily onto an overstuffed couch, the cushions protected by clear plastic covers. She reached into her crochet basket, dug beneath the yarn, and removed the satellite phone Santos had given her.

She studied the controls, recalling the instructions she'd read last night. She held the phone at arm's length, cocking her head so she could see through the correct part of her bifocals. When she was able to read the buttons, she jabbed the power button with her index finger, then watched the display come to life. Santos had told her that it would take a little while for the phone to connect to the satellite network, so she waited patiently for the phone to do its thing. When the display indicated that it was ready, Margaret dialed the single contact programmed into the phone.

"Hello, Margaret. Calling so soon?"

Margaret was taken off-guard that Santos immediately knew who she was. Although it made sense that he'd keep track of the phones he handed out, she still hadn't expected it. She could hear the diesel locomotive in the background, the sound of the train making its way down the tracks. "Good morning, Mr. Santos. I know you said to only call for certain things, but one of those certain things just happened."

"What was that?"

"A couple of men showed up here asking about the train."

Santos sighed into the phone, like he was disappointed that she'd bothered him over so trivial a matter. *"That's to be expected. People are surprised when they hear a train on tracks that have been silent for so long. I appreciate you taking your responsibility seriously, but I'm sure it's just natural curiosity. Nothing to be alarmed about."*

"I'm not so sure, Mr. Santos. The fellow asking all the questions had a lot of guns and was wearing military-looking gear."

"*A soldier?*"

"Nah, I don't think so. Hard to describe really. He looked half-soldier, half-cowboy, if that makes any sense. He said he was from a nearby town that had some trouble with strangers and since then they try to keep an eye out for any strangers showing up in the area. He also knew about the Chinese."

There was a long silence. So long that Margaret pulled the phone away from her head and stared at the display to see if it was still working. "Mr. Santos?"

"*Yes, I'm here. I'm just processing your report. Maybe there is more to it than natural curiosity. I'll make a mental note in case there are further developments.*"

"I asked him if he thought you all were trouble and should be run off if you came back around. He said no, that he just wanted to ask you some questions."

"*Did you get a name?*" Santos asked. "*Just in case this man pops up again.*"

"He said his name was Hugh."

"*Thank you. I made a note.*"

"Well, I just thought you should know," Margaret said, uncertain of what else to say. "Did I make a mistake? I apologize if I bothered you for nothing."

Margaret wondered if she should just have kept her mouth shut. She wasn't sure what kind of reaction she'd expected from Santos, but this wasn't it. When he'd visited Finney, he'd demonstrated that cooperating with him brought rewards and she needed more rewards. Even the tiny aid package he'd given her was enough to improve her situation.

"*You did nothing wrong. I appreciate you taking your obligation seriously. Just continue to monitor the situation,*" Santos said. "*If the men come back, I'd appreciate an update. Otherwise, I'll speak with you the next time we're passing through the area.*"

"Yes sir. I'll do my best. You take care now. Bye!"

Santos hung up without returning her goodbye. Margaret checked the screen to see that the call had indeed ended, then she powered down the phone. She worked her way back to her feet and retrieved a pot of hot water from the top of the woodstove. She closed her blinds and made herself a cup of the instant coffee that Santos had included in the *special* box he'd given her for accepting the phone. Even though it was instant, the smell was intoxicating.

40

Honaker, Virginia

Later that afternoon, Santos stood along the twisted rails, hands on hips, staring at the charred remains of the trestle before him. He used his phone to take a couple of pictures documenting why he'd be unable to proceed any further along this section of track. Clearing felled frees or a mild landslide was one thing, but replacing a trestle was beyond the scope of this mission.

Seeing two of his men climbing back up the embankment to the tracks, Santos hailed them. "Find anyone who'd talk?"

One of them grinned. *"Muy borracho."*

The other nodded in agreement. "An old man in that village said the men got very drunk and set fire to the bridge. Apparently, no one liked the railroad very much. What now?"

Santos jabbed a thumb back toward the train. "Luis is plotting an alternate route." He rolled his shoulders. "We expected there would be inaccessible routes. We've been luckier than some of our colleagues, but that luck has run out. We'll backtrack to the next junction and try another direction."

One of the men, dressed in black cowboy boots, jeans, and a denim jacket lined with wool, indicated the cluster of houses in the distance with the tip of his rifle. His name was Miguel and he was one of Santos' most loyal men. Whether Santos needed his cigarette lit, his glass refilled, or a dozen people beheaded, Miguel did any job put before him without batting an eye. "The old bastard down the hill wanted to know if we brought him anything. We going to feed these people?"

Santos considered the idea for a moment. "I guess there's no reason not to. We're here and this will be the last town we reach along this rail line. We might as well plant the seeds of goodwill while we're here."

"We handing out care packages too?" Miguel asked.

"Let's do it. I don't think I'll leave a phone with these people since this community is so close to the last one, but we can still hand out basic aid packages. Use the ATVs since it's a long walk down that hill. Once the supplies are loaded, we'll go down together."

41

Honaker, Virginia

From a hill to the west, Hugh, Charlie, and Garnet watched the men unload several ATVs and trailers from a flat car. They hooked the trailers to the ATVs, then staged them in front of the box cars and began offloading supplies into them.

"What do you reckon is in those boxes?" Charlie asked, watching the scene through binoculars.

"Looks like relief supplies," Hugh commented, his eye glued to his rifle scope. "Most of those boxes are labeled as food or medical supplies."

"That woman back at Finney didn't say anything about relief supplies being distributed," Garnet commented. "Of course, I probably wouldn't be bragging about that either."

"No, *she* didn't mention it," Hugh said. "But that boy I talked to did. He said they were given supplies for helping clear the tracks. The old woman conveniently left that out of her story."

"Well, you can't blame her for not wanting to tell a bunch of shady-looking men like us," Garnet laughed.

Hugh nodded. "That might be true."

"I'm confused," Charlie said. "They're giving out supplies. Are these bad guys or good guys?"

Hugh sat up. "Hell if I know. I'm not sure what to think."

"So, what do we do?" Garnet asked. "Give it up and go home? The whole thing still seems odd to me. What the hell are these people doing here?"

"It's odd to me too," Hugh said. "If they are cartel, this isn't a charitable mission. Everything with them is about making money. Since no one here has money to pay for the goods that are being distributed, I'm guessing this is some kind of investment on the cartel's part."

"An investment?" Charlie asked.

"Against future earnings," said Hugh. "They're spending money in hopes of the investment paying off later. Like buying people's loyalty by handing out things they need. Of course, I'm just guessing at this point."

"Well, we might never know. They can't go any further on this section of track," Charlie pointed out. "I guess they'll have to reverse out of here and go home or wherever they're going next."

Hugh got to his feet. "I *want* to know. I'd feel better knowing."

"Then what do you propose?" Garnet asked.

Hugh slung his rifle over his neck. "I'm going to walk down there and talk to the man in charge."

Charlie burst out laughing. It was only when he noticed Hugh wasn't laughing along that he quit and grew concerned. "Are you serious?"

"Sometimes even the best intel doesn't paint an accurate picture of the situation on the ground. You have to get your hands and boots dirty."

"We could do that after the train backs out," Charlie said. "Seems safer to talk to the locals than the armed strangers."

Garnet shook his head. "That woman back in Finney didn't tell us the whole story. Same thing might happen here."

"Once that train is gone, the truth might be gone with it," said Hugh.

"What if they shoot you?" Charlie asked.

"They didn't shoot anyone in Finney and there's no indication they have hostile intent here. If things do get spicy, I'm hoping you guys can lay down some cover fire so I can get out of there."

Charlie folded his arms, frustrated by Hugh's plan. "I'm glad to help, but it looks like you'll be outnumbered thirty to one. I'm not sure how much we can do to save your ass if things go downhill."

"Do your best," Hugh said. "That's all I'm asking for. I'm an adult making my own decision. If it's my time to go, there's nothing I can do about that."

Charlie's expression was sour. "I don't like it."

Hugh adjusted some of the gear on his chest rig, taking a couple of items from pouches and tucking them into the packs draped over his horse's back. There was no sense carrying unnecessary weight into a situation he might have to leave at a run. "I've been in a lot of intense situations, Charlie. When I was in Central America, sometimes I'd go on these operations with CIA or Special Forces. Even if we knew we were going into a hostile village, those guys would make contact with the head man. Even if we couldn't sway their loyalty, we could often find out who among the enemy forces was running the show and that's valuable intel."

"I guess." Charlie scuffed the ground with the toe of his boot. "Just be careful."

Hugh grinned. "Always."

"Bullshit," Charlie laughed.

Garnet laughed too. "I barely know you, Hugh, and even I know that ain't true."

42

Honaker, Virginia

HUGH'S RIFLE was slung around his neck, and he held it by the grip to keep it from bouncing off his body. He kept his finger clear of the trigger guard, not wanting his "friendly" visit to be misinterpreted as something else. Most of the men were clustered around the train's boxcars, offloading packages onto ATV trailers. Hugh was walking casually down the tracks when one of the men spotted him. He didn't hear what was said, but two dozen men were suddenly holding rifles. Even those who'd been loading the trailers stopped what they were doing to monitor Hugh's approach. They didn't immediately take aim at him, but the message that he should be on his best behavior was clear.

Hugh noted a lack of trigger discipline as the men brandished their AKs, which made him glad those rifles weren't pointed at him. He figured it was safe to assume that those might be full-auto rifles as well. If something popped off, even if it was a random shot from a deer hunter somewhere within hearing range, it was likely that thousands of rounds would turn Hugh to ground chuck in less than a minute. One of the men spoke into a radio, presumably notifying the head honcho of Hugh's approach.

Hugh stopped about thirty feet from the closest man and greeted the party in Spanish. When there was no response, he asked if he could speak with the man in charge, though he assumed he'd already been called to the scene. Hugh's obvious familiarity with their language got no reaction from the men. He didn't do it to shock them but in hopes it might put them at ease. So far it didn't appear to be working. Hugh's command of the language wasn't textbook, but colloquial. He'd learned Spanish in the jungles, working for years on end alongside native speakers. He knew the idioms, the expressions, and the inflection that he hoped would demonstrate he might have shared some of the same experiences that these men knew.

Despite his fluency in their language, none of the men spoke to him in either Spanish or English. Hugh didn't take it personally. He assumed it was training and the men were disciplined. They were soldiers, at least in terms of their rank in the cartel he imagined they belonged to. Hugh had seen it before in those affiliated with cartels. The price of breaking rank could be high. Fatal even.

Hugh and the men stood in awkward silence until another man, presumably the one who'd been radioed, approached the scene. He was better dressed and didn't carry a rifle, though he wore a .45 Kimber automatic in a hip holster. He walked past his men without speaking, up to within ten feet of Hugh, and rested his hands on his hips. It wasn't an aggressive or defiant stance, but clearly one of authority.

"To what do I owe the pleasure of this visit?" Santos asked in English, studying Hugh closely.

Hugh plastered a smile on his face, hoping it didn't make him look like a psycho. "Yes, sir. I couldn't help but notice that you had an operational train. That's something we're not accustomed to seeing around these parts. At least not lately."

Santos nodded in acknowledgment of the obvious. "Yes, I'm aware that the United States is at somewhat of a standstill these days."

Hugh cleared his throat. "Don't take this wrong, but I'm curious as to what you're doing here. We've seen United Nations troops, and we've heard rumors of Chinese combatants. We've also seen every manner of American bureaucrat and turncoat that you can imagine. Is this an aid mission that you're conducting?"

Santos switched to Spanish. One of his men had told him over the radio that the gringo spoke their language, but he wanted to see it for himself. "Would your name happen to be Hugh? Are you the same man who inquired about our train after we left the last village?"

Hugh hid his cards well, but he was shocked at what Santos said. Not only had Santos provided someone in Finney with a method of communicating with him, whomever he'd entrusted with the task had actually done it. Hugh suspected it was Margaret. Hugh had only given his name to her and the boy from the trailer, but Margaret was definitely the sharper of the two. Whatever Santos had paid for her loyalty had worked and she was firmly tucked into his pocket. That she and Hugh were both Americans, both from the same local area, meant nothing to her when weighed against the bounty of an aid delivery.

Seeing no reason to lie, Hugh replied in comfortable Spanish. "Yes, my name is Hugh and I'm the one who asked about your train. Surely you must understand that a man cannot ignore the presence of strangers in his community during such challenging times. I can't begin to tell you how many battles, both large and small, we've been forced to wage against people who came into our community with bad intentions. I decided that I could lurk in the shadows and guess as to why you're here, or I could just come out and ask you. I favor the direct approach."

Santos smiled. "Your command of our language is impressive. It's obvious it's not from the classroom. You've spent time with native speakers."

It wasn't a question, so Hugh didn't answer. Like Margaret, he didn't offer information freely. In a moment, Santos continued, switching back to English.

"I appreciate directness, Hugh. To answer your question, we are not here with ill intentions. We are offering aid, though I admit it's a small gesture when weighed against the tremendous scale of the American disaster. However, it's only a start. We hope there will be more relief forthcoming."

"Can I ask who provides this aid?" Hugh didn't take his eyes off Santos.

Santos shrugged innocently. "It's not the Chinese. It's not NATO. It's not the traitorous politicians within your own government. Isn't that enough?"

Hugh smiled like he and Santos were both party to an inside joke. "There was a time in my life when I didn't have the luxury of asking who signed my checks. These days I prefer to know who's filling my pockets. Maybe it's not so much wisdom as experience that prompts me to ask those questions. Nothing in this world is free. Wouldn't you agree?"

Santos gestured down the tracks. "Would you believe that no one else has asked? Over a thousand miles we've come with thousands of hungry mouths asking to be fed. No one else seems to care who hands them a bag of food as long as they receive it."

"As I said, I know that all things come with a price. If people don't realize that, they're foolish."

Santos conceded that with a shrug. "Questions are the luxury of the well-fed. The hungry cannot afford to be so virtuous."

Hugh tilted his head. "Your point has merit as well."

Santos folded his arms across his chest. When he spoke, there was a twinkle in his eye. "You said it yourself, all things come with a price. What if the answer to your question comes with a price?"

Hugh didn't look away. "Then hopefully it's one I'm able to pay."

Santos laughed. "You have big balls, my friend. You come strolling into an unfamiliar situation, totally outnumbered, and make demands of someone with dozens of armed soldiers at his disposal."

Hugh held up a hand. "I make no demands. I'm simply asking questions. We're two men having a polite conversation. As to your army of men, who's to say that I don't have just as many encircling us right now? Who's to say that this conversation isn't being observed through dozens of rifle scopes?"

For a moment, Santos looked uncomfortable, then he burst out laughing again. "I don't believe you, Hugh. And even if I did, I don't scare easily."

Hugh grinned, but there was nothing friendly about his smile. "Nor do I."

Santos stared into Hugh's eyes for a long time, taking measure of the man. Finally, he said, "I work for a private business interest. An alliance of men of means who, for one thing, don't see Chinese control of the United States as being good for business. They believe their interests would be better served by getting in on the ground level of reconstruction."

Hugh nodded while Santos was speaking. When he was done, Hugh cocked his head to the side and squinted. "We're doing a lot of dancing here. Can I be blunt?"

Santos opened his arms. "Certainly."

Hugh gestured toward Santos' men. "I've never been to Mexico, but I spent a lot of time in Central America. I've met hundreds of cartel soldiers and even some lieutenants. My gut tells me that you men represent a cartel or perhaps even a conglomerate of several cartels. I'm practical enough to understand that in itself isn't necessarily a bad thing, but I'd feel better if you explained to me in blunt terms what the cartel's goal is here in America. I know you're not here to make me feel better, but it might save some hurt feelings down the road if you do."

"Whose feelings? Mine or yours?"

"I don't have feelings," Hugh said. "A man attempting to hurt mine has a full day of work ahead of him."

Santos laughed long and loud. "Again, the balls on this guy."

Hugh shrugged. "You gave me permission to be blunt."

"Yes, I did. May I ask you a question of you?"

"Go for it."

"Do you represent your own interests, Hugh? I know you said you were part of a group, but are you in charge of this group? Are you part of the leadership of this group?"

"I'm an advisor to the leader. We have a community that we

control or are responsible for, depending on how you want to look at it."

"Ah, I see," Santos said. "So, you are an advisor to the local warlord?"

Hugh was taken aback at that assessment of the situation. To an outsider it was probably accurate, and perhaps it even *was* representative of reality of the situation, but how would Jim respond to being characterized as a warlord? Hugh couldn't imagine it was a title he'd embrace since he'd been so hesitant to accept the mantle of leadership to begin with.

"I guess you could say that," Hugh finally conceded. He figured any attempts to reframe the description would be pointless. Maybe Santos' assessment of the situation was the most accurate for now.

"Is this warlord of yours a powerful man?"

"I think he is," Hugh said. "More powerful than he understands sometimes. He struggles with the responsibility of leadership, but he commands respect. People believe in him."

"Could I meet with this warlord? Do you think he would speak with me?"

"I believe he would," Hugh said. "But I can't speak for him, and it will take me at least a full day to return home and ask him."

"Assuming he agrees to meet, where would be a convenient place to hold this meeting?"

"The day after tomorrow in the town of St. Paul," Hugh replied. "It should be on the GPS or maps you're using for navigation. You passed through there about twenty-five miles ago. It's a bigger town, right on the river."

"Ah, I remember."

"My friend will ask what the meeting is to be about. What should I tell him?"

Santos considered this. "Obviously, my employers are businessmen. I wouldn't be here, and they wouldn't be spending the money they are if there wasn't an opportunity here for them. Do they want to profit? Yes, but they are also interested in getting the American marketplace back up and running. That requires goodwill and cooperation. Tell your warlord it's a friendly visit to discuss how we might be able to help each other."

"How do I know that you aren't trying to get our 'warlord' to a meeting so you can kill him?" Hugh asked.

Santos smiled. "You don't."

"So perhaps we show up with an army of our own."

"I would expect no less, Hugh. Before you go, I'm going to give you a satellite phone with my number programmed into it. If something changes, let me know. Otherwise, I'll expect to see you the day after tomorrow."

43

The Reset Roadhouse

"How's the bean counting going?" Jim stepped into a back office at the roadhouse and leaned against the door jamb.

Josie and her people were tabulating census data on their laptops, outside of the view of the public. "We're not done yet, but close. The teams still have a few outlying homes to visit, so maybe another couple of days and we'll have preliminary numbers."

"I'm sure that takes longer," Jim said. "There's more distance between houses."

"We also had to reduce the number of teams. There weren't enough spare horses for everyone."

"We asked Shade about hauling us around in the wagon," said Yana. "He said he had to get his work done first."

Jim cocked his shoulders. "Survival before census."

Josie cut him a look. "Have you been sitting on that line, waiting to use it?"

Jim laughed. "No, it just popped in my head."

"We think we found a house," Lamar blurted out. "That's a positive thing."

"Excellent! Which one?" Jim asked.

"A Victorian that was being used as an office before the collapse. It must have been an apartment at one time because it was pretty chopped up."

"The downstairs is contemporary, but the upstairs is very dated," said Yana. "Seventies paneling, avocado appliances, and this 1990s teal and purple paint scheme."

"Sadly, you've landed in a town with no interior decorators," Jim said. "What about the more important features?"

Josie ticked off items on her fingers. "It has a working woodstove, good windows, and no broken plumbing that we could find."

"Was it empty?" Jim teased. "Or did you have to boot some old lady to the curb?"

Josie smiled. "We ran into the owners while we were working on the census, and they overheard us talking about looking for a place. They said the house was winterized so the pipes wouldn't freeze, and they confirmed the woodstove worked. The house has been sitting empty since the collapse."

"I'm surprised it's in habitable condition," Jim said. "We had a lot of arson in the last year and a half. Then there were the people stripping old buildings of anything they could burn to stay warm."

"I don't know how it survived, but I'm glad it did," Josie said. "While I appreciate your hospitality, living in a bar isn't helping my productivity or my liver."

"I can relate." Jim chuckled. "Owning a bar has the same impact on my life. The other day my daughter asked me when I was taking up the banjo. I think she was trying to make a point."

Yana giggled. "Daughters."

"I know," Jim said. "So, when are you moving out?"

"Tomorrow," Josie told him. "Once Shade helps us haul our stuff over there, we're going to split into teams. Two of us will try to straighten the house out while Shade takes the other two to cut firewood."

"Food will be an issue," Jim noted.

"We'll probably be taking our meals here for a while," said Yana. "We're glad to trade our services for basic meals until we can come up with long-term provisions."

Josie raised a finger in the air. "Speaking of which, we hid some supplies at the armory, hoping we might be able to go back one day and retrieve them. We discussed making the trip with Shade. We included some weapons and ammunition in the cache. I told Shade he could have the pick of them if he'd take us up there."

"I'm sure he will," Jim said. "He likes to get out of town. He knows people everywhere. You'll need to take more shooters, though, in case things get hairy. Why don't you wait a few days and you can take Hugh, Ian, Conway, and Charlie. Hugh and Charlie might need a day or two to recover from the recon mission they're on now."

Jim tipped his head back and stared down the hallway toward the main room of the roadhouse. "I think I hear Cookie. He's been running around with Clay looking at infrastructure projects. Clay has a lot of good ideas."

"His Uncle Tim has been very enthusiastic about the census," Yana said. "I believe he's been conducting his own census, building a list of eligible women in the town."

Brendan snickered. "Yeah, he's been rating them each with some code he uses. I don't even want to know what it means."

"It's something to do with fruit," Lamar said. "Some get peaches, some get cherries, and some get pineapples. There's a few others."

Josie rested her head in her hands. "God help us. This was *not* what I intended when we discussed a census."

Jim laughed. "Oh, I can't wait to hear what Ellen has to say about Tim." He ducked out of the office, headed into the main room of the roadhouse, and spotted Clay and Cookie at the bar.

"How's it going?" Jim asked, leaning on the bar beside Clay.

"Not bad. You were right about Cookie. He knows the town inside and out. We've managed to locate nearly everything we need to get indoor grow operations going in four different locations."

Cookie was nodding along. "I've got people building raised beds.

I've got another guy who is putting together the oil burner stoves Clay designed for us. Other people are finding soil. I've got a whole team collecting jugs of oil that we can use to fuel the waste oil burners."

"Any trouble finding oil?" Jim asked.

Both Clay and Cookie shook their heads.

"You'd be shocked how much oil is sitting around this town once you start looking for it," Cookie said. "We'll end up with hundreds of gallons in just a few days and most of that will be from auto parts stores. Shade is supposed to make the rounds and deliver all of it in his wagon."

"What about lighting?" Jim asked.

"That took more time, but we found lights that will work," Clay said. "They're not perfect, but they'll get us started."

Jim was getting excited about this project. After bouncing the idea around with Hugh for nearly a year, getting the right people on the job had made it come together in a matter of days. "What about batteries?"

Clay and Cookie's faces sagged, taking Jim's along with them.

Randi delivered two beers and Clay took a sip of his. "Not ideal. We found more solar panels that were designed for powering highway caution signs, but the battery situation is lacking. We definitely need to find better batteries."

Jim sighed. "We need to go talk to Wrong Way. I had a few drinks with the guy last night and he said he'd let us take a look at the equipment in the building. I don't know what I'm looking at, so I need to take someone who does."

"Can we go now?" Clay asked.

"I don't see why not," Jim said. "Drain those beers and let's hit it."

It was a decent day for early winter. Jim guessed the temperature to be in the upper 40s with sun and no wind. While he had a horse, the others didn't so they chose to walk. It was less than a mile to the technology park and the walk would give them time to brainstorm without being interrupted. Getting sidetracked happened often when meetings were held at the roadhouse.

With the ideas flowing, the walk passed quickly. Jim lost track of time until they were closing in on their destination and Cookie stopped dead in his tracks. Jim started to ask him what was wrong but saw him staring at something in the distance. That was when Jim noticed Wrong Way crawling in the weeds on his hands and knees.

Assuming he'd been shot, Jim slung his rifle around, shouldered it, and scanned their surroundings. "Down!" he shouted at Cookie and Clay.

Then they all heard a protracted gagging and choking. Not the sound of someone gut shot or stabbed, but the sound of someone puking in the grass.

"Oh shit!" Jim rushed in Wrong Way's direction.

Still assuming the man might have been injured, Cookie demanded, "What's wrong? Did someone do something to you?"

Wrong Way turned to look at them with watery eyes, saliva dripping from his mouth. He raised a finger and pointed at Jim.

Jim rolled his eyes and slung his rifle around to his back. "Don't blame me for this! You're the one who said you could hold your liquor. You're the one who said you had a year and a half of drunks to catch up on. I guess you shouldn't have tried to catch up on them all in one night, huh?"

Wrong Way's reply came in the form of more projectile vomiting.

"Geez." Cookie shuddered and turned away. "I'm a sympathetic puker. I can't watch this."

Clay gagged. "*No one* wants to watch this."

"Why'd you let me drink that...poison?" Wrong Way moaned.

"I drank it too," Jim countered. "There was nothing wrong with it."

Clay and Cookie were standing about twenty feet away, their backs to Jim and Wrong Way. Cookie had his ears plugged with his fingers.

"We wanted to look at some of that battery backup equipment you mentioned," Jim mentioned.

Wrong Way tipped over onto his side and laid in the grass. "You're really going to ask me about that now?"

"We walked all the way down here."

Wrong Way rolled back onto his stomach and began throwing up again.

Cookie jammed his fingers into his ears even harder and began singing to drown out Wrong Way's sounds. "Lalalalalalalalalalalalalalalalalalalalala!"

Jim couldn't help but smile at the absurdity of the situation. Among his group of friends, only Hugh and Randi would have seen the same humor in the moment as he did. "Listen, man, I know you're not in any condition to do a tour right now."

Wrong Way shot Jim a complicated look. One that accused Jim of having a keen grasp of the obvious. One that warned there would be payback for this one day. "No shit."

"Is there a master key or something? I'm sure this building had biometric locks when the power was working, but there had to be a key. You think you might be able to let us in for a self-guided tour? I promise we won't take anything without asking."

Wrong Way rolled his eyes, then ran a shaky hand down to his belt, where he unclipped a ring of keys. He clumsily sorted through the ring, selected a key, and held it out to Jim. "Master...now let me die in peace."

Jim plucked the key from Wrong Way and patted the ailing man on the back. "Thanks, man." Jim walked away, digging his radio out of his vest.

"Is he done yet?" Cookie asked, barely unplugging his ears.

Wrong Way answered with an explosion of vomit. Cookie jammed his fingers back into his ears, crushed his eyes shut, and began singing again.

Jim stepped away and keyed the mic on his radio. "Jim for the roadhouse, Jim for the roadhouse."

"*Go for the roadhouse,*" Randi replied. "*You get lost?*"

Jim laughed. "No, but we found Wrong Way laying in the grass worshipping Ralph and claiming we poisoned him."

"*No one wants to accept responsibility for their own actions,*" Randi mused. "*Why am I always the bad guy?*"

"He's going to need some assistance. He's in rough shape."

"*That's not in my job description,*" Randi fired back in a sarcastic tone. "*I just create drunks, I don't fix them.*"

"I wasn't going to ask you to, Princess, but you think you could whip up one of your hangover helper concoctions? Find someone who can deliver it and sit with him for a while. Maybe Conway or somebody."

"*Conway is here. I'll send him.*"

"Thank you, Randi. Wrong Way will owe you one."

"*You'll owe me one,*" Randi corrected. "*You're the one who asked.*"

Jim ended the transmission without acknowledging Randi's comment, then rejoined Clay and Cookie. "I've got help on the way for him. The rest of us are going to take a tour."

"I don't think he heard you," Clay said, pointing at Cookie.

Cookie was humming loudly to himself, fingers jammed into his ears. Jim hooked a hand under Cookie's bicep and guided him toward the door.

44

IT WAS NEARLY dark when Jim, Clay and Cookie returned to the roadhouse. Randi's hangover helper drink, complete with electrolytes and pain meds, had settled Wrong Way enough that they were able to get him back inside the data center before they left. Conway had spent most of the afternoon with Wrong Way, then headed back to the roadhouse on his horse when Jim finally excused him from drunk-sitting.

Despite Wrong Way's condition, it had been a very productive trip. The amount and quality of the battery backup equipment they found had exceeded their expectations. It was state-of-the-art gear. Jim knew nothing about what he was looking at, but Clay estimated the batteries had cost more than a million dollars. They hadn't removed anything yet as they were way too heavy to extract without a team of men, rigging, heavy carts, and Shade's wagon. They had made an extensive list, however, complete with the specs on all the batteries they found. Clay said this list was the final bit of information required for him to design the solar grow rooms Jim wanted to build.

"I hate going into the season of darkness," Jim complained as they turned onto the street that held the roadhouse. "I need my daylight."

In the distance, music reverberated from the roadhouse. The few windows in the old brick building glowed from the solar lights strung across the ceiling. The air carried the smell of fires blazing in the woodstoves and the odor of some variety of meat roasting over a spit. They were halfway down the street when they heard the sound of hooves behind them.

Jim swung around, never comfortable with not knowing who was behind him. He saw three riders in silhouette in the distance. He not only recognized the weariness in their posture, but their profiles as well. He waved, uncertain of whether they could see him or not. Jim kept walking and by the time they reached the roadhouse, the riders had caught up with them.

"Welcome home," said Jim.

"Glad to be home." Charlie slipped off his horse. "I'm exhausted and my ass is killing me."

"We put in some miles," Hugh agreed.

Clay nudged Jim with his elbow. "Cookie and I are going to head inside and warm up. We'll catch you in a few."

"See you inside," Jim said, returning his attention to Hugh. "Eventful trip?"

Hugh climbed off his horse, put his hands on his hips, and arched his back. There was an audible pop. "There's a *lot* to talk about."

"I reckon I'll be heading back to the house," Garnet said. "It sounds a little noisy in there for me and the boys."

Garnet started to climb off his horse, but Hugh put a hand on his leg and stopped him. "You take the horse for tonight. Bring it back tomorrow and we'll see about getting you set up with one of your own. That sound fair?"

Garnet shook his head. "Don't sound fair at all. What have I done to deserve a horse?"

"You went on this operation as part of our team, and I'd be proud to ride with you again if you're willing to go."

Garnet shrugged uncomfortably. "If you say so."

Hugh unclipped one of the backpacks from his horse and hung one of the shoulder straps over Garnet's saddle horn. "Take this too. It's the food we didn't eat."

Garnet stared at the pack. "I ain't used to charity. Not so much to kindness either."

"Garnet, I don't think the problem is you not being used to charity. I think the problem is you're not used to being part of a group. You're not used to being valued for the person you are. We appreciate you and hope you'll come around on a regular basis."

Garnet was silent for a long time. He couldn't bring himself to speak, but he didn't have to. The silence that emanated from him wasn't one of protest, but of something unfamiliar stirring inside. Something he was afraid to give voice to for fear that voice would crack and through that crack would pour emotions that he cared not expose to the light of day.

Finally, Garnet turned his horse. "Come on, boys. Let's go home."

"He's an interesting character," Charlie said when Garnet was out of earshot. "It was fun hearing his stories. I got some new ones on Hugh too. I can't wait to tell Pete."

Jim patted Charlie on the shoulder. "He's inside now. Feed and water that horse before you go in."

"I was planning on it," Charlie said with that tone of a teenager who feels like he's too old to have an adult looking over his shoulder.

"I'm sure you were," Jim said.

Hugh pulled his pack off his horse. "Charlie, do you mind taking mine too?"

Charlie grabbed the reins. "I don't mind a bit."

When Charlie was gone, Jim asked Hugh, "Who was Garnet talking about?"

"What do you mean?"

"The boys? He kept talking about the boys. Said it was time for them to get on home."

Hugh mulled it over, looking for the words. "There's a lot of men with demons, Jim."

"I reckon I know a little bit about that," Jim admitted. "I'm sure you do too."

"I ain't never met a man who knew his demons quite the way Garnet does. Most of us get a break from them. I don't think Garnet's ever leave."

"That's a hell of a thing to think about."

"That's a fact," Hugh said. "I'm sure it's a hell of a thing to live with too."

Ian was working the door and he ushered Jim and Hugh inside. The dim lights of the roadhouse were a little brighter than the outside, but not so much as to hurt the eye. It was a soothing, comfortable darkness that was almost as much of a home to Jim now as his place in the valley. That realization had been unsettling the first time it came to him as he'd never considered himself a town person. At the same time, he'd never considered himself a leader, either, and here he was shouldering that responsibility now.

"The bar?" Jim asked.

Hugh thought about it for a moment, then shook his head. "We need privacy, but I need food first. Are Josie and her people around?"

Jim searched the bar. "They should be here somewhere. Maybe in the back."

"Let's you and I talk first, then we can involve them later."

"Copy that. You talk to the kitchen and find some food. I'm going to let Ellen know I'm back, then we'll take over an office."

After a few minutes of searching, Jim found Ellen having a drink with Josie, Yana, and some of the census crew. He told her that Hugh had something he wanted to discuss in private, but he'd find her when he was done. She seemed curious about what they were going to discuss but didn't ask. She knew Jim would tell her when he had time to go into detail.

Jim started for the back, then made a slight detour to the roped off area where Ed manufactured most of the liquor sold at the road-house. He opened a locked cabinet to which only he and Ed had a key, then removed one of the special bottles of liquor from the cabinet. When a batch of liquor turned out especially well, Ed used a Sharpie to label the cap with the letters "ER", which stood for Ed's Reserve. Those letters meant it was among the "shiniest" of the shine they produced. Jim grabbed two glasses and headed for the back office.

Hugh was already there, eating heartily from a plate he'd put together in the kitchen. It was beef stew ladled over rice, a meal that was not only filling, but delicious. Jim had some earlier and was impressed. It wasn't always easy to come up with varied dishes when the supply of spices and ingredients was so inconsistent.

"Good, huh?"

Hugh nodded with his mouth full. He was often like this when he returned from a recon mission. He might barely eat for days when he was on the trail, but he returned with a ravenous need to balance his caloric deficit.

Giving Hugh a little more time to eat, Jim said, "Clay, Cookie, and I visited the data center this evening. Clay came back with an extensive list of the batteries we found in the backup equipment. He says it should be enough to get some of our grow room projects off the ground."

Jim uncapped the bottle of Ed's Reserve—blackberry obviously—and poured a few fingers in each glass. He capped the bottle and slid one glass over to Hugh, then leaned back in his chair with his own glass. The chair came with the office and it was comfortable. Jim would have propped his feet on the desk, but it seemed rude when Hugh was eating at the same desk, only a few feet away.

"How did Garnet do?"

"He did fine," Hugh said. "He's a troubled man, but a good man. We enjoyed having him along."

"Is he solid? Did you feel like he had your back?"

"Yeah. I wasn't sure what to expect as we learned more about his problems, but his instincts are good. I felt certain he'd have been an asset if we ran into trouble."

"That's good to know."

"We caught up with that train," Hugh said between bites.

Jim was glad Hugh finally broached the topic because he was getting antsy waiting for a report. He was determined to let Hugh offer up any information at his own pace. He had a way of organizing the data in his mind so that he remembered the most detail. Jim knew by this point in their relationship that pushing him only disrupted Hugh's systematic presentation and increased the chance he might leave out something important.

"I'm kind of surprised you located it," Jim said. "I figured this would be more of a detective mission really. Finding people who'd seen the train and trying to build a picture from their eyewitness reports."

"It was like that up until the train headed into Honaker and had to stop at the burned-out trestle. That's where we caught them."

Although the questions were piling up in Jim's head, he did his best not to burst out with fifty of them in one breath. "You were able to observe the train directly?"

Hugh scraped his plate clean and placed the fork on it, then drained the last of his water bottle. Only then did he pick up the blackberry moonshine and lean back in his chair facing Jim. "I observed them from almost as close as we're sitting now."

Jim raised his eyebrows. "How'd you do that?"

"I walked right up to them and asked to speak to the man in charge. We had a nice conversation."

Jim's jaw practically hit the ground. "Hugh! Think that's a little risky?"

Hugh shrugged and took a sip of the liquor. "Sometimes it's the only way. We spoke to some people in Finney who had interacted with the men on the train. From that information I gathered that the people on the train were on a mission to build goodwill, just like the cartels are known to do in in their native countries. I felt speaking to them was a reasonable risk as long as I behaved myself."

"So, what is it they do in in their native countries?"

"In Mexico and Central America, the cartels sometimes build loyalty among poorer communities by distributing food and goods there. Cartels will run truck caravans through villages and hand out microwaves and other appliances. People remember things like that. So, when one of the residents of Finney let slip that they'd received aid from the train, I started to think that might be their mission instead of something more violent."

Jim leaned forward and placed his glass on the desk so he could talk using both hands. "But it's still the cartel, right? They don't do anything for free or out of the goodness of their hearts. There has to be a motive. There has to be something in it for them."

Hugh reached into his coat pocket, retrieved the satellite phone that Santos had given him, and slid it across the desk to Jim. Jim stared at the phone without touching it.

"Is that Josie's phone?" Jim asked.

"No, it was a gift from Santos, the man in charge of the train we were following."

"Why did he give you a phone?"

"He didn't," Hugh said. "It's for you."

Jim pointed at himself. "Me?"

"Santos wants to meet with the local warlord."

Jim met Hugh's eye, the impact of that comment settling on him. He leaned back in his chair, a confused look on his face as he tasted that word. "Warlord?"

45

The Reset Roadhouse

THE NEXT MORNING Jim convened the first meeting of his advisory council. The membership wasn't locked in stone and Jim assumed he'd tailor the invitations to match whatever situation that he needed to take before them. This morning's membership included some of the people he most trusted in the world. The roadhouse wasn't yet open for the day, and they opted to meet in the immense dining room and bar area because it was much warmer than the conference room in the back, which had no woodstove or other heat source.

"If we were holding this meeting two years ago, I'd be offering you coffee and donuts," Jim said, pacing around his seated guests. "Best I can offer this morning is liquor and leftover bread."

"We might be able to do a little better than that. The kitchen is putting together some ham biscuits," Gary offered. "You're welcome to drink liquor if you want, but we have water also."

"Thanks, Gary," Jim said. "Funny how the person least suited to be a host ends up running a roadhouse."

Randi emitted something between a laugh and a cough. "Not

nearly so ironic as how the person who hates people the most ends up accepting responsibility for so many of them. Now *that's* freaking funny."

Jim cringed at the truth of it.

"You know I'm right!" Randi said.

She was. Jim couldn't argue. He looked around at the assembled group of people he'd come to accept as his tribe. There was Ellen, who'd been by his side all along, and Hugh, who was one of his oldest friends. Lloyd was also one of his oldest friends, though not exactly suitable as an advisor, so he wasn't participating in this meeting. While he was great for comic relief, he wasn't the guy you went to with potentially life-changing tactical and political situations.

Others who'd gathered for the meeting were some of the people Jim had become closest to in this new life. There was Gary and Randi, the two with whom he shared an indescribable bond from the experiences they went through trying to make it home from Richmond. They'd seen each other at their lowest and most miserable. They'd supported each other when it seemed all was lost. Perhaps most importantly, they'd literally helped each other dispose of the bodies when they'd been forced to take lives. They might not be related by blood, but the three of them shared a bond that went beyond friendship.

Jim brought in some relative newcomers who, by one way or another, found themselves dumped there in that place and time. There was Shade, Ian, Cookie, Clay, Josie, and Wrong Way. They were also part of the tribe now, united by the single, imperative goal of survival and success.

"As most of you know, I'm a reluctant leader," Jim began, "but this is where the road led me. When I accepted this role, I imagined that most of what I had to contribute to the people of my community would be along the lines of setting up infrastructure projects to improve our living conditions. Now, for our very first meeting, we find ourselves facing a situation that stands to have a significant impact on our future."

Jim looked around the room and saw that he had everyone's full attention. Some of them knew what he was about to talk about. Others would be hearing it for the first time.

"I don't consider myself to be a violent man, but I've often become one to get my family and friends this far. Despite what some might think, I don't wake up each morning and pull on a shirt that says Choose Violence."

Randi barked out a laugh, which Jim acknowledged with one of his crooked smiles.

"I don't think I'm being overly dramatic when I say that the situation we're facing is major. It could be a crossroads where the choice that I make—that *we* make—determines how the foreseeable future goes. I need your help to make sure I do the right thing here. Hugh, tell the group the story you told me last night. Tell them about the train."

It took Hugh about thirty minutes to thoroughly retell his story. With Jim's advisory council potentially playing a role in his decision-making process, Jim felt they needed to hear it all. They didn't ask as many questions as Jim had the previous night, but they listened intently. Jim caught some interesting looks when Hugh mentioned Santos referring to Jim as a "warlord."

When they were done, Wrong Way repeated the word just as Jim had last night, as if it couldn't be understood without speaking it aloud.

"Warlord...?"

"I had the same reaction to that title," said Jim. "I've been wondering for days if this job came with a title, but that sure as hell wasn't the one I imagined. I was quick to reject it when Hugh told me the story since 'warlord' has so many negative connotations, but maybe it's a mistake to reject it. If that's a term these people understand, then perhaps that's the title I need to assume when I meet with them."

The room exploded, though it wasn't from Jim potentially adopting the title of warlord. It was from the idea of Jim meeting with the people on the train. Ellen, Randi, Gary, Josie, and Ian were all protesting at the same time. Jim was a little surprised to see Ellen protesting so vehemently. She'd had the opportunity to voice her concerns last night when he told her Hugh's story, but she must have been too tired. With a full night's sleep under her belt, she'd come out swinging.

"It was bad enough when you'd make trips into town a year ago, knowing everyone here hated you and wanted to kill you. I never knew if you were coming home or not. This cartel guy sent you a phone. Just call him and talk with him. What's the point of meeting him face-to-face? Why put yourself in danger?"

Jim tried to keep his voice neutral. "This is different than those trips into town. That was about protecting you and the kids. It was about refusing to submit to intimidation. That was about warning people to leave us the hell alone. In this case, we *know* China is coming and they'll reach us at some point. We have to do something. Josie, were you able to find out anything about their progress?"

Josie looked grim. "After we talked last night, I spoke to my counterpart at the Charlottesville aid distribution center. They were forced to close just like we were when the wireless grid collapsed. They abandoned their center much sooner. She said people rumored to be Chinese military contractors had been active there in Charlottesville for about two weeks. The contractors are weeding out pockets of resistance and assuming control of the area. They're clearing roads, setting up checkpoints, and distributing pamphlets explaining their mission in America so people will know what to expect."

"Shit, how far is that?" Wrong Way asked. "Two hundred and fifty miles or so?"

"About that," Jim acknowledged.

"How are these Chinese contractors traveling?" Gary asked. "Are they on foot?" His hope was evident in his voice.

"Primarily," Josie said. "They do have some air support available, according to observers. Not enough for mass troop transport, but sufficient to move elite teams. The choppers launch from merchant ships anchored off the East Coast or from bases in Mexico."

Shade sat up straight, scooting to the very edge of his seat. It was the most agitated Jim had ever seen him. Something had rattled him. "Okay, I clearly haven't been taking this seriously enough. Somehow, I had the impression that Chinese contractors had a presence on the coast, but it sounds like you're talking about something along the lines of an *invasion*."

"It's a soft invasion at this point," Josie explained. "Once the rest of the world gets over their pearl-clutching and outrage, the assumption is that China will ramp up their efforts. In fact, China is already trying to draw world attention away from what's happening here by increasing military tension with Taiwan. Once the international community is thoroughly distracted, more contractor teams will most certainly be appearing on our shores."

"Why contractors?" Ian asked. "Isn't China legendary for their massive army? Why don't they just send troops?"

"Contractors are a gray area," Wrong Way said with the certainty of someone who knew that world from the inside. "Every nation in the world enjoys using contractors in ways they could never use troops. The use of a nation's military forces triggers all this international scrutiny that isn't applied to contractors in the same way. No nation can afford to be too outraged by the presence of contractors since they all do it."

"That's true," said Hugh. "I've been there."

Wrong Way met Hugh's eye. "As have I."

Nothing Shade had heard had served to calm him down. He raised a hand in the air, though that wasn't necessary for him to keep the group's attention. At his size, with the volume of his voice, he commanded attention through sheer presence alone. "So, if these Chinese contractors walk here, we could potentially run into them in the next two weeks, depending on how much resistance they run into as they move across the state. If they use air assets, we could run into these special teams you're talking about any day now. Like even *today*."

"All that is possible," Jim said. "Which is why having this meeting right away was so important. Which is why I feel like I can't ignore the people on the train."

"These people on the train basically admitted to being cartel, right?" Wrong Way asked Hugh.

"They did," said Hugh. "I had enough experience with cartels in Central America to make an educated guess, but the man in charge of this train, Santos, admitted that he worked for an alliance of cartels. He sugar-coated things and referred to it as a private business interest, but the truth is obvious."

Wrong Way wasn't excited by what was being suggested. "Getting in bed with the cartels is risky business. I have friends who were involved with anti-cartel operations through federal agencies and the stories they told were horrifying. It's stuff you'll want no part of."

"I understand all that," Jim said. "But a choice has to be made or it's going to be made for us. Do I meet with the train people and hear what they have to say, or do we choose to go it alone and fight it out with the Chinese?"

"I got no problem with a fight," said Shade.

"If we're only facing small units one at a time, we might have half a chance," Gary said.

Jim's expression was utterly serious as he faced his old friend. "Think about what half a chance means, Gary. These are small units of highly trained men with better weapons and better gear than us. We're short-handed already and we'd inevitably lose some of our people. Look around this group and consider that."

Shade leaned back and folded his arms across his chest. "I don't go down without a fight."

"I'm not suggesting we surrender," said Jim. "I'm suggesting we should probably do the thing that best increases our odds of survival and buys us some time. We just need to decide which curtain that choice is behind."

"Would we have to fight the cartel if we refuse their help?" Gary asked. "Would they come after us?"

Jim deferred to Hugh on that one.

"That's undetermined," Hugh said. "I'm not sure they're in a position to wage war against every community who refuses their help. I can't imagine very many do, though—not when they're handing out food and gear. We would likely be small fish to them, and they'd have no need to bother with us. In the end, they're businesspeople, not invaders. They want wealth and markets for their goods, not conquest."

"So, what would the cartels get out of helping us drive the Chinese out?" Randi asked. "What's in it for them?"

"That's a question I'll specifically be asking if I meet with Santos," Jim said. "After talking with Hugh, we think their goal is to re-establish markets. They need America to function on some level, so they have customers for their products, whatever those products happen to be."

Josie spoke up then. "While the Chinese have been longstanding suppliers to the cartels, selling them the precursor chemicals for the drugs that flood America, the cartels understand that the Chinese will not tolerate them operating in America if China succeeds in taking over the country. They only helped flood the country with drugs so they could weaken America. If China takes over, there will be new rules, and the cartels understand they probably won't be favorable for them."

"It's a long-term play on the cartels' part and I'd bet it's way bigger than you people imagine," Wrong Way said. "With no law enforcement to stop them, the cartels will root themselves so deeply in America that they'll never be driven out again. America may get back on its feet again one day, but we'll be a third-world nation with no constitutional rights. The cartels will set the rules and establish the standard of justice. That's why they're working together in an alliance. They want to own this country."

"We need to zoom in," said Hugh. "Let's not blow this up to the point we can't decide on what's before us today. Jim isn't responsible for single-handedly determining the fate of the United States. This exact debate will probably take place thousands of times around the country. Maybe it has already, though admittedly we're up against the wall because the Chinese are getting closer."

"What do you need from us, Jim?" Cookie asked. "I've lost track of the question in all this discussion. Do you need an opinion from us or just support?"

Jim took a deep breath. "I feel like I need to call this Santos guy and take his offer of a meeting. I just wanted you folks to understand the potential consequences. It's more than a meet and greet with a stranger passing through the area. I might be asked to agree to certain conditions, and I won't be able to run each and every decision by you under the circumstances. If I go, I have to go into this meeting with the ability to negotiate and set terms. You have to trust me. If anything, I guess that's what I'm asking for."

"Well hell," Shade boomed. "You had that all along."

"And my support is obvious," Ellen said.

Randi nodded. "Mine too."

"And me," Gary said, raising a hand.

Jim nodded as he took in the show of support. "So, is there anybody dead set against it?"

Wrong Way stared at Jim. "I'm dead set against you going *alone.*"

"Copy that," Hugh said. "I agree we need a team in place."

"What are you doing?" Ellen asked. "Are you calling him?"

Jim looked up from the satellite phone, which was in the process of powering up. "Yeah."

"Then I guess trying to talk some sense into you is over?" She crossed her arms and bobbed her foot.

Jim winked. "Never was much point to that."

"Truth!" Randi laughed.

The phone began ringing and Jim held up a hand to silence everyone as he pressed it to his ear.

"*Hello.*" The voice was deep, with a Hispanic accent. The greeting wasn't a question, but an acknowledgement. Santos knew to whom he was speaking. He obviously kept track of who had his phones. "*Can I assume I'm speaking to the warlord of this region?*"

Jim leaned into the title. "Yes, you can, Mr. Santos. I'm here with my security council right now and we were just discussing the meeting you proposed."

"*What is your decision?*"

"I accept your invitation. St. Paul is a day's ride for us. Can we meet tomorrow at sunset?"

"I'm agreeable to that," Santos replied. *"I'd rather not stop our train in town, though. It draws too much attention."*

"Do you have access to maps or GPS?"

"Both."

Although Jim was working from memory here, he was familiar enough with the area that he was certain he was recalling it accurately. "Directly south of the town, both the river and the tracks make a hard bend near a rock quarry."

"Give me a moment to see if I can locate that."

Jim heard Santos breathing into the phone as he pulled up whatever navigational device he was using. Nearly a minute passed before he spoke. *"Ah, I see exactly where you're talking about. That looks private enough that the townspeople won't be an issue."*

"Excellent," Jim replied. "I'll find you there around sunset then. I'll be bringing my advisor with me. I believe you two already met."

"Please do," Santos replied. *"And if you have one available, bring a spare horse. I'll send you home with a few gifts from the outside world."*

"I'll do that. Goodbye, Mr. Santos."

Jim ended the call, but held onto the phone, contemplating the weight of what he'd just done. Like so many other moments since the collapse, he'd acted in the only way he knew how, fully aware that it was impossible to understand all the possible implications of the things he did. When he looked around the room, at the silent faces of his people, he could see that they understood the gravity of the moment as well.

"So, it's on," he said. "What now?"

Hugh stood and pushed his chair beneath the table. "I'll get a team together. I want to be out of town by afternoon. If we ride into the night, we can be in position by morning and catch a few hours' sleep." He pointed at Wrong Way. "You in?"

"Wouldn't miss it," Wrong Way replied.

46

The Valley

SIX HOURS LATER, a group of men were gathered in Jim's barn, double-checking their gear and loading horses. They'd chosen to leave from the valley because Jim and Hugh had so much of their "special" gear stored there. Not all the battlefield pickups they'd accumulated since the collapse were sold at the roadhouse. Weapons with full-auto or burst fire capability went into Jim or Hugh's armories. Suppressors, night vision gear, or thermal scopes were retained for situations just like this one. Same with body armor, holsters, and load-bearing gear.

They'd found a horse for Wrong Way and brought him to the valley with them. He said he hadn't ridden a horse since he was a kid, but he'd done fine between the town and the valley. Wrong Way had an impressive load of gear and seemed excited about the opportunity to go on an operation again, even if the hope was that this one wouldn't turn into a firefight. In addition to Wrong Way and Hugh, the team consisted of Shade, Conway, Ian, Gary, Charlie, Pete, Garnet, and Cookie. They were all men Jim and Hugh had determined were capable behind a gun and had the temperament for an operation like this.

"I was at the rock quarry recently and there's no one living there," Hugh told the group. "There's a lake for watering the horses and enough overgrown grass to give them something to graze on while we're there. Charlie and Pete, you guys are watching the horses."

"Got it," Pete said.

There was a day when Pete and Charlie would have argued over being assigned a duty like that, but they were growing up, certainly through experience if not by age. They understood that someone had to watch the horses, and the mission was best served by not whining about being assigned one of the less glamorous jobs.

"Does everyone have a warm sleeping bag?" Jim asked. "We've got extras so don't be shy about asking if aren't sure about the one you brought."

Two of the men weren't sure about theirs so Hugh upgraded them from Jim's Daddy Shack, the storage building where Jim stockpiled his best gear. Once that was out of the way, those with the most horse experience helped the others load their horses. While this was taking place, Jim, Shade, Wrong Way, and Hugh stepped outside.

"We should make it to the quarry early in the morning," Hugh said. "I'll get Pete and Charlie set up with the horses, then the rest of us will get into position in the woods. Wrong Way is going to run the overwatch tomorrow evening since I'll be going with you."

"I don't know who your strongest shooters are," Wrong Way said. "I'll need Hugh to school me on that while we're riding. I'd like to have four strong snipers, including myself, in the best positions. The rest of the team will be there to provide muscle if all hell breaks loose."

"Put me down as one of your snipers," Shade said. "I brought my long-range setup and I know how to run it. I can shoot the balls off a billy goat at eight hundred yards if it comes to that."

Hugh patted Shade on the shoulder. "Hopefully, it won't come to that. Ideally no has to fire a shot, whether at cartel soldiers or billy goat balls."

"Definitely," Jim agreed. "Everyone has comms?"

Hugh nodded. "Radios have been tested and distributed. Wrong Way and I have codes established so I can let him know during the meeting if things are starting to go downhill. Everyone on the team has a list of those codes."

"No offense, but can they remember them?" Jim asked. "I don't want any crossed signals, someone shooting when they should be standing down."

"They should be able to remember them," Hugh said. "I personally wrote them down on everyone's arms with permanent marker. I'm not taking any chances."

Jim smiled. "Good man."

"So what time are you leaving?" Hugh asked.

Jim blew out a breath. "I'll leave at first light tomorrow. I'll meet up with Pete and Charlie at the quarry, then reach out to you. We can coordinate from there."

"That'll work," Hugh said.

Jim approached the rest of the team. It looked like everyone had finished securing their gear and was awaiting the order to mount up. Jim went to each man and shook his hand.

"I feel like I'm in good hands," he said. "You men be safe tomorrow. Don't just watch out for me. Watch out for each other."

When he reached Pete and Charlie, Jim pulled the two into a hug. "I'll be seeing you boys tomorrow. The same warning goes for you. Be safe and watch out for each other."

"Love you, Dad," Pete said.

"I love you too, Pete," Jim said. "And I love you too, Charlie."

"I love you, Jim," Charlie said.

Jim remembered that age and the awkwardness he'd felt then at expressing emotions. These boys didn't have that. There was a finality that hung over each and every moment in this world, the understanding that this could be the last opportunity they ever had to express how they felt about someone. They wanted there to be no confusion or misunderstanding. They left nothing on the table.

When they loved someone, they made sure that person knew without a doubt.

Once they'd said their goodbyes to Jim, the boys ran to the front porch to hug Ellen and Ariel. Jim watched from the barn knowing that it ate at Ellen's soul to see Pete ride off into a situation like this. At the same time, she understood that making him stay home when everyone else was going would embarrass him in a way that would make him resentful. He had to go and they had to let him.

Finally, Jim shook Hugh's hand. "I'll see you tomorrow, buddy. Be safe."

"You be safe as well. If anyone can manage to find trouble on a peaceful ride across the countryside, it'll be you."

"Let's hope not," Jim said. "I'm determined to play nice...until I can't."

Jim stepped to the side as the last of the men mounted their horses and rode off. They were taking the shortcut through the field, where they'd cross the river, ride through town, then continue down Route 71. They had a long day ahead of them, a day Jim would repeat tomorrow. He turned toward the house and met Ellen's eye long enough to see hers were filled with tears. She went inside without waiting on him, preferring to work through her emotions before they burst out of control.

Jim knew she didn't blame him for the situation. This world wasn't of his making. Not what was happening today, not what had happened over the last year and a half. Even if she didn't blame him for the state of the world, Jim wasn't sure that he could ever stop blaming himself. He remembered those days before the collapse when people whined incessantly on social media. He'd been one of those who wished for a reset, not fully grasping what the consequences of such a reset would be. He knew he hadn't singlehandedly brought this disaster down upon his nation, but there would always be that memory, that guilt.

47

The Reset Roadhouse

THE MOOD at the roadhouse was somber that evening with so many big personalities absent. Most of the patrons didn't know about the train and Santos. They had no reason to know. It was Jim's role now to deal with things like that. Yet the absence of their friends, their coworkers, their family, had all the staff behaving in a more subdued manner than usual. Jim was in the store portion of the roadhouse, hanging clothes on racks, when Lloyd marched up to him.

"You got a minute?"

Jim took in his oldest friend. He appeared more serious than usual. "You look like a man on a mission."

"I am. Can we go outside a second?"

Jim grinned. "You gonna whip my ass or something?"

Lloyd smiled back. "If that was my plan, I'd do it on stage for everyone to see. It'd be like the good old days when they had wrestling in the high school gym with Ric Flair, the Macho Man, and the Mongolian Stomper."

"Do I need a jacket?" Jim asked.

"Nah, it'll only take a minute."

"You resigning or something? Giving up the banjo?"

"None of that," Lloyd said. "How about you just shut up for a minute and come on?"

Jim sighed and followed Lloyd out the front door. The night was cold and silent, as if the world itself was feeling the same melancholy that the roadhouse crew was feeling.

"So, what's going on?" Jim asked.

"I'm going with you tomorrow."

Jim didn't answer for a moment. They hadn't kept the council meeting or the ensuing operation from Lloyd. They weren't a secret, but Lloyd knew there was nothing he could contribute to either of those efforts, so he hadn't complained. Yet here he was with something clearly on his mind.

"We all have our areas of expertise, Lloyd. I explained to you why I didn't need you at that council meeting. I'm not saying you won't be needed at a future one, but this one didn't mesh with any of your strengths." Jim couldn't let it pass, so he added, "Assuming you have any."

Lloyd didn't take the bait. "To hell with that meeting. I don't care about that, and I damn sure don't care about sitting in the woods all night like the rest of them are doing. I ain't talking about any of that. I'm talking about you setting out toward St. Paul on your own tomorrow. I'm not letting that happen."

"Did someone put you up to this?" Jim asked. "Ellen? Randi?"

Lloyd blew out a frustrated breath. "No, dammit! You're my oldest friend. My best friend. You know I'm not a fighter, but you're not headed out alone tomorrow and that's final. What time are you leaving?"

"Sunup."

For a second, Jim caught a flash of Lloyd's expression in the light coming from the roadhouse and it looked like he might be regretting his decision. Sunup came early for a man who enjoyed drinking and playing music all night, whether he was onstage or not.

"I'll be ready," Lloyd said. "Where are you leaving from?"

"Home."

"I'll be outside your house waiting at sunup," Lloyd said. "Don't leave without me or I'll be highly pissed. That a deal?"

Jim nodded.

"You promise?"

"Yes, I promise, Lloyd. I won't leave without you."

Lloyd put his hands on his hips, satisfied with himself. "Good. Now that we've got that solved, I need to get my ass on stage. I taught the band a special number that we're debuting tonight."

"Oh yeah?"

Lloyd grinned. "You betcha. We're doing 'Dead Skunk in the Middle of the Road' by Loudon Wainright III. You remember that one?"

"Of course I remember it and I feel honored to be here, Lloyd. Truly."

"You should be." Lloyd headed for the door.

48

The Valley

JIM WAS PERFORMING a final check of his loadout the next morning when he heard a horse approaching the house. He cracked the curtain and saw Lloyd, true to his word, sitting atop one of Randi's horses. Jim's horse was already saddled, loaded, and tied off to the porch rail. He gave Ariel and Ellen one last hug, then stepped out the door.

Jim made it halfway down the steps before he got a good look at Lloyd in the gray light of morning. "What the hell is that around your neck?"

Lloyd looked down. "Oh, this little thing?"

"Yes, that! It damn sure ain't a banjo."

Lloyd took it by the grip and held it in the air. "It's a Thompson machine gun."

"Is that the one Nooner gave you? I thought you couldn't hit the broad side of a barn with it."

"The one Nooner gave me was a semi-automatic replica. This one is the real deal."

"You've got a banjo *and* a full-auto Tommy gun? These are indeed dangerous times for the American people."

Lloyd grinned mischievously. "It came with a half-dozen drum magazines and a thousand rounds of ammo. I got it off a retired trooper. Apparently, it was being held as evidence in a drug case up until the collapse, then it mysteriously went missing, along with a lot of other things."

"What did it cost you?"

"I'm almost embarrassed to say."

Jim cringed. "Now I'm almost afraid to ask."

Lloyd waved him off. "Nothing that bad, but it's a little strange."

"You need to just come out and tell me because it's getting worse in my head every minute you drag this out!"

"The trooper's ex-wife hated the banjo almost as much as he hated her. The deal is I have to go to her grave once a week for an entire year and play for an hour. He gave me a list of the songs she hated the most and I built a playlist around it. She especially hated 'Sally Ann', so I play that one twice."

"Hell, I don't even know what to think about that, Lloyd. I don't know what's worse—him offering the deal or you taking it."

Lloyd raised the Thompson in the air again. "I don't see a thing wrong with it. It ain't like she can hear me, and I finally got the gun of my dreams. Wanna burn off a mag and wake up the neighborhood?" He laughed an evil laugh.

Jim mounted his horse. Once he was in the saddle he adjusted his gear until everything was settled and positioned comfortably, his rifle hanging across the front of his body. "How about you save your ammo in case we really need it, Al Capone?"

Lloyd seemed disheartened for a second then shrugged. "This horse would probably appreciate me wasting some. Its legs nearly buckled when I loaded my ammo."

Jim swung his horse around and the two of them headed off through the pasture toward the river.

"Still packing that .32?" Jim teased.

"No, you'd be proud. I'm .45 caliber all the way this morning. I'm carrying my old friend Buddy's 1911."

"I'm impressed."

"What are you carrying?" Lloyd asked.

"This M4 has a giggle switch for full-auto, and I've got my Beretta on the chest rig. Then I've got a baby Glock in my waistband and a North American Arms .22 in an ankle holster. Rounding out my ensemble is three blades, two grenades, and a partridge in a pear tree."

Lloyd chuckled. "No one does paranoia like Jim Powell."

"Well, I've lost track of how many times people have tried to kill me, so I leave the house each day assuming I might be fighting for my life."

"Hell, I'm a banjo player. I know a thing or two about people trying to kill me."

Jim cracked up. "You just told a banjo joke on yourself. Now that's funny."

"Ain't no wonder. All your banjo jokes have eroded my self-esteem. I hope you feel bad about it."

"I'd venture to say that playing the banjo has eroded your self-esteem," Jim shot back. "Can't be good for a man's sense of value and personal well-being. Hell, I'd hate to speculate on how bad a man must hate himself to carry one of those infernal things around and perform in public with it."

"You'd think a sonofabitch would be more appreciative of his best friend riding into danger with him. We haven't even left your property yet and you're flogging me like a rented mule."

"You started the banjo jokes," Jim said. "Not me."

"Well, if you'll allow me to change the subject, I have to admit I'm kind of excited about this trip. You and I haven't had a good road trip since we went over to the music camp that time."

"I'm hoping this one will be less eventful."

"Me too." Lloyd sighed. "Still, it reminds me of the old days. Road trips and cruising around in some of those old beaters I had."

"*Pushing* those old beaters as much as riding in them. Repairing them with coat hangers so we could get home. Having to use vise grips to shift. Having to sit on cinder blocks in that old Chevy when you tore out the interior."

Lloyd stared off wistfully. "Yeah, those were the good old days."

"You don't seem too miserable right now."

"You mean this minute or in general?"

"In general."

Lloyd leaned in Jim's direction like he was sharing a conspiracy, then he giggled. "I'm not miserable at all. I love this. Sometimes I feel bad that so many people died or are suffering, but this is the world I feel like I was missing my entire life."

"The apocalypse?" Jim asked. "You watch too much *Mad Max* as a kid? Read *The Stand* too many times?"

"Nah, man, not the apocalypse. That's not what I meant at all. What I see is the world of the early twentieth century. To hell with the internet, computers, and television. I'm back in 1900 and having the time of my life. I don't get up each day looking at what we've lost in the world. I look at what we've gained."

Jim had his own ideas about it, but he wanted to hear Lloyd's. "What have we gained? What have *you* gained?"

"We devote our time to what matters. We take care of each other and spend time together like a big family. We've gained community and found new values. You can't put a price on that."

"There was a heavy price and eighty to ninety percent of the country paid it," Jim said. "Those who survived are still paying that price every day."

Lloyd jabbed a thumb at his own chest. "In my opinion, it's still worth it. A lot of people died, but I'm still here and I have to make the best of it."

Jim was silent for a moment as he processed what Lloyd was saying. "This isn't the world I dreamed of. I mean, there were times I wished for bad stuff to happen to shut up the whiners, but I didn't want this. Not then and not now. When I was a teenager, and I imagined you and I would still be having adventures at this age, they didn't involve horses, guns, and cartels."

"What did you imagine?"

Jim smiled at the memory. "I thought we might be exploring ruins in the jungle, drinking in tropical bars, or driving across the country. Things like that. Things we wanted to do when we were in high school."

"We're a far cry from all that. Not sure if any of those things will ever be an option again in our lifetime."

"That's part of why I started the roadhouse. I know I talk all the time about using it as a way to monitor what's going on in the community, but it also gives people a sense of purpose. People have jobs. You have a place to play. It forces us to interact with our community."

"And you have a place to boss people around," Lloyd teased.

Jim ignored him. "It's about finding peace and purpose in the world you live in because that's the only world you have at this moment in time. I'm not one hundred percent there yet, but I'm trying to get there. I work on it every day."

When Lloyd didn't say anything, sarcastic or otherwise, Jim looked over expectantly. Lloyd had an odd look on his face. Something was obviously on his mind.

"What is it?" Jim asked. "Might as well spit it out."

"Speaking of finding happiness in the world you live in, I'm going to ask Randi to marry me."

Jim about fell off his horse. "I didn't think either of you would be up for going down that road again."

"I admit I thought marriage seemed pointless considering the world we're living in. But I've been reconsidering that. It's like the roadhouse. It's a way to bring some normality to the chaos."

Jim smirked. "The chaos of the world or the chaos of you and Randi being together?"

"The world, smartass. The chaos with Randi is fun. The chaos of the world, not so much."

"You needing a best man? Again?"

"If she says yes."

"I do have plenty of experience at being your best man. What's it been? Three times already?"

Lloyd shot Jim a frown. "Come to think of it, maybe I need a new best man. The one common denominator in all those failed marriages was having you as the best man. I wonder what Nooner is doing on my wedding day?"

Jim laughed. "You don't have a day set, but it wouldn't matter anyway. Nooner does the same thing every day. He drinks."

"You say that like it's a bad thing."

Instead of laughing at Lloyd's comment, Jim fell silent.

"Now you're the one getting quiet. You pouting because I might replace you with Nooner?"

"Nah, it's not that. It just seems like bad luck to be talking about future plans when you're riding into a potentially dangerous situation. If this was a western or war movie, your ass would be the first to get killed."

Lloyd's eyes went wide. "Thanks a lot! I was feeling pretty good about helping a buddy out until you started talking like that. You ever think about something, then decide maybe you shouldn't say that out loud?"

"Not really," Jim admitted.

"You should *seriously* consider it."

49

Outside of St. Paul, Virginia

IT WAS late afternoon by the time Jim and Lloyd turned their horses off Highway 58 and rode around the rusty yellow pipe gate blocking the quarry entrance. After a year and half without maintenance, the wide gravel road was littered with potholes and mud puddles. Wheel loaders and dump trucks sat idle, their windows pockmarked with bullet holes. The conveyor belts that normally carried stone between crushers, screens, and various piles sagged with the weight of whatever they'd held when they were shut down.

The pit from which most of the stone came had filled with water, creating a cold, deep lake. The water looked clear now but reflected a turquoise green color on a sunny day, the result of calcium carbonate and other minerals that leached into the water. It was the kind of place that made a good swimming hole in the summer but permanently swallowed the bodies of anyone who drowned there. The same could probably be said of any bodies *tossed* in there for disposal, which gave Jim pause. It was always good to know of a convenient spot where a guy could lose a dead body if he happened to cause one.

Jim caught a whiff of smoke on the air. He assumed Hugh had told the boys they could have a fire, since there was no reason for them not to. Those men deployed across the hillside near the river might have to maintain a low profile, but Pete and Charlie were far enough from the tracks that it shouldn't matter.

A voice hailed Jim from the distance and he caught sight of Pete waving at him. He and Lloyd headed in that direction, reaching the boys several minutes later.

Lloyd slithered off his horse and groaned. "That was way more time on a horse than I'm used to."

Charlie pointed at Lloyd's pack. "Untie that and we'll put your pack with the others. We've got them under a tarp so they'll stay dry."

Pete pointed at Lloyd's Thompson. "What the hell is that? I've never seen one before."

Lloyd proudly hefted the weapon into the air. "This, my uncultured young friend, is a Thompson submachine gun. A weapon that proudly served this country in several wars. It was a favorite of gangsters and bootleggers."

"Oh, so it's an antique, like you," Pete teased.

"A very *capable* antique," Lloyd confirmed. "Just like me."

Charlie got on his radio. "Charlie for Hugh, Charlie for Hugh."

"Go for Hugh."

"Jim and a very capable antique just reached camp." He cracked a grin at Pete.

"Come again?" Hugh said.

Jim held out his hand and Charlie handed over the radio. "This is Jim. I just reached camp. Lloyd came with me for the ride."

"Copy that. You sit tight and I'll come to you."

"Got it. Jim out." He returned Charlie's radio to him, then faced Lloyd. "Lucky for you, that name isn't likely to stick as a nickname. Capable Antique just doesn't roll off the tongue."

"You need me to go with you?" Lloyd asked.

"It'll just be me and Hugh meeting with Santos, but we'll see if Hugh needs you anywhere else. If not, you can stay here with Pete and Charlie."

"He didn't bring a banjo, did he?" Pete asked warily.

Jim pointed at the Thompson. "Lloyd could only handle one implement of death and destruction at a time."

Pete patted Lloyd on the back. "Then he's welcome to stay."

"I was staying anyway," Lloyd harrumphed. "We have something to talk about."

Charlie shook his head. "Whatever it is, I don't want to know."

"Well, I'm telling you anyway. I'm thinking about asking Randi to marry me and I might need you two to be the flower girls for the wedding."

Pete and Charlie weren't laughing.

"They're getting big enough to take you," Jim warned Lloyd. "You better hush. I don't want to come back to find you floating face-down in that lake."

Lloyd scoffed at the idea, though he kept his mouth shut.

Once their horses were unloaded, they circled round the fire to warm up. Fifteen minutes later Hugh came jogging into camp. He rolled up to the fire and sucked down a long drink from his hydration bladder.

"It's easier when the horse does the running," Hugh said between breaths. "I'm a little out of practice at running long distances in gear."

"We'll be walking back," Jim said. "I'm not much of a runner unless I'm being chased."

"The train is there already and parked on the tracks," Hugh said. "We've been watching them for a while. Our people are in position and everyone knows their role. Wrong Way is in charge while you and I are in the meeting."

"Any activity at the train?" Jim asked.

"Nothing suspicious. They have a couple of sentries standing watch on the cars. They're outfitted about the same as when I last saw them. I don't think they're expecting a fight."

"Good," Jim said. "I don't want one either."

"You ready to go?"

Jim nodded slowly. "As ready as I'm going to get, I suppose."

"You need me, Hugh?" Lloyd asked.

Hugh studied Lloyd with an appraising eye. "Though you do seem like a very capable antique, especially carrying that Thompson, I believe we'll be fine. You should stay with Pete and Charlie."

"Funny," Lloyd said. "That's exactly what Jim suggested."

Pete gave Lloyd a light punch in the arm. "Welcome to the kids' table, Lloyd."

50

The Train

JIM WAS ALWAYS in awe of the Clinch River. There was no escaping the ancientness of it, the sense of prehistoric time that it brought forward across the eons. The jumbled boulders, the carved valley it traveled through, all distorted Jim's sense of time and place in the universe. He imagined the long-extinct creatures that must have watered, swam, and hunted this same stretch of river. Today, Jim had bigger concerns than daydreaming about the history of this waterway.

Jim and Hugh were on the same side of the river as the train tracks, which they intersected after a thirty-minute walk from the quarry. Sunset had already come and gone, the color slowly draining from the world, and adding to the sense that this was a place outside of time and the normal way of things. The mood was ominous but not foreboding. Jim understood this was an important moment and a test of his leadership, but he wasn't afraid. The risk of the moment was immense, and there was always the chance that he might not be going home. The outcome of that was beyond his control. If he died, he knew his family would miss him, but they'd be in good hands. That was all he could ask for.

They were behind the train, which sat on the tracks approximately a quarter mile past them, so Jim and Hugh began walking the tracks in that direction. Without moving his head, Jim scanned the woods around him for any sign of his people. He knew they were there and could feel their eyes upon him, but he didn't see any sign of them. Hugh and Wrong Way had done well in helping them find concealed positions. Jim hoped beyond all hope that those men would still be hidden in those positions when he walked out of here later. He didn't want anyone to die today, especially not because of a decision he'd made.

The sentries on top of the train must have spotted their approach and relayed the information. More men spilled from the rearmost car, all of them armed, but their rifles pointed at the ground. They didn't block Jim's approach, and moved to either side of the track, creating a funnel that would direct Jim where they expected him to go.

"Think it's too late to change our minds?" Hugh asked.

"Yes." As much as a part of Jim wanted to call this off, a bigger part of him understood that this was an unavoidable moment. It was where fate, destiny, and the future collided. It was where all those moments since waking up without power in that Richmond hotel room had led him.

Another man appeared on the rear platform of the train. He paused there, then dropped to the ground and started toward Jim and Hugh. This man didn't carry a rifle and the smile on his face seemed incongruous with the tension of the moment. Jim felt no discomfort coming off the man. He wasn't afraid, but there was no reason he should be. He was probably a man who never showed fear. His position didn't allow it.

Though Jim tried to not show it either, there were certainly moments he felt it. Oddly enough, the man's demeanor relaxed Jim, yet in the back of his mind he understood that he shouldn't let himself feel too relaxed. Any attempts to make him feel comfortable might be designed to intentionally distract him and provide a false sense of security. Shit, with all the feelings going through his head, he didn't know which to settle upon and actually feel. Anxiety was nipping at his heels like a chihuahua.

"Good evening, my name is Santos. Thanks for joining me here along this beautiful stretch of river." He stuck out a hand.

Jim shook it, rolling with the moment. "Good evening. I'm Jim Powell."

"Wonderful to meet you, Jim." Santos shook Hugh's hand. "And good to see you again, my friend."

Hugh didn't return the greeting but smiled his crooked smile and shook Santos's hand.

Santos gestured back toward the train. "Will you gentlemen join me inside? It's more comfortable."

"Certainly," Jim said. What else could he do at this point? In for a penny, in for a pound.

They followed Santos to the train and the hair on Jim's neck prickled as he walked through the gauntlet of two dozen armed men. Several of them had the gold-plated AKs that had caught Garnet's attention when he first saw the train. Besides those rifles, all Jim saw were tattoos, cold eyes, and men willing to kill him at the drop of a hat. Seeing these men up close just reaffirmed that he didn't want his people to have to fight these men. While these men might not be Chinese contractors or special operators, they weren't to be trifled with. They were killers accustomed to stacking bodies and not losing sleep over it.

Jim expected he and Hugh would be asked to leave their weapons outside, but Santos made no such request. It would have been a big ask and Jim wasn't sure he could have gone into such a meeting unarmed. He probably would have, but it wouldn't have been comfortable. As it was, both he and Hugh were armed to the teeth and as ready as they could be for whatever the world hurled at them.

Aside from whatever guns and knives they had concealed on them, Hugh and Jim had both switched to close quarters weapons before they made the hike to the river. Jim carried a 9mm AR pistol that had been modified to full auto. Hugh carried an MP5 that the local sheriff's department had once obtained through a government reuse program. If they had to fight on a train, these weapons might serve them better than their rifles. Like Jim, Hugh also carried two high-explosive grenades that had been a gift from Barb, daughter of the infamous Mad Mick.

Santos led them through several crowded cars. "Excuse the mess, gentleman. We've been on the road for a while and my men are not good housekeepers."

Finally, they stopped in the cleanest car they'd seen yet, half of which was set up as an office. A plastic folding table had been set up in the room and covered with a black tablecloth. There was an oil lamp burning in the center of the table, despite all the cars they'd passed through being illuminated by electric lights. It seemed like an attempt to throw some ambiance into the otherwise stark setting. Somewhere, a muffled generator was running, but it was the only sound they heard.

Santos gestured at the table. "Please, have a seat."

Both Hugh and Jim had left their packs at the quarry camp. They only carried their weapons and combat loadout. When they hesitated for a second, Santos began laughing, then took a seat at the head of the table.

"Gentleman, I can read your minds. Neither of you wants your back to the door. Neither of you wants to leave your weapons out of reach. I'll not be offended if you shift your chair to a spot at the table that makes you more comfortable. Nor will I be offended if you keep your weapons alongside you. I would offer my assurance that you are safe here, but I don't take you as the kind of men who'd take my word on that."

Jim shrugged at Hugh, then shifted his chair so that he had a view of both doors into the train car. He unsnapped his AR pistol from his sling, took a seat, and placed it on the floor beside him. Following his lead, Hugh did the same with his MP5, placing it alongside his chair after he sat down.

Santos brought a radio up and addressed Jim and Hugh. "Gentlemen, I'm going to radio for some refreshments to be delivered to us. Please don't shoot my cook. His importance in my organization is not to be underestimated."

Jim nodded in agreement, though that agreement was entirely contingent upon whether the cook came in shooting or not. Under the right circumstances, he'd kill a cook as easily as he'd kill a cartel soldier.

Santos keyed the mic and spoke in Spanish. Jim didn't understand the language but knew that Hugh did. Jim saw nothing on Hugh's face to indicate that Santos had said anything other than what he'd said he was going to. A moment later, they heard the sound of footsteps approaching and two men entered the office with large trays. They sat them on the table, then placed small plates and silverware in front of Jim, Hugh, and Santos, along with two bottles of wine. When the trays were unloaded, the two servers retreated, closing the door behind them.

"We do have water, but would you care for a glass of wine?" Santos asked. "It's one of my favorites, the Casa Madero 3V. It's a little-known fact, but Casa Madero was one of the first wineries established in the Americas. They opened in 1597."

While normally, Jim preferred not to mix alcohol with potentially life-threatening situations, it seemed as if protocol demanded it in this case. Besides, he could use something to take a little of the edge off. "I'm not normally a wine guy, but I'll have a glass."

"Same here," Hugh said.

Santos opened the bottle and poured three glasses. He handed them out, then gestured at the platters on the table before them. "Usually, we don't eat in this fashion, but this is a special occasion and the cook has outdone himself. Perhaps you can see now why I didn't want you to shoot him."

"It smells delicious," Jim said.

"What are these dishes?" Hugh asked.

Santos began pointing them out. "We have tostadas with smoked marlin or duck carnitas. The shot glasses are ceviche shooters, which have sea bass in a citrus marinade with a splash of mezcal. Then we have guacamole and a variety of salsas. For dipping, there are chicharrónes—pork rinds—and plantain chips."

"It looks amazing," Hugh said.

Santos regarded Hugh. "With your proficiency in our language, I'm wondering if you've had any of these dishes before?"

Hugh shook his head. "We didn't eat this well in the places I frequented."

"What places were those?" asked Santos.

When Hugh hesitated to reply, Jim answered for him. "Stories like that are best shared among friends and we're not there yet." Leave it to Jim to set a friendly tone for the meeting. It was a skill he'd perfected at his old job.

Santos wasn't offended by Jim's abruptness. He gestured at the heaping platters. "Then let us eat and talk. Perhaps we'll be friends by the end of the night."

Jim dipped his head. "Perhaps."

At Santos's urging, they filled their plates and ate. The food was indeed amazing, perhaps the best Jim had eaten since the collapse.

"So, tell me why you're here," Jim asked between bites. "Hugh told me what you told him already, but I'd like to hear it for myself. Also, I'll go ahead and warn you that I'm a blunt man, if you haven't noticed that already. There's no need to sugarcoat things."

Santos smiled at Jim's disclaimer. "I admire that you are plainspoken. I'm much the same. It's best not to obscure truth under layers of nonsense and flowery language."

"Good," Jim said. "Then let's not speak like you're a politician and I'm one of your constituents. We're two guys shooting the shit over dinner and a glass of wine."

"I have to admit I'm not used to that," Santos said. "On this journey across America I've spoken to many influential people, and they typically like to be wooed and pampered. They like to be treated like they're as important as they once were. They miss having their egos stroked."

Jim frowned and waved a hand in front of his face. "That's not how I roll, Santos. That's for people who hold their meetings in the parlor or the boardroom. I hold mine in bars, barns, and workshops."

Again, Santos laughed. "As you wish, my friend. If we go back two years in time, business was booming for my employer and their counterparts. Our primary trade partner was the United States. If you're familiar with business, you can understand how the loss of a primary customer impacts you. If you supply car parts to the automative industry, how are you affected when car sales bottom out? If you sell mining equipment, what happens when no one is buying coal?"

"I understand that our collapse must have hurt your bosses. What is your employer's primary export?" Jim thought he knew, but he wanted to ask. It was a test to see whether Santos was ready to cut through the bullshit or not.

"There's a trinity of ...*product*...that generates most of our income," said Santos.

"Drugs and guns?" Jim suggested. "What else?"

"Human trafficking," Hugh said, beating Santos to the punch.

Jim looked at Santos and cocked an eyebrow. Santos nodded somberly. "It's the fastest growing business in the world."

Jim gave Santos a look of disgust. "That doesn't mean you have to become involved in it."

Santos shrugged indifferently. "When there is a market that produces that level of revenue, smart businessmen want their piece of the pie, and my employers are *very* smart men. Yet one also has to ask, is it the fault of the supplier that this market exists, or does this market exist because of a sickness in American society that demands to be satisfied?"

"That's a valid point," Jim conceded, "but I can't look at someone who abducts women and children as blameless. To be honest, that level of ruthlessness is why your presence here in my community concerns me. It's why I took this meeting. I need to know why you're here and what you want from us."

Santos popped an olive in his mouth and washed it down with a sip of wine. "Well, if it makes you feel any better, this is not a mission of plunder. I'm not here to kidnap people or steal what few resources you have. My employers have a vested interest in getting American markets back up and functioning again. We need your economy restored so Americans will begin spending money with us. Since no one else in the world seems interested in helping the 'old' America get back on its feet, a group of businessmen from my part of the world formed an alliance for that very reason."

"The Chinese seem interested in doing something here," said Hugh. "I'm surprised you're willing to go against their wishes since they supply you with many of the chemicals required for your drug operations."

"Yes, but they don't want the old America back," Santos said. "They want to plunder America to loot its resources. My employers think that's bad for business. They got together and decided to distribute aid in hopes it would generate goodwill with the American people. Assuming we can help you with your China problem, there will be no purging us when order is restored. Our roots will be woven into the fabric of America. Our market penetration will be deeper than ever."

"The question is, which devil do we partner with?" Jim summarized.

Santos opened his hands. "Basically, that is the decision before you. But with the understanding that one choice will preserve the way of life you are familiar with, while the other will entirely reshape your nation into being little more than a Chinese satellite."

"I talked to the people in Finney," Hugh said. "You made quite the impression there. How have other communities responded to you?"

Santos pointed to a map on the wall. "We came through Texas and Louisiana, then headed north in this direction. We're nearly out of aid packages so we'll be headed back after this meeting. Surprisingly, every community we've visited has welcomed us with open arms. In fact, they anxiously await our return. Not once have we been met with hostility. I think it's safe to say that people prefer us over a Chinese invasion."

"Until you pass through towns and people turn up missing," Jim said. "Or until people start overdosing on your drugs."

"And bodies are found hanging off overpasses," Hugh added.

"I could offer you promises that we aren't here to kidnap people, but you wouldn't believe me."

Jim looked Santos in the eye. "I wouldn't."

"Being suspicious of people with whom you are in an alliance is okay," Santos said. "It doesn't mean you can't find any common ground at all."

"Then assuming our relationship is not to be built on trust, what's it to be built on?" Jim asked. "What do you need from us and why should we provide it?"

"My train is the easternmost train of several that my employers sent out. We are closest to the anticipated path of the Chinese invaders. Since my operation confirmed that we can get this far by train, my employers have already prepared a second, larger operation. The next one won't stop in every town as we've done. It will drive straight through and deliver five hundred men with trucks, ATVs, weapons, and supplies to the front line of this battle. Once we get a handle on how entrenched the Chinese forces are, there may be several more trains behind the first."

Hugh was wide-eyed at this revelation. "If this fighting force is already being readied, then what's the point of meeting with us? Is this just a courtesy notification that there's about to be a war in our backyard?"

Santos cocked an eyebrow. "Do I look like the kind of man who does things out of courtesy?"

The obvious answer was that he didn't, but Jim was struggling to find a polite way to say it. Finally, he said, "Uh, no."

"Thank you," Santos replied. "No, this isn't a courtesy visit. It's important for our men to know that they have the support of the local population. They can't focus on fighting the Chinese if they have to be watching their backs."

"So far everyone is onboard?" Hugh asked.

"They are and it's hardly surprising. When people are desperate enough, loyalty can be purchased cheaply. It's a system we've perfected over decades."

Hugh added another tostada to his plate. "From what I've seen of your business model, don't you have a backup plan for when loyalty can't be purchased? Isn't your fallback to murder those who don't support you?"

Santos waved a finger in the air. "We don't kill those who fail to support us, only those who choose to work *against* us. There's a difference."

"What would that mean for us?" Jim asked. "Whether we choose to support you or not?"

"If you don't want our help, it's not that we would target you. Our focus is on the Chinese. What would happen, instead, is that we'd ignore you. Your villages wouldn't get our help, either in the form of soldiers or supplies."

"Would your men pose a threat to us?" Jim asked. "If your soldiers were active in our area, would I have to warn people to stay inside and hide out?"

The look Santos gave was complex, but his answer was not. "Men in the field, a long way from home, sometimes act in ways that we might not approve of, but what can you do? I cannot answer that question."

There was an implied and nonchalant threat there that pissed Jim off, though he wouldn't let it show. The stakes were tremendous. While part of him wanted to snap up his weapon and pop this two-bit hood in the forehead, it was about more than him. It was about his people outside. It was about his family and friends. It was about the whole damn community that applauded when Jim announced he was taking charge of them. For just this one moment, Jim wished he could throw off the mantle of leadership long enough to cap this guy, but that wasn't how it worked.

As Jim saw it, his job wasn't to keep his people alive at all costs. Some costs were too high, such as surrendering their freedom or accepting a situation that would have them living in fear. Jim would make some sacrifices, though with limits. He drained his glass of wine and slid his plate away. Across the table, he saw Hugh watching him with concern. His old friend knew him well enough to understand that if Jim was going to make a dumb move, this was when he'd make it.

Jim placed both his hands on the table in front of him. "As I said, I'm a blunt man and I have a keen awareness of the kind of flexible morality that our times demand. I understand that our current situation sometimes requires choices that would never have been acceptable in our old world. While I don't like your business and I don't like the violence that your presence brings with it, I like the idea of Chinese occupation even less. I can support your efforts but only up until a certain point."

Santos began tapping his finger on the table. He wasn't a man who negotiated for things, but he respected Jim's bluntness and felt like it was best they understood each other. When you knew where a man's line in the sand was, it was much easier to avoid it. Or should you reach the point where you no longer cared whether you stepped over it or not, then there was still a benefit to knowing when you crossed it.

"If your people are operating in our community, we will fight *with* you, but I won't watch the people under my protection be pushed around or threatened," Jim said. "If your soldiers try to run over my people, there will be consequences. Do we understand each other?"

Santos stared Jim in the eye. "As long as you understand that your consequences might produce further consequences. That's a dangerous game to play with me. I can assure you my resources are vast."

Jim didn't look away. "When two dangerous men meet, manners become very important." He stuck out his hand. "Can we agree to try and play nice?"

Santos took Jim's hand and shook it, although Jim saw a spark in those eyes. It was a hint that while Santos probably wanted to kill Jim about as much as Jim wanted to kill Santos, they both had larger obligations. They both had people to answer to.

"You are a hard man, hillbilly warlord. Are there more of you? When I return and travel north through these mountains, am I going to meet more stubborn, violent men at every stop?"

"You'll encounter some who won't even meet with you," Jim warned. "You'll meet those who shoot at your train simply for the pleasure of it. I know you and your men are hard, but you're not the only hard men."

"Do you want your phone back?" Hugh asked, trying to break the tension of the moment.

Santos waved him off. "Keep it. We might need to speak again in the future."

"Thank you for your hospitality," Jim said, only because he'd been raised to say such things.

"With our meeting complete, we'll be leaving the area now," Santos said. "We're returning to Mexico to resupply. We'll leave the last of our supplies beside the tracks. Come back in an hour and you're welcome to them."

Jim nodded, pushed back from the table, and stood. "Don't make me regret this decision, Santos."

Santos stood. "I could say the same, Jim Powell, hillbilly warlord. But before you go, I have a small gift." Santos walked to a cabinet and retrieved two bottles and two boxes. He handed one bottle and box to Jim, the second to Hugh.

"Patron Platinum," Hugh said. "That's good stuff."

Santos offered a hollow smile. "Drink it in good health. The boxes are Don Luis cigars. They're a personal favorite."

"Thank you, Santos," Jim said. "Safe travels home."

51

Outside of St. Paul, Virginia

JIM AND HUGH exited the train, walking back through the same gauntlet of cartel soldiers they'd passed through when boarding. It was dark now and the hair on Jim's neck stood up at the idea of those armed men behind him. Jim and Hugh had headlamps, but they didn't use them yet. There was no need making themselves easier targets if killing them was the plan. Jim imagined Santos stepping onto that railing and giving the order that the two of them be mowed down as they walked away. Jim's men, positioned in the woods, might be able to take vengeance afterward, but it might be too late to save Jim and Hugh.

Jim turned the volume up on his radio and keyed the mic. He assumed those of his men using thermal or nightvision had updated the others that they'd left the train. "Gentlemen, Hugh and I are almost clear of the tracks. Stay in position. The men on the train say they're leaving within the hour. I'd like eyes on them until they do. Jim out."

Only when they reached the trail to the quarry did they begin to breathe easier.

"Well, that could have gone worse," Hugh said.

"Indeed it could have, but they're not gone yet. And once they're gone, it sounds like we'll be seeing them again in the future. I'm not sure what I think about what just went down back there. It's certainly not leaving me feeling all warm and fuzzy."

"It'll take some time to process," said Hugh. "You did the only thing you could do, though. It was the right call."

"Still sucks."

"Decisions are different when the world has fewer guardrails. We're freer people than we were before the collapse, but that freedom damn sure came at a cost."

"I guess we should just hang out here until the train clears out," Jim suggested.

Hugh pulled a tiny red LED light from a pocket and turned it on. It provided just enough of a glow that they could see each other without broadcasting their position.

Jim blew out a breath. "I wish I felt better about that meeting. It was multiple choice and every choice was shitty."

"That's why you are the right guy for this job, Jim. You don't want to care about all those people, but you can't help it. There was a minute, though, where I thought you were going to pop the guy right there at the table."

"I'd probably feel better about the meeting if I had," Jim admitted.

"Or we could be dead."

Jim didn't answer, which was all the confirmation Hugh needed that he was right. The two of them stood in the dark woods, listening for the sound of the train starting up, and talking about the evening. About thirty minutes after Jim and Hugh had stepped off the train, the diesel locomotive powered off, taking Santos and his men home.

"Jim, I want to check that load before we call the men down," Hugh said. "Just in case it's booby trapped or something."

"You think they'd do that?"

"I'm not saying they did, but they're perfectly capable of it."

"Then be careful," Jim warned. He raised his radio. "This is Jim. The train left us a package. Hugh is going to check it out first. Stay in position until my signal."

It was only as Hugh walked away that Jim started to become concerned for his friend. Hugh walked into danger on a daily basis, sometimes with Jim but often alone. He was comfortable with risk and danger in a way that would have eaten away at the nerves of most people. If the cargo was booby-trapped and Hugh was killed or injured, Jim had no clue what he'd do without him. It had been sheer chance that the two of them had reconnected after the collapse, and Hugh had become indispensable. Outside of Ellen, Hugh was the person who perhaps knew Jim best, the person who understood his struggle.

For a moment, Jim started to call Hugh back, but he didn't. Hugh wouldn't have returned anyway. He'd have considered the risk to be justifiable. If Santos left items they could use, they needed to get them before someone else did. Watching his friend walk down the tracks in the glow of his headlamp, Jim struggled to breathe, his chest tight with the residual anxiety of the evening.

Hugh reached the pallet sitting beside the tracks and examined the stack of boxes from all angles, first from a distance and then closer. He carefully unstacked the pallet, making sure there was nothing concealed in the stack. Finally, holding his flashlight in his mouth, Hugh unsheathed his knife and carefully opened each and every box until he was certain there was nothing there to be concerned about.

"All clear," Hugh said into his radio. *"All elements converge on my position."*

Jim raised his radio. "Jim for Pete or Charlie. Jim for Pete or Charlie."

"Go for Pete."

"Can you guys bring the horses down the trail to the tracks? Leave Lloyd watching the camp."

"Is everything okay?" Pete asked.

"Yeah, it's fine. We just have some items we need to haul back to camp, so bring some tarps and ropes with you."

"Copy that. Pete out."

Jim could hear his people trailing out of the woods, shuffling through the carpet of leaves that littered the slopes of these hardwood forests. He returned to the tracks and joined Hugh at the pallet. "What's the score?"

"Food, medical, batteries, .22 ammunition, spices, sports drink mixes, powdered milk, and some other stuff. It's an interesting assortment."

"We'll take it back to the roadhouse and split it up there," Jim said. "I don't know how far it'll spread, but Josie and her people need some supplies to get started out, and I'm sure Garnet could use some things too."

"Good plan," Hugh said.

"You had me a little nervous there, Hugh. Once I started thinking about booby traps, I couldn't stop thinking about it all blowing sky high and taking you with it."

"I wasn't too concerned. The cartel need bodies and customers. Dead people are useless to them." Hugh reached into a pocket and retrieved the satellite phone Santos had given them. "I programmed Josie's number in there before we left. You might want to give her a call and ask her to quietly let people know that all is well."

Jim took the phone, feeling the weight of it in his hand. There was so much technology that he didn't miss, like the poison of social media, but this phone felt like a small miracle in his hand. It was the power of connectivity, the ability to push a few buttons and ease the mind of someone hours away. Jim walked off and took a seat on the rail. After a brief conversation, during which Josie promised to update everyone back at the roadhouse, Jim stood up and joined his friends at the pallet. With his adrenaline ebbing, he was suddenly tired, aware of just how long and tense the day had been.

Hugh was smoking a cigarette and giving everyone an overview of what had taken place with Santos. There were some details he left out. He'd let Jim decide how deep to drill down. However, everyone who'd sat out in those woods with a weapon tonight deserved to know the basics of what had gone on. They'd trusted Jim and he trusted them back.

"Did I see a case of Modelo in there?" Jim asked.

Hugh nodded. "Two cases. I don't think we got the conventional aid package. This looks like a supply dump to me. A mix of aid and things they wanted to get rid of before they headed home."

"Crack open a case of beer. These guys deserve it," Jim said.

"Me too?" Charlie asked, riding up the tracks alongside Pete, both of them leading strings of horses.

Jim considered this for a moment. "Sure, you boys can have one, but remember that what happens on the operation stays on the op."

"Got it!" Pete dismounted with a grin on his face.

The men drank one of the cases of beer while they transferred the pallet of goods to their horses, strapping the cargo on in whatever manner they could secure it. They only had to get it as far as the quarry today. They could worry about packing better tomorrow. Once they had everything loaded, they tossed the pallet and their empty bottles into the weeds. Jim hated littering, especially alongside the river, but they didn't have the capacity to haul empty bottles back home just to throw them into a sinkhole near the roadhouse.

Back at the quarry, they set up a watch and split up the second case of beer. Jim struggled with the idea of letting men drink when they were out in the field, but these weren't soldiers. They were ordinary men pulled into extraordinary circumstances. They were regular guys asked to do things they never expected life would demand of them. They weren't trained for it, but they'd performed well, and Jim thought they should be rewarded. Perhaps it wasn't the most disciplined way to behave, but he was figuring this out as he went, just like they were, just like everyone was.

"Can I speak to you a second?" a voice asked.

Jim was zoning out, sitting by the fire and lost in the flames. He was almost too tired to think, the details of his conversation with Santos fading off from an immediate concern to something he'd dwell on tomorrow. He looked over his shoulder and found Wrong

Way standing there with a beer in his hand. There was something in Wrong Way's tone that implied he wanted this to be a private conversation.

Jim stood up. "Sure."

They walked over to a rubber-tired loader settled onto four flats. Jim was chilled now, missing the embrace of the warm campfire. He hoped this wasn't to be a long, drawn-out conversation. He didn't have the brainpower for anything taxing.

"I was kind of bummed after our conversation the other day," Wrong Way began.

"Which one?"

"The one where I called my employer and found out I'd been wasting the last year and a half guarding empty servers."

Jim offered a sympathetic smile. "Understood, man. Most people would probably feel the same."

"I've thought a lot about my predicament since then. I've been studying maps and thinking about the buddies I could connect with. I remember lots of conversations with dudes over the years where we talked about hooking up if the shit hit the fan. I thought about visiting some of those guys and seeing if that was still an option, but without comms or a vehicle, I'm talking about weeks of walking just to find out if someone is home or not."

"Not to mention that travel isn't safe now. People will ambush you just to see what you're carrying. The world is dumb and dangerous."

"Which is why I wanted to ask if you would have any objection to me sticking around. I promise I won't be a burden on you guys. I'll help out where I can. I can run a gun and I'm trained. From what I've seen, you and Hugh might know what you're doing, but a lot of these guys are just winging it. They might need trained up and that's something I could help with if you wanted."

"Owning guns was sexy to a lot of people," Jim said. "Training was work. A lot didn't want to put in the work."

"I'm not criticizing, I'm just saying I'd be glad to help where I can."

"You don't have to sell yourself, brother. We'd be glad to have you.

We have a good thing going and I don't want to lose it. That's the only reason I agreed to step up and lead this group. Now, if you don't mind, I'm freezing my ass off."

"One more thing," Wrong Way said.

"What's that?"

"I have a laptop that I haven't used for much more than playing solitaire lately, but if I could get access to the internet, I have connections I could explore."

Jim had been staring longingly at the warm fire, but he turned and met Wrong Way's eye. "I assume you've heard us talking about the gear Josie's people have?"

"Satellite modems."

Jim nodded. "I don't know how it all works. I don't know if those are connections they can share out to other devices or if only approved computers can access the networks they're using. It's something you'd have to talk to those guys about."

"It's not so I can play Call Of Duty online. I have Signal and Protonmail accounts. Through those accounts I have access to a worldwide network of friends and associates."

"I had those same accounts, man, but they don't help if the people on the other end don't have internet access."

"I'm assuming that's because most of your friends are stateside," said Wrong Way. "The military contracting industry is global. I have friends doing personal protection in the UK, Dubai, Saudi Arabia, and all over the damn place. I know people running companies out of these places because that's where the work is."

"I'm exhausted and not putting the pieces together. Explain it like I'm a three-year-old crotch goblin asking the same damn question for the fiftieth time."

Wrong Way laughed. "I *might* be able to get intel and scuttlebutt that Josie's people don't have access to. Those guys don't travel in the same circles I do. Who knows? If I reach the right people, I might even be able to set up a supply drop. I'm sure there's things we need from the outside world that we're not getting."

Now Jim was following along. His puzzle might be rusty, but the pieces finally slid into place. "That's intriguing. How about you, Hugh, and I have a sit-down when we get back to town tomorrow?" He stuck out his hand. "I appreciate your decision to stay. I look forward to having you as part of our community."

Wrong Way shook it. "Thanks for not killing me."

Jim frowned. "Have my people been telling stories again?"

"Maybe a few."

52

The Roadhouse

It was late afternoon the next day when the riders returned to town. Those who'd borrowed horses dismounted along the way and walked on home while the rest of the group headed for the roadhouse, leading the spare horses with them. Once they reached the roadhouse, the supplies they'd brought back were offloaded into the storeroom. Everyone had agreed to split them up among the people who needed them.

They turned the horses out in the corral behind the roadhouse and carried their personal gear in. Wrong Way had come with them even though they'd passed his building on the way there. Now that he'd decided to join up with Jim and his people, he seemed anxious to put the isolation of his previous life behind him. He had making up to do.

While Shade was hugging Becky and telling her how much he'd missed her, the rest of the crew settled at tables and at the bar.

Randi came and stood before them. "Welcome home, gentlemen. And Lloyd."

Lloyd frowned. "I was all prepared to be a smartass with you, but I decided I'd be nice instead. Despite the way you just addressed me, I'm going to continue to be nice. I missed you and it's good to see you again."

Randi looked concerned. She stuck out a hand and pressed it against Lloyd's forehead, feeling for a fever. "You feeling alright? You fall off your horse and hit your head or something?"

Lloyd turned away, offended. "Ain't nothing wrong with me that a good woman can't fix."

"Many have tried and failed," Jim muttered.

Lloyd and Randi both glared at him, equally offended by that remark.

Jim plastered an awkward smile across his face. "We miss anything?"

Randi placed glasses on the bar and started pouring everyone's favorite drinks, which she knew by heart. Wrong Way was the only exception to that, so she poured him some of the blackberry moonshine she'd poured for Lloyd and Jim.

"Well, Tim has been enjoying the census. He's come in several times to get a drink and tell me about all the 'feisty broads' he's met."

"He starting a harem?" Jim cracked.

Randi shook her head and grinned. "No, a pickleball league."

Jim, Hugh, Wrong Way, Lloyd, and Shade all cringed at the same time.

"Pickleball?" Jim asked.

Randi said, "Yeah, it's like—"

Jim rolled his eyes. "I know what it is, I'm just not sure why the hell anyone would want to play it *or* why that seems like an important thing to do in the apocalypse."

"Especially with the days already being short because of winter," Shade said. "Seems like their time would be better spent doing... damn near anything."

"On the other hand," said Hugh, "if it takes their mind off their problems for a few hours a week, what's the harm?"

Jim raised his glass and tipped it to Hugh. "Good point, my friend.

Thanks for the reminder that working until we collapse is not the end goal."

"Hell, I could have told you that," Lloyd griped.

Jim elbowed his old friend. "Yeah, but it means less coming from someone who never works."

Lloyd unleashed his most sarcastic fake laugh.

Ellen came in then, holding hands with Ariel.

"You're lucky," Lloyd says. "I was about to get off this stool and kick your ass. I'm only holding back because of your little girl."

"I figured it was because you fought like a little girl, and you were afraid she'd kick *your* ass."

Before Lloyd could respond, Ariel was at Jim's side, giving him an aloof hug. She'd missed him but she didn't want to show him too much affection or it might go to his head. Ellen went behind the bar so she could talk to Jim face-to-face. She leaned across the bar and welcomed him back with a kiss, which was met with a chorus of "ooohs."

"Simmer down," Ellen teased. "We're married."

"Where's my kiss, woman?" Lloyd demanded of Randi.

She shrugged. "We're not married."

Lloyd stood, reached in his pants pocket, and came out with a green leather box. He opened it and the yellow lights of the roadhouse reflected off the stone. He held it out to Randi. "Would you like to be?"

Randi narrowed her eyes and crossed her arms over her chest. "Is this some kind of joke?"

Lloyd wasn't laughing. He wasn't even smiling. "I'm dead serious, woman, but I'm too sore to get on a knee, not to mention I've stood in horse stalls cleaner than this floor. Will you marry me, Randi?"

Tears started rolling down Randi's cheeks. She jabbed a finger at Jim. "Yes, I'm crying, and you better not laugh if you know what's good for you."

Jim held his hands up in surrender. "No one is laughing, Randi." He glanced back over his shoulder to find the entire crowd watching what was taking place at the bar. "In fact, no one in this entire place is laughing. We're all waiting for your answer."

You could have heard a pin drop.

Randi exploded toward the bar, throwing both arms around Lloyd as she burst into a fit of crying. "Yes! Yes, I'll marry you. Don't make me regret it."

"You'll regret it every time he picks up that banjo," Jim cracked.

Randi smiled at Jim with a joy he'd never seen in her before. "If that's the only regret I have for the rest of my life, I can live with it."

Ellen leaned across the bar toward Jim. "Let them celebrate. I want to hear about your trip."

Jim looked around and spotted an empty table toward the back. "Let's go over there. It's quieter."

Ellen came back around the bar and the two of them settled into chairs at a table near one of the large woodstoves.

"I was worried. I'm glad you were able to call Josie and let her know everyone was safe. I can't remember the last time I had such anxiety over you going off to deal with something."

Jim took a sip of his drink. "This one felt different. The weight of responsibility was different. All my earlier decisions impacted fewer people. I felt like everyone I knew would suffer if I screwed this up. Who the hell has a frame of reference for decisions like this anyway? Nothing in my life ever prepared me for this."

"How did it go?"

Jim smiled. "Well, I didn't kill anyone—or *everyone*, which is what part of me felt like I should have done."

"Really? You considered doing that?"

"Nothing I've ever heard or read about cartels made me want to sit down with them. I won't accept anything they say as truth, except for the things I've been able to verify through other sources. They're right about the Chinese heading in this direction. They're right that we can't deal with them alone. Still, a part of me wanted to annihilate all the men on the train, then destroy every railroad bridge for a hundred miles."

"But you didn't."

Jim tapped a fingernail on the rim of his glass, then stopped, realizing his hands were overdue for a good washing. "I didn't. We can get along fine without the supplies they were handing out. We have for this long. What we do need are the bodies. We need soldiers, killers, shooters, whatever the hell you want to call them. But I can't help feeling like I made a deal with the devil."

Ellen reached across the table and laid her hand atop Jim's. "Deals with devils are not binding. That's why there are so many stories about men turning the tables on them."

Jim sighed. "Well, if that's the case, I hope I have what it takes to turn things around when that time comes."

"You look tired."

"I'm exhausted to the point of nausea."

Ellen scooted away from the table. "Then finish that drink and let's go home. This place can run itself for the night."

"You don't have to ask me twice."

"You let everyone know while I find Ariel."

Jim drained his glass, returned it to the bar, and said his goodnights. He grabbed his gear and was waiting at the back door when Ellen and Ariel showed up.

"If we go home, who's going to boss Lloyd around?" Ariel asked.

Jim smiled at his snarky daughter. "He asked Randi to marry him. He's her problem from now on."

Ariel's brow furrowed. "Poor Randi."

53

The Reset Roadhouse

THE FOLLOWING weeks were eventful for Jim, his people, and their community. Less than a week after Lloyd's proposal, the roadhouse hosted its first wedding. In these times, when death could strike suddenly and with no warning, people knew it was best not to put off those things they wanted to do. The event brought a huge crowd to the roadhouse. Jim was Lloyd's best man yet again and the ceremony was performed by one of the community's only remaining ministers, a Presbyterian named Revered Homer. Both of Randi's daughters served as bridesmaids.

As with many pastors, Reverend Homer was loathe to give up the pulpit once he'd planted his feet there. He stood on the roadhouse stage and waved his hand in the air. "While I have you all here, while we have a band and a good crowd assembled, I would just like to say that this might be a good time to check off any of those things in your life that require a preacher. Anyone out there needing baptized, converted, married, or anything other than a funeral?"

"Can you just get this over with?" Lloyd complained. "This tie is choking off my breathing."

Reverend Homer jabbed a finger at Lloyd. "Son, if you'd learn a little patience, you might not be standing up here for the fourth time."

Lloyd blushed when he felt Randi's hand tighten. He knew it wasn't a gesture of reassurance. It was the prelude to her throwing a punch. He leaned over and whispered in her ear. "Don't hit the preacher until it's over, then I'll hold him for you."

Everyone in the crowd was looking around, waiting to see if anyone was moving forward toward the stage. All eyes turned toward the bar as a hand slowly went up—a large, scarred hand attached to a large, loud man.

Shade gulped. "Reckon it'd be a shame to let this moment slip by without doing what my heart is telling me to do." He dropped to a knee, which still left him almost as tall as the woman whose hand he held. "Miss Becky, would you do me the honor of becoming my wife?"

Becky was overwhelmed at first, unable to do anything but tear up and nod. Then the reality of the moment hit her and she was like a woman possessed. She jumped, squealed, and flapped her arms. "I'm getting married! Yes! Yes! Yes, Shade! I'll marry you!"

A laugh rolled across the room as her enthusiasm infected everyone in attendance.

Reverand Homer smiled and pointed at Shade. "Let me finish up with these two and we'll get you up here in fifteen minutes."

"Don't go anywhere, Jim," Shade called out. "Reckon I'll need a best man and you've already scrubbed up for the job."

Jim grinned. "I'd be honored."

"And Ellen!" Becky shouted. "Will you be my matron of honor?"

"I'd be honored."

Two hours later, Reverend Homer finally stepped off the stage after having married four couples and performed several baptisms. It was as lighthearted a night as the roadhouse had seen in a long time. There was music on the stage, people dancing, and free drinks were flowing. Like many in attendance, Jim had several drinks and let his hair down more than usual. He was actually relaxed, which only served to remind him of how much tension he carried with him most of the time. The apocalypse didn't leave much time for unwinding.

"You having a good night?" Jim asked, finding Garnet in the crowd.

Jim almost didn't recognize him. The old man had cleaned up, slicked down his hair with something oily, and was even wearing a suit.

"I'm having a damn fine night," Garnet said. "Thank you all for including me."

Jim patted him on the back. "You're welcome here anytime. You're one of us."

A waving hand caught Jim's attention. It was Yana at the back of the room, trying to catch Jim's eye. He excused himself and worked his way through the crowd, which was no easy task on this bustling night. Finally, the crowd spat him out at the back of the room.

"Everything okay?" Jim asked.

Jim couldn't help but feel a gnawing anxiety when things were going well. He'd learned over time that people usually didn't interpret their gut feelings correctly. He couldn't recall how many times he'd heard people in the old world say that they *knew* something bad was about to happen because they just felt it in their gut. Jim had come to understand that most often this gut feeling was actually generalized anxiety and not the precursor to some major event. There was a difference and Jim was still learning where that dividing line was.

"Yeah, I'm fine but do you have a second? There's something in the back that you might want to see."

"Let's go," Jim said.

Yana went through the door into the office section of the building. Josie and her people had already moved into their house, but they often worked from the back of the roadhouse so they could share information with Jim and his people. Yana led Jim into the conference room where Josie, Wrong Way, and Hugh were seated behind laptops.

"What's going on?" Jim asked. "I was just getting ready to bust a move on the dance floor." The comment didn't even get a smile. Jim looked from face to face, trying to read the room. He didn't see fear, but he saw *something*.

"We added Wrong Way to our network so he could access email and messaging," Josie said.

"He mentioned that. How's it going?"

"I've been messaging contacts for a few days now," said Wrong Way. "I was hitting up everyone in my address book and everyone who'd ever emailed me about job opportunities. When I found an old work-related email that went out to a group, I messaged everyone in that group, just trying to see if anyone was active and had news."

"Any responses?" Jim asked.

"Not until now." Wrong Way gestured at Josie and Yana. "I saw these guys had snuck away from the festivities so I assumed they might be working. I had my tablet with me, so I took the opportunity to link up and see if I had any responses. I had one."

"From whom? And just as important, from *where*?"

"When I first got out of the service, I did a couple of years with Black Canopy. Ever heard of them?"

"Of course," Jim said. "Probably the largest private military contractor in America."

"It's a huge outfit and I have nothing but respect for the guy who owns it. He's a true patriot and one of the smartest damn people I've ever met in my life. I loved working for him, but I eventually figured out I needed to step back from the adrenaline and get my head together. I took a couple of years off, then hired on with the company I work for now."

Jim hated being rude, but he was too impatient to listen to a life story right now. "You're killing me, dude. Who did you hear from?"

"Sorry, man. I knew a lot of the Black Canopy guys worked internationally so I was hoping one of them might get my message. I heard from one of them today."

"What did he say?"

Wrong Way stared at the screen for a moment, then got up from his seat. "Maybe you should come read it."

Jim circled the table and leaned over to view the tablet propped up on the table with a folding keyboard. A message was open against the white screen. It was short and to the point:

Good to hear from you, brother. Hang in there. BC has something in the pipeline. Help is on the way.

Jim looked at Wrong Way, then at Josie and Yana, who were both staring at him. "I'm assuming you all have discussed this? What do you think it means?"

Hugh lit up a cigarette and rested his elbows on the table. "In my opinion it means Black Canopy might be preparing to launch an operation. Help *could* be on the way."

"We're trying to verify this with other sources," Josie said. "But it's possible this information is so compartmentalized that no one in our network is aware of it."

Jim's mind was reeling from what he'd just read. While he didn't want to leap to conclusions, it was hard not to. Could it mean they had an option besides the cartel or Chinese invasion?

Jim pushed away from the table. "Message him back and see if you can get more info. Offer to share what intelligence we have if that helps."

"We should definitely offer to serve as a resource," Hugh added. "If they truly are setting up an operation, we should do everything we can in support of it."

"Agreed," Jim said.

Wrong Way was nodding. "Already on it. I'm hoping to set up a call. I'll update you as soon as I hear back from him."

"This could be huge," Jim said.

"Or it could be nothing," said Hugh. "Don't get too excited yet. Sometimes operations die on the vine for one reason or another."

"Agreed," Josie said. "Look how far Lightspeed got before someone pulled the rug out from under him."

Jim winced. "That's true. We should keep this under wraps until we know more. Is there anything else? I should get back to the party. I'm supposed to offer up a toast to all the couples."

"One more thing," Josie said. "We just finished compiling the census data today. Would you like to know what we learned?"

"Yeah," Jim said. "I've been dying to know."

"We only counted within the boundaries that you drew on the map," Yana said. "The area you considered to be your area of operation."

Jim twirled his hand, gesturing for Yana to get on with it. "I know all that. Just give me a number." He wasn't trying to be rude, but it had been an overwhelming week. His brain was as tired as his body.

"One hundred and thirty-seven," Yana said, leaning back in her chair.

Jim frowned, blinked, and shook his head. "Wait...what?"

"One hundred and thirty-seven," Yana repeated.

Josie was nodding slowly, as if verifying that number was indeed accurate.

Jim blew out a breath. "That's just a fraction of what I was expecting. I thought we might have three times that. It *seemed* like we had more."

"You might have up until the second grid collapse," Josie explained. "The death toll from that event added up. It greatly reduced what was an already decimated population."

Jim wandered out of the room without a word. He needed a drink. He wondered if he'd been better off not knowing, assuming that his town remained much larger than he imagined. He stepped from the back hallway and into the roadhouse where the music was loud and the crowd boisterous. In his head, he did a rough count of how many people were in the building tonight. Certainly, there were some from outlying communities that hadn't been included in the census, but it was devastating to realize this might almost be everyone.

This room contained the majority of his town, his community, and his world. Every time he'd addressed them, he'd seen them as a sample, a representation of the larger group that existed out there *somewhere*, but now he knew it didn't. This was it. This was his tribe.

It took a certain number of people to raise and gather food, to haul wood, and to defend the town. They were on the very edge of not having enough people to sustain themselves. He would have to do his very best to make sure that he protected them. If the census was correct, they couldn't spare a soul.

The End